Estacada Public Library
825 NW W...

WIT...

D0443635

WINTER'S END

WINTER'S END

Jean-Claude Mourlevat

translated by Anthea Bell

CANDLEWICK PRESS

This is a work of fiction. Names, characters, places,
and incidents are either products of the
author's imagination or, if real, are used fictitiously.

Copyright © 2006 by Gallimard Jeunesse
English translation copyright © 2008 by Anthea Bell

All rights reserved. No part of this book may be reproduced,
transmitted, or stored in an information retrieval system in
any form or by any means, graphic, electronic, or mechanical,
including photocopying, taping, and recording,
without prior written permission from the publisher.

First U.S. edition 2009

Library of Congress Cataloging-in-Publication Data

Mourlevat, Jean-Claude.
[Combat d'hiver. English]
Winter's end / by Jean-Claude Mourlevat ;
translated by Anthea Bell. — 1st ed.
p.   cm.
Summary: Fleeing across icy mountains from a pack of
terrifying dog-men sent to hunt them down, four teenagers
escape from their prison-like boarding schools to take up
the fight against the tyrannical government that murdered
their parents fifteen years earlier.
ISBN 978-0-7636-4450-5
[1. Fantasy. 2. Despotism—Fiction. 3. Adventure and
adventurers—Fiction. 4. Orphans—Fiction.]
I. Bell, Anthea. II. Title.
PZ7.M8646Wi 2009
[Fic]—dc22   2009008456

09 10 11 12 13 14 BVG 10 9 8 7 6 5 4 3 2 1

Printed in Berryville, VA, U.S.A.

This book was typeset in Baskerville.

Candlewick Press
99 Dover Street
Somerville, Massachusetts 02144

visit us at www.candlewick.com

In memory of Rony,
my boarding-school friend

CONTENTS

PART TWO: AS THE RIVER FLOWS

PART ONE

MILENA'S VOICE

*There is something in the human voice
that, coming from the soul, moves our
own souls profoundly.*

—Janet Baker, British mezzo-soprano,
on the voice of Kathleen Ferrier

THE RULES

At a sign from the supervisor, a girl in the front row rose to her feet and went over to press the metal switch. Three unshaded electric bulbs flooded the study room with white light. It was so dark that reading had been almost impossible for some time, but the rules were strict: in October the lights came on at six o'clock in the evening and not a moment sooner. Helen waited ten more minutes before making up her mind. She'd been counting on the light to dissolve the pain she'd been feeling in her chest since the morning, but now it was rising like an oppressive lump in her throat. She recognized it for exactly what it was: sadness. She'd felt it before. She knew that she couldn't fight it off and that waiting would only make it worse.

So yes, she'd go and see her consoler. Too bad if it was only October, very early in the school year. She tore half a page out of her notebook and wrote on it: *I want to go and see my consoler. Will you come with me?* There didn't seem any point in signing it. The girl who read it would know her handwriting anywhere. She folded the piece of paper into eight and wrote the recipient's name: *Milena. Third table by the windows.*

She slipped the paper in front of her neighbor Vera Plasil, who was dozing, open-eyed, over her biology textbook. The little note passed discreetly from hand to hand down the line of tables next to the aisle where Helen sat, reached the fourth table, then sped on invisibly down the middle line, moved to the line beside the windows, and so on to the far end of the classroom and Milena in the row second from the front. The whole thing took only a minute.

It was an accepted rule among the girls: messages must circulate fast and freely and must always reach their destination. You passed them on as a matter of course, even if you hated the girl sending the message or the girl she was writing to. The boarding school demanded absolute silence, so these little forbidden notes were the only way of communicating during study periods and classes. In over three years at the school, Helen had never seen a message go astray or come back, let alone be read by someone it wasn't meant for. Any girl who did that would have paid heavily for it.

Milena skimmed the message. Her masses of blond hair cascaded down her back like a lion's mane. Helen would have given a lot for hair like

4

that, but her own was short and straight like a boy's and she couldn't do a thing with it. Milena turned and frowned, as if in disapproval. Helen knew exactly what that meant. *You're crazy! This is only October! Last year you held out until February!*

Helen gave an angry little shake of her head and narrowed her eyes. *Maybe, but I want to go now. So are you coming or not?*

Milena sighed. So that was all right, then.

Helen carefully tidied her things, rose to her feet, and crossed the room under the curious gaze of a dozen girls. When she reached the supervisor's desk, she noticed that Miss Zesch, in charge during the study period, had a sour smell of sweat about her. In spite of the cold, her forearms and upper lip shone with unhealthy-looking perspiration.

"I want to go and see my consoler," Helen whispered.

The supervisor showed no surprise, just opened the large black register in front of her.

"Name?"

"Dormann. Helen Dormann," said Helen. She was sure the woman knew her name perfectly well and just didn't want to show it.

The supervisor ran a greasy finger down the list of names and stopped on the letter *D*. She checked that Helen Dormann hadn't used up all her outings yet.

"Very well. Companion?"

"Bach," said Helen. "Milena Bach."

The supervisor ran her finger up the list again to

the letter *B*. Milena Bach hadn't gone out as another girl's companion more than three times since term began in September. Miss Zesch raised her head and shouted in such a loud voice that half the girls jumped, "BACH, MILENA!"

Milena rose and went to stand in front of the desk.

"Are you willing to be Helen Dormann's companion going to see her consoler?"

"Yes," said Milena, without looking at her friend.

The supervisor glanced at her watch, noted down the time on a piece of paper, and then said expressionlessly, as if reciting something learned by heart, "It is now eleven minutes past six p.m. You must be back in three hours' time, at eleven minutes past nine p.m. If either of you is not back, another girl will be put in the Sky and will stay there until you return. Any particular girl you'd like to name?"

"No," said Milena and Helen at the same time.

"In that case," said Miss Zesch, running her finger down the list, "in that case it will be Pancek."

Helen felt a pang. It was awful to think of little Catharina Pancek in the Sky. But another of the unwritten rules was that you never picked the girl who would be punished instead of you. The choice was left to the supervisor. Of course, if she liked, she could choose the same person ten times running, but at least that way solidarity among the girls was maintained. No one could be accused of deliberately causing someone else to suffer.

The Sky did not deserve its name. Far from being high in the air above, the detention cell was underneath the cellars. You reached it from the refectory, down a long, spiral staircase with cold water dripping from the steps. The cell measured about seven by ten feet. The walls and floor smelled musty, earthy. When the door closed behind you, all you could do was grope your way over to the wooden bed, sit or lie on it, and wait. You were alone in the darkness and silence for hours.

People said that when you went in it, you needed to try to take a quick look at the top of the wall opposite the door, where someone had painted the sky on the beam — a patch of blue sky with white clouds. Catch a glimpse of it before the door closed, if only for a split second, and you could find the strength to bear the darkness better without despairing. That was why the place was called the Sky. Everyone was terrified of being sent there or even of unintentionally getting someone else sent there.

"And you'll miss supper," Miss Zesch went on. "Did you think of that?"

"Yes," Helen replied for both of them.

"Off you go, then," said the supervisor.

She wrote the date and time of the girls' outing on their cards, stamped them, and took no more interest in the matter.

Milena went to put her things away under her desk and then joined Helen, who was waiting for her in the corridor, already muffled up in her hooded coat. Milena took her own coat off its hook and put it on, and they both walked along the corridor, which was lit on both sides by the lights from the study rooms. They went down the worn steps of the wide staircase to the ground floor. Then they followed another corridor, a dark one this time because the classrooms were empty after six in the evening. It was cold. The enormous cast-iron radiators were all turned off. Had they ever worked at all? In silence, the girls crossed the school yard, Helen in front, walking quickly, Milena following with a gloomy look on her face.

When they reached the barred gate, they went into the Skeleton's lodge, as the rules required. The old crow, alarmingly skinny and always surrounded by a cloud of acrid smoke, ground her cigarette out in a brimming ashtray and looked at the two girls.

"Names?"

You could see the bones beneath her skin, almost piercing her cheeks and fingers, where the blue veins traced intricate patterns.

"Dormann," said Helen, showing her card. "Helen Dormann."

The Skeleton studied the card, coughed over it, and handed it back to her.

"What about you?"

"Bach. Milena Bach," said Milena, placing her own card on the desk.

The Skeleton looked up with sudden interest. "You're the one with the good singing voice?"

"I sing a bit," said Milena cautiously.

"Well?" the Skeleton persisted.

It was hard to make out her tone. Was it jealousy or admiration? Or a mixture of both? When Milena didn't reply, she went on, "So do you sing—better than me, for instance?"

This time it was obvious that the Skeleton was determined to pick an argument. "I don't know. Possibly," said Milena.

Three years in the boarding school had taught her how to answer the supervisors and teachers: stay neutral, make no positive statements, always agree with them. Then you had a quiet life.

"So you don't sing better than me? Come on, let's have an answer!"

The old bag of bones was clearly out for a bit of fun. She lit another cigarette. The forefinger and middle finger of her right hand were stained yellow by nicotine. Helen glanced at the clock hanging on the wall. They were wasting so much time!

"I don't know," said Milena calmly. "I've never heard you sing."

"And I expect you'd like to?" the Skeleton simpered. "You'd like to hear me sing a little tune, but you don't dare ask, is that it?"

Helen had no idea how her friend was going to wriggle out of this, but the Skeleton broke into hoarse laughter, which quickly turned into an uncontrollable coughing fit. Unable to say another word, she put a bunched-up handkerchief in front of her mouth and, still coughing, signaled to the girls to hurry up and get out.

It was almost half past six when the two friends were finally through the barred gate and out on the road.

"Totally off her rocker!" said Milena.

To their right lay the small town, with its dimly lit streets, to their left the old bridge, with its street lamps and the four stone statues of armed horsemen. They made for the bridge.

"Are you mad at me?" asked Helen. "For missing supper? I'm sure my consoler will give me something for you. She cooks really delicious things."

"I couldn't care less about supper," said Milena. "It's not worth eating. It'll just be burned soup this evening. I'm mad at you for wasting a visit to your consoler in October. You know we need at least two to get us through winter. We'll want them as soon as it gets darker and the nights are longer. How are you going to manage when you don't have any left?"

Helen knew her friend was right. All she said was, "I don't know. I just needed one today."

An icy drizzle made them screw up their eyes. They wrapped their coats around themselves and instinctively moved closer together. The uneven pavement shone below their feet, and the black, sluggish water of the river ran under the bridge. Milena took Helen's arm and heaved a deep sigh of exasperation. They looked at each other and smiled. Their arguments never lasted very long.

"How does the Skeleton know I sing?" asked Milena.

"Everyone in the school knows," said Helen. "There aren't many good things about the place. Something like that gets noticed. People talk about it."

Her mind went back to the unforgettable after-noon three years earlier when she had first heard Milena sing. Four of them, all new girls, had been sitting on the steps near the refectory, bored to tears. There was Doris Lemstadt, who only stayed six months before she fell so sick that she had to leave; Milena and Helen, still at the start of their friendship; and a fourth girl—had it been Vera Plasil with her gentle blue eyes? Probably. Doris Lemstadt had suggested passing the time by taking turns singing songs. She started with a song from her own part of the country down in the plains. The song was about a soldier's wife waiting faith-fully for her husband, but it was clear that he was never coming back. Doris didn't sing badly at all, and the other three clapped—quietly, so as not to attract attention, since it was forbidden to sing or listen to any song not on the syllabus, according to School Rule 42.

Helen had followed with a comic song from the old days, about the troubles of an old bachelor who didn't know how to get along with girls. She couldn't remember all the words, but it was funny enough to make her three friends laugh, especially the bit about a poor man whispering sweet noth-ings to a nanny goat, thinking it was his fiancée. Vera didn't know any songs, so she passed.

Then Milena had sat up a little straighter to

expand her chest fully and closed her eyes, and a pure sound like the notes of a flute had risen from her throat:

"Blow the wind southerly, southerly, southerly,
Blow the wind south o'er the bonny blue sea. . . ."

The other three girls were astonished. They hadn't known that anyone could play with her voice like that, modulating it, making it vibrate, lingering on a note that swelled and then faded.

"But sweeter and dearer by far 'tis when bringing
The barque of my true love in safety to me."

In the stupefied silence that followed the last notes, all Doris could whisper was, "What was that?"

"A traditional folk song."

"It was lovely," said Doris.

"Thank you," Milena said softly.

That was three years ago, and Milena hadn't sung more than half a dozen times since. When she did sing, it was a rare and precious gift, given when she chose to whomever she chose—one evening in the dormitory at Christmastime, for a group of ten girls, for instance, or in a corner of the yard just for Helen on June 14, as a birthday present, or, last time, on a summer afternoon during a long walk beside the river. As soon as she opened her mouth, you felt a tingle down your spine. Her singing, even if they didn't understand the words, somehow spoke straight to all the girls. It brought back old faces, and you could almost feel a hug you thought you'd forgotten. And above all, even if you were sad when you heard it, it gave you strength and courage. The rumors had spread very fast: Milena did indeed "sing well," but she revealed none of her gift in Old Ma Crackpot's music lessons and choir practice. Her voice was like anyone else's then, ordinary, with no special charm. Old Ma Crackpot taught nothing but theory in music lessons, and she made the girls sing the three authorized songs until they were completely sick of them, particularly the dreadful school song:

"Happy of heart and pure of soul,
In unison we sing. . . ."

Now the two girls were in the middle of the bridge, at its highest point. Ahead of them in the distance was the hill where the consolers lived.

"Think we'll meet any of the boys?" asked Helen.

"That really would surprise me!" Milena said with a laugh. "They don't come here as often as we do; everyone knows that. And no one but Helen Dormann would think of visiting their consoler at this time of the evening in October!"

"We might meet some coming back down, all the same."

"Dream on! They hide in the undergrowth when we come along! You'd have to shake the branches and shout, 'Hey! Anyone there?'"

Helen burst out laughing. She was relieved to see her friend back in a good mood.

"Do you think the consolers hug the boys too?"

"I'm sure they do!" said Milena. "But the boys wouldn't admit it even under torture."

They started down Donkey Road, which was steep and poorly lit. You could imagine families sitting over supper in yellow lamplight behind the narrow windows and drawn curtains. Another world. Sometimes you caught the sound of laughter or a raised voice. They passed the cobbler's. He was just closing his shop for the night and gave them a vague nod without really looking at them. Boarding-school girls, that's what they were to everyone, and people avoided speaking to them.

At the end of the road, they came to the country-side—no more houses except where the consolers lived, at the very top of the hill. They stopped for a moment to get their breath back and look at the town below on the far side of the river. Now they could see the glistening slate rooftops, the church towers, the roads shining in the light of the street lamps. A few cars were driving around, silent at this distance and looking like big, pot-bellied beetles.

"It's lovely," sighed Helen. "I would like the town if it wasn't for—" She stopped, jerking her head at the huge building they had just left: the girls' boarding school on the other side of the bridge.

"And if we could go there now and then." Milena finished her sentence, pointing to the other building: the boys' boarding school a couple of hundred yards from the girls' school.

They had just set out again along the trodden earth road when a couple of figures came around a bend higher up. The two boys were striding downhill fast. They disappeared from view for a moment and then came into sight again, closer now, where the road began to run straight. The first boy was tall and thin. Helen noticed the way he looked straight ahead in a challenging way, his firm chin jutting out. The second, who was rounder in the face and shorter, followed close behind him. She saw the curly hair under his cap and his laughing eyes.

"Hi!" said all four of them at almost the same time, and they stopped face-to-face in the road.

"You're going up?" asked the boy with the cap, rather stupidly.

"Looks like it, doesn't it?" said Helen. Then she was annoyed with herself for sounding sarcastic, and to apologize added, "And you're going down again."

"That's right," said the boy.

"Who was whose companion?" Helen ventured. "If it's OK to ask?"

The boy said nothing for a couple of seconds, looking undecided, and finally made up his mind and pointed to his taller friend. "He's my companion."

Helen got the impression that he was blushing as he made this confession. She liked that. Not wanting to embarrass him, she pointed to Milena and said, "And she's mine." Which meant, *I'm going to see my consoler too — it's nothing to be ashamed of.*

15

The boy was obviously grateful. He smiled and said, "What are your names?"

"I'm Helen," said Helen, "and this is Milena."

"I'm Milos," said the boy. "He's Bartolomeo. We're in the fourth year. What about you—which year are you in?"

"We're both in the fourth year too," said Helen.

The little coincidence amused them. Then they didn't know what to say next, so they said nothing, feeling rather awkward. The two boys couldn't bring themselves to go on down the hill or the girls to go on up it. There were very few opportunities for the students in the two schools to meet like this; it would have been stupid to part so quickly. Helen noticed that Milena and Bartolomeo couldn't take their eyes off each other and thought her friend seemed unafraid. Looking from one to the other, she wondered desperately what to say next. But it was Milena who spoke first.

"We could exchange messages through the Skunk, couldn't we?"

Helen felt the blood rise to her face. She had always thought that messages delivered by the Skunk were only for the fifth- and sixth-year students. Milena's suggestion seemed incredibly daring. It was as if she had suddenly crossed a forbidden frontier without warning.

The Skunk was a wizened little old man who hobbled across the school yard and back late in the morning on Fridays, laboriously hauling his handcart after him. It contained, first, a load of clean sheets and, on the way back, a pile of dirty sheets, which he was taking to the laundry in town. As the only person who could pass freely between both schools, he was someone of considerable importance: he could deliver messages and bring the replies back next week or the week after. All you had to do was leave your letter tucked in the laundry along with payment—a banknote in an envelope or, even better, a bottle of spirits if possible. The Skunk suffered from some kind of gastric disorder that gave him appallingly bad breath. A disgusting smell of rotten cabbage hit you ten feet away from him even if he'd hardly opened his mouth. The poor man tried to keep this misfortune at bay by drinking cheap rotgut that could be bought for him in the town.

"We've never tried it before," said the taller boy, the one his friend had called Bartolomeo. "But the older guys say it works."

His voice was both deep and soft, almost a man's voice.

"Let's write our names down," said Milena. She was already tearing a piece of paper into four.

They all searched their pockets for a pencil or a pen, and then each of the four carefully wrote his or her name. Standing close together in their long overcoats, they formed a little island of warmth in the cold. The boys had their collars turned up, the girls had pulled their hoods over their heads, and there was almost nothing of them to be seen except their hands and faces. Helen finished writing *Helen Dormann, the girls' school, 4th year*, then handed the paper to Milos without hesitating. He handed his note to her at the same time, and their fingers touched. They smiled and put the two scraps of paper in their pockets unread. Milena and Bartolomeo had already exchanged theirs.

"We don't want our letters to cross each other," said Milena, always practical. "Helen and I will write first."

"Fine," said the two boys.

"Right." Helen shook herself and took Milena's arm. "We're going on up. I don't have much time left."

"We'd better get a move on too," said Milos. "Or we're going to be late. I don't fancy sending a friend to the detention cell."

And they rushed on downhill.

"You'll write first, then?" the taller boy confirmed, turning back for a moment.

"Is that a promise?" asked Milos, forefinger raised as if to threaten them.

"It's a promise!" said the two girls at the same time, laughing.

THE CONSOLERS

As Helen and Milena walked into the consolers' village, the chilly drizzle surrounded them like liquid dust, its tiny droplets glittering in any light from the street lamps or windows. The brick houses, crowding close to each other all along the road, looked like miniatures. You went down a few steps to reach most of them, and you almost had to bend to get through the doorway.

Milena stopped at the first house. "I'll wait for you here. And don't forget me if your consoler's cooked something nice. I'm starving."

"Don't worry, I'll remember. I just hope it's warm for you in the library."

To make sure, Helen followed her friend into the tiny, low-ceilinged room. A flame was flickering behind the glass door of the wood-burning stove, and it was indeed warm.

"They never forget, do they?" said Milena.

A lighted lamp on the table welcomed visitors, and halfway up the wall were two shelves with a hundred or so well-worn books on them. As Milena took her coat off, she was already looking at them, deciding which to choose.

"I'm off, then," said Helen. "See you soon. Have a nice read!"

She herself had been here several times as companion to Milena or one of the other girls. She loved the library, a place cut off from the rest of the world where no one ever disturbed you and you could read and dream in peace. It was like a nest or a cradle, she thought—somewhere warm, in any case, where no one ever wished you harm. And no one else would come in except, from time to time, a quiet man who must be married to one of the consolers, coming to add a log to the stove on the hearth. He would ask kindly, "Enjoying your book?" You assured him that you were, and he went away again. She had only once had to share the room with another companion, a boy who read for a few minutes but then sat huddled up in a corner with his head on his knees and went to sleep.

All the girls loved being chosen as companions and having the chance of two hours in this library. Sometimes, of course, they would rather have visited their own consolers, but Rule 22 was quite clear: Girls acting as companions are not allowed to visit their consolers. And the severe punishment didn't encourage anyone to disobey: no outings for the rest of the year.

Helen went straight ahead, turned left at the fountain, and started along a sloping road. As she reached Number 47, she found herself smiling. She knew in advance what happiness she was going to give and receive. She went down the three steps and tapped lightly on the window rather than the door. The panes were steamed up inside. In a moment a small hand rubbed one of them and a bright little face appeared. The child's mouth opened wide, and Helen could see his lips shaping the two syllables of her name: *He-len!*

A few seconds later Octavo was throwing himself into her arms. She picked him up and kissed his chubby cheeks. "You're so heavy!" she said with a laugh.

"I weigh fifty-seven pounds!" said the child, very proud of it.

"Is your mama here?"

"In the kitchen. I'm doing my homework. Will you help me like last time? I like it when you help me with my homework."

They went into the living room. It was not much larger than the library, but stairs to the right went up to the second floor, where there was a bedroom, and a door at the back of the house led to the kitchen. This door opened to reveal the monumental form of Paula.

On one of her first visits, Helen had cried her heart out and then fallen asleep in Paula's arms. When she woke up, she had murmured, "How much do you weigh, Paula?"

She was only fourteen at the time, and this tactless question had made the fat woman laugh. "Oh, I don't know, my dear. I've no idea. A lot, anyway." When she hugged you, it was hard to make out where her arms, shoulders, breasts, and stomach were. Everything merged into a sensation of sweet warmth, and you wanted to stay there forever.

Paula opened her arms now for Helen to snuggle up in them. "It's been a long time, my beauty."

Paula often called her "My beauty" or "My pretty one." And she would hold Helen's face between her hands to get a better look at her. Helen had heard herself described as a number of things—emotional, odd, a tomboy—but no one else ever said she was pretty or beautiful. Paula did, and she meant it.

"Yes, last time was before the summer," Helen said. "I wanted to wait until December at least, but I couldn't manage to hold out."

"Well, come on in. I'm just making supper for Octavo. Baked potatoes, and there's some of the pear tart we had for lunch left. Will that be all right?"

"Couldn't be better!" said Helen happily. Everything she ate here, far away from the hated school refectory, tasted delicious.

Octavo was already impatient to get back to his homework. "Come on! I can't do it on my own."

As Paula went back into the kitchen, Helen rejoined the little boy and sat down beside him. "So what are you learning at school, then?"

"Words that go in pairs for males and females."

"Right. Like what?"

"The teacher gave us the first one. It was husband and wife. We have to write down three more pairs."

"Have you thought of your three?"

"Yes, but I'm not quite sure about the third."

"Go on."

"Wizard and witch."

"Very good."

"Bull and cow."

"That's fine. How about the third?"

"That's the one I'm not sure of."

"Never mind, let's hear it."

"Fox and foxess."

Helen found it hard not to laugh. At the same time a deep, strong wave of melancholy swept over her. Did she have a little brother of her own somewhere? A little brother puzzling over his homework? Sticking his tongue out as he concentrated on the past tense of the verb *to do* or a problem like 3 × 2? No, she didn't have a brother or sister anywhere. Or parents either. She thought of the orphanage where she had spent her childhood, and the autumn day when she left it. How could she ever forget?

Three grim-looking men push her into the back of a large car. They lock all the doors and drive off in silence.

"Why have you locked the doors?" she asks the man next to her. "Do you think I'm going to jump out or something? Where are we going?"

He doesn't reply, doesn't even turn his head. All the way she smells the strong odor of his leather jacket and the cigarettes that the other two are smoking in the front of the car. They drive through the countryside for hours, and then the road runs beside the river to the nameless little town and the gray boarding school building.

About a hundred other girls are waiting in groups of five or six, coats over their arms and small books in their hands. They are all surprisingly quiet. She is led along shabby corridors to the room outside the headmistress's office, where she has only a few minutes to wait. Then the door opens and a girl comes out, also with a coat over her arm and a book in her hand. She is small, wears thick glasses, and looks even more downcast than the others. This, as Helen will learn later, is Catharina Pancek. She just murmurs, "Your turn to go in," and then walks away. Helen cautiously goes through the doorway.

"Name?"

This is the first time Helen hears the headmistress's voice.

"Dormann. My name's Helen Dormann."

"Age?"

"Fourteen."

"Come here."

Helen goes up to the desk, where a massive woman with short gray hair is sitting. She wears a man's jacket, and her shoulders are wide and powerful. Helen will soon discover that the girls' nickname for her is the Tank. The Tank searches some papers, finds a file on Helen, and runs through it. Then she opens a drawer and brings out a leaflet.

"Here, take this."

The leaflet is well worn; its cover has been mended many times.

"These are the school rules. You must have them with you at all times. There are eighty-one rules. Learn ten a day. If you have to come back here, which I hope you will not, you must know them all by heart. Go into the cloakroom next door, find a coat that fits you, and go out. If there's anyone sitting outside my door, tell her it's her turn."

Helen goes into the room next to the office, which is full of dozens and dozens of coats hanging there like theatrical costumes. Except that all these costumes are identical: heavy wool overcoats with hoods. It's like a maze. If I ever need to hide, *thinks Helen,* I'll know where to go. *She chooses a gray coat that looks a little less threadbare than the others, tries it on, and decides that it fits. She takes it off, puts it over her arm, and goes back through the headmistress's office. The Tank ignores her.*

A tall, pale girl is sitting on the bench in the waiting room, bleeding slightly from the nose into a handkerchief stained with red. Helen will learn later that her name is Doris Lemstadt; she will become so ill that she leaves the boarding school. "Your turn!" *Helen tells her, and she goes out into the yard where a faint ray of sun falls on the girls standing there motionless, with their coats and their booklets of rules.*

"I know—I'll say duck and drake instead. Is that better?"

Helen came back to the present and smiled at Octavo. "Yes, that's better. Not as funny, but better."

The delicious smell of baked potatoes was

25

coming from the kitchen, and Paula called, "How's your friend Milena? Is she all right? Do you admire her as much as ever?"

"She's fine," said Helen, laughing. "And yes, I do! She's waiting for me in the library. Can I take her something from supper?"

"Of course, and a slice of tart if there's any left."

Paula was always cooking: for herself, for Octavo, for people who happened to drop in. It was impossible to go to her house and not eat anything, or come away without something to eat: a helping of bread-and-butter pudding or chocolate cake or just an apple. She had one child, Octavo, but no husband. When Helen asked her about that, she had said she didn't need one. The village on this hill belonged to the consolers, and it was no place for men unless they were very discreet. Like the man who comes to put wood in the stove, Helen had thought. He must be one of those shadowy men who were allowed to live on the hill. Other men didn't feel at ease here; they lived in the town and seldom came up to the village.

Most of the consolers were of considerable girth and made sure they stayed that way. How could you give someone a proper hug, how could you comfort people, if your bones were sticking out? Some of Helen's friends didn't agree; their consolers were slender and fragile, but they wouldn't have exchanged them for the world. Catharina Pancek, for instance, said her consoler was like a little mouse scurrying about, and she loved her like that. She wouldn't have wanted to drown in a mass of soft flesh like Paula's.

Helen hadn't chosen Paula for herself. The supervisor who took her up to the hill the first time, three years ago, had stopped outside Number 47 without asking her opinion and said in dry tones, "Her name is Paula. I'll come back for you in two hours."

Helen had gone down the three steps and knocked at the door, and Paula had opened it and burst out laughing at the sight of her.

"Oh, what a lost little kitten! Come in and have something to eat. Are you thirsty? How about a mug of hot chocolate? Yes, hot chocolate will warm you up."

Since that day, Helen had visited Paula only six times, just as often as the rules allowed. About fifteen hours in all, no more. And yet she felt she had known Paula forever. She occupied a huge place in Helen's heart.

Octavo put his school satchel away, and they set the table for supper. The baked potatoes were so fluffy and so delicious that Helen's first few mouthfuls almost made her feel unwell.

"Oh, this is so good!"

She spared a fleeting thought for the other girls back at school having to put up with insipid soup. But their turn would come. She might as well forget them for the moment and enjoy the happiness here. Over supper they talked mostly about Octavo, his school, the practical jokes he played there. His teacher must be kept on her toes with a character like Octavo in her class. At eight o'clock he went upstairs to his room and came back down in pajamas to kiss Helen and his mother.

"I like it when you come to see us," he told Helen, "but not in the evening because then my mommy can't cuddle me."

"I'll come up and see you later," Paula promised. "Go to bed now. Helen only has half an hour left. I've explained to you: it would be very serious for her to be late."

"Is it true they'd put another girl in a black hole instead of Helen?" asked Octavo.

"Who told you that?"

"Some of the kids at school say so."

"Well, it's not true. Off with you now. Go to sleep."

The little boy slowly climbed the wooden staircase. His eyes were full of anxiety.

There was a large and rather worn-out armchair against the left-hand wall. Paula dropped into it. "Well, my pretty one, what do you have to tell me today? Come over here."

Helen went to sit at Paula's feet and put her head in her lap. The plump woman's two warm hands stroked her head slowly from her forehead to the nape of her neck.

"I don't have anything to tell you, Paula. Nothing ever happens at the boarding school."

"Tell me about before you were there, then."

"I can't. You know that."

For a moment they were both silent.

"You talk to me," Helen went on. "About when you were a little girl. I always like imagining you little. Were you already—"

"Fat? Oh yes, I always have been. And one of my cousins made it very clear to me one day. I remember, my sister, Marguerite, and I had caught a hedgehog—"

"You have a sister? I didn't know."

"Yes, an elder sister. She's ten years older than me and she lives in the capital city. Well, as you know, hedgehogs look very round and fat, and . . ."

Still stroking Helen's head, Paula told the story of the hedgehog, then another anecdote about a lost purse, and then yet another. She never told you what you should or shouldn't do in life. She just told stories. A moment came when Helen felt herself falling asleep. She didn't want to. She hauled herself up and buried herself in her consoler's bosom like a small child. Paula put her arms around her and sang songs that flowed into each other with a sweet, dreamlike sound.

"Helen, are you asleep? You'll have to go back now."

"I wasn't asleep."

The clock said eight thirty. She slowly shook off the lethargy that had come over her and went to get her coat.

"Can I have something for Milena? And the end of the tart that we kept for her?"

"I'll put it all in a basket. Just leave the basket at the library and I'll collect it tomorrow. When will you be coming back to see me?"

"I don't know. I'll try to wait until January for my second outing. I hope there won't be too much snow to get up here then."

They stood on the doorstep in each other's arms for a long time. Helen breathed in Paula's scent: her apron, her sweater, her hair.

"See you soon, Paula. Thank you. Give Octavo a kiss for me."

"See you soon, my beauty. I'll always be here for you."

Helen hurried along the village streets, carrying the basket. It was still drizzling, and hard to see. She hurried into the library, looking forward to seeing Milena enjoy her baked potatoes. She'd just have time to eat them and the pear tart before they set off to go back to the boarding school.

But when Helen entered the room, she stopped short. It was empty except for the end of a log burning out in the stove.

After the first moment of shock, Helen thought her friend might be upstairs. There was a door at the back of the room, and probably a staircase beyond it.

"Milena! Are you up there?"

She tried to open the door, but it was locked.

"Where are you, Milena?"

Terror rose in her. Why would Milena have gone back ahead of her? Was she afraid of being late? They had plenty of time.

Then she saw a book on the table with a piece of notepaper folded in half sticking out of its pages. Helen snatched it up. Milena's elegant handwriting covered just four lines:

Helen, I'm not going back to school. Don't worry. I'm all right. Ask Catharina Pancek to forgive me.
    Milena
    (Please don't hate me.)

Helen stood in horror for a full minute, unable to react. Then she felt rising anger. How could Milena do such a thing? How cowardly to leave like that, without any explanation, either! She felt betrayed. Tears of rage came to her eyes. *Please don't hate me.* How could she not? At that moment she really did hate her friend. Selfish and irresponsible, that's what she was! What could she do? Go back to Paula and tell her what had happened? That wouldn't be any use. Run away? Not go back to the boarding school herself? After all, she might as well take her chance, because little Catharina would be put in the Sky anyway. But where would she go? And suppose Milena came back after all? Then she, Helen, would be to blame for Catharina's imprisonment. Questions came thick and fast in her mind, but no answers.

She put the note in her pocket and left, leaving

behind the basket containing the plate of baked potatoes, still warm and wrapped in a cloth, and the slice of pear tart.

As she carefully walked back in the dark, it occurred to her that this would cause a sensation: never in living memory had any girl at the school not returned. If they were allowed out from time to time, it was because of the certainty that no girl would dare to condemn another perfectly innocent comrade to the torment of the Sky. The most cruel punishments stipulated in the school rules sent you there for a few hours, but never for days or weeks. *You might even die there,* thought Helen.

She retched with anticipation of the shame she'd be feeling in a few minutes when she had to confess to the others that Milena hadn't come back. *"Did she have an accident?" "No, she just hasn't come back—that's all."*

The shame of being Milena's friend . . .

She crossed the bridge, and the memory of her friend's arm in hers a few hours earlier as they walked over these same paving stones hurt her. It was a few minutes after nine when she reached the lodge and presented herself to the Skeleton. The woman, seeing Helen on her own, realized that her hour of glory might be about to come: after twenty-five years keeping watch at this gate, she would at last be able to tell the headmistress that a pupil had failed to return. *"That's right, Headmistress. She hasn't come back!"* She took her time savoring this once-in-a-lifetime moment.

"You went out at . . . let's see, at eleven minutes past six?"

No, not until six thirty, and it was your fault, thought Helen, but she had learned to control herself.

"Yes, eleven minutes past six," she said.

"And now it's only seven minutes past nine, so you're back on time."

"Yes, I'm back on time," agreed Helen, thinking *Go on, spit your venom out. You're just dying to.*

The acrid smoke of cigarettes got up her nose and into her eyes. Did no one ever open the window here? The Skeleton hemmed and hawed for a few seconds, and then breathed, in a barely audible voice, "So . . . what about the girl who sings?"

"She isn't here," was all Helen said.

"She'll be back by eleven minutes past nine at the latest, of course?"

"I don't know."

"You don't know?"

"That's right. I don't know."

"Well, we'll wait for her together. Then we will know. And we can keep each other company. Do you like company?"

Her small, bloodshot eyes held the sheer cruelty of a snake.

"Yes, I like company," said Helen in an expressionless voice, gritting her teeth and trying to suppress her urge to hit this sadist.

The minute hand went around the dial of the clock on the wall three times. It seemed an eternity.

33

Come back, Milena. Please walk into the lodge. Bring this nightmare to an end.

"Still not here," remarked the Skeleton, pretending to be upset, though her delight was obvious.

Her cigarette was burning out in the ashtray. Forgetting about it, she lit another. Her hands shook as she pushed in a plug on her switchboard and picked up the phone. After a few seconds she had an answer on the line.

"Good evening. This is Miss Fitzfischer in the lodge . . ."

Miss Fitzfischer! Well, at least I've learned something new today, thought Helen. *Who'd have guessed that the Skeleton's name was Fitzfischer?*

"May I speak to the headmistress, please? It's urgent."

The conversation was very short. Helen thought the Skeleton was going to have a stroke as she told her news, her voice was shaking so much with excitement.

". . . Yes, that's right. One of the pupils has failed to return. . . . Her name? Milena Bach, year four. . . . Definitely, Headmistress. . . . Yes, Headmistress. . . . Yes, the other girl is back. She . . . oh, absolutely, Headmistress. . . ."

"May I go back to the dormitory?" Helen asked when the Skeleton had hung up. She realized that she was breaking Rule 17, which forbade the students to ask adults any questions.

But the Skeleton was in such a state that she didn't notice. "Yes, you can go."

* * *

The dormitory, a vast room with fifty or so bunk beds and gray metal lockers, was above the refectory. In the faint glow of the night-lights Helen passed through the first part, where the youngest girls slept, amid whispers and the rustling of sheets. There was still a light on in Miss Zesch's cubicle in the corner, casting vague shadows on the ceiling. When Helen reached her bed, near the windows, she sat down on the edge of it to take her shoes off. For the first time in more than three years, Milena's bed, the one above hers, would be empty. She undressed, put on her nightgown, and disappeared under the covers, head and all. Less than ten seconds later, she heard Vera Plasil, in the next bed, whispering.

"Where's Milena?"

Helen timidly emerged. "She hasn't come back."

"Will she be coming?"

"I don't think so."

Vera groaned. "Oh, no! I don't believe it! So who was picked for punishment?"

"Catharina Pancek."

"Oh, my God!"

The dormitory where the fifth-year and sixth-year girls slept was on the other side of a partition. One of the other supervisors suddenly burst through the door and marched straight toward Miss Zesch's cubicle. Helen quickly recognized Miss Merlute, a tall, round-shouldered woman whose huge nose looked like a false one. People said she was the Tank's lapdog, ready to do anything for her, obeying her orders without a moment's hesitation. There was a low-voiced conversation, then both supervisors came out of the cubicle and made straight for the part of the dormitory where the fourth-year girls slept.

"PANCEK!" thundered Miss Zesch. "CATHA-RINA PANCEK!"

The girls started and sat up in bed.

"Catharina Pancek, get up, get dressed, and come with me!" ordered Miss Merlute.

"And the rest of you lie down again and stop talking!" shouted Miss Zesch.

In the next row, little Catharina sat up, unable to believe it. But a glance at Milena's bed, impeccably made and empty, immediately told her what was in store for her. She looked at Helen, but Helen turned her head away.

"Hurry up!" said Miss Merlute impatiently.

Catharina put on her glasses, which she kept hooked over the metal bedhead, opened her locker, dressed, put on her shoes, and went out with her coat under her arm. As she passed close—the supervisors were waiting farther off—Helen called in a low voice, "Catharina!"

"What is it?"

"Milena asks you to forgive her."

"What?"

"Milena asks you to forgive her," repeated Helen, and her voice broke.

Catharina didn't answer. She made her way past the rows of beds, while a chorus of voices rose as she went by.

"Good luck, Catharina! You can do it, Catharina! We'll be thinking of you."

One girl ran over to her and kissed her cheek. Helen thought she saw her slip something into Catharina's hand.

Miss Merlute, impatient, seized the girl by the arm and led her away almost at a run. They both disappeared through the doorway.

"Bitches!" said one girl savagely.

"Bloody cows!" agreed another.

"Stop talking, I said!" shouted Miss Zesch, and the voices died down.

Once peace and quiet were restored, Helen hid under her sheet and blankets and curled up into a ball. In the darkness she tried to persuade herself that this was only a nightmare and best forgotten, and she did her best to distract her mind by thinking up male and female couples, like Octavo: husband and wife; wizard and witch; fox and vixen; boy and girl. And she trembled as she whispered, very quietly, "Milos and Helen."

ANNUAL ASSEMBLY

The next day was Friday, the day the Skunk came. Helen would have to get a move on if she was going to write her letter to Milos and leave it in the laundry cart before the old man arrived. She took advantage of Miss Mersch's math lesson, which was from nine to ten. The math teacher was confined to a wheelchair and wouldn't rush at her to snatch away her half-written letter shouting, "And what, young lady, is this?" She might have an eagle eye, but Helen, like the rest of her friends, was good at covering up.

For a moment she wondered how to begin. *Dear Milos?* They hardly knew each other. . . . *Hi, Milos?* You might say that to anyone. She decided on just *Milos*. He could take it any way he liked. She told him how she had found the library empty, about her return to the boarding school without Milena, and above all about how miserable she felt when she saw little Catharina Pancek taken away to the detention cell. She wrote about Milena's amazing voice, saying she'd never have thought her capable of letting anyone down like that. And she asked him to reply soon, adding that she'd be *waiting impatiently* for his letter. Then she cobbled together a makeshift envelope out of another piece of notepaper folded in half and glued together. She took the piece of paper that Milos had given her the day before out of her sock, where she had tucked it away, and carefully copied his name: *Milos Ferenzy. The boys' boarding school. Fourth year.* Before slipping her letter into the envelope, she paused for a moment to think, and added, under her signature: *By the way, I haven't even told you anything about myself. I'm seventeen. I like books and chocolate (and I'm glad I met you).*

Writing that last line, she felt doubtful and uncertain. Had she said too much? Not enough?

At ten o'clock break, she unobtrusively joined a group of fifth-year girls in one corner of the school yard and asked straight out, "How does the mail service work? Does someone put the letters in the laundry cart and then the Skunk takes them away?"

A tall, slim, and rather pretty girl stared hard at her. "Who do you want to send a letter to?"

"A boy from over there."

"What year are you in?"

"The fourth year."

"What's your name?"

"Helen Dormann."

"And what's his?"

"Milos Ferenzy," said Helen. She blushed, and felt furious with herself.

The older girls conferred by exchanging glances. None of them knew Milos. He'd probably be too young to interest them.

"Give it here," said the tall girl, and the others spontaneously formed a little barrier around them so that Helen could hand her letter over unnoticed.

"You're the one who leaves the letters?" Helen asked.

"That's right."

"I . . . I don't have a present for you. Or for the Skunk. I don't have anything. I didn't have the time to . . ."

"That's all right. I'll bring you the reply. If there is one."

A little before midday, Helen was looking out the music-room window, which had a view of the yard, and saw the Skunk arrive with his jolting cart. He disappeared into the laundry and came out with a pile of white sheets. The day's letters must be hidden among them.

I sent a letter to my love
And on the way I dropped it.
One of you has picked it up
And put it in your pocket.

Helen hummed, amazed to find how easily the nursery rhyme came back to her from her early childhood.

40

* * *

The days that followed were unbearable. Helen expected to be called to the Tank's office at any moment. But the summons never came. The lack of reaction to what had happened was worse than anything. It meant that the school staff were sticking to Rule 16: If any pupil does not return after her three hours' absence, another girl will be sent to the detention cell immediately and will stay there until the runaway is back. Everything was in order; the matter was closed.

None of the girls dared mention Catharina, but everyone thought of her the whole time. Was she managing to sleep? Did they give her anything to eat and drink? Helen questioned a fifth-year girl who had spent a whole night and half the next day in the Sky last year for throwing her soup plate at the refectory wall and shouting that she was "Fed up! Fed up! Fed up!" She wouldn't say much and seemed mainly anxious to know if Catharina would have had time to get a look at the picture on the beam.

"Is it that important?" asked Helen. "Did you see it yourself?"

"Only for a second or so, but it kept me from going around the bend. Was it you Milena went out with?"

"Yes."

The girl turned her back. Helen felt that everyone held her responsible for what had happened, or at least thought she had been Milena's accomplice. As Milena wasn't there, they couldn't tell her what they thought of her, so they took their fury and resentment out on Helen. Only Vera Plasil hadn't turned against her.

"It isn't your fault. How could anyone think it was? She'll come back, I'm sure. I expect she had something really important to do. You wait and see; she'll do it and she'll be back."

"Then why didn't she tell me anything about it?"

Vera Plasil had no answer to that. She just looked at Helen with sympathy in her big blue eyes.

From Sunday onward Helen was counting not the days but the hours until Friday, when the Skunk came. Time just wouldn't pass. She made herself imagine the worst to avoid feeling too bad when the moment came: the worst was if she didn't get a reply from Milos this time and had to wait another week. The mere thought of it was disheartening.

And Milena still didn't come back. Might never come back . . . until Catharina died in that black hole. The worst moment was suppertime. Since the detention cell was under the refectory cellars, the girls knew that Catharina was close to them, and they had difficulty forcing down what was on their plates.

At last Helen woke up in the morning and it was Friday. At ten to twelve, punctual if none too steady on his feet, the Skunk wheeled his cart of clean sheets across the yard. From the music room, Helen saw him disappear into the laundry to exchange them for the dirty bed linen.

"Happy of heart and pure of soul,
In unison we sing.
Midst fields and forests we will stroll . . ."

Old Ma Crackpot made them repeat that verse for the twelfth time, but Helen wasn't listening to the others singing anymore. *Oh, let there be a letter for me,* she thought. *Let there be a letter! I can't wait another whole week.*

On her way out of the refectory, a sixth-year girl came up to her. "Are you Helen Dormann?"

"Yes."

"Here's your mail, then! And don't forget the little present next time."

"I won't—I promise!" said Helen, beside herself with delight as she put the two envelopes in her pocket. There were two of them! All week she'd been afraid of not getting a letter, and now she had two!

Feverishly, she searched the school yard for Vera Plasil. "Vera, could you wait at the door for me, please?"

The lavatories were dilapidated, but the only place where you could be left in peace on your own for a few moments, so long as there was someone to stand guard at the door. Once inside, Helen took the envelopes out of her coat pocket. Her name was on both, *Helen Dormann, the girls' boarding school,* and her class, *fourth year,* but the handwriting on them was different. The first envelope was in Milos's writing, which she easily recognized, large and neatly connected. The second, an inimitable, almost adult hand, was Milena's! She opened Milos's letter first. After all, this was the one she'd been waiting for all week. It was short:

Helen

I got your letter, and here's mine. I hope it won't be too Skunk-scented! Bartolomeo didn't come back the other evening. I have something serious to tell you. Be at the corner of the east and north walls of your school at midnight on Friday. Promise?

Milos
I haven't told you about myself either. I'm seventeen. I like Greco-Roman wrestling and eating (and I'm very glad I met you too).

Helen wondered if what she was holding was her first-ever love letter. The repetition of the last sentence of her own letter almost word for word suggested that Milos wanted a close friendship. Emotion almost made her dizzy. So many extraordinary things had been happening these last few days. She put the letter back in its envelope and opened Milena's, which was longer.

Dear Helen,

I can imagine how angry with me you must be, and I really do understand. But you have to know that I didn't let you down on purpose.

What happened is this: Bartolomeo came back to the library just after you left. We talked for over two hours, and at the end of that time, I decided to go on the run with him. We're leaving tonight. I'm never coming back to the boarding school again.

We were hiding behind the fountain when you passed just now carrying a basket. I don't know what was in it, but thank you for bringing it for me!

At the moment we're at my consoler's house, where I'm writing you this letter. She'll send it on to you via the Skunk.

There's so much I'd like to tell you, but I don't have time. Milos knows all about it. He'll explain. Ask him.

I hope we'll meet again. You've been my best friend all these years. I'll never forget you. I'm very sad to say good-bye.

Love and kisses,

Milena

P.S. I feel terrible about Catharina, but I had to do what I'm doing now.

"Helen, I'm getting cold out here. And it's raining too."

Waiting at the door, Vera was getting impatient. Helen wiped her eyes with her handkerchief, hid the two envelopes in the inside pocket of her coat, and emerged from the lavatories.

At evening study time, it was as if the ghosts of Milena Bach and Catharina Pancek occupied their empty places in the third row and the front row respectively. The absence of the two girls weighed

45

on everyone's mind. Miss Zesch, sweating more than ever, was almost falling asleep.

"What's Greco-Roman wrestling, Vera?" Helen whispered.

"I think it's men in swimsuits flinging themselves on each other and each tries to get the other guy down on his back."

"God—really?"

"And they stink of sweat and grunt a lot."

"Oh."

"Why do you want to know?"

"Just wondering."

Helen couldn't stop thinking of Milos, telling herself all the time that she must be crazy to go falling in love with a boy she'd seen for less than five minutes, and in a dim light too. Another thing was that she couldn't conjure up his face. The harder she tried to remember it, the more elusive it was. She thought she remembered that Milos wasn't very tall; his cheeks were rather round, yes; he had curly hair, yes; and a nice smile—yes, yes, and yes again—but she couldn't visualize him anymore. She decided that what she really wanted was to fall in love, and the first boy to come along would do. She just hoped she wasn't going to be too badly disappointed.

And what did he want from her? The idea of meeting him by night fascinated her, but it scared her too. *I have something serious to tell you.* What did that mean? And she'd have to get out of the dormitory in the middle of the night. Luckily Miss Zesch, who was their supervisor again tonight, snored like a pig as soon as she fell asleep, and she didn't surface again until early morning. She was by far the easiest of all the supervisors to deceive. Much more than Miss Merlute, a silent, cunning insomniac who went poking her long nose around among the rows of beds at any time of night. No, the real danger was from the other girls. Especially Vera, who was always a light sleeper and would want to know where she was going. Helen was tempted to tell Vera what was going on but decided against it. Sensible Vera was capable of waking the whole dormitory when the moment came, just to save Helen from putting herself at risk.

Under the covers, Helen looked at the luminous hands of her watch; it was after ten, and Miss Zesch wasn't snoring yet. She still wasn't snoring at eleven. That was very strange. The light was on in her cubicle, but no other sign of life came from it. Was she determined to stay awake through the night now, of all times, and imitate Miss Merlute by prowling around the beds looking like a bird of prey? Helen strained her ears desperately. In the absence of the usual roaring sounds, a gentle little snore would have been enough for her, but even that didn't come.

At quarter to midnight, her patience exhausted, she decided to try her luck and go out anyway. She glanced at the next bed. Vera was sleeping peacefully with her mouth half open. Reassured, Helen ventured to sit up. She was going to get out of bed to go to her closet and get her clothes when Miss Zesch opened her cubicle door. Helen first froze like a statue and then lay down again, eyes wide.

Miss Zesch was obviously not in her normal state of mind. Taking care to make no noise, she slipped out of her cubicle as slowly and surreptitiously as an assassin. What was more, although Helen felt she must be dreaming this part, she was wearing high-heeled shoes and an evening dress! Never, ever had she been seen with anything but clodhoppers on her feet, wearing huge pants or, on her good days, a thick woolly skirt. She closed the door behind her and tiptoed away. Helen waited for her to disappear entirely, restrained herself for a few more minutes, just in case the supervisor came back, although that seemed unlikely, and then, since nothing was moving, she dressed and made for the dormitory door in her own turn.

It was a clear, cool night. Several long clouds were drifting in shreds across the full moon. Clutching her coat around her, Helen skirted the east building, going around by the back of it. The perimeter wall rose on her left, dark and threatening. She followed it. A gray outline stood there at the corner. Milos! She waved and hurried toward him. He moved forward himself, smiling, and kissed her on both cheeks.

"Helen! You had me scared. You're late."

She was surprised to find him so much taller than

she remembered. Bartolomeo must be extremely tall for his friend to seem short by comparison.

"I'm sorry. I couldn't get out. Our supervisor wasn't asleep. And now she's gone out herself—can you believe that? She left the dormitory just before midnight."

"Did she really? Then I know where she's gone, and I'm going to show you. If you're good at gymnastics."

"I'm great at gymnastics."

"Excellent. Can you climb a rope?"

"Like a squirrel!"

She wasn't sure whether squirrels climbed ropes or not, but she felt like saying yes to everything tonight. She'd have jumped into a fire with Milos if he'd asked her to.

"Wait for me here, then. I'll be back in a couple of minutes."

"Can't you explain a bit first?"

"Later!"

Milos was already stuffing his cap in his pocket and beginning to climb. Helen was amazed by his strength and agility. Clinging to the gutter, he climbed as easily as a monkey. His fingers, hands, arms, and legs were moving all the time, and he didn't stop except to get his breath back with his foot on a second-floor windowsill.

"Be careful!" begged Helen down below.

But in reply he just kept on climbing, and next moment he was just below the roof. He stayed hanging from the gutter for a few seconds, then swung from side to side a couple of times and threw his right leg over it. As he recovered his balance, something slipped out of his pocket and fell at Helen's feet.

"My knife!" he called down. "Can you pick up my knife?"

She bent down, and retrieved a heavy pocket knife that must have at least six blades.

Then there was a long silence. Milos had disappeared. She felt the cold seeping in under her coat. What was she doing here with this acrobatic boy who had something serious to tell her?

She was still looking up at the roof in vain when a slight rustling noise attracted her attention. A little way off, a rope was passing over the gutter and dropping straight down the wall. She quickly unbuttoned her coat so that it wouldn't hamper her, wedged the rope between her ankles as she had often done before, and began climbing. When she was level with the third story, she glanced down and was overcome by vertigo. She'd never climbed this high in gym lessons. And there was no mat here to soften the impact if she fell. *Weird kind of first date,* she thought. *Is it always like this?* She took a deep breath and went on. When she reached the gutter, she had no time to wonder how she was going to get up on the roof. Milos was already reaching a hand out to her.

"Give me your right hand and take hold of my wrist. Not my hand, my wrist!"

She took his wrist, and he took hers. Next moment

Helen felt herself being lifted into the air. She hardly had to help herself at all with her knees and elbows before she was sitting beside Milos, who seemed as relaxed forty feet from the ground on top of this roof as he would have been on a sitting-room sofa.

"That's called a cross hold. It doubles your strength," he explained.

"I thought I was going to die," breathed Helen.

"Rest for a minute. We've done the toughest part."

"I should hope so."

They clambered over the damp slates of the roof and reached a skylight to which Milos had fastened the rope. He hauled it up now, coiled it, and fixed it to his belt. Then he opened the skylight far enough for them to slip in. It was easy to hang from the edge and then let yourself drop to the floor inside. Milos went first and landed silently, bending his knees to break his drop. Helen copied him with ease and felt that she had just impressed him twice in a short time: first by climbing the rope so well, then by jumping down into this loft. When Milos caught her, she felt light as a feather in his strong hands. He took a flashlight out of his pocket, switched it on, and swept the beam over the space around them.

The loft was empty and dusty. There was nothing between the massive roof structure and the oak floorboards. They could stand upright in the middle of it but had to bend as they moved closer to the sides.

"What are we doing here?" Helen asked.

Milos put his forefinger to his lips and pointed down. "Shh! Listen!"

The confused, muted sound of conversation came from the story below. There was even a sudden burst of laughter.

"What's going on?" Helen whispered.

All Milos said was, "Got my knife there?"

She handed it to him. He worked his way cautiously forward, eyes lowered, as if looking for something. When he reached the other side of the loft, he knelt down and signaled to Helen that he had found it and she could join him.

"Give me a light," he said, handing her the flashlight, and with the point of his knife he made an incision about four inches long where one of the floorboards looked weaker than the others.

"Are you allowed knives in the boys' school?" Helen marveled, crouching down beside him.

"If we did only what's allowed," said Milos with a smile, "I wouldn't have a rope or a knife, and I certainly wouldn't be here with you in the middle of the night."

"When are you going to explain? I've earned the right to know, haven't I?"

"Hang on a little longer. I'm nearly finished. If you like surprises, you won't be disappointed."

He worked away for several more minutes, removing tiny wood shavings. Then he opened another blade of his knife and used it as a lever. The floorboard groaned slightly and resisted, but then it gave way. Milos signaled to Helen to switch off the flashlight, and he slowly raised the oak board. At once the voices, barely audible a moment ago, could be heard clearly.

"You go first!" said Milos, inviting Helen to look down.

She lay flat on her stomach and placed her face against the narrow rectangle of light. What she saw seemed so unreal at first that she wondered if she was going out of her mind.

There were about fifty people. At the back of the large room stood a buffet laden with food and carafes of wine. Rows of chairs faced a platform with an oak table on it. The rows on the left of the central aisle seemed to be reserved for women, and Helen immediately spotted the Tank standing near the front row with her inseparable ally, Miss Merlute, beside her. Squeezed into a purple evening dress too tight for her beefy shoulders, the headmistress was smiling. Beside her, Miss Merlute wore an extraordinary structure like a helping of sauerkraut on her head, which was bobbing this way and that. Her nose could have been a sausage sticking out of the sauerkraut.

Behind her sat other familiar figures, although they were barely recognizable this evening: first the Skeleton, who had tried unsuccessfully to plump herself up with shoulder pads and other devices; Old Ma Crackpot, breasts swelling like mortar shells under a bottle-green outfit; Miss Mersch in her wheelchair, made up like a birthday cake and clutching a sparkly black evening bag in her white-gloved hands; and finally Miss Zesch as Helen had seen her emerge from her cubicle, but now further adorned by an improbable little yellow hat. Standing on his own near the buffet, the Skunk was fiddling with his cap while eyeing the wine carafes.

Helen almost burst out laughing. Then some men she didn't know took their seats on the right of the aisle. Helen straightened up in astonishment. "Is this some kind of a fashion parade?"

"No, it's the annual assembly of the staff of both boarding schools."

"What sort of assembly? And how do you know all this?"

She had to wait a little longer. Fascinated by the spectacle below them, Milos was taking it all in. Sometimes he shook with silent, suppressed laughter. After a few minutes, he propped himself on his elbows and looked at Helen. The light coming up through the gap he had made in the loft floor faintly illuminated their hands and faces.

"Listen, Helen," Milos whispered. "No other student at either school has ever seen what we're seeing now. When I told you to go first, it was a historic privilege! Did you recognize the staff of your school?"

"Yes, they're all there. And they're all dressed up! Anyone would think they were crazy."

"They are crazy. And the men are the staff of my school. Mad too in their own way."

"Milos, you're scaring me . . . and anyway, what are they all doing here together?"

"I told you: it's their annual assembly, and it's super-secret. They're getting together to welcome a man called Van Vlyck. He's a leading figure in the Phalange, one of its top security bosses, and in particular he's in charge of boarding schools like ours. Apparently they're all scared stiff of him. We'll see."

Alarmed, Helen lowered her voice even further. "What if they catch us? You said this was super-secret. You could have warned me!"

"They won't catch us. No one ever catches me."

"So why wouldn't they catch you sometime in the future?"

"Because I'm lucky, see? Always have been."

"Lucky? You expect me to be satisfied with that?"

"Yes, I do!"

Helen wanted to lose her temper with Milos, but somehow she couldn't manage it. There was such confidence in his smile that she found herself believing what he said without the slightest doubt: no, they'd never be caught.

"Milos, you said boarding schools like ours. Meaning what?"

"Oh, there's too much to explain all at once, Helen! I'll tell you about it all later. That's a promise."

"OK, so why is this man Van Vlyck coming here?"

"To see if everything's in order, I imagine.

Checking up to make sure his lunatics are as crazy as ever. Wait a minute! Something seems to be happening down there. Your turn to have a look, and remember everything you see!"

Helen took up her observation post again. The men and women down below had risen to their feet to applaud the energetic entrance of a powerful man with a red beard, in a sheepskin-lined jacket so worn that it was shiny at the elbows. He certainly hadn't gone to the trouble of putting on evening dress, and his muddy boots could have done with a good polishing. Two men, apparently under his orders, followed close behind him. He made straight for the platform, sat down on a chair, which disappeared under his large posterior, and didn't even take off his jacket. Evidently he didn't intend to stay long. With a gesture, he invited the Tank and a man who must be headmaster of the boys' school to come and sit on either side of him. The Tank was preening like a fat goose as she joined him on the platform. The headmaster, with a flower in his buttonhole, looked equally proud. The newcomer's two henchmen stationed themselves at the door and never moved from the spot.

"Ladies and gentleman, my dear colleagues . . ." There was total silence as Van Vlyck addressed them. His blazing eyes swept over the audience. "My dear colleagues, here we are again. As you know, I really enjoy these nocturnal meetings. They give us all a chance to get together every year, and . . ."

"Can you hear all right?" asked Helen, who was in the best position.

"Not great," Milos admitted.

"Come on, if we shove up a bit . . ." She moved a little way until they were lying side by side, almost cheek to cheek. "Better?" whispered Helen.

"Perfect," Milos replied.

"As tradition demands," Van Vlyck went on, "we'll begin by reviewing the months that have passed since my last visit. Let's start with the girls' school. It is my pleasure to convey the congratulations of the Phalange to the headmistress for the firm and rigorous hand with which she runs the establishment. She is confirmed in her post."

The Tank murmured bashful thanks, but Van Vlyck gave her no time to luxuriate in these compliments.

"Congratulations also to the supervisory staff, in particular Miss Zesch and Miss Merlute, for their conscientious devotion to duty. Congratulations to Miss Mersch, the mathematics teacher, whose exemplary commitment . . ."

As these commendations were handed out, heads turned to those who were fortunate enough to have earned them and were practically swooning with self-satisfaction. Other staff members tried to smile, but jealousy distorted their faces. The Skeleton in particular tightened her lips and craned her scrawny chickenlike neck.

After dealing with the girls' boarding school, Van Vlyck went on to take stock of the boys' school just as rapidly and with the same indifference. Then he suddenly raised his voice.

"We are fighting a hard battle, my dear colleagues. A battle that calls for perseverance and determination. I want you all to know that you are supported in your efforts by the Phalange, which I have the honor of representing here. But I also want you to know that the slightest weakness on your part will be severely punished. For instance, as I am sure you are well aware, we regard allowing letters to pass into or out of the schools as a major misdemeanor . . ."

At the back of the hall, the Skunk made a face and kept his eyes on the toes of his shoes for the rest of the speech.

"Let me repeat this," continued Van Vlyck. "If you ever doubt yourselves, if at any time you find yourselves beginning to feel some compassion for one of your charges, remember: these people are not like us!"

He emphasized this remark by tapping the table with his forefinger, and then went on, pale with anger.

"Secretly, these people despise you, and you must never forget it!"

"These people?" whispered Helen. "Who's he talking about?"

"You and me," Milos whispered back. "Listen . . ."

"They are a threat to our society, just as their parents were."

Helen was trembling. "What's he saying? Our parents? Milos, what does this mean?"

Milos moved a little closer still to her. "Shh. Hear him out."

"We offer them the chance of reeducation in the establishments into which we have generously received them," Van Vlyck was going on. "Our essential mission is to keep the bad seed from germinating. We must crush it underfoot, showing no pity. The rules are there to guide you in your task. They are not complicated; observe them and you will be safe. Forget them and the retribution will be severe. Finally, let me tell you, face-to-face, that the Phalange will tolerate no treachery."

Having delivered these threats, Van Vlyck jutted out his powerful jaw, while an uneasy silence fell over his audience.

"And now I will take up no more of your time," he concluded, clearly satisfied with the effect he had made. "I know there's an excellent buffet supper waiting for you. If anyone has anything to say, speak up now. Otherwise I'll close the meeting."

He spread his arms, sure that no one would venture to raise any other subject, and he was about to conclude proceedings when something extraordinary happened.

The Skeleton, mortified by the lack of any special commendation for herself, rose from her chair, pale as a corpse and skinnier than ever.

"Mr. Van Vlyck," she began in nervous but clipped tones, "if I may ask, have you been told that one of our students has run away?"

Van Vlyck, who had already been rising to his feet, slowly sat down again.

"Has . . . run away, Miss Fitzfischer? Really? Kindly explain."

"Yes, sir," replied the Skeleton, overwhelmed to be mentioned by name. "I told the headmistress a week ago. The runaway is a girl in the fourth year."

Van Vlyck turned slowly to the Tank, who changed color three times within a few seconds: her face went first white, then red, and ended up with a tinge of green.

"Yes, it's true, Mr. Van Vlyck. But we instantly brought the rule for such cases into force. Another student is at present in the detention cell, and—"

"A week ago?" asked the incredulous Van Vlyck, articulating every syllable. "The girl ran away a week ago?"

"Yes, Mr. Van Vlyck," babbled the Tank, suddenly sounding as nervous as a small child. "But I thought—I thought there wasn't any point in—"

"In telling me?" Van Vlyck finished the sentence, with terrifying calm. "You thought, Headmistress, there 'wasn't any point' in telling me, is that correct?"

"Yes," admitted the Tank as she bent her head, unable to utter another word.

"Miss Fitzfischer," said Van Vlyck, turning back to the Skeleton, who was still on her feet, "what is the name of the young person who has run away, if you please?"

"Her name is Bach, sir. Milena Bach."

"Milena Bach," Van Vlyck slowly repeated, and it seemed to Helen that he had turned deathly pale.

She shivered. Even hearing her friend's name spoken by this ogre made her feel as if he almost had Milena in his dirty hands already.

"And what's she like?" he went on. "I mean, describe her physical appearance."

"She's quite tall, a very pretty girl . . ."

"Her hair, please. What color is her hair?"

"Light—light brown," stammered the Tank, in a faint voice, although he had not been asking her.

"Light brown?" asked Van Vlyck, surprised.

"Oh no, she's blond, sir," the Skeleton corrected the headmistress. "Very blond."

The Tank found the strength to raise her head and look at the woman who had watched over the gate of her school for twenty-five years, and the glance the two of them exchanged was pure poison. There was silence while Van Vlyck passed his hands over his face at some length, as if to wipe mud off it.

"This girl," he went on at last in a very low voice. "Miss Fitzfischer, does this girl have any . . . any special talent or quality?"

"Yes," replied the Skeleton, relishing what she was about to say in advance.

"And . . . and what is this special quality, please?"

"She has a very fine singing voice, sir."

There was a long and oppressive silence.

"One final question, Miss Fitzfischer," said Van Vlyck at last, "and then I shall be able to offer you the thanks and congratulations that are your due. Did this girl run away on her own?"

The headmaster of the boys' school, sitting on Van Vlyck's left, had already been wringing his hands for some time. The prospect of having to confess to the same dereliction of duty as the Tank turned his stomach.

"It so happens . . . Mr. Van Vlyck . . . it so happens that, unfortunately, our own institution has also had a similar—"

"What's the boy's name?" Van Vlyck interrupted him forcefully.

"His name is Bartolomeo Casal, sir, and—"

He never finished his sentence. Van Vlyck had appeared to keep calm until now, but at this he closed his eyes, his chest swelled, and he did something no one would have thought possible: he raised his enormous, hairy fist, brought it down on the oak table where he was sitting, and broke the top of the table in two. The dreadful cry he uttered at the same time froze his audience with horror.

"Someone tell Mills!" he shouted, beside himself. "Someone take Mills and his Devils an item of clothing, a handkerchief, a shoe—something, anything carrying the scent of those two vermin!"

"Milos," gasped Helen, terrified, "what are they going to do to them? I don't understand any of this. Explain."

The two of them straightened up, kneeling face-to-face. Milos opened his arms, and Helen, on the brink of tears, flung herself into them.

"Oh, Milos, this is a nightmare."

They heard chairs being overturned down below, and the sound of running feet.

"Get out of here!" bawled Van Vlyck hoarsely. "Get out, all of you, before I murder you!"

The racket died away, and ended with a door slamming violently. Helen looked down through the hole in the floorboards one last time. No one had stopped to put the lights out, and the hall was silent and empty again. Empty except for the Skunk, the only one left, still beside the buffet table with his cap on a chair beside him. He poured himself a glass of white wine, sipped it, clicked his tongue appreciatively, put the glass down, and began making himself a ham sandwich.

POLICE CHIEF MILLS

Bombardone Mills, an apron around his waist, was breaking the eighth egg for his omelette into a chipped bowl when the phone rang. Automatically looking at his watch, he saw that it was a few minutes past two in the morning. Once again hunger had woken the regional police chief in the middle of the night and forced him to get up, sure that he'd never fall asleep again unless he methodically satisfied his appetite. He had the stomach of a hippopotamus. He took time off to throw a generous handful of diced bacon into the pan, then wiped his hands on a greasy dishtowel and turned toward the living room, wondering why someone was calling him in the middle of the night. No one was allowed to disturb him at this hour except for something very important, and the mere idea of that set off a pleasant tingling in his chest and his guts.

Back in his kitchen less than a minute later, he celebrated the good news by breaking two more eggs into the bowl. He enjoyed all aspects of his job, but manhunts had always given him more of a thrill than anything. Finding the scent of your quarry, tracking it down, running it to earth, capturing and killing it—how could anyone feel more alive than at these moments? More powerful? More pitiless? And this time the quarry wasn't single but double. Twice the pleasure lay ahead!

He beat the eggs vigorously, added salt and pepper, and slid the omelette into the pan, where the bacon was already sizzling. Then he went back to the living room, picked up the phone, and dialed a number.

"Is that the barracks? Mills here. Put Pastor on the line, would you? . . . Hi, Pastor, get the pack ready. No, not the full pack, five or six. The best. Yes, at once."

A shape on the sagging sofa moved in the dim light.

"Hear that, Ramses? Going to enjoy this, are you?"

A strange head emerged from under a moth-eaten rug. The lower part of its face was elongated like a dog's muzzle, but the rest of it was human: its eyes, its hairless skin, its flat skull covered with short hair.

"You heard that. You got it, right? We're going hu-u-un-ting! Hu-u-un-ting!"

Mills lingered on the *u* sound, and then spat out the last syllable abruptly.

Ramses started whimpering and directed a still-sleepy eye on his master.

"Uuuu-in," he laboriously articulated.

"Hunting!" Mills corrected him. "Hunting! Say it after me, Ramses: hunting."

"Uuuu-in."

"OK, Ramses, get dressed and join me in the kitchen."

The omelette was ready. Mills slipped the whole thing into a soup plate that had been standing on the table since he ate his supper. He cut a huge chunk of bread and took the top off a tall bottle of beer. The aroma of the omelette and the prospect of the hunt delighted him. It struck him that life was a beautiful, simple thing when you made no particular demands on it. He began eating with a hearty appetite. Ramses, in a jacket and pants, sat down opposite him. He had done up the buttons of the jacket in the wrong holes, so that its front hung oddly. Mills felt slightly moved. Good old Ramses could always give him a laugh. But he'd never managed to teach any other dog-man to do up his own shoelaces!

"Eat? Want something to eat?"

"E-e-e-eee," the creature replied, with a trickle of saliva running down his chops.

Mills pushed part of the omelette across the table to him and handed him a spoon.

"Here, and watch what you're doing. Neat and clean, right? Neat and clean!"

Ramses laboriously stuck the spoon between the

three fingers of his right hand, which had nails like claws, and concentrated on conveying a little food to his mouth.

They were finishing their meal when someone rang the doorbell. A thin, pale man was standing out on the landing, holding a travel bag.

"I'm a supervisor at the boys' boarding school. I've come from Mr. Van Vlyck to bring you the——"

"Yes, I know," Mills interrupted him. "Come in." He led the man into the kitchen. "Sit down."

The man gingerly perched on a corner of the chair. He never took his eyes off Ramses, and his hands were trembling.

"Forgive me, but this is the first time I ever . . . I've never seen a——"

"Never seen a dog-man before? Well, better take your chance now and have a good look. His name's Ramses. Say hello, Ramses!"

"L-l-o-o-o!" the creature got out, twisting his mouth into a distorted smile that uncovered two rows of powerful teeth.

The man flinched so abruptly that he almost fell off his chair. Beads of sweat shone on his forehead.

"Right," said Mills. "So show me what you've got there."

The man opened his bag and took out a pair of leather boots.

"Here. They belong to the young man. I hope they'll do. And for the girl, I've brought this."

He dug into the bag again, and, still staring fixedly at Ramses, produced a scarf.

"She often wore it. We asked."

"No perfume to mask the girl's own odor?" asked Mills.

"I don't think so," replied the man warily, not daring to say for sure.

Mills took the scarf from his hands, buried his nose in it, and sniffed noisily.

"That's OK. You can go."

"Thank you," the man mumbled. "Thank you and—er—good-bye, Mr. Mills."

At the kitchen door, he turned. He was probably hoping to hear the dog-man's disturbing voice again. The terror he had felt when Ramses uttered his inarticulate greeting a moment before told him to run for his life, but his fascination was stronger than his fear.

"And good-bye to you too, Mr. . . . er . . ." he repeated, to Ramses.

The dog-man didn't move a muscle.

"Don't bother!" said Mills. "He reacts only to my voice. And my orders."

"Oh—oh, is that so?" faltered the man.

"Yes," Mills replied. "For instance, if I tell him to attack you here and now, then you have twenty seconds to live, no more."

"Twenty seconds—really?" said the man, choking.

"Just enough time for him to leap at your throat and virtually tear your head off your body."

"My head off—my body?" the man repeated. He gave a small, nervous laugh and then slowly backed out into the corridor, followed by the gentle gaze of Ramses. Mills could hear his steps accelerating, the front door of the apartment slamming, and then the sound of his feet running downstairs.

There was still half a saucepan of black coffee left over from the evening before. Mills put it on the stove to warm up while he dressed. He didn't wash; he never did before setting out on a hunt. Nor did he wash at any time during the hunt, even if it was likely to last for weeks. He didn't shave either. The dirt that built up in the folds of his stomach and between his toes, the beard spreading over his face as if to consume it, all made him feel he was turning into an animal. When it was over and the prey was caught, he liked to go home, exhausted, filthy, and hungry, take a hot bath, and then spend three days eating and sleeping and never showing his face outdoors.

He put on his boots and a leather jacket, swallowed the coffee on his feet, and threw a few clothes, a pair of snowshoes, and a chunk of rye bread into an old canvas knapsack. As he left, he picked up the travel bag containing the boots and the scarf.

"Coming, Ramses? Let's have fun!"

The two of them set off for the barracks through the night. The deserted roads echoed under their feet. The police chief went ahead. Ramses followed a little way behind him, walking upright. Like all dogmen, he could maintain a vertical posture without much difficulty, but he had the hunched shoulders and rounded neck typical of his kind, making him look like a hunchback. His arms seemed too short and too rigid, as if they had atrophied. "Stand up straight!" Mills often told him. Then Ramses would straighten his shoulders and put his head back, but next moment he had forgotten again.

Soon they were in the suburbs.

"Walk beside me!" ordered Mills. "You know I don't like to have you following me. Anyone would think you were a farmyard dog snapping at my heels!"

Ramses came up level with his master, and they walked side by side for ten minutes. Then, gradually, the dog-man fell back until he was walking behind Mills again. Mills gave up. This was one of the things he couldn't get Ramses to do, although when he'd taken him to live in his own apartment five years earlier he had cherished high hopes of this exceptionally gifted member of the pack.

Ramses was one of the third generation of dog-men in Mills's service. The first generation, which he had inherited when he was appointed to his post, consisted of twenty animals — or twenty men, whichever you preferred — who had been given the names of stars. The second generation, ten years later, bore the names of Roman emperors: Caesar, Nero, Octavius, Caligula. The third was named after ancient Egyptian pharaohs: Chephren, Teti, Ptolemy, and so on. Thus Ramses was the son of Augustus and Flavia, and the brother of Cheops and Amenophis. Mills had quickly seen the remarkable potential of the big dog-man with the dreamy look in his eyes, and one day it gave him the idea of adopting Ramses and keeping him in his own bachelor apartment.

They had made rapid progress over the first few weeks. Ramses had learned to write his name and read easy words like *taxi* or *bike*. He could soon say over forty words, beginning with *hello, thank you, eat, hunt,* and *Bombardone*—although they became *"L-l-o-o-o! . . . an-koo . . . e-e-e-eee . . . uuu-nt,"* and *". . . aaardone!"* Then Mills had tried to do more, and that was harder: teaching him to play cards, whistle a tune, make an omelette.

Those days were over now. It had been obvious for some time that Ramses wasn't getting any further.

"Why do you keep him?" Pastor the dog-handler asked. "Take him back to the barracks. He'll be happier with his own kind. Isn't he bored, living with you?"

The chief of police couldn't bring himself to tell the truth: he had become attached to his strange companion's quiet presence and absolute loyalty. Sometimes he woke suddenly at night, a prey to uncontrollable fears, and eating didn't help. Then he went to lie down beside Ramses on the living-room sofa and spent the rest of the night there, reassured by the dog-man's regular breathing.

There was a light on in the barracks, on the second floor. They entered the building and went up a metal staircase. Pastor was waiting for them in his office, smoking a cigarette. He was a flabby, fat man with thick lips, and at present he had the untidy hair and reddened eyes of someone who has been hauled out of bed.

"Hi, Bombardone! Hi, Ramses! Couldn't it wait until tomorrow?"

"No, it couldn't wait," Mills said. "Is the pack ready?"

"I picked the five best: Cheops, Amenophis, Chephren, Mykerinos, and Teti. I suppose you're taking Ramses, so that makes six. OK?"

"OK."

"When do we leave?"

"Right away."

Without further comment, Pastor rose to his feet, put on his heavy sheepskin-lined jacket, and picked up the knapsack hanging from a hook. He was obviously anticipating an immediate departure.

"Starting where?"

"Starting with the consolers. That's where they were last seen."

"Off we go then."

Pastor liked his dogs but not manhunts. Chasing around the mountains for days and nights like an animal, shivering with cold under a blanket, going without food for days on end did not appeal to him. He had never had the predatory instinct of a man like Mills, who would put up with anything for the thrill of the chase.

The five dog-men were waiting in the dark near the barracks gate, rigid arms hanging by their sides. Two of them were smoking. They wore clothes and shoes, and from a distance might have been taken for factory workers waiting for a bus to pick them up at dawn. When Ramses joined them, they hardly looked at him.

Pastor crossed the yard, dragging his feet, a bunch of keys in his hand. He yawned, opened the gate, and whistled through his teeth—a short, sharp sound. The little troop set off behind him. Mills brought up the rear, glad not to have Ramses trailing along behind him anymore.

They reached the consolers' village just before three in the morning. Mills stopped the pack outside the library, the last place the fugitives had been traced. He pushed the door open with his foot and glanced inside. The lighted lamp was on the table; a flame was still dancing behind the glass door of the stove. He went into the room on his own and gave it a brief inspection. The two young people had run away over a week ago, and he couldn't expect to find any sign of them here now. Mills went over to the bookshelves and swept his forearm over the lower one, sending twenty or so books flying to the ground. He scattered them farther with a kick.

"Found anything?" asked Pastor, putting his head round the door.

"No, nothing," said Mills, leaving the library. "We'd better give the dogs their things to get the scent."

Pastor opened the travel bag and took one of the boots out of it. "I'll give this to Cheops, Amenophis, and Teti. And we'll let the other three have the girl's scarf. That way we'll know if our two birds parted company."

"Good thinking, Pastor!" remarked Mills with sarcastic approval. "Brighter than you look, aren't you?"

"I just want to get this over and done with quickly," grunted the dog-handler, and he held the boot out to Cheops. "Here, Cheops, find! Find!"

The dog-man stuck his entire muzzle into the boot. He tilted his head to one side in a comical way and kept his eyes closed. When he had sniffed it at his leisure, he passed the boot to Teti, who did the same. Mills watched them out of the corner of his eye, observing the agitation that gradually came over them. He had always been fascinated by the moment when the dog-men shed their humanity and became all dog. Seeing them quiver with excitement and hearing them whine made him jealous. He too would have liked to be able to register his prey's precise scent in the appropriate part of his brain and begin tracking it down, nose raised to the wind.

"Find, Ramses, find!" he said, holding the scarf out to his favorite.

"Uuu-nt," said Ramses.

"Hunt, yes, that's right," Mills encouraged him.

Pastor's opinion was that Mykerinos had the best nose in the pack, and as soon as he had smelled the scarf, he set off along the main road through the village. All the others followed. It was a strange sight to see the six hunched figures striding along in the pale moonlight like vampires after blood. When

74

they reached the fountain, they didn't hesitate for a moment but turned into a small, sloping road on their left. Halfway along it, they stopped in silence outside Number 49.

The dog-men never barked. All they ever did, at the height of their excitement, was to utter faint whines barely audible to the human ear. Nothing ever gave warning of their presence or their approach. If they were after you, you could expect to see them appear suddenly only a few feet away—by which time it was already too late.

The little house was sleeping. Mills didn't bother to knock at the front door, which was just below street level, but stood in the road itself and threw a handful of gravel at the second-floor windows.

"Who's there?" asked a woman's voice.

"Police," said Mills.

"What do you want?"

"Open up!"

The curtain at the window was drawn a little way to one side. The presence of the dog-men showed that this wasn't some kind of joke. Whoever was inside the house could be heard grumbling for a moment and then coming slowly downstairs. The front door opened to reveal an enormous woman in dressing gown and slippers.

"You are Mrs. . . . ?" asked Mills.

"I'm known as Martha. What do you want?"

"You're a consoler?"

"Would you believe me if I said no, I'm a professional cyclist?"

Having no sense of humor himself, Mills didn't care for jokes. He had to make an effort to keep calm.

"And you are Miss Bach's consoler?"

"I only know their first names."

"Milena," Mills said, and even in the mouth of such a brute, those three syllables were still surprisingly beautiful.

"I could be," replied Martha.

"Yes or no?" asked Mills.

The large woman looked straight into his eyes without showing the slightest sign of fear. Mills felt his annoyance increasing.

"She came here last week," he said, "with a young man, and they left together. Where did they go?"

"My dear sir," whispered Martha, narrowing her eyes, "you know very well that no consoler will ever tell you about the visits a young person pays to her, still less what's said on those occasions. We're like priests, you see, like confessors. And if you don't understand that, then let me put it in simpler terms for your benefit: it's a trade secret."

Mills was a hot-tempered man. In half a second he was beside himself with rage.

"Go indoors!" he ordered, as if the place were his own. Once he was in the house, he closed the door behind them both, forced the consoler down into a chair, and sat astride another facing her, his arms on the back of the chair.

"My good woman," he whispered, "you and your

colleagues are paid by the authorities, meaning me, to give these young people a chance of leaving their schools for three outings a year. At first you were simply called their contacts. I don't know who thought up the stupid term *consolers*. But you can be sure of one thing. I have only to do this," he said, snapping the fingers of his right hand—"this," he repeated, snapping them again—"and all the jokey stuff will be over, understand? You can come down from this hill of yours and get on with your career as—a professional cyclist, was it? So I'm asking you for the last time: did Miss Milena Bach come to see you last week?"

"My dear sir, I really think you ought to drink verbena tea in the evenings. You'd sleep better. And then you wouldn't have to go around in the middle of the night with those unfortunate creatures who—"

"Did that girl visit you or did she not, ma'am? I strongly recommend that you tell me."

"Or there's orange-flower water. You're naturally high-strung, and it would help you to—"

A slap stung Martha's left cheek. She was astounded. No one had ever slapped her, not even her father when she was a little girl, and Mills had a heavy hand. For a moment, stunned and distressed, she almost burst into tears, but she had no time for that. A sound like the booming of a gong was heard outside, followed by a creaking noise, and the door opened.

"Some kind of problem, Martha?"

Four consolers came in one by one, filling two-thirds of the room with their large bulk. The leader was Paula, Helen's consoler, holding a frying pan. The other three were armed with rolling pins.

"No, none at all." Martha smiled, with tears in her eyes. "We were just having a little chat, this gentleman and me — and a real gentleman he is too! But he was about to leave, or that's what I think. . . ."

Mills, still sitting astride the chair, had been quick to assess the situation. In spite of his physical strength, he was far from sure that he could overcome those four mountains of flesh. And for a police chief who was a bachelor into the bargain to die at the hands of women armed with rolling pins would be a shocking humiliation. Of course, he had only to whistle up Ramses and tell him to attack, but setting a dog-man on the consolers would not look like a glorious feat either.

"That's right. I was about to leave," he grunted, rising from the chair.

The four huge women drew back, leaving a narrow passage through which he had to walk like a naughty boy running the gauntlet. Outside, Pastor was rubbing his head with both hands.

"Look what they did to me, Bombardone!" he said furiously. "The bump coming up on my head — you wouldn't believe it. Those madwomen aren't even afraid of the dogs!"

Mills ignored him. The six dog-men were grouped together a little way off. They were all turning to look north, muzzles pointing in the air and quivering. Mills joined them.

"They're somewhere over there? They made for the mountains, right?"

"Uuu-nt," said Ramses, craning his neck.

"I knew it," muttered Mills. "Fugitives always try escaping over the mountains, never down the river."

The other dog-men didn't move, but as he came closer to them, Mills heard their impatient whining.

THE SKY

Although Catharina Pancek was only fifteen, with a childish face, she was resourceful. While pretending to give her a hug, a friend had slipped something into her hand, and whatever happened, she must hide it before the inevitable search was carried out. As she put it in her pocket, she recognized the tiny, familiar sound of little pieces of wood knocking against each other: matches! The best present anyone in her position could be given.

Miss Merlute propelled her on ahead through the dormitory where the older girls slept. They didn't know Catharina's first name, but their encouragement accompanied her all the way past their rows of beds.

"Be brave! You'll be fine! Don't be afraid."

And as she went through the doorway, she even heard one last cry, uttered without any fear of the consequences. "Look at the Sky! Don't forget!"

Catharina shivered. In the last few years she herself had tried to comfort girls being taken away to the detention cell, but she could never have imagined being condemned to it herself someday. As she walked past the beds, she felt her fear recede slightly as if the solidarity and sympathy of so many friendly voices were weaving her a garment of courage with light touches.

Once out of the dormitory, they walked quickly down straight, deserted corridors that Catharina had never seen before. Their shoes disturbed dark balls of dust fluff. These corridors couldn't be swept very often. Miss Merlute went ahead, switching lights on and off as they passed. Sometimes she turned to make sure that her prisoner, whose legs were shorter than hers, was still following, and in profile her huge nose looked so long as to be almost unreal. Without slowing down, so as not to attract the supervisor's attention, Catharina took the matchbox out of her right-hand pocket and thrust it into her thick hair. With a little luck she wouldn't be searched there. They went through several doorways and suddenly, indeed entirely unexpectedly, they were outside the headmistress's office. Miss Merlute quickly knocked twice on the door, then, after a pause, knocked for the third time. *That's their code*, Catharina told herself.

"Come in!" called the voice of someone with her mouth full on the other side of the door.

Miss Merlute took Catharina by the collar, as

if she'd been caught stealing, and pushed her into the room.

"Pancek!" she announced.

The Tank, seated at her desk, was just finishing her meal. The leftovers were spread out in front of her: some lettuce, a chicken carcass, a bowl of mayonnaise with a spoon dug into it, a plate of cheese, some jam, a bottle of beer.

"Well, Pancek?" she asked, masticating noisily.

Well what? Catharina would have liked to ask.

"Do you know where you're being taken?"

"Yes, I know."

"You can do mental arithmetic in there. It will pass the time."

Catharina didn't know exactly what the headmistress was getting at and said nothing.

"Are you afraid?" the Tank went on.

"Yes," Catharina said untruthfully, guessing that it was better to say so. "Yes, I'm afraid."

In fact she felt nothing at this moment, except anxiety that her matches might be discovered. Baffled, the Tank looked her up and down. "Have you been in the detention cell before?"

"No, never."

"Excellent. It'll give you something to tell the others when you get out. If you get out."

You can say what you like! thought Catharina.

Meanwhile Miss Merlute had sat down at a corner of the desk in front of her own plate and was stripping remains of meat off the chicken carcass with the point of her knife.

"Empty your pockets!" the Tank ordered.

Catharina put a handkerchief and a hairbrush on the desk.

"You can have the handkerchief back. It may come in useful. But give me your glasses and your watch. Glass can cut. You'll get them back when you come out."

Catharina's confidence instantly evaporated. She had been shortsighted from birth and wore glasses with thick lenses.

"Oh, please let me keep my glasses!"

"What did you say?" thundered the headmistress. "Giving orders now, is she? Where you're going, child, you won't need any glasses."

"I wasn't giving orders, I only——"

"Your glasses!"

Catharina felt her eyes blurring, and sobs rose in her throat. She took her glasses off and put them on the desk with her watch. Everything around her looked hazy. She was in a mist, and her tears made it sparkle.

"Search her!" ordered the Tank.

Miss Merlute didn't have to be told twice. Her nasty paws scurried over the girl, who gritted her teeth. The supervisor's breath smelled of cold chicken and mayonnaise. *Just so long as she doesn't search my hair,* Catharina silently prayed. She didn't.

"Take her away!" the Tank concluded.

Their wild careen down the corridors began again. Catharina slowed down, arms stretched out in front of her to avoid bumping into obstacles.

When Miss Merlute had had enough of that, she seized her prisoner by the collar again and did not let go. Soon they were in the refectory. It was strange to be there in the middle of the night. The heavy tables, cleared after supper, seemed to be sleeping like large animals. Sounds echoed through the room. Miss Merlute opened the door at the far end of the refectory and switched on a flashlight, and, side by side, they both started down the steep staircase. After a few feet, they passed the cellar on their right and went on down. The steps glistened with moisture; sounds were muted. It felt like walking into a tomb. The spiral of the staircase finally came to an end, leading to a tunnel about thirty feet long, its roof propped up in a makeshift way and with a trodden mud floor. The detention cell was at the far end. Miss Merlute turned an enormous key in the lock, pushed the door open, and ran the beam of her flashlight over the furnishings inside.

"That's the toilet," she explained, pointing to a tin bucket. "Emptied once a day. You'll get a meal once a day too. And that's your bunk."

The Sky! thought Catharina, eyes raised to the top of the wall. *Light up a bit of the Sky, you old witch! Even if I can't see it clearly! I don't mind about the bucket!* But Miss Merlute wasn't going to linger here. She was probably in a hurry to finish her meal in the Tank's company. She turned on her heel and left the cell. The next moment, the place was plunged in darkness. Catharina heard the key turn in the lock, then the supervisor's rapid footsteps as she went away, and after that all was silent. Groping in the dark, Catharina made her way to the bunk and sat down on it. It was made of planks and had no mattress. She took the box of matches out of her hair, where it had been resting safely, and carefully opened it. She counted the matches three times, taking great care not to drop any on the damp floor. There were eight exactly. *How many seconds of light do eight matches come to if you let them burn right down to the end in your fingers? Sixty-four seconds? Seventy-two?* She remembered what the Tank had said about mental arithmetic. *What did she mean by that, the mad old bag?* Anyway, it would be better to hold out as long as possible before using them. She must save them up, a bit like saving up visits to the consolers. Catharina felt a pang when she thought of her own consoler, her kind little mouse. How sad she'd be to think of her in here! With her right hand she pulled the blanket up to her nose and found that it didn't smell as bad as she might have feared. She wrapped herself up in it to sleep. It must be ten in the evening. A long night lay ahead.

When the cold woke her, she couldn't tell whether she had slept for only a few minutes or several hours. Was it morning yet? She thought she heard an insect moving close to her ear. Or a spider? She pulled her coat close around her, hauled the blanket up again, and tried to go back to sleep. It was no good. Gloomy thoughts kept coming into her mind, like an army of insidious beetles scuttling over her. *Where have you gone, Milena? Will you be back soon? Who's going to come looking for me here?*

She held out for what seemed an eternity, although perhaps it was only an hour, and then made up her mind to strike the first match. She would burn one after each meal, so that would be one a day, and she wouldn't be using them up too quickly. She got up and pulled her bunk over to the back wall. If she stood on it, she was very close to the beam they talked about. Just as she was about to strike the little sulfur head of the match on the side of the box, she felt sudden anxiety: suppose there was nothing on the beam after all? No sky, no cloud? No picture of any kind? What a disappointment that would be! And if there really was something, would she be able to see it without her glasses? She hesitated for a few seconds and then finally decided. The match caught fire at once, and Catharina was amazed to see how it lit up the entire cell. She raised her trembling arm toward the beam, and she saw it.

Yes, a patch of sky was painted on the half-rotten beam. It measured only about twelve by six inches, and the azure blue had certainly faded, but it definitely showed the sky! You could tell from the cloud to the left of the picture. A billowing white cumulus cloud like a cotton ball. The flickering flame made its shape swell and seem to move and change: it was an elephant, a mountain, a dragon. Catharina watched, fascinated. It seemed to her that the sight of those colors, even blurred by her short sight, had plucked her out of the dark depths of the earth and brought her back to the land of the living. It was as if the wind were blowing in her hair and the blood running through her veins again.

The sudden return of darkness and the sharp burning pain at her fingertips brought her back to reality: she had just used up her first match. Now there were only seven left. But never mind: she had seen the Sky, and it made her feel stronger. She lay down again, full of courage now.

Don't worry, Milena! Go where you have to go and do what you have to do. I can hold out—for you, for Helen, for all of us. Never fear, girls, little Catharina Pancek has seen the Sky and she'll hold out. You'd be surprised!

Her handkerchief was drenched with tears, but to hell with the Tank. The Tank could get lost—they weren't tears of misery or fear.

Miss Merlute had told the truth. Someone visited Catharina next day. The sound of the key turning in the lock made her jump. A flashlight dazzled her.

"Your meal."

A small woman put a tray down on the side of the bunk. It held a piece of bread, a plate, a jug of water, and a glass.

"Eat it while I take the bucket away to empty it."

"What time is it, please?"

"I'm not allowed to talk to you," replied the woman, and she went out, taking care to lock the door again behind her.

Catharina drank half the contents of the jug in a single draft. She realized that she was incredibly thirsty. Feeling around on the tray, she found a spoon and gingerly tasted the contents of the plate. Beans, barely warm. She swallowed a mouthful, bit into the bread, and thought it was almost nice. *I'll keep it,* she told herself, *I'll eat it bit by bit and make it last.* She hid it under the blanket and forced herself to finish the beans.

A couple of minutes later, the woman was back. She put the bucket down in the corner of the cell and came over to the bunk, shining her flashlight on the tray.

"Finished?"

"Yes," said Catharina. "Do you . . . do you work in the boarding school? Are you new? I don't know you."

"I'm not allowed to talk to you," the woman repeated. "I'll be back tomorrow."

She picked up the tray and went away.

Alone again, Catharina lay on her back for a long time with her eyes wide open, in a very strange, dreamy state. She could have sworn that she knew the woman's voice.

Passing the time was difficult. Catharina exhausted all possible games. She tried to remember poetry she had learned as a child. She went through the names of all the countries in the world in alphabetical order, then boys' first names, then girls' first names, then trees and animals. How much time did all that take? Hours or minutes? How could she know? *Do mental arithmetic* . . . Why not, after all? She started saying her multiplication tables.

On the second day, the same woman came back, and it was all just as it had been the day before. The only difference was that she had boiled potatoes instead of beans.

On the third day—had her hearing grown sharper?—Catharina thought she could just hear the sound of mealtimes in the refectory above her: footsteps, plates and cutlery clinking, chairs being pulled over the floorboards. But the sounds were so faint that she didn't know if she was imagining them or not.

On the fourth day, when she was about to light her fourth match, she struck it clumsily and the flame went out at once. This tiny incident plunged her into deep despair. That same day the small woman stopped dead in the open doorway as she was leaving the cell and asked, "Is your name Pancek?"

"Yes," replied Catharina.

The woman stood there perfectly still for a few more seconds, saying no more, and then she went away.

On the fifth day, Catharina began coughing, and she had a sore throat. She realized that she was finding it more and more difficult to keep count of the days she had spent in the cell. Everything in her head was completely mixed up. The only certain way she could check was by counting the number of matches she had left, because she burned

89

only one a day, and she couldn't prevent herself counting them over and over again. Three matches left . . . three. Three more days when I can see the Sky . . . and then what? Where would she find the strength to keep going after that?

On the sixth day, the woman stopped in the doorway again and continued with the question she had been asking the day before. It was as if she had thought of nothing else since.

"Pancek—Catharina Pancek?"

"Yes," said Catharina. She was sitting on the bunk, trembling feverishly.

There was a long silence, and then the woman said, "It's nine in the evening. I always come at nine in the evening. I'll leave the jug of water close to the door for you. I'll be back tomorrow."

That voice. . . . Just for a second Catharina felt she would be able to put a name to the woman any moment now; it would spring to her lips. She had it on the tip of her tongue, deep in her heart. But as soon as the door closed again, she knew the name had escaped her and she couldn't remember it. She had confused dreams. They were full of fires, the sound of keys turning, swarms of insects, and the Tank shouting, "I beg your pardon?" She searched for the matchbox in her hair for at least an hour before remembering that it had been in her coat pocket since the first evening.

On the seventh day, she couldn't get up when her tray was brought in. The woman came over to her, put her flashlight down on the bunk, and helped her to sit up. "You must eat, Miss Pancek," she said.

Catharina sat there with her teeth chattering. The little woman helped her to drink, then put the spoon in her right hand, but her fingers were trembling so badly that the entire contents fell on her lap. Then the woman took the spoon and fed her like a baby.

Once she had swallowed the first mouthful, they stayed sitting there side by side. The woman appeared to be hesitating.

"Don't you recognize me?" she murmured at last.

"I recognize your voice," said Catharina, hardly surprised to hear the gentle tone in which the woman spoke. "But it's so long ago. . . ."

The woman picked up the flashlight and shone its faint beam on her own face. "Can you see me better now?"

Catharina raised her head and narrowed her eyes. But the sad, heavy face meant nothing to her.

"I knew your father well," the woman went on, and her voice was unsteady. "His name was Oskar Pancek. I worked for him as a maid."

"My father?"

"Ah yes, your father. He was a fine man. He was very good to me."

"I don't remember anything. . . ."

"Or look at me this way," said the woman, turning her face to show her right cheek. "Do you remember me better now?"

The whole right side of her face was covered

by a birthmark, a large port-wine stain. It ran from the middle of her forehead all down her cheek, covering half her mouth and jaw.

"Theresa," Catharina murmured. The three syllables escaping her mouth spread an instant gentle softness through the cell. "Theresa," she repeated. It was like a door opening or a veil being lifted. She saw herself in a large drawing room with a sweet tobacco smell in the air. The curtain of the open bay window was moving in the breeze. Someone was playing the piano, a bearded man wearing a velvet jacket. His fingers caressed the piano keys. She could see him only in profile and came closer to climb up on his knees. "Oh, Cathia, leave your father in peace!" said a voice, and Theresa was bending over her to pick her up.

"My father . . . did he play the piano?" Catharina ventured. Her heart was racing.

"Yes, yes, he did," replied the woman, rising to her feet.

At the door she stopped again, and added, in a voice full of sadness, "Yes, he played the piano, but only for his own pleasure. Most of all he was a great mathematician. And a great figure in the Resistance. I'm not allowed to talk to you. Here are your glasses, your watch, and your hairbrush. I'll put them down beside the jug of water."

Catharina thought she was about to leave now, but the woman hadn't quite finished yet. "There's no one watching the place tonight. After one in the morning, there'll be no one on supervision duty in the school."

Catharina sat there for a long time, feeling stunned as she took in what the woman had just told her in those few words, and above all realizing that the key had not turned in the lock. She staggered over to the door, ran her fingers over the inside of it, and pulled it toward her. It opened easily. Emotion made her fall on all fours. She groped for the jug of water, found her hairbrush, her watch, and her glasses, and put the glasses on at once.

I'm free, she told herself as her thoughts raced through her head. *I'm free. I have my glasses and my watch back. . . . There's no one on supervision duty tonight. . . . My father was a great mathematician and a great figure in the Resistance. . . . I still have one match left for a look at the Sky.*

Trembling all over in spite of her coat and the blanket, she lay down on the bunk. She fell asleep and woke up again more than five times before she thought the right amount of time might have passed. As best she could, she pulled the bunk over to stand under the beam, climbed on it, and struck the eighth and last match. Her watch said nearly two o'clock. For the first time she was seeing the Sky with her glasses on, and she was amazed to find what a vivid blue it was. The white cloud was like a huge feather bed.

She drank from the jug again, trembling with fever, and went along the mud-brick tunnel, stepping carefully. *My consoler,* she told herself. *I must go to her. I must get there somehow.* Every step she took echoed painfully in her head. She climbed the damp spiral staircase, groping her way up it. She had gone about halfway when the door above her creaked. The beam of a flashlight fell into the stairway. Someone was climbing down. Was it Theresa coming back? Someone else? In panic, she just had time to take refuge in the space to her left by the cellar entrance. Flattening herself against the wall, she held her breath.

"Careful, the steps are slippery!" a voice whispered.

"Put your hands on my shoulders," another voice replied. "You said this place is underneath the cellar?"

"Yes. Keep going! We'll have to go right to the bottom of the stairs."

The two figures passed Catharina without seeing her. The way ahead was clear again. She started up the staircase again, but suddenly felt dizzy and thought she was about to fall into the void. Her fever was consuming her, draining all her strength. She knew she'd never get to the top of the steps alone. So she'd have to gamble that the two people down there might be on her side. They'd soon see that the detention cell was empty and turn back. They'd be here again in a few seconds. She sat down on a step to wait for them.

ON THE ROOF

The wet slate shone sparkling black. Sitting on the roof ridge of the boarding school, Helen and Milos wrapped themselves in their coats and looked down at the little town. It was still sleeping between the steel-colored river and the dark northern hills.

"Isn't it beautiful!" Helen gasped. "Have you ever walked in the town?"

"Yes, every time I'm companion to a friend visiting his consoler," said Milos. "I never go to the library—I'm not all that big on reading. It sends me to sleep. So I go back down the hill, over the bridge, and into town. That's what three-quarters of the boys do."

"But what if you get caught?"

"I've told you already. I never get caught. Look down there, where the smoke is rising—it's almost purple. That's the slums; they're full of bars and hoodlums. People go there to drink and fight."

"You're scaring me! Have you ever been there?"

Milos roared with laughter. "I've been through them, but don't worry, I never drink and I don't fight either. At least, not in bars."

"That's right, you said you're a wrestler, didn't you?"

"Greco-Roman wrestling."

"What's that like?"

"Same as freestyle wrestling except you're not allowed to grab your opponent's legs. Or punch or bite or put a stranglehold on him."

"So what's the idea of the sport?"

"You have to get the other man down on his back by attacking just his upper body and make his shoulders touch the ground. It's called a fall."

"It sounds primitive."

"I am primitive."

"I don't believe you. Are you good at . . . at Greco-Roman wrestling?"

"I'm not bad."

"The best in your school?"

"Yes, I think so."

Milos said this without sounding arrogant. Helen had asked him a question and he was answering it truthfully, that was all. She was impressed. Once again, she felt she could be in no danger beside this boy with his large hands, even though she hardly knew him. They both looked up. The countless stars seemed to be blazing unusually brightly. Their sparkling, silent, distant light filled the frozen sky. Helen shivered.

"Are you cold? Do you want to go back?"

"Not until you've told me what you had to tell me, Milos. You promised."

He hesitated for a moment. A cat put its head out from behind a chimney, watched them briefly, surprised to find two humans up here, and then moved gracefully away.

"We must look weird up here on the roof!"

"Come on, tell me, Milos!"

"OK. Are you ready?"

"I'm ready."

"Then let's begin at the beginning. It was last spring. A new boy arrived at the school. Odd kind of guy, about our age, taller than average but sturdy too, shoulders like a furniture mover, long face, blunt features, right thumb very crooked, nose had been bashed in, scars on his arms and hands, hair standing up in tufts. In fact the sort of tough-looking character I'd be very wary of in the ring. Out in the yard his first evening he came over to us and spoke to Bart, hesitating a bit. 'Seems like you're Bartolomeo Casal?' Bart looked him in the face and said yes, that was him. I wondered for a moment if the guy was going to throw himself at Bart and attack him. But no, he opened his huge mouth, buried his face in his hands and kept on saying, almost groaning, 'I don't believe it! I don't believe it!' He seemed so shattered that we took him off into a corner of the yard where no one would see us. 'You certainly kept me on the run!' said the boy. 'Three years I've been looking for you! Three years I've been getting myself chucked out of every boarding school I could find on purpose, trying to track you down! The detention cells I've been in! The beatings I've taken! Look at my face, will you?'

"He was all choked up with emotion. He took a dirty handkerchief out of his pocket, cried into it for a bit, and blew his nose. 'Explain yourself!' Bart said. 'We don't have a clue what you're talking about. First of all, who are you?'

"'I'm a cart-horse,' says this boy.

"'A what?'

"'A cart-horse! Don't you know what that is? I'm the sort that wears themselves out chasing after clowns like your kind! We're told there's mail to be delivered; we deliver it, even if it means ten years searching and the person it's for can't be found. We're ready to go through hell and high water to deliver it. Mind you, not for just anyone. Not for those Phalangist bastards! My dad never could stand them. Me neither. To think I'm the one who's found you! I just can't believe it! You swear you really are Bartolomeo Casal?'

"'Yes, I swear it,' says Bart, feeling more like laughing than anything else by now. 'But why are you looking for me?'

"'I just told you,' says this boy, sounding annoyed. 'Are you deaf or what? I have a letter for you! Sewn into the lining of my jacket, that's where your stupid letter is. It's been going around sewn into people's linings for twelve years! I'm the fourth cart-horse to carry it. Unpicking the lining and stitching it up again every time I change my jacket or coat, I'm sick of it. I'm a cart-horse, not a fashion designer! See my hands? Right, I'll go off to the bathroom to fetch it out and then you can have it. Wait here.'

"Bart and I looked at each other, stunned. A minute or so later the guy was back. 'Thanks,' said Bart, slipping the worn envelope into his pocket. 'What's your name?'

"'Basil, and you know what I'm going to do now?'

"'No,' we said.

"'I'm going to watch my step, I am. I'm going to be an angel, a little lamb, that's what. And most of all I'm going to get some rest, because I've done my job.'

"Then he shook hands with both of us and lumbered off like a bear. We could hear him snorting ten yards away.

"After that, Basil became friends with Bart and me. It was fascinating to hear his story. He'd been in over six boarding schools; he knew all kinds of secrets. You just had to ask him. The annual assembly, Van Vlyck, the rest of it—it's through Basil I know about all that."

"I see. And he must have read the letter too. No one can keep a letter in his pocket for three years without being tempted to read it."

"Of course not. Unless that person can't read."

"You mean Basil can't?"

"No, none of the horse-men can."

"The what?"

"Horse-men. Basil was making fun of himself, saying he was a cart-horse; he's really one of the horse-men. I'll explain more about them another time, but it's a fact; they can't read. From the start, Basil sat in the back row in the classroom. Everyone caught on quickly, and the teachers left him alone."

"Poor boy. And what was in the envelope?"

"A letter for Bart."

"Yes, of course, but what was the letter about?"

"All in good time. Bart read it right away in the bathroom while I kept watch at the door. Like in your school, they never leave us in peace. When he came out, he was white as a sheet. 'Aren't you feeling well?' I asked. 'Who was writing to you?'

"'My father,' he said. 'It's a letter from my father. . . . I never even knew I had one! He wrote it to me fifteen years ago.'

"Over the next few days, Bart changed. He's not the talkative sort, but he started questioning lots of our friends one by one. And it was always the same question he asked. 'Do you remember your parents?' They'd have turned around and thumped anyone else, but somehow people don't turn on Bartolomeo Casal. It was odd: he'd go up to boys he hadn't said a word to in three years and ask them straight out: 'Do you remember your parents?' Most of the time the answer was no. But if someone did say yes, he'd go on asking questions for hours."

"What for?"

"To check up on something his father explained in the letter."

"Meaning?"

"Bart told me in the end, and that's the serious thing I wanted to tell you."

"Go ahead."

"We . . . how can I put this? We're not ordinary orphans."

"Not ordinary orphans?"

"No. Our parents all had something in common."

"What?"

"They all fought against the Phalange organization when it seized power."

Helen's heart was in her mouth. In her seventeen years of life, she'd never been able to form any kind of idea of her parents. She'd often tried imagining what they were like, but in spite of all her efforts, they slipped away from her memory like a fish slipping out of your hands. Hearing someone mention them, even so vaguely, seemed unreal. She felt as if after all this time those two shadowy, ever-elusive figures were giving her a loving wave from infinitely far away. She pressed close to Milos's shoulder to convince herself that all this was real: the rooftop where she was sitting, the pure, cold night all around her, and this calm, quiet boy on the point of revealing extraordinary secrets.

"I don't understand. You mean they rounded us up and put us together because of our parents?"

"That's right."

"But why?"

"Because our parents all died at the same time, more or less."

"You mean they were . . ."

"Murdered, yes."

"Murdered? Who did it?"

Milos hesitated for a few seconds. "The Phalangists. Bart's father describes them very simply: barbarians, he calls them. They seized power by force a little over fifteen years ago. It was a coup d'état. They arrested and assassinated anyone who dared to resist, wiped out all trace of them, banned any mention of their names, destroyed their works if they happened to be artists."

"But Bart's father must have escaped if he wrote that letter."

"He was one of the Resistance leaders, and yes, he did manage to get away. In the letter he writes that he's up near the peaks of the northern mountains, and so far he's succeeded in eluding the Devils, the dog-men under the police chief, Mills. But he won't get much farther, he says. He's exhausted and his feet are frozen. And he says he's giving the letter to a companion in the hope that someday it will end up in his son Bartolomeo's hands."

"It took fifteen years, but it arrived in the end!" marveled Helen. "Thanks to Basil!"

"Exactly. And at the end of the letter," Milos went on, "Bart's father tells him that while he was on the run, he met an extraordinary woman, a singer. Everyone loved and protected her. The barbarians couldn't silence her—as long as she was able to sing, they feared her and her voice. Her name was Eva-Maria Bach, and she had a daughter, a little blond girl who looked exactly like her."

"Milena," Helen murmured.

"That's right. Those barbarians tracked her mother down to the mountains where she'd gone with Bart's father and a handful of other partisans. The dog-men were let loose on them . . ."

Helen shuddered. "My God! Surely Bart's not going to tell Milena that, is he?"

"I don't know."

They said nothing for a few moments, and then Helen went on. "So all those people—I mean our parents—they're dead? There's nothing left of them?"

"No, nothing," Milos said sadly. "There's nothing left of them." And then he added, very quietly, "Except us."

His voice was strangely resonant in the clear night air. At that moment, perched side by side on the slate roof, they felt like the survivors of a terrible, long-ago disaster, two fragile and miraculous birds.

"I always knew Milena wasn't ordinary," said Helen, smiling. "She had that secret deep inside her—something greater than any of the rest of us had. It's a unique gift. You only have to hear her sing to understand."

"Bart's not an ordinary boy either," said Milos.

"Those two were bound to meet. Remember the evening when we all met on the hill? They couldn't take their eyes off each other! And on our way back to the boarding school, Bart stopped dead in the middle of the bridge and asked me, 'Did you hear what she said? Her name's Milena! It's her!' I knew at once that nothing would keep him away from her, not even the thought of sending an innocent person to the detention cell. It was stronger than anything else. We didn't need to say any more. He just gave me a hug and he went off. When he'd gone a little way, he turned back and called, 'We'll meet again, Milos! We'll meet again . . . somewhere else. We'll all be together then, the living and the dead!' And then he was gone. I was left alone on the bridge feeling like an idiot, just like you a few hours later."

"They won't be coming back, then?"

"They won't be coming back."

"But what about Catharina in her cell? We can't leave her there to die!"

"You're right. We have to get her out of there tonight. With the annual assembly, and what happened at the end of it, I don't suppose supervision will be very tight."

"There must be another boy in the detention cell in your school too."

Milos dug both hands into his hair and then sighed deeply. "There was. But not anymore."

"What do you mean? Did they let him out?"

"No, it was like this. A terrible thing happened.

104

When Bart and I left the school last week for me to go and see my consoler, the supervisor picked a boy for punishment instead of us if we failed to come back. And guess what—he picked Basil. The poor guy found himself in the cell without doing anything wrong for once. All he wanted was to keep quiet and out of trouble! He was in there for five days and five nights, and on the Thursday morning I saw two men carrying his body out on a stretcher. His skull was all battered, and there was blood congealing on his face and shoulders. They loaded him into a van and took him away. I don't know where. I think he couldn't bear the idea of being punished unjustly. I think he went crazy with rage in that hole, and then flung himself at the door to kill himself. That's what I work out happened. . . ."

Milos's voice cracked. Helen turned to him, and thought his eyes were suspiciously bright for a boy who claimed to be primitive.

"Come on," he said, pulling himself together. "We must find Catharina before she goes crazy too. Let's get moving!"

They left the rope where it was on the roof and came back down through the skylight. The lock on the door at the far end of the loft didn't stand up to Milos's knife for long. They went down the stairs and into the hall where the assembly had been held. The Skunk, replete and dead drunk, had collapsed beside the wall, fast asleep with his mouth wide open. A plane crashing into the room wouldn't have woken him. When Milos got a close-up view of the buffet—the old soak hadn't been able to make any real inroads into it—he practically fainted.

"The pigs! Look at that: pies, ham, pâté, apple tart!"

"Chocolates!" moaned Helen.

They fell on the food and ate everything that came to hand. Then they helped themselves, not feeling at all guilty, to anything they could carry easily, stuffing their pockets with bread, cheese, and crackers. The doors had all been left unlocked after the guests fled in disorder. They opened them one by one and reached the ground floor unimpeded. In the dark they made their way along the corridor that ran the full length of the building. Milos didn't switch on his flashlight until they reached the refectory, where he felt sure no one would find them at this time of night. The little door at the back of the room was open too. Milos started down the stairs first.

"Careful, the steps are slippery!" whispered Helen.

"Put your hands on my shoulders," Milos replied. "You said the cell's underneath the cellar?"

"Yes. Keep going! We'll have to go right to the bottom."

After about ten feet, a space opened out on their right. Milos ran the beam of his flashlight over it, saw nothing, and went on down. Following him along the mud-brick tunnel, Helen felt her heart thudding violently. What state would little Catharina be in? How would she have survived when Basil, who must be much tougher, had lost his head?

How could they have left her alone for a whole week in that nightmarish cell? Shame and fear overwhelmed her.

"It's not locked!" exclaimed Milos, incredulous. "Look, Helen, the door's wide open!"

She joined him, snatching the flashlight from his hands. If the door had been left open, it could mean that Catharina wasn't in any shape to escape. Perhaps she too . . . Helen swept the beam of the flashlight around the cell. It was empty.

"She isn't here! I don't understand. What have they done with her?"

"Come on!" Milos interrupted. "We can't hang around here!"

They turned back, baffled, not knowing whether to be glad or anxious to find Catharina gone. They were about to start climbing the stairs again when Milos stopped so suddenly that Helen bumped into him. Little Catharina Pancek was sitting on a step farther up the staircase, huddled in her coat. She smiled at them.

"Helen—oh, Helen, I'm so glad to see you."

Helen rushed forward to take Catharina's hands. They were burning hot, and the girl's hair was sticking to her forehead. She smelled of earth.

"Catharina, what are you doing here? You're shivering! Who let you out?"

"Theresa," Catharina replied. "It was Theresa. . . . Would you . . . would you like to see the Sky?"

Helen realized that in her amazement at finding the cell empty she had completely forgotten to look up at the legendary picture on the beam. The girls at the school both feared to see it and dreamed of the sight.

"Yes . . . yes, I would. You mean the Sky really exists?"

"Oh yes, and it's beautiful. I'll show you, but . . . but help me. My . . . my legs won't carry me."

They took her under the arms, and all three went slowly back to the cell. Milos turned the flashlight on the beam, and they looked at it in silence. The sky was deep blue; the white clouds were crowding each other close as the wind chased them. A large gray bird soared through the air, wings spread wide. They could almost hear its cry.

"I never knew there was a bird," whispered Helen, impressed.

"It wasn't there just now," said Catharina faintly. "It wasn't there at all while I was in the cell. . . . It's just appeared. . . . That means I'm the bird, and the bird has flown away. . . ."

"Are you sure it wasn't there?" asked Helen.

"My father was a mathematician," Catharina replied.

"What? What are you talking about?"

"My father was a mathematician. . . . Theresa told me so."

"Let's get out of here," Milos breathed into Helen's ear. "She's feverish; her teeth are chattering."

"Right, but where do we take her?"

"I want to go to my consoler," Catharina declared.

The other two exchanged a swift glance and agreed. They helped Catharina up the stairs as best they could and left the refectory. They had expected the fresh night air to revive the sick girl, but the opposite happened: she almost fainted, and they had to support her to keep her from collapsing in the yard. They skirted the perimeter wall as far as the Skeleton's lodge. There was no light on in there. Was the old battle-ax watching in silence from behind her venetian blinds? They bent double, keeping below the windows as they made their way silently on until they reached the gate. Milos tried the handle. No luck. It was locked.

He was turning back to tell Helen, who was still supporting Catharina, when an acid voice froze them where they stood. "Going for a little walk, were we?"

The Skeleton was standing ten feet away. Her skin looked yellow in the moonlight. She hadn't taken off her evening dress or her makeup, and the ash of her cigarette glowed in her hand.

"And what are you doing here, young man?"

Helen opened her mouth to invent some story, but she closed it again at once. There was nothing to explain—or rather, there was too much to explain, and Milos was slowly moving toward the Skeleton.

"Don't you come any closer, young man! One more step and I shall scream!"

"In that case, ma'am, I'm very sorry," said Milos, "but—"

And he did something very simple and decidedly primitive: he knocked her out with a single upper-cut to her chin. She uttered a strange, mouselike squeal, staggered a little way back, and collapsed like the bag of bones she was.

"Oops!" said Catharina, laughing.

Milos made for the Skeleton, lifted her with one hand, and carried her into the lodge. The next moment, he came out, locked the lodge door, and unlocked the gate.

"I've shut her in there and unplugged the phone, but we'll have to hurry."

Even with the two of them supporting her, one on each side, Catharina was terribly slow. After they had gone a little way, Milos stopped, took her glasses off her, draped her around his shoulders like a scarf, and set off again, striding vigorously. They started over the bridge under the indifferent gaze of the four stone horse-men.

"Watch out!" breathed Helen. "There's a boat going under the bridge."

"What's it doing here in the middle of the night?" Milos wondered, and he moved a little way back from the parapet to escape the eyes of the oarsman, who seemed to be watching him.

They went up Donkey Road as fast as they could. The street was dark and silent. Soon they reached the place where they had met for the first time a week earlier.

"Do you remember?" Helen ventured to ask.

Their situation didn't prevent her from feeling romantic.

"Could I forget it?" replied Milos breathlessly.

Still on his back, Catharina was muttering disjointedly.

"What's she saying?" Helen asked.

"She's delirious. She's talking about matches, a piano, spiders, I think. Do you know who her consoler is? And where she lives?"

"Yes, her name's Emily. I think I can find the house. Can you make it to the top of the hill?"

"I can make it."

Once they reached the fountain, they went around it and on up the road, which now ran straight ahead of them.

"This is it," said Helen, stopping outside a brick house with blue shutters. She knocked on the door three times. "Open the door! Please open the door!" she called. "We have Catharina here!"

"Just coming," a faint voice replied from the second floor.

They waited. Milos, dripping with sweat and still out of breath, stood the sick girl on her feet, put her glasses back on her, and held her upright, close to him. He could feel her burning in his arms. At last the door was opened by a woman in her dressing gown. She was so tiny and delicate that you couldn't help thinking of a mouse. Her eyebrows shot up, revealing large eyes full of surprise and concern. She clasped her hands in front of her breast. "Catharina, my poor child! What have they done to you?"

"She's been in the detention cell," Helen replied.

"Oh, Holy Virgin Mary! Come in, quick, come in!"

Milos carried Catharina to the bedroom and laid her down in the warm bed that the little mouse had just left.

"I'll give her something to bring her temperature down. My God, how can people be such savages? How they can do it I don't know! Do you know?"

Milos and Helen had no answer. The little woman was bustling eagerly about Catharina. She washed her face and hands, caressed her, breathed softly on her forehead, murmured comforting words. A few minutes later, Catharina was fast asleep. Her consoler sat with her for a little longer and then came downstairs to sit at the kitchen table, where the two young people were talking in low voices.

"Can you keep her here, Emily?" asked Helen.

"You know my name?" said the consoler, surprised.

"Yes, Catharina's often talked to me about you."

"She's a good girl. I'll keep her here until she's better. I'll hide her; don't worry. But what about you two? You have to be back before dawn, don't you?"

"We ought to be back by dawn, yes," said Helen gloomily.

In the silence that followed, they thought they heard sounds out in the street, and a man's muted voice giving orders.

"Put the light out! Quick!" Milos ordered.

Emily ran for the switch at once and turned the light off. They waited, keeping absolutely still, and then cautiously ventured over to the window. Gray shadows hovered like ghosts in the twilight. They were slowly moving away. One of them, lagging behind the others and passing close to the window, showed his long profile: a dog's muzzle.

"The Devils!" whispered Milos. "Mills and his dog-men. They're on their way to hunt Bartolomeo down."

"And Milena," said Helen, shuddering with horror.

They dared not move or put the light on again until the last shape had entirely disappeared at the far end of the road.

"Come along, I'll make some coffee," said the consoler when the dog-men had gone. "And you must eat something."

Helen wasn't very hungry after helping herself to the buffet supper in the assembly hall, but Milos managed to eat a slice of roast pork and some quiche.

"We'll have to go back now, I suppose," said Helen, once they had finished their coffee.

Milos took a deep breath, and his features suddenly hardened. "I'm not going back there, Helen. I'm never setting foot in that school again."

"What do you mean?"

"I'm not going back. Ever!"

"Then what will you do?"

"Follow the pack of dog-men, catch up with Mills

and his Devils, and stop them from taking Bart. I know him; he'll never be able to defend himself! He's finished without me, and Milena with him. Those filthy dogs will eat them alive."

"Don't do it," the consoler begged. "They'll eat *you* alive."

"No one's going to eat me! I'm off, and that's that!"

"But someone else will be sent to the cell instead of you. You know that," Helen objected.

"Yes, I know. But you're talking like them now, and I don't want to hear that kind of thing anymore! They've always controlled us by threatening to punish someone else instead. Bart was the first to defy them, and he was right! Basil's shown us another way to do it, though not one I'd go for. Well, I'm leaving too, and not feet first! I'm off, and that's that!"

Helen had to accept it: Milos had made up his mind, and he wasn't going to change it. In silence, she and the consoler packed him a bag full of food and warm clothes. It was three in the morning when they left the little house.

At the fountain, where their ways parted, they stood face-to-face for a moment, distraught, not knowing how to say good-bye. Then—and it was hard to tell which of them moved first—they came together, embraced, and held each other close. They kissed each other's cheeks, mouth, forehead, hands. The cold welded them together.

"I can't leave you," Helen cried. "I can't!"

"Do you want to come with me?" asked Milos.

"Yes. Yes, I do."

"You won't blame me for dragging you away?"

"Never."

"You realize I don't know how all this will end."

"I don't care. I'm coming."

"We'll stay together for good?"

"Yes, we'll stay together for good."

"Promise?"

"Promise."

They went back to Emily to tell her what they had decided. The little consoler could only moan, "Oh, my children, my poor children!" But she didn't try to make them change their minds. She found some spare clothes for Helen too and said good-bye, promising to take good care of Catharina.

When they had climbed above the village, they turned to look back at the sleeping town. They gazed at it in silence, guessing that they would never see it again.

"I'd have liked to say good-bye to Paula and Octavo," said Helen, and tears rolled down her cheeks.

"Who are they?"

"People who live here. I love them."

"Then don't go to say good-bye. They'd stop you from leaving."

A large, gray bird turned north in the moonlit sky, wings spread wide. They heard it utter its cry.

MOUNTAIN REFUGE

On the evening of their own flight, a week before their friends followed, Milena and Bartolomeo got on a bus that had crossed the whole country and was now driving north. They wanted to get over the mountains as quickly as possible. What awaited them after that they had no idea, but anything would be better than falling into the hands of the Phalangists again.

Martha, Milena's consoler, went with them as far as the road that skirted the hill, and they all waited in the drizzling rain for the bus to arrive. It was a monstrous, old bone-shaker with a square hood that made it look like an angry animal. The night was dark. As soon as she heard the engine, Martha planted herself fearlessly in the middle of the road and waved her arms to stop the bus. She pushed the two young people inside, and when the driver asked where they were going, she gave the name of a town one hundred miles farther north in the foothills of the mountains.

"That's where they're going, and here's the money."

The man glanced suspiciously at the long coats worn by boarding-school students, and asked cunningly, "So where do they come from?"

"Out of their mothers' bellies, same as you," replied Martha smartly. "Keep your eye on the road and leave them alone!"

The man did not reply but handed Bart the two tickets. Experience had taught him to avoid quarrelling with the consolers—you weren't likely to win! He pressed a button on his dashboard, and the concertina pleats of the folding door closed with a shrill, screeching sound, forcing Martha off the step. She blew Milena a kiss from the roadside. Milena, still standing, blew a kiss back and then waved as long as she could while the bus carried her away, waved until night and the mist swallowed up the large form of her consoler.

"Good-bye, Martha," Milena murmured.

They put the voluminous bag that Martha had given them in the luggage rack overhead and sat down side by side on a dirty, scuffed leather seat—he by the window, she on the aisle side. Bart was short of space for his long legs. There were no more than ten passengers scattered around the bus, some in front of them, some behind. Most were asleep under blankets with nothing but their hair showing. After taking a nasty look at his new passengers in the rearview mirror, the driver put out the dim lights inside the bus, and suddenly there was nothing but the yellow beam of the headlights in the night and the persistent snoring of the engine.

"So this is freedom?" whispered Milena.

"That's right," Bart agreed. "What do you think of it?"

"Wonderful! How about you?"

"I didn't imagine it quite like this." He smiled. "But I like it all the same. Anyway, let's get some rest. We'll be there in a few hours' time, and we'll need all our strength to get across the mountains as fast as we can."

"You're right."

She leaned her head against her companion's shoulder, and they tried to sleep. After half an hour, they had to admit that they weren't going to manage. The bends and bumps in the road kept them awake, but so, most of all, did the turmoil in their minds. Milena sighed.

"Are you thinking of Catharina Pancek?" whispered Bart.

"Yes," Milena confessed.

"Sorry you came?"

"Yes . . . no . . . oh, I don't know. What about you? Are you thinking of whoever's in detention instead of you?"

"Yes. Particularly because he's the one who brought me my father's letter."

"What's his name?"

"Basil."

They fell silent, their hearts suddenly heavy with guilt. The driver lit a cigarette. There was nothing to be seen on either side of the road but lines of trees standing in the mist as if petrified.

"Did you notice how old this bus is?" said Milena after a while, scraping her fingernail over the dry, blackened leather of her seat. "Maybe our parents were in it too when they got away."

"Maybe. Perhaps they even sat where we're sitting now!"

"You're laughing at me!"

"No, I'm not. My father doesn't give any details in his letter. He just says he met your mother while they were on the run."

"And he doesn't say what happened to her?"

"No," lied Bartolomeo, "he doesn't."

"Perhaps they both got across the mountains. Perhaps they're still alive. . . ."

"I don't know about that."

"What does he say about her?"

"I've told you about ten times already, Milena. He says she sang beautifully, and everyone adored her."

"Sang . . . adored. Was all that in the past tense in his letter?"

"Yes . . . no . . . I don't remember."

"Would you open it and look, please?"

Bartolomeo put his hand in his coat pocket and then changed his mind. "I won't be able to read it. Too dark in here. Leave it till tomorrow."

"Bart, are those words in the past tense in the letter?" Milena persisted.

He hesitated for a moment, and then said, "Yes. They're in the past. But that doesn't mean anything except that they were leaving this country. So it makes sense for him to have written in the past tense."

The road wasn't winding so much now. They fell asleep at last, leaning against each other. Milena had a very odd dream in which Old Ma Crackpot had brought a symphony orchestra into the classroom, but the musicians weren't playing. Instead, they were sitting on the tables and making friendly conversation with the girls, who were delighted. The Tank and Miss Merlute, perched on the top rung of a ladder, were looking in through the window, their faces red with fury as they angrily tapped on the panes in protest. But no one took any notice of them except Old Ma Crackpot, who made gestures of powerless despair in their direction.

Milena woke up with a start. Two pale, washed-out eyes were staring at her from a few inches away. She realized that her head had slipped off Bart's shoulder and was now hanging down over the aisle. The man on the next seat was scrutinizing her with frank interest. He wore a farm laborer's jacket and pants, and his large, chapped hands rested on his knees. There was a cage containing two fat gray rabbits at his feet.

"Eva-Maria Bach," he muttered in a thick voice.

His flat face, which wore a blissful smile, suggested that he wasn't quite right in the head.

"I'm sorry?" said Milena. "What did you say?"

"Eva-Maria Bach . . . that's you, right?"

"No, I . . . Who do you mean?"

The man did not reply but nodded, looking satisfied, as if Milena had said yes to his question. Seeing that he was still staring at her as hard as ever, she turned away. Bartolomeo was asleep beside her, his head against the window. She dug her elbow into his ribs.

"Wake up, Bart. There's a weirdo on my other side."

The boy opened his eyes, leaned forward, and spoke to the man on the other side of the aisle. "What do you want?" he asked.

The man, still beaming, picked up the cage so that they could get a better view of his two rabbits.

"Never mind him; he's a bit simple," Bartolomeo whispered into Milena's ear. They smiled at the man and agreed: yes, they were very handsome rabbits; he should be proud of them.

Day was dawning now, and they were close to the town. Patches of light fell on the countryside here and there. Farmhouses with slate roofs sometimes came into sight as they turned a bend. Soon they were going along an endless straight road full of potholes, but instead of trying to avoid them, the driver was driving as fast as the engine would go. The bus raced furiously on. Tuned between two channels, the radio was blaring out appalling music at full volume. Very soon the travelers, shaken like plums falling off a tree, were emerging from under their blankets one by one and beginning to get their things together.

"You don't like music?" bawled the driver, laughing at his own joke.

"Yes, we do. That's the trouble," Milena murmured.

A few minutes later they had reached the suburbs of the town and then the bus station. The driver parked his vehicle beside a dozen others, all lined up by a building with flaking walls.

The place was deserted. It was bitterly cold. Milena put the hood of her coat up over her head. "Do you think that's the café over there? We could get a hot drink before we start out."

"It would be better not to let people see too much of us," Bart suggested.

But the glazed door they were facing, with a pattern of a cup with a small spoon in it, did look as if it led to a café. They made for it. Inside, three men drinking white wine at the bar were half hidden by the smoke of their cigarettes. Bus drivers, perhaps. A fat man, the café manager, was sweeping the floor in a desultory way. Reassured, Milena and Bart opened the door and went to sit at a table by the opposite window. From there they could just make out the first hills, with the dark mass of the mountains beyond them.

"Yes?" asked the fat man, his three chins quivering.

"Two coffees, please," said Bart.

They sipped slowly, holding the hot cups of coffee between the palms of their hands. Now that she felt a little warmer, Milena put her hood back, letting her luxuriant, blond hair tumble over her shoulders. One of the men at the bar immediately turned. He stared at her, and went on staring. A second man soon followed his example. There was nothing pleasant in the grins on their faces.

"What are they after, Bart? They keep on looking at me."

"You'll have to get used to it," said Bart, jokingly. "Looking at you isn't exactly a hardship, you know."

At any other time Milena would have liked the compliment, but her uneasiness spoiled any pleasure she might have felt. "Stop it; it's not that. It's more as if something about me intrigues them."

By now the three men were talking in low voices and openly looking her up and down.

"That's enough," said Bart firmly. "I don't like this. Let's go!"

Milena swallowed the last of her coffee, the sweetest mouthful at the end, and they both got to their feet, leaving some of the money that Martha had given them on the sticky tablecloth.

"Good-bye," they said to the men as they went out.

"Good-bye," one of them growled in return. Bartolomeo was just shutting the door when the man's hoarse voice caught up with them, followed by a coarse laugh from his two companions. "Think she'd give us a song before she goes?"

Milena stopped dead. "Did you hear what he said?"

"I heard."

She took hold of the collar of Bartolomeo's coat, almost hanging on him. "Bart, you don't understand!"

"What is there to understand?"

"They think I'm my mother! You can see they do! In the bus earlier, and now too . . ."

"A simpleton and three drunks, Milena! Come on. Please."

She resisted him. "No, I'm going to ask those men! They must know. The one in the bus called me Bach. He said my name, do you hear? And a first name too. He said my mother's name, Eva-Maria; I'm sure he did."

"You may be right, but we can't hang around here. They'll be after us, remember. All it takes is for the manager of that café or one of his customers to make a phone call. So come on."

He took her arm, and regretfully she let him lead her away.

The rain never stopped all morning. They walked on side by side through the drizzle, their steps in time with their breathing. The road went uphill, but they could see almost nothing of the plains they were leaving behind or the mountains ahead of them. Milena was feeling gloomy, and they didn't talk much. A few cars slowed down as they caught up with them. They saw surprised faces and suspicious glances behind the windows.

"Let's get off the road," Bart said. "I'm sick of the way they're staring at us."

Late in the afternoon they caught up with a horse-drawn cart going up a stony path. A small, swarthy man was leading the horse by its halter. Milena, whose feet were beginning to feel sore in spite of her boots, put on her prettiest smile and asked, "Could you give us a lift?"

The farmer stopped, grudgingly, and let them step in over the side rail.

Inside the cart a woman of about sixty, wearing a coarse woolly cap on her head and a black apron, was sitting on a sack of potatoes. She greeted them with a smile, and then her small, deep blue eyes rested on Milena and stayed there, the intensity of her gaze at odds with the rest of her rather ordinary appearance.

"Do you . . . do you know me, ma'am?" Milena asked uneasily.

"Acourse I knows you," the woman replied. Then, very quietly, she began to hum a tune with her mouth closed. Her voice was unsteady, and it was hard to follow the melody, but you could tell that as she sang, the woman was hearing another voice, a beautiful one, and was trying to imitate it.

Milena got goosebumps. "That . . . that's very pretty. Where did you hear that tune?"

The woman ignored the question and went on humming dreamily. It was as if, looking at Milena, she were looking inside herself at the same time, seeing her own memories. She was concentrating on every note.

"Who sang that song?" Milena persisted when she had finished.

"Why, you!" the woman said. "We had your records at home, we did. A shame it were . . . Oh, it were a crying shame what happened."

The cart stopped just then. The farmer unhooked the chain keeping the tailgate in place and flung it abruptly back. "You two get out! We're here!"

"Wait a moment," said Milena. "I just wanted to ask this lady—"

"There ain't nowt to ask!" said the farmer, pushing the woman toward the house. "I never should've took you two up. You clear out of here, quick!"

They spent the next two nights in ruined houses. The walls protected them from the wind and the cold well enough to let them snatch a few hours' sleep. As soon as they were up, they went on walking north. Hungry as they were, they tried to save their provisions as far as possible. They drank the icy water of mountain streams from their cupped hands.

At midmorning on the third day, the mist suddenly lifted, and they were amazed to see the unreal beauty of the landscape surrounding them. Green moorland stretched out ahead, sprinkled with gray rocks and small, sparkling lakes. Far away the snowy peaks of the mountains rose to the sky. Sharp air filled their lungs.

"Oh, my God!" exclaimed Milena. Words failed her and she couldn't say any more.

"This is freedom," Bartolomeo breathed. "What do you think of it now?"

"Oh—not bad!" she replied after a moment. "Let's celebrate."

She went up to a rock and sat down on it. When he was about to sit beside her, she pushed him away. "No, go farther off. Like that, yes."

She straightened her back, put her hands on her knees, and took a deep breath.

"A poor soul sat sighing by a sycamore tree;
Sing willow, willow, willow!"

From the moment when she sang the first notes, the air around her seemed to be transfigured. Her pure voice spun invisible threads between earth and sky.

"With his hand in his bosom
And his head upon his knee;
O willow, willow, willow, willow!"

Milena sang effortlessly, her eyebrows drawn slightly together, her eyes closed. She didn't open them until the last vibration of the last note had died away.

Bart, entranced, didn't dare break the silence. His throat was tight with emotion.

"Did you like it?" asked Milena.

"Yes," he said. "Yes, I liked it a lot. And I liked the little lines it gives you between the top of your nose and your forehead."

"I know it does. They come as soon as I open my mouth to sing. I can't seem to make them go away."

He came over to her again and sat down on the rock beside her. "Where did you learn that song?"

"I feel as if I've always known it. I must have learned it when I was very small. From my mother, I suppose. I can understand that now. I know about twenty songs by heart, and I've always sung them to myself, first in the orphanage, then at the boarding school . . . always. I can sing them to myself in silence and hear them in my head. Sometimes I choose one and decide to sing it properly—I mean out loud."

"What makes you decide to do that?"

"I don't really know. The right moment. The right person."

"I see—and was this time the right moment or the right person?"

"Take a guess!"

She took his hand as they started walking again. It was that evening that they decided not to go any farther.

*   *   *

The mountain refuge hut, in the shelter of a group of trees, stood just on the line reached by the first snows. The door was unlocked. The single room had a bunk bed pushed against the back wall, a huge fireplace, a table, two benches and a cupboard cobbled together out of rickety planks. They lit a fire and ate some of their provisions. Then they talked all night. They talked feverishly until they felt exhausted, and by the small hours of the morning, they had come to their decision.

Bart found a pair of rusty scissors in a drawer and sharpened them at length on a hard stone. Milena sat astride a wicker chair in front of the fire with her head facing the back of it and bent her neck, "Go on."

Hesitantly, Bartolomeo slipped a heavy handful of blond hair between his fingers. "Are you sure? You won't hold it against me later?"

"Look, I'm the one asking you to do it. We know we must go down again, and I don't fancy having three-quarters of the population take me for a ghost. Go on, Bart."

The first snip of the scissors gave them both a pang. After that Bart set to work as well as he could, sending locks of blond hair flying around them. Soon the feet of the chair were surrounded by a silky, golden carpet. When Milena had nothing left on her head but a short, untidy boyish haircut, he put the scissors down.

"All right?" he asked, going around to kneel down in front of her.

Milena's face was covered with tears. "It's hard," she said sadly. "I've had long hair since I was four. About the age when I learned the songs. It's as if you'd cut my arms off."

"But your hair will grow again. Don't cry."

"What do I look like?"

"I don't know . . . well, like Helen Dormann, maybe."

She found the strength to laugh. Seeing her like that, her face tear-stained, her eyes reddened and her hair shorn, Bartolomeo Casal thought he had never seen such a beautiful woman in his life. *A woman,* he told himself, *not a girl.*

They took off their school coats, threw them on the fire, and watched them burn until there was nothing left but the charred buttons. Then they went out to the little lake nearby. It was perfectly circular, reflecting the deep green of the spruce trees surrounding it. The silence and calm were absolute.

"First to say 'This is the first morning in the world' has lost!" said Milena, laughing.

"This is the first morning in the world!" shouted Bart, and he raced for the bank. Stripping off his clothes quickly, he plunged into the icy water. He swam fast, churning up the water with his arms and legs.

"Come on! Come on in!" he called when he had reached the middle of the lake.

She hesitated, and then undressed too and went to the edge.

130

"Come on in!" called Bart again.

She couldn't help it: she shouted out loud and flung herself into the water. It felt like having a thousand red-hot needles pierce her body. They met in the middle of the lake, choking, shaking with laughter, unable to utter a word.

When they were back on the bank again, the air seemed bitter cold. They ran to the refuge and piled the fire high with dry branches, all the logs that were left, and their own clothes, which they had carried back under their arms. The wood crackled, sending up sparks, and then the flames rose high. They pulled a mattress in front of the fireplace and slipped under the covers. Their skin, warm from the fire, was still cold in patches from the icy lake. Some drops of water were still running down Milena's white back. They held each other close, kissed and embraced, amazed to find themselves here naked, body against body for the first time, without any fears at all.

Much later, when they woke up, the sun was high in the sky. They considered the clothes that Martha had packed in the bag for them. Bart's pants were four inches too short, and they had to let the hems down to lengthen the legs. Milena was decked out in a dress that could have belonged to her grandmother and a black coat with a fur collar.

"Just look at me!" She laughed, pointing to her hair, which resembled a recently harvested wheatfield. But Bartolomeo's eyes said, *You could wear anything at all; nothing would make you ugly.*

131

"Anyway," he said out loud, "if any dog-men get up here, they'll find themselves faced with quite a problem. Our trail ends in this mountain refuge. Sorry, gentlemen, but we're on our way back down."

The idea of escaping by crossing the mountains had soon seemed to them unbearable. Their own parents had fled in the past, but at least they had fought before they ran away. They had defied the Phalange. And some people were surely still ready to do the same. Like the woman in the horse-drawn cart who had said it was a shame. They had decided last night they had to find those people and join them. Brute force was obviously on the barbarians' side, but how could they not believe that the precious memory of life before the Phalange didn't still live on, lying low in people's hearts? There must be embers that could be rekindled before darkness covered the world entirely. In their excited conversation at the refuge, Bart and Milena had worked out that there must be a link between the rekindling of that fire and Eva-Maria Bach's voice. The barbarians had silenced it, and Bart knew how, but it now vibrated on in Milena's throat. Perhaps anything was still possible.

And Milena, who had only just found her mother's trail, couldn't resign herself to giving up so quickly. Every step she took northward was a denial of her heart, a denial of her wish to know more about the woman who had been so like her.

What was more, they had said to each other, how could they leave Catharina Pancek and Basil behind them, imprisoned in detention cells? Their sacrifices called for something better than just hiding.

Bart couldn't get the secrets revealed by Basil out of his mind. After all, the terrifying Van Vlyck was only a man, and an order from him would surely be enough to open the doors of all the boarding schools. They had to find the man and make him give that order. How? They had no idea, but at least they would have tried. They'd have fought back.

It was with this crazy hope that they had made up their minds: they would stop trying to escape and go to the capital city in the south of the country. Neither Bartolomeo nor Milena had ever been there.

They walked for a long way, came to the river, stole a small boat tied up to a dock, and let themselves be carried downstream, stopping only to sleep and stretch their legs. The great river seemed ready to protect them, offering them its soft murmuring and its slow waters. It cradled them.

"Sing," Bartolomeo sometimes said, and Milena let the lines appear on the little patch of skin between her nose and her forehead for him.

In the middle of the third night, they passed under a bridge. The clear sky was sprinkled with stars. Bart recognized the four stone horsemen.

"Wake up, Milena! It's our little town. Look, there's your school!"

Milena, sleeping under a blanket at the bottom of the boat, put her chin above it and sat up to see better. "You're right. It feels funny going under the bridge, when I've walked over it so often. Look, there are people crossing it now! They look like students from the schools with those coats. What on earth are they doing here at this time of night?"

Sure enough, two figures were hurrying toward the hill. The first seemed to be carrying something heavy on his back, perhaps a sack. The second, who was a little smaller, no doubt a girl, was following close behind. But as the current swept the boat on, they were unable to see any more.

THE NIGHT OF THE DOG-MEN

Pastor got out of the bus in a very bad temper. Three of his five dogs had been vomiting for half the journey, and they'd had to drive with the windows open to let in some fresh air. The other passengers, already terrified by the presence of their strange traveling companions, had been freezing cold all night, and couldn't sleep. The horrible, sour stench made them gag. The other two dog-men, Cheops and Teti, weren't much better than their comrades. Green in the face, they had been belching disgustingly the whole time, not even bothering to wipe away the saliva slobbering down their chops. Only Ramses had behaved decently. He was sitting beside Mills, and they had both managed to sleep, heads close together like a pair of lovers.

"Told you so," muttered Pastor, kicking the wheel of the bus. "These creatures don't travel well. Amenophis threw up all over my jacket. I'll be stinking right through the hunt."

"No worse than usual, I can assure you," said Mills dryly.

When Pastor asked the bus driver why he hadn't reported the two fugitives last week, he said one of the consolers had told him to "leave them alone," and he for one didn't go asking for trouble. The big dog-handler, who had a bump on his head to remind him of an unpleasant experience, had no difficulty in understanding the man's meaning. They went into the café, where the manager greeted them with a sleepy "Morning." He confirmed that yes, he had certainly seen the young couple. They'd been sitting at that table by the window over there. Where had they gone after that? No idea. Pastor ordered a large basin of coffee for "his dogs."

"Your dogs?" asked the surprised manager. "Dogs taken to drinking coffee these days, have they?"

"Mine have, yes," said Pastor, jerking his head in the direction of the stooping figures visible beyond the curtain over the glazed door.

"Oh, I ... yes, I see," stammered the café manager, and he went off with his fat face shaking.

Less than ten minutes later, the two men and their pack were off along the mountain road. Mykerinos had sniffed Milena's scarf together with Chephren and Ramses, and he led the others with his nose raised to the wind. Mills had given the other three dogs—Cheops, Amenophis, and Teti—Bartolomeo's boot to smell again, and they too immediately set off.

"Good," said the police chief. "They went along

136

the road on foot. We can take shortcuts and save time."

Although the two young people had a head start, he didn't doubt for a moment that he would catch up with them before they were over the mountains. He had seen the same thing happen more than ten times before: fugitives lost their way, suffered injuries, gave way to exhaustion. Sooner or later they were always tracked down, and then . . . well, official instructions might be to bring them back alive, but Mills had never been able to resist the dubious pleasure of taking a different line. He and Pastor had known each other so long that they didn't need to discuss it when the time came. Mills would merely nod, and the big dog-handler understood and whispered a single word into the ear of one of his beasts. A word of just two syllables, very simple, but pitiless and deadly: "Attack!" The sight of the kill disgusted Pastor, and he put his jacket over his head rather than watch. When it was all over, he called his dogs to heel and congratulated them. By then he couldn't even recognize the bodies. Mills, on the other hand, made himself watch to the very end, with his stomach heaving but his eyes wide open. All he had to say in the report was that the fugitives had been armed, their behavior had been threatening, and the police party had been forced to defend themselves.

They started along the uphill path on their right. After a hundred yards, Pastor was sweating profusely. "Bombardone," he muttered, "I'm telling you, just so's you know, this is my very last hunt. You'll never get me going up this damn mountain with you again."

"You've said that before, and you were always right there with us next time. You love the hunt— admit it!"

"I hate it. Anyway, I'm retiring in six months' time. You know I am. My wife and I are off to live in the south. You know what kind of pet we'll keep then?"

"No."

"A cat! A nice, big, neutered kitty-cat who'll sit on my knee and purr. Ha, ha, ha!"

Three hundred yards lower down the mountain, Helen and Milos heard Pastor's laughter ringing through the air, echoing back from the rocks. They stopped.

"If he laughs like that often enough, we're in no danger of losing them!" said Helen.

It had been a hard night for them both. They had taken Emily's advice to leave their school coats at her house and caught the same bus that Bart and Milena had taken a week before. They sat at the back to attract as little notice as possible. But there had been a terrifying moment as they left: a massively built man had stationed himself in the middle of the road to stop the driver, who opened the bus door. The huge man had gotten in, followed by the alarming pack of dog-men.

"Don't be afraid, ladies and gentlemen," Mills

had boomed at the frightened passengers. "They won't hurt you."

"That's right, don't worry," Pastor had added. "They obey my slightest word. In theory."

And he had made his dog-men sit in the empty seats.

Two of them, addressed as Cheops and Teti by their master, sat down just in front of Helen and Milos. From behind they were an intriguing sight, with flat skulls that seemed to have no room in them for any brain.

Then the unhappy animals' ordeal began. The stink of their vomit, the constant stops, and the icy air coming in through the windows had made the journey seem endless, but Milos had a chance to notice something that he thought could come in very useful later. Apart from the dog-man sleeping against Mills's shoulder, the others seemed to obey only one man: their master, the handler whom Mills called Pastor. The police chief had been obliged to use him as a go-between several times when he wanted the pack to do something: tell them this, make them do that, and so on.

"If I could just manage to—how can I put it?—overpower him," Milos had whispered.

"Overpower him?" Helen had replied. "You think you're on a wrestling mat or something?"

For the rest of the night, the two fugitives had kept quiet, sometimes dropping off to sleep for a few minutes, but always woken by the cold. Toward morning one of the two dog-men turned and looked at them for a long time, vacant-eyed. His pale, expressionless face looked as if he had just emerged from a nightmare. Helen almost screamed.

Now they themselves were hard on the heels of the pack, and the climb was beginning. Up above, the autumn sun was bathing the crest of the mountains in color.

"Nice day for an outing!" said Milos. "Know any good walking songs?"

Mills, Pastor, and their dogs went rapidly ahead for two days. It was a forced march, and they ran when the terrain was good enough. Whenever they could take a shortcut, Mills didn't hesitate to lead his pack along steep or overgrown paths. They came to the mountain refuge on the second evening, scratched and grazed, exhausted, stupefied by the open air. Pastor could go no farther. The dogs were starving. As for Mills, he was in seventh heaven as he kicked the door of the refuge open and went in.

"Hey, take a look at this little love nest, will you? They went at it right here on this mattress! Bet you it's still warm!"

"Could be," grumbled Pastor. "But they've burned all the wood, the vandals! I'll go and find some for the night. Ramses, Chephren, come and help me, you lazy brutes!"

The two dog-men followed him. The others lay down on the floor, waiting for their master's next orders.

"Move over, will you?" Mills snapped at them. "I can't get by."

They looked at him as if he'd spoken in Hebrew.

"Move, I said! It's not that difficult to understand!"

They didn't budge. It made Mills feel vaguely uneasy, and he left the room until Pastor was back. Raising his eyes, he saw that the weather had changed within a few hours. Low gray clouds covered the sky.

That night snow began falling, heavily and steadily, and it didn't stop. It wrapped the hut in silence, like cotton balls, and soon they felt a long way from civilization, as isolated as if they were in the middle of the ocean. From time to time Mills went out on the doorstep and came back at once, covered with snowflakes.

"We'll leave tomorrow at dawn. Just think how infuriating it would be if they freeze to death before we catch up with them."

They lit a fire, ate some bread, and drank a little of the spirits that Pastor had brought. The big dog-handler would have liked the snow to prevent them from going on at all the next day, but you couldn't count on Mills agreeing to that. He would track his prey as far as hell itself, even at the risk of his own life. The two men lay down side by side on the mattress, fully dressed. Mills had merely hung his jacket on the hook behind the door. The dogs slept on the floor a little way off. Mykerinos seemed to be galloping in his dreams; under his jeans, his thin legs jerked convulsively.

For the first time since they had left, it occurred to Helen that she shouldn't have gone with Milos. She had ventured on this crazy expedition, and now they were going to freeze to death a hundred yards from a refuge with a fire burning in it. A hundred yards from its door, and they couldn't knock at it. She had lost all feeling in the fingers of her left hand. She'd blown on them, tucked them inside her shirt. Nothing helped. And now she couldn't stop her teeth from chattering. Milos, kneeling behind her, was holding her close and trying to warm her by rubbing her with his own large hands, but he wasn't in a much better state himself. He was shivering all over too, and he didn't know what to say to cheer her up.

They had approached the mountain refuge as night was falling, exhausted, and the smoke coming from the chimney told them that the hunters were already there. They had hidden behind rocks, then it began snowing. The cold, their discouragement . . . what could they do? Move away from the refuge and lose themselves in the night? That would mean certain death. Knock on the door and ask for shelter?

"Don't expect them to feel sorry for us," said Milos. "No chance. They're barbarians, and don't forget it."

They had seen Mills appear in the doorway three

times to breathe in the night air, and then go back to the fire that was keeping them all warm in there, men and dogs both.

"It's the other one I need," Milos said at last. "The other man, the dog-handler. He has to come out eventually."

"Suppose he does? What will you do to him?"

"I'm not too sure. But it's our last chance. I'm going to leave you alone for a few minutes. If I can't manage anything, I'll come back to you and then—well, too bad, we'll knock at the door. OK?"

"OK," said Helen. "But be careful. Promise!"

"I promise," he said. He hugged her, dropped a kiss on her hair, and went toward the refuge, skirting it and going around behind the building.

Helen wondered what Milos was planning. In spite of the cold and her fear, she couldn't help smiling when she saw him reappear on the roof three minutes later. Milos must have been a cat in a former life.

Pastor got up to throw a log on the fire and watched it burn, brooding, sometimes stirring the flames with the poker. All around him the room looked like a battlefield after a defeat. The sleeping dog-men lay about on the floor like corpses. He noticed, with amusement, that Ramses had moved close to Mills and laid his muzzle against his master's hip. Pastor crossed the room, taking care not to tread on the bodies lying there, stepped over Amenophis, put on his sheepskin jacket, and opened the door. The cold hit him full on. Snow was still falling, though perhaps not quite as hard as at the beginning of the night. *Good thing we brought snowshoes,* he told himself, looking at the thick layer that had settled.

"Where you going?" grunted Mills, who was only half asleep.

"For a piss," said the dog-handler.

"OK, but close the door after you. It's freezing."

Pastor shut the door and took a step out into the snow. Then he walked a little way along the wall to his right and stopped to urinate. He took his time. When he had finished, he did up his fly and yawned. A snowflake landed in his mouth, and then another. They melted at once on his warm tongue. It was a pleasant, delicate, tickling sensation. He kept his mouth open on purpose to go on with this little game. *Like a kid!* he thought, laughing. *I'm playing like a kid! Hey, if Mills could see me!* That was the last thought he had before the shock hit him.

Crouching on the edge of the roof ready to jump, Milos knew that he couldn't do it. To drive the blade of his knife into the back of the man standing motionless six feet away was beyond him. So what could he do? He still held the opened knife in his right hand, just in case. Then he concentrated on the two things that his life and Helen's depended on: knocking Pastor out at the first blow and next, at all costs, preventing him from alerting his dogs. They were sleeping only a few yards away, and their keen ears would pick up the slightest hint of a groan. He was lucky that Pastor had positioned himself just below him. In spite of the darkness, he easily recognized the man's thick sheepskin jacket. Now he must make up his mind to jump.

Never, not even before his toughest fights, had Milos felt a quarter of the tension flooding through him now. He realized that all he had ever experienced so far on the wrestling mat was just a game. Yet he had entered into it entirely, body and soul; he had trained hard. He'd never given up the sport in spite of suffering hard blows, sprains, and broken bones. Over the last year he had defeated all the other boys he faced, even fifth-year and sixth-year opponents who were older and heavier than he was. But this time it wasn't a matter of winning or losing. It was a matter of life or death.

How would his stiff muscles respond when he told them to jump? Would they let him down, for the first time ever? This man Pastor seemed rather thickset—he was massive. Milos guessed he must be about two hundred twenty pounds. Quite a weight difference when he, Milos, fought in the under-one hundred forty-five pounds category! And his opponent was still warm from the fire, and had probably had something to eat.

Frozen and feeling sick inside, Milos still hesitated. *Now! Now!* he urged himself. *In a moment that fat lump is going to turn. He'll see you, and he'll shout, and then it'll all be over. Jump, Milos, jump!*

The snow giving way under his feet made his

mind up for him. He began sliding and couldn't stop by holding on to anything. He had no choice now. He gathered all his energy together and launched himself into the void.

His knees hit Pastor's backbone with violent force. Pastor collapsed in the snow headfirst, and Milos flung himself furiously on the man. He got his right arm around Pastor's neck under the chin and locked the hold with his left arm. The arm-lock was banned in wrestling. No strangling. All his trainers had said the same to him ever since the day when, still a little boy, he had first put on a wrestler's uniform. No strangling.

The rest of his body had instinctively gone into the on-top position, which prevents the other wrestler from disengaging. Legs, hips, pelvis—he had brought them all into action without stopping for a moment to think about it. The hundreds of hours he'd sweated out on the training mat came from concentrating on a single swift, sure, precise move. Up to this point, he was sure, Pastor had made no sound at all. And it must stay that way. It must stay that way *at any price*. And those words really meant something. Milos braced himself, consolidated his grip, and then tightened his hold.

Bombardone Mills, about to drop off to sleep, felt as if he had heard a muted thump somewhere outside. Had poor old Pastor thrown a snowball? Or had he slipped and fallen flat on his face? He was tempted to get up and go out to take a look, but the feel of Ramses nestling against his stomach overcame any idea of moving. He patted the dog-man's long head with the back of his hand. Without opening his eyes, Ramses growled faintly, as if in thanks. Mills closed his own eyes. He had to get some sleep. Tomorrow would be a tough day.

Helen had seen Milos launch himself off the roof and land on the man. She immediately forgot the cold and her exhaustion and fear. There was nothing over there but the shape of the two motionless bodies. The snow was already beginning to cover them. What was Milos doing? Surely he wasn't going to—? Through the window of the refuge she could see dancing shadows thrown by the flames on the hearth. A cruel man and six dogs were sleeping there only a few yards away, ready to tear Milos to shreds if they found him. Perhaps they weren't even asleep. And he had gone to face them alone, armed only with his big hands and his courage. "I never get caught!" he kept saying cheerfully. But suppose they did catch him all the same. Suppose they did catch him.

How long does it take to strangle a man? Every time Milos relaxed his armlock, even very slightly, his opponent shook faintly but convulsively and groaned. The sound might rouse his companions. Milos braced himself again to keep the man silent and immobile. The muscles of his right arm were beginning to seize up under the strain of his intense effort.

Suddenly he saw Pastor's large hand begin to move, slowly creeping closer to something shining in the snow. *My knife!* he thought. *The knife I dropped. The knife I opened myself! He's going to grab it!* His first impulse was to free one of his arms to block Pastor's hand, but then he thought better of it. Relaxing the stranglehold for a single second would allow his opponent to call out, and that meant certain death. Unable to do anything to prevent it, he saw the hand groping, reaching, finally grasping the handle of the knife, and picking it up. For a few seconds Milos was vaguely aware of the effort Pastor was making to move his arm underneath his body, and then he felt a burning pain in his right thigh. He managed not to cry out, and with a defensive reflex action he tightened his stranglehold even more.

The knife stabbed again in the same place, and he couldn't suppress a groan. He managed to move his leg slightly to immobilize Pastor's arm and prevent him from stabbing a third time. Unable to draw the knife back to strike again, Pastor dug around with the blade in the wound he had already made. The pain was excruciating. Milos knew he couldn't endure it much longer. He had to finish this. Very slightly, he shifted his position. His head was now jammed against the dog-handler's; the man's dirty hair stank of sweat. Their two bodies, welded together, were a single entity.

Milos tried to think of nothing but Helen, who

would die if he failed, and of Bart whom the dog-men would tear to pieces without a moment's hesitation. He imagined them sinking their pitiless fangs into Milena's flesh. *These are barbarians,* he told himself again. *The man pressing so close to me that I can feel the warmth of his body is a barbarian.*

"I'm sorry," he whispered, without knowing whether the other man could hear him. "I'm sorry." And with the aid of his shoulder he began twisting Pastor's neck. He put all his strength into it until he heard the cracking sound he was waiting for. His opponent's body gradually seemed to relax. Milos maintained his hold for another ten seconds and then slowly let go. Pastor's body subsided, inert as an enormous doll. Milos lay there beside it for a moment, almost fainting with pain and exhaustion. No strangling. His eyes blurred with tears. Shame and disgust nearly made him throw up. Strangleholds are banned. Then why hadn't the referee stopped him? And what were the spectators doing? He'd won, hadn't he? They might give him a little applause!

He used his forearms to haul himself up to a kneeling position. The silent snowflakes were falling lightly and gracefully all around. He was on a wrestling mat, yes, but it was a mat made of snow. There were no seats for the audience, just a few black spruce trees, hardly visible in the night. There wasn't even a towel for him to wipe away his sweat.

And his opponent was dead.

He picked up the knife, rose to his feet, and put a hand to his leg. His jeans were drenched with blood. He'd see to that later. Taking the dog-handler's body by the collar of his jacket, he dragged it, with difficulty, toward the rock where Helen was waiting.

Bombardone Mills woke with a sudden start. A branch, probably full of resinous sap, had just exploded on the hearth with a sound like a fire-work going off. He turned over and saw that his colleague wasn't back yet. Some of the dog-men opened an eye. Ramses yawned.

It wasn't like Pastor to go for a stroll in the middle of the night, with snow falling. It wasn't like anyone, come to that. Mills gently moved Ramses' head and got to his feet. As he went out, he bumped into Teti's left leg. The dog-man showed his teeth.

"That's enough," growled Mills. "Don't overdo it."

Snowflakes whirled in the beam of his flashlight, but too densely for him to be able to see more than thirty feet ahead. The police chief followed Pastor's half-covered tracks to the right and found a place where the snow was packed down strangely flat.

"Pastor! Hey, Pastor!" he shouted.

No reply. Looking more closely, he saw a trail beginning here, leading toward the rocks. More than that, he saw drops of blood tracing a scarlet dotted line in the white snow. He didn't like this at all. He was about to follow the trail when he realized that his boots were nowhere near tall enough to cope with this snow. He hurried back into the refuge to put his snowshoes on, but his glance fell on the travel bag with Bartolomeo's boots in it. They'd come higher up his legs.

Leaning back against the room partition, he put on the first boot and then the second. They were a little large for him, but supple and comfortable. As he straightened up, he was surprised to see Cheops standing in front of him. The dog-man had risen without a sound and was glaring at him.

"What do you want?" asked Mills uneasily. "Are you thirsty?"

Cheops let his eyes wander slowly down to the police chief's feet. His muzzle was quivering, and a vicious light gleamed in his eyes.

"Oh, I see!" Mills laughed. "It's the boots. So you think they're—"

Teti too came over and sniffed the air near the boots. A low growl rose from the depths of his throat. It made Mills shudder.

"They're not my boots, you morons!" he said, and swore at them. "It's not me you're looking for. We've been on the march together for three days—don't you recognize me? Are you thick or what?"

He walked around the two dogs, making for the door. But now Amenophis, lips curling back to show the white ivory of his teeth, barred the way.

"Let me by, idiot! Your master's out there. He's in danger."

The dog-man took a step forward, and Mills had to retreat. He stumbled against the mattress and fell over backward.

"I'm taking them off, look! Here, watch, I'm taking them off!"

His heart was thudding. He sent the boots flying through the air to the far end of the room, but the three dog-men took no notice. A very simple line of reasoning was forming in their poor, deranged brains: they'd been given a scent to follow, and the man lying on the mattress in front of them carried that scent. They didn't need to know any more.

"Pastor!" bellowed Mills at the top of his voice. "Pastor, for God's sake!"

Then he looked for Ramses, who had taken refuge in a corner of the room and looked utterly dazed.

"Ramses, here! Defend me!"

The three dog-men were suddenly transformed. Their eyes were bloodshot; their fangs were bared. In a few seconds they became hatred personified. Chephren and Mykerinos, who had been given Milena's scarf to sniff, let the heat of the moment carry them along and joined the others.

"Ramses! Hell, can't you see they're going for me any minute?"

The unfortunate Ramses was in torment, torn between his brothers and his master. He writhed, groaned, wept.

"Ramses, help me!"

That appeal made up his mind for him. He

leaped forward, jaws slobbering, to stand beside Mills. He was big and strong. The others took a step back.

"Attack, Ramses! Attack!"

The loyal dog-man flung himself on Mykerinos, the nearest of his assailants. He was looking for the creature's throat but found only his shoulder. The two of them rolled over on the floor, fighting furiously. Then everything happened very fast. Chephren and Teti attacked together. Teti closed his jaws on Ramses' throat and bit hard. The other two went for his arms, legs, and belly. Struggling, Ramses tried to break free but couldn't. Mills saw red blood flowing over his black trousers and his jacket, the jacket he had once taught the creature to button up for himself.

"Aaar . . . done," begged Ramses, groaning. "Aaar . . . done." And then, making a huge effort, he added, "Ell-ell-ell . . ."

Mills realized that his companion was calling to him for help. A new word, a word he'd just learned. He felt sobs rising in his chest.

"Let go of him!" he shouted.

Then he saw Ramses roll his eyes until only the whites showed. Next moment it was all over.

And when the five Devils turned to Bombardone Mills, he knew that hell itself was very close.

Milos had joined Helen behind the rock over an hour before, and they were waiting in vain for any sign of life in the mountain refuge. Mills must be worried about his colleague's absence. Surely he was bound to come out soon. Helen wasn't shivering so much now with Pastor's warm sheepskin jacket over her shoulders. Milos, lying beside her, held a handkerchief pressed to his leg and was fighting the pain. Every movement he made, however tiny, brought warm blood flowing over his thigh. The dog-handler's body lay under the snow a few yards away. Neither of them dared to look at the small mound forming there. Suddenly the door of the refuge opened and Mills finally appeared. They saw him walking out of the doorway, hesitating, and going back inside. Later they heard him shouting—first for Pastor, then calling to Ramses for help. Then came that terrible outburst of noise, and they realized, with horror, just what was happening. At last, as silence returned, they froze with amazement as they watched an unreal spectacle.

The five dog-men came out of the refuge, raised their muzzles to the sky, and began howling like wolves. The sound pierced the night. But it was not a howl of menace; it sounded joyful. Teti was the first to tear off his jacket and throw it away in the snow. Mykerinos did the same, and then in their own turn Chephren and Amenophis stripped off shirts and jeans. Soon they had all cast off their human clothing, and they leaped away in the direction of the mountains. Within a few seconds, they were lost from sight in the mists.

"The dog-men!" breathed Milos, fascinated. "Reverting to savagery."

"No," said Helen. "Reverting to freedom. They're leaving savagery behind. Come on, the refuge is empty now."

She supported Milos as well as she could. Every step he took sent a stabbing pain through his leg. The wound must be deep.

Helen was astonished to find that she had the strength to drag the bodies of Mills and Ramses outside all by herself. She laid them beside Pastor and covered them up with snow. Her own movements, slowed by exhaustion, seemed strange to her. She returned to the refuge like a sleepwalker, picking up one of the dog-men's shirts in passing. She turned over the mattress, drenched with Mills's blood, so that Milos could lie on it, and put a makeshift dressing on his injured thigh.

There was a large loaf of rye bread on the table. "Could you eat something?" she asked.

"No," said Milos, "but you eat. I think you're going to need enough strength for both of us."

She put some wood on the fire, sat down at the table, and managed to swallow a few mouthfuls. Then they lay down side by side, while the flames cast moving shadows on the ceiling.

"All right?" asked Helen.

"All right," Milos murmured, "except that I've killed a man." And he buried his head in the crook of his elbow and wept quietly.

"You killed a man who would have killed us," she said. "Was that what you wanted?"

"Strangling's not allowed," Milos sobbed. "It's

not allowed. And I did it. I never want to fight again."

She stroked his hair for a long time until he calmed down. Then she said, low-voiced, "Listen, we can't go on tomorrow. We'll never get across the mountains in this snow, not with your injury. We must turn back. What do you think?"

But Milos wasn't thinking anything. He was asleep.

She took his large hands in hers—they were hardly warming up yet—and kissed them. They were not the hands of a killer.

THE GIANT PIG

Helen woke up early in the morning. The fire had gone out, and the acrid smell of cold ashes caught her by the throat. She was shocked to see the belongings of Mills and Pastor scattered around her, useless, in the pale light of dawn. So she hadn't dreamed last night's events: the fight to the death between Pastor and Milos, the wound in Milos's leg, the carnage inflicted by the dog-men.

She turned to Milos and gently touched his shoulder. "How are you feeling?"

"All right," he said, smiling. But he didn't move.

She got up and went to open the door. More snow had fallen overnight. The dog-men's clothes were covered up, and over by the rocks, the buried bodies of Mills, Pastor, and Ramses showed only as three gracefully curved little mounds. She went back indoors and set to work making a fire with some dry twigs and small pieces of kindling. Kneeling in front of the fire, she blew on the flames. Milos, who was still lying on the mattress, watched her out of the corner of his eye.

"Seems you can do anything! Hide bodies under the snow, light a fire, cheer people up. I'm tempted to ask you for a coffee just to see what happens!"

"Want to bet?" she said, pretending to be cheerful. Hurrying off, she opened drawers and cupboards until she found what she was looking for: an old saucepan without a handle. She went out to fill it with snow and then put it over the fire. Less than ten minutes later she was handing Milos a mug of steaming hot water with a few drops of the spirits Pastor had brought added to it.

"Sorry, not very strong as coffee goes," she said.

He drank it in small sips, leaning on one elbow.

"Will you be able to walk?" asked Helen. "We'll each have a pair of snowshoes; that should help us get down. Because we are going to turn back, aren't we? We can't go on now."

Milos put the empty mug down and looked at her sadly. "Thanks for the 'coffee.' You're very kind, but I can't walk at all. I can't even get up. I didn't sleep at all last night—it hurt too badly. And look: I think the knife went almost right through my thigh."

He raised the blanket. Blood had soaked the dogman's shirt, and he carefully moved the torn denim of his jeans aside.

"Oh, my God," Helen gasped at the sight of the gaping wound. "I'll change the dressing for you."

158

"That won't stop it from bleeding," said Milos. "All I can do is keep the wound compressed by trying to move as little as possible. There's nothing else to be done unless you can stitch wounds too. Got a needle and thread with you?"

But neither of them laughed. Last night Milos had said, "I think you're going to need enough strength for both of us," and now Helen realized how right he was.

"I'll go down to the valley to get help," she said, trying to keep her voice steady. "I'm sure I can find a farmer with a sleigh, and we'll get you back down to have that wound seen to. Or I could bring a doctor up here?"

"Do you think you can manage it?"

"I don't see any other solution, do you? We might wait hundreds of years for someone to come this way."

Milos sighed. He didn't like the idea of letting Helen go on her own.

"The snow will have changed the whole land-scape. You won't recognize anything."

"I won't even try finding the path we took up here. I'll go straight ahead downhill and knock at the first door I come to."

Wasting no more time, she stood up and began getting ready to leave. Mills's snowshoes were better than the other pair; the wood was almost new, and they had supple leather straps. She adjusted them to fit her and took a few steps out in the snow to try them. Of the two knapsacks, she chose Pastor's, which was smaller. She took out the contents, a packet of hard crackers, and two apples, and left them beside Milos with half the loaf of bread.

"You must eat a little or you'll just get weaker."

"I'll try," he promised.

She melted another full saucepan of snow and gave it to him to keep in reserve. Then she arranged anything that might keep him warm around him: the blanket belonging to the refuge, one of the dog-men's pullovers, and Mills's jacket, which was still hanging behind the door. She rolled up Pastor's sheepskin jacket and put it in her knapsack with the rest of the rye bread.

When the time came for her to leave, she crouched down beside Milos and took his curly head in her hands. "It took us two days to come up here. I won't need that long to get down again. We saw some houses on the way, remember? With a bit of luck I'll be back tomorrow, the day after tomorrow at the latest. You won't run away, will you?"

"I'd have my work cut out for me to do that!"

They said nothing for a few seconds.

"I thought I was going to protect you, and now I'm the one who needs your help." He sighed. "That was clever! I should have stayed at the school."

"Stop it!" Helen interrupted him. "You wanted to keep the pack from catching up with Bart and Milena, and you did it! It's because of you they have nothing to fear now."

"Yes, but what about you?"

"I'll be all right — don't you worry. Well, I'd better

leave. Shall I look for some more wood for you first? Dead branches? You could burn them this evening."

"No, don't waste time doing that. I'd rather you left at once."

"You're right. I'll be off." But she was still hesitating. "Is there anything else I can do for you?"

"Yes, come back!"

"Of course I'll come back!"

"Promise?"

She merely nodded. *If I open my mouth,* she thought, *my voice will fail me, and this is no time to burst into tears.* At the door, she turned and gave him a last smile. He waved good-bye with the fingers of one hand.

"I'll wait, Helen. Look after yourself."

She walked straight ahead for hours, going downhill, running when she could, thinking only of saving time. The wooden snowshoes crunched at every step she took over the fresh snow. *Go on! Go on!* their little rhythmical tune seemed to say again and again. The sun made the ice crystals glitter. *How beautiful this would be,* she thought, *if Milos weren't up there with his leg bleeding!*

Whenever she stopped, she was surprised by the noise of her breathing and the frantic beating of her heart in the silence of the mountains. She swallowed a mouthful of bread, let a little snow melt in her mouth, and went on again. Her secret hope was to find shelter before nightfall, but the sun was already sinking behind the mountain peaks in the

161

west, and she hadn't yet seen any sign of a human dwelling.

At last the slope became less steep. She couldn't be far from the plains now. Since it was slowly growing darker, and a sharp chill was penetrating her sweater, Helen put on Pastor's sheepskin jacket and quickened her pace. She didn't like the idea of sleeping outside. Luckily some rocks soon appeared ahead of her, and then came the green grass of the plains. She took off her snowshoes and tied them to her knapsack by their straps. A path went downhill past a wood of silver birch trees. She followed it, and she hadn't gone five hundred yards before a small stone cottage appeared to her right on the far side of a meadow.

The cottage was certainly very old, but it looked well maintained. A thin plume of white smoke rose from the chimney. A giant pig was squelching around in the mud of its enclosure, two huge, dirty ears flapping against its sides. Helen had never seen such an enormous pig. It must weigh almost two tons. She went up to the wooden door and knocked, waited in vain for someone to answer the door, and knocked again. She thought briefly of Goldilocks: Would there be three bowls of porridge on the table? And three chairs? And three beds? The enormous pig was watching her from a distance, with unearthly grunts emerging from its throat.

"Anyone there?" called Helen.

She walked all around the cottage, but she

couldn't see a sleigh or any kind of cart, only stocks of firewood under a lean-to. Back on the other side again, she tapped at the window panes.

"Anyone there?"

She put her face against the glass. The room inside was lost in the dim light, but in the faint glow of the fire in the stove she saw someone sitting on a chair, both legs propped on a foot warmer.

"Please, sir!" called Helen, and the man raised his eyes and saw her. "Please, may I come in?"

She decided that the vague movement of the man's head meant yes and opened the door. The room had a low ceiling. Its entire furnishings were a cupboard, a table, a clock, and two benches standing on the trodden-earth floor. Helen went over to the stove.

"Excuse me, sir, but I saw the smoke and . . ."

The man was even older than she'd thought. Or perhaps he was sick. Deep wrinkles lined his tired face; the last of his scant white hair lay over his forehead like a funny little comma. He was keeping his hands warm under the blanket that covered his knees.

"I've come down from the mountain refuge," Helen ventured. "The refuge—you know, in the mountains?"

The old man didn't seem to understand. He was watching her without alarm but without any real curiosity either. His large ears stood out from his bald head.

"Do you live alone here?" She took a closer look

around the room and saw a second wicker chair drawn up close to the stove. "Do you live alone here?" she repeated, raising her voice and pointing to the chair. "Is there anyone else here with you?"

She was already resigning herself to further silence when he opened his mouth and, in a hoarse voice, uttered a short and totally incomprehensible sentence, something like, "Sjo ce adji?"

"I'm sorry, what did you say?" she asked.

He repeated the same words, but raising his voice and sounding annoyed.

"I'm afraid I don't speak your language," Helen apologized. "I . . ."

He brought a thin arm out from under the blanket and pointed his shaking hand at her. "Bjoy? Gjirl?"

"Oh, I see!" said Helen, laughing. "A girl! I'm a girl!"

With her short hair, her square face, and wearing Pastor's jacket, she could indeed have passed for a boy. As soon as the old man knew that she was a girl, he seemed better disposed to her. He signaled to her to draw up the other chair and sit down. But that was as far as communication went, and they sat there face-to-face, now and then exchanging rather awkward smiles. Helen was just wondering how the evening was going to turn out when the door opened and a little old woman wearing a head scarf came in. She closed the door after her, quickly hung up her coat on a nail, and stopped dead in the middle of the room when she saw the visitor, who had risen from her chair. However, after the old man had said something in his own language, she walked toward Helen at once with her arms spread wide, "Hugo's fiancée!"

"No, I'm not Hugo's fiancée," replied Helen, glad to find someone who could understand her at last. "I got lost in the mountains, and—"

"Oh, I see," said the old lady, obviously disappointed, but she hugged Helen warmly all the same. Her cold cheeks felt soft as silk. "And you're lost?"

"That's right. I've come from the refuge up in the mountains. You know it?"

"Yes, yes, I know the refuge."

"My friend's up there, he's injured—badly injured—do you understand? It's his leg. I came down to find help, he needs medical attention."

As she told her story, the old man was trying to talk to his wife too, and the poor woman didn't know which of them to listen to.

"He thinks you're Hugo's fiancée," she told Helen at last. "Stubborn as a mule, he is! Just tell him Hugo's well and then he'll leave us in peace!"

"Hugo's well," Helen told the old man, smiling and articulating clearly. "He's very well."

"Ah," he said, satisfied, and then he was quiet.

The old lady gave Helen a conspiratorial wink, as if to say, *Now we can talk sensibly*.

"As I was telling you, my friend's in the mountain refuge," Helen tried again. "He's badly injured. I need to find a sleigh to go and get him down, or a doctor to go up and treat him."

"Oh, is there a doctor in the mountain refuge?"

"No! No, there isn't a doctor in the refuge! My friend's all alone up there. He's injured. Do you know a doctor?"

"Well, my son . . ."

"Your son's a doctor?"

The expression on the old woman's face suddenly changed. She looked at Helen in astonishment. "My son's a doctor, is he? My youngest son?"

Oh, my God, Helen thought, *what on earth have I landed in?* But she persisted all the same. "Yes, you just told me your son is a doctor. Didn't you?"

"Oh, I don't know. . . . Would you like a little soup?"

For the first time, Helen noticed a cast-iron pan heating up on the stove. Steam was escaping from under the lid. Why not take advantage of the offer? Night had fallen now, and she would have to eat and sleep somewhere.

The little old lady lit an oil lamp hanging from a beam in the ceiling and took a large bowl out of the table drawer. "I'll see to my man first. He shakes too much to feed himself. He's not quite right in the head, you know. He hasn't spoken anything but his mother tongue for some time. Oh, it's so sad, my dear. You should have seen him when he was young!"

Helen watched her feeding her husband the soup, standing close to him. It was touching to see her patience and the delicacy of her gestures. Then she and Helen sat down at the table for their own

166

meal. Sadly, the soup wasn't as good as Helen had hoped. She could hardly swallow the lukewarm pieces of potato and turnip floating in a broth that tasted of nothing much.

"Is there anyone else living near here?" she asked. "Other houses?"

"My son . . ." said the old woman.

"Your son the doctor?"

At this moment the old man in his chair repeated a question, several times. Helen caught the name Hugo.

"What's he saying?"

"He wants to know how many children you and Hugo have. He's rambling—wait a minute."

She answered volubly in her husband's language, and then stifled her laughter in the dishtowel she was still holding.

"What did you say?"

"I said you had seven, all boys, and two of them twins into the bargain! He'll leave us in peace while he thinks that over!"

Sure enough, the old man nodded and immersed himself in his own thoughts again. Helen repressed her desire to laugh. This little old lady, so lively and so confused at the same time, was full of surprises.

"You were telling me your son lives here. Your son the doctor."

"Oh, the doctor? Does he live here too?"

"Yes, your son . . ."

"Ah yes, my son. He'll be coming tomorrow morning. Would you like a glass of wine, my dear?"

"What time will your son be here? Because my friend is injured up there in the mountain refuge."

"Yes, yes, didn't you say it's his leg?"

"That's right. His leg is injured. Will your son the doctor be able to help him? Do you think he'll be able to treat him?"

The old woman trotted over to the door at the back of the room and opened it. A flight of steps led up to the second floor and another went down to the cellar. She picked up a half-full bottle of wine from the first step and took two glasses out of the cupboard.

"I don't drink wine," said Helen. Her impatience was getting her down. "I'd rather have—"

"Ah, you should have seen him when he was young!" the old lady interrupted her, filling the glasses. "Sixteen and a half, I was, working in the café. He was a woodcutter. We happened to pass them in a clearing, my friend Franciska and me. A dozen foreign workmen. They'd stopped for their break; they were bare-chested, playing boules with round stones. There was a lot of talking and laughter. He was better-looking than the others. Much better-looking. He had his stone in one hand and a piece of cheese in the other. His shoulders were shining with sweat. 'Ooh,' said Franciska, 'did you see that one? Such a handsome man!' What a laugh we had! And I made sure I passed that way alone over the next few days. One day he came up to me and we told each other our names. He was even better-looking up close than from a distance. And another time we agreed in sign language to meet that evening."

Helen turned her head and looked at the old man's liver-spotted skull, wrinkled neck, and thin shoulders as he dozed by the stove. In spite of her own impatience, she felt touched.

"And . . . so you got together?"

"Yes, that we did. Try keeping a boy and a girl apart! I waited for him behind my father's workshop. I'd prettied myself up on the sly. Lipstick and everything. When I saw him come around the corner of the street and walk toward me I was bowled right over! He was wearing a white shirt, with an open collar showing his chest, and as for the crease in his trousers—oh, what a crease! Ironed in! And there he was, sleeping in a hut in the middle of the woods, but it didn't keep him from looking elegant. Eighteen years old, he was, and there was I, sixteen and a half . . ."

"What a memory you have!"

"No, no, I forget everything these days, but not that. Come along, let's drink to our health, my dear."

They clinked glasses. The wine was rough as it went down Helen's throat, and she found it hard to swallow the first mouthful.

"So then you had children?" she went on, a little ashamed of bringing the conversation back to what really interested her.

"Children, oh yes. We had . . . we had four. No, five."

"And now the youngest is a doctor? Is that right?"

"I don't remember . . . oh, you must forgive me. I'm like him; I forget so much these days. Come along, time for bed. We sleep down here, in the little room next door, and you can have the room upstairs. Just take a candle from the drawer before you go up, dear."

She went over to her husband, whispered something to him, and helped him to his feet. They both crossed the room, moving very slowly. Helen watched them pass her as she drank her wine. It was already going to her head. When the door of the little room next door had closed behind the two old people, she rose and went to sit by the stove to absorb a little warmth. It was sure to be cold upstairs. She was about to go up when the old lady came back in her nightdress, with a nightcap on her head.

"Look, dear."

The photo in the wooden frame showed the head and shoulders of a young man wearing a tie. He had a black, neatly shaped beard, and he wore a peculiar flat cap on his head as he looked confidently into the lens.

"My son! Read what it says on the back."

On the cardboard at the back of the frame someone had carefully written a date—it was thirty years ago—with the new graduate's first name, Josef, and his qualification: doctor of medicine.

"Your son! That's your son who's coming tomorrow?"

"Yes, he comes every Tuesday. Good night, dear."

Helen swiftly counted days. She and Milos had run away from school on Friday evening; two nights had passed since then. Maybe the old lady was right.

Although she was so tired, she found it hard to get to sleep. The bedroom was cold, the bed sagged, and the enormous eiderdown slipped to the floor at the slightest movement. She was haunted by her mental picture of Milos losing blood in the mountain refuge. She didn't drop off until the small hours of the morning, lulled by the giant pig's deep grunting. It shook the windowpanes.

The doctor arrived at ten in the morning in a muddy, high-built car, which was backfiring noisily. He was a dark-eyed man of about fifty. With his gray hair, bald patch, and shaggy beard, he didn't look much like the photograph of his younger self. Helen ran over the meadow toward him before he even had time to get out of the car. It was a relief to talk to someone who could understand her!

"We'll go on around the mountain in the car," he said. "Then two hours on foot from a place I know will get us to the refuge."

"You mean we'll be up there by this evening?"

"Yes, that's right."

"Do you have your medical bag with you? Will you be able to treat him?"

"I have everything I'll need. I'll just leave my parents their provisions and then we'll start."

Helen could have kissed him. Her good-byes to the two old people were quickly said.

"Come back and see us soon!" said the old lady. "We enjoy a visit."

"Gjirl!" the old man informed his son, pointing to Helen. And he embarked on a long and incomprehensible torrent of words in which the name of Hugo came up several times.

"What's he saying?" asked Helen.

"He says you're very young to have had seven sons with Hugo. I wonder how on earth he took such an idea into his head."

"Who is this Hugo, anyway?" asked Helen, smiling.

"My son," said the doctor. "He'll be twelve in November."

Then he put a toboggan into the trunk of the car and turned the starting handle. The pig gave them one last grunt by way of good-bye and they set off, with the old lady waving her dirty dishtowel from the doorstep.

The road went uphill along a gentle slope, but there were so many rocks that it was a bumpy ride. The car jolted along, and Helen had to hold on to the door handle beside her seat to keep from being thrown up into the air. Talking through the roar of the engine wasn't easy.

"What were you doing up at the refuge at this time of year?" shouted the doctor.

"A walking trip!" Helen replied, surprised to find how much easier it was to shout a lie than tell one in a normal voice.

"The snow took you by surprise?"

"Yes."

"I see. I'm Josef—what's your name?"

"Helen."

They said no more for a few more miles, and then the doctor jerked his head in the direction of a bag on the backseat. "There's something to eat in there. Bread and dark chocolate, I think. Help yourself."

Chocolate! Helen made an effort not to fall on it too desperately. She reached behind her for the bag and put it calmly on her knees.

"How exactly did your friend injure himself, by the way?"

"Cutting a piece of wood with his knife," said Helen, a bar of chocolate in her hand. "Would you like some?"

"Yes please, I'll have a small square," said the doctor, laughing. "My little weakness!"

As she gave him the chocolate, a jolt even stronger than the others made them both rise briefly into the air and they both burst out laughing.

Helen considered telling him the truth as she ate the chocolate. Once they got up there, he'd soon realize she'd been lying. He'd see how deep the cut was, and the blood all over the place. And if the snow had melted, he'd even see the bodies. He was a doctor; he'd treat Milos, but then what? Would he give them away?

She realized that it was a risky business to take this unknown man up to the scene of the violence. But how else could she help Milos?

They drove on for a little longer, exchanging a few commonplaces about the landscape and the poor state of the road. The doctor, concentrating on his driving, asked no more questions. Dark ravines lay on their right now. On their left, the summit of the mountain disappeared into the mists. A large bird of prey clipped the windshield, flapping its wings, and made them jump.

"Is it much farther?" asked Helen.

"No, we're nearly there," the doctor told her. And less than a quarter of an hour later he stopped the car by the roadside.

A snow-covered path led straight toward the mountains. They put on their snowshoes and started along it. The doctor took large strides, pulling the toboggan that was to bring Milos down again. Sometimes he stopped to wait for Helen, who was carrying his medical bag and had some difficulty in keeping up. They walked for over two hours before they came to a small spruce wood.

"The refuge is on the other side," said the doctor. "You'll recognize the place."

Sure enough, as soon as they had gone through the wood, she could make out the gray shape of the hut about two hundred yards above them. Her heart beat faster. *I'm coming, Milos. Don't worry. I'm bringing a doctor. Everything will be all right . . .*

She was about to step out of the woods when the doctor laid a hand on her shoulder. "Wait!"

"What is it?"

"Men—look!"

Three men with spades were standing close to the rock where Mills, Pastor, and Ramses lay buried. They could be heard cursing under their breath as they uncovered the bodies. A fourth man was busy with a sleigh standing outside the door of the refuge. They all wore leather coats and boots.

"Phalangists," said the doctor in a low voice. "What are they doing here?"

The door of the refuge opened, and two more men emerged. They were carrying a limp body by the shoulders and feet, and threw it roughly down on the sleigh. One arm dangled over the side, looking half dislocated.

Helen felt ill. "Milos!"

She took a step back and sat down on the toboggan. Everything was reeling around her: the dazzling snow, the spruce trees, the gray sky.

"Milos," she said, and wept.

"Shh!" the doctor ordered her. "Keep quiet."

Outside the refuge, the men were putting on their snowshoes. The three of them pushed the sleigh toward the downward slope. "We're on our way!" one of them called to the men by the rock.

A few seconds later, the sleigh was out of sight.

"They didn't even put a blanket over him," moaned Helen. "Is he dead?"

"I don't know," the doctor whispered. "We can't stay here. Come on!"

Although the heater was on full blast, Helen was shivering as she sat in the car. The doctor stopped, took off his jacket, and gave it to her.

"Put that on and try to calm down. I don't think your friend is dead. You saw what a hurry they were in to take him away. When someone's dead, people can take their time, can't they?"

Helen had to agree, but it wasn't reassuring. They drove on in silence for some time, going far more slowly than on their way to the hut, and then the doctor turned and looked at her with a kindly expression.

"Now, tell me everything, please. What exactly happened in the refuge?" And as she still hesitated, he added, "You have nothing to fear from me, I assure you."

She wanted to believe it. She began at the beginning, unable to keep back her tears. "We ran away from our boarding schools. . . ."

And she told him all about it: the flight of Bart and Milena, little Catharina Pancek in the detention cell. She told him about Basil's death, the annual assembly, Van Vlyck, Mills, Pastor, and his Devils. She told him about their bus journey through the night, their exhausting climb up into the mountains, their wait near the rock, freezing; she told him about the dreadful fight between Pastor and Milos, his wound, the frenzy of the dog-men. She told him everything, and when she had finished, she added to herself alone, in silence: *And what I'm not telling you, Doctor, is that Milos is my first love. I'm sure of that now . . . and I've already lost him.*

He listened to the end of the story without interrupting her, and then simply asked, "Do you know anyone who could take you in?"

"My consoler would," Helen murmured. "She's the only person I know outside the school, but I can never go back to her now."

When they reached the stone cottage, night was already falling. The doctor turned off the car engine but didn't get out. In the sudden silence his voice was calm and full of certainty. "Listen, Helen. I've been thinking. This is what we'll do. First we'll have some supper here with my parents. It'll be better than yesterday; don't worry. I brought some good food up with me. Then I'll take you home with me, to the little town where the bus took you, and you'll meet my wife—and your fiancé, Hugo! But you can't stay long. There's going to be all hell to pay in this part of the country, as you can imagine. They don't like losing their own men like that. You can't go back to that school of yours either.

"So early tomorrow morning I shall put you on the bus going south, with the money for your fare and a little extra. You'll arrive in the capital city the next night. Ask your way to the Wooden Bridge and go there. The Wooden Bridge, don't forget, because there are a great many bridges in the city. This one is to the north, upstream of the river. People sleep under it; they may look alarming, but don't be afraid of them. They won't hurt you. Ask for a man called Mitten. Remember that: Mitten. Tell him you come from me—Josef the doctor. He'll help you and tell you where to find other people like us in the city. I've lost track of them all. The network's always on the move."

"People like us?"

"People who don't go along with the Phalange. Is that enough of an explanation for you?"

"Quite enough. Thank you very much, doctor."

"My name's Josef."

"Then thank you, Josef."

"Don't mention it, Helen. It's the least I can do. May I give you one more piece of advice?"

"Of course."

"Get rid of that jacket and knapsack very soon. They could mean bad trouble for you."

She realized that she was still wearing Pastor's sheepskin jacket and carrying the knapsack that had once belonged to Mills. "Oh, God, yes, of course! But what should I do with them? I'd hate them to be found in your parents' house. I could bury them, I guess, or burn them. . . ."

"I have a better idea," said the doctor. "There'll be nothing left of them at all, not even ashes. And my wife will give you a coat to replace the jacket tomorrow."

As they passed the pig's enclosure, he threw the knapsack and jacket over the wooden fence. The huge boar snuffled at them for a moment with his vast snout, then opted for the knapsack. Within a few seconds he had swallowed it, metal reinforcements and all. It took him a little longer to appreciate the interesting flavor of sheepskin mixed with mud.

At dawn next day, they went to the bus station together, Helen warmly wrapped in a woolen coat that the doctor's wife had given her. Josef gave her the money he had promised, with some food and a book for the journey. First he shook hands, then he changed his mind and kissed her on both cheeks.

"The Wooden Bridge — and the man is known as Mitten. Whatever you do, don't forget those names. Good luck."

She got into the same bus that had brought her there four days ago — a century ago, in a distant time when Milos was still with her. As she watched the mountains move away in the dirty rectangle of the rear window, she felt her heart breaking. They'd caught Milos. Even though he'd told her he never got caught. What would they do to him? What would she do alone? They'd said they'd never leave each other. He wasn't going to die, was he? *We will meet again, won't we?* she thought. *Promise me, Milos. Please!*

ANGEL ON A BIKE

Helen arrived at the bus station in the capital city in the middle of the night, feeling more alone than she had ever been in her life. Where were Milena and Bart? What was she doing in this place? When she asked the way, a passerby just pointed without bothering to open his mouth: the Wooden Bridge was over there. She set off. Tall, dark buildings rose on her left like cliffs, silent and menacing. She went down to the river and walked along the bank. The Wooden Bridge, Mitten — she didn't know anything about either of them, but her only hope was to find them.

At least six fires were burning under the bridge, their dancing flames reflected on the rippling surface of the river. Helen stooped at the top of the stone steps leading down, glad to have arrived at last. She had walked a long way, passing at least six bridges before she reached this one. A dozen ragged derelicts were sleeping under burlap sacks around the largest of the fires. Loud snores rose in a kind of disorderly concert, interrupted from time to time by a kick or an elbow in someone's ribs. Now and then one of the sleepers got up to relieve himself in the water or put a branch of wood on the flames. Other, smaller fires were crackling gently in the darkness. Men sat by them eating, drinking spirits, and smoking in silence.

The clock of the nearby church was just striking midnight. Helen went down the steps and walked under the arch of the bridge, repeating the doctor's words to reassure herself: *People sleep under it; they may look alarming, but don't be afraid of them. They won't hurt you.*

"Hey, whaddya think you're doing here?" asked a rasping voice very close to her.

The woman addressing Helen was sitting against the wall in the shelter of a buttress. It would be difficult to guess her age, but perhaps she was around fifty. Her face, flushed with broken veins, was half hidden under the peak of a fur cap, and a mongrel dog lay asleep at her feet.

"I'm looking for Mitten."

"So what's your business with Mitten, then?"

"I just want to talk to him."

The woman pointed to a small fire that had almost gone out fifty feet away. "That's him over there. Give him a kick; that'll wake him up!"

Helen approached the shape lying huddled under a pile of blankets. "Er . . . please, sir," she began timidly.

The woman burst out laughing. "No need for any 'sir' around here! Give him a kick, like I said!" And when Helen didn't look as if she would, the woman shouted, "Mitten! Hey, you, Mitten. You got a visitor. Pretty little chick. A blonde!"

"What?" grunted the man, raising his shaggy head and long face. He could have been around forty. Thin as his face was, there was something cheerful about it. "What d'you want?"

"Are you Mitten?" asked Helen.

"Looks like it. So who are you?"

"I've come from Josef. Dr. Josef."

The man yawned at length, showing a mouth with half his teeth missing, noisily cleared his throat, and sat up a little. "And how's good old Doc Josef? Still getting paid to kill his patients off?"

"He's fine," said Helen, smiling.

The tramp pushed back his covers and stood up with some difficulty. He was wearing large, woolen gloves with the fingertips cut off to expose the last two joints of his dirty fingers.

"You're from up in the hill country, I reckon. Know your way around here?"

"No, that's why Dr. Josef . . ."

"Right. Well, let's show you around for a start."

Helen, who was already worn out by cold and weariness, didn't feel at all like going back up to the icy sidewalks of the city, but a surprise awaited her at the top of the steps. Mitten kick-started a motorbike that looked a positive antique, with an enormous yellow tank rather like the curved body of a wasp.

"Get up behind and hold on tight!"

The monster motorbike, which had no front light, chugged noisily off along the roads and began climbing north up a hill.

"Where are we going?" cried Helen, who was numb by now. "I'm freezing!"

"To the cemetery!" replied Mitten. "There's a good view!"

As they went on uphill, the city revealed itself below. Helen had never imagined that the capital was so big. More than ten bridges crossed the river, and she found it difficult to believe it was the same river that she knew. *If you could see how wide it is here, Milos! Four times as wide as when we were looking down at it from the roof of the school! If you could see this city! Dozens of towers and belfries, wide avenues, hundreds of alleyways, tiled roofs going on and on forever. The tiles are prettier than slates. Oh, it's a shame you aren't here; it's a shame.*

The motorbike had no stand. Mitten leaned it up against the cemetery wall and led Helen on. They crossed the road and were soon standing on a grassy mound like a promontory above the drop below. As she turned, Helen saw the crosses and tombstones on the graves shining in the cold moonlight.

"Never mind the dead!" said Mitten. "Take a look at the view. Not bad, eh? The bridge to the north there, that one's mine. You can tell it by the fires burning there. The biggest bridge in the middle, that's Royal Bridge, the one with the bronze statues. This side of the river, you got the Old Town, right? Other side of the river, you got the Castle—up on that hill, see it? Down below is the New Town. The Phalange hangs out in that tall building." He spat the way he was pointing and then turned back to his motorbike. "OK, you seen it all. Guided tour's over, and if we don't move, we'll freeze to death."

"Where are we going now?" asked Helen.

"I'm taking you to Jahn in the Old Town."

"Who's Jahn?"

"You'll soon see."

They were already on their way down the slope when Mitten half turned and shouted, "Hey, you know those two as arrived by boat last week?"

"What two?" she asked, with a sudden surge of excitement.

"Tall, thin guy and a blonde with her hair cut short. Watch out. Hold on—the road's bumpy here!"

"A blonde with short hair?" Helen asked. "Do you . . . Do you remember their first names?"

"No . . . yes! Him, he was Alexandro, something like that, and she . . . um . . . Helena, that's it! Yup, Helena!"

"Bartolomeo and Milena!" she shouted into Mitten's ear.

"You don't need to yell like that! Want to

burst my eardrum? Yeah, like you said: Barto-thingamajig and Milena, that was it."

"Where are they now?"

"At Jahn's, of course. Where you're going, love."

Helen had been under so much stress for days and nights on end. Now, suddenly, she was relaxed. She immediately forgot about the cold, her anxieties, the grief of being alone. She was going to see Milena again! Maybe even tonight. She laid her forehead against the back of Mitten's neck. *This is an angel taking me there on his motorbike!* she thought. *Maybe he doesn't smell too sweet as angels go, but he's an angel all the same because we're on our way to Milena.*

They rode through a maze of narrow alleys and reached a small paved square. It was deserted. Mitten stopped outside a restaurant with an old-fashioned facade running at least sixty feet along one side of the square. The glazed door bore the name of the place, JAHN, in gilded lettering. Behind the curtained windows Helen could just make out rows of tables with chairs perched on them upside down, a forest of legs sticking up into the air.

"This is it," said Mitten, without turning off his engine. "Off you go. I won't come in. You ask for Mr. Jahn, get it? Not just Jahn, right? Mr. Jahn. You tell him you want work. He'll tell you to clear out. So then you say, 'I'm ready to wash dishes.' And then he says, 'Ready to wash dishes?' And you say, 'Yes, I've already mashed potatoes for

Napoleon . . .' and he'll take you on. Easy as pie. Got all that, have you?"

Helen wondered if she was in the middle of some crazy dream. "I don't understand. Who's Napoleon?"

"Why, Dr. Josef's giant pig. Didn't you see him up in the hills?"

"Yes, but I never knew his name."

"He's our mascot, Napoleon is. When we've seen those Phalangist bastards off, we're going to build a great big bonfire, have a hog roast, and eat Napoleon, in tribute to him, like. Off you go, then. I'll wait to see if you're OK. Give me a wave from the window, right?"

"Right," said Helen. "I'll go in—and thank you for everything."

She was on her way to the entrance of the restaurant when Mitten called her back. "Wouldn't have a little cash for the gas and the guided tour, would you?"

"Oh, of course!" cried Helen apologetically, ashamed of herself for not thinking of it first. She gave him a few bills.

Then she opened the door and found herself in the comfortable warmth of the building inside. Dim standby lights faintly illuminated the large restaurant. She made her way between the tables, passing double doors that must lead to the kitchens. At the back of the restaurant there was a wide oak staircase with a faint light at the top of it.

She climbed the stairs in silence, drawn as if by a magnet to the line of light showing under a door. She had almost reached the landing when she tripped on one of the steps.

"Anyone there?" asked a deep voice from the lighted room.

"Yes," said Helen. "I . . . I'd like to see Mr. Jahn."

"You want to see Mr. Jahn?"

"Yes, please."

"Come on in, then, and you'll see him."

A chubby-cheeked man was sitting at a desk, poring over accounts books. He glanced rapidly at Helen and went back to his calculations. Classical music was playing on the radio, but the volume was turned down, and Helen had to strain her ears to pick it up.

"So what brings you here, young lady?"

"Work. I'm looking for work."

"No vacancies."

His thick lips gave the impression of a sulky pout. Helen stood her ground.

"I . . . I'm ready to do any kind of work. I can wash dishes. . . ."

Still writing with his stub of a pencil, the man muttered, "Ready to wash dishes, are you?"

"Yes, I've already mashed potatoes for Napoleon, so . . ."

She had the odd sense of speaking lines in a play, but a play that would determine the whole course of her future life. Jahn glanced up. This time he was really looking at her, and his eyes were very gentle.

"Ah, so that's it. Potatoes for Napoleon. And how old are you?"

"Seventeen."

"Did you run away from your boarding school too?"

"Yes."

The stout man put down his pencil, took off his glasses, and ran both hands through his curly hair. Then he sighed, as if all the cares of the world were weighing down on his shoulders.

"Right," he said at last. "Right. I'll show you to your room. It's up in the attic. You can begin tomorrow morning. But I already have more than enough people washing dishes. You can . . . Let's see, yes, you can sweep up in the restaurant and wait on tables. The others will explain the job to you. Your salary won't be very much, but you'll get your board and lodging. Are you hungry?"

"No," said Helen. She hadn't even finished the food Dr. Josef had given her for the journey.

"Then off to bed with you now. It's late."

He switched off the radio, rose, and led her up more stairs. They climbed two floors higher and reached a dilapidated, low-ceilinged corridor with a dozen small closed doors on each side of it.

"Your colleagues' rooms," said Jahn.

When he reached the end of the corridor, he

opened the left-hand door and stood back to let Helen in.

"Here we are. This is your room, and here's the key." He stepped back out into the corridor, and then turned back. "What's your name?"

"Dormann," said Helen. "My name is Helen Dormann. Please . . . is there a girl called Milena Bach here?"

"Milena sleeps in the room next to yours," said Jahn as if in passing, "but don't call her that anymore."

"What should I call her, then?"

"Anything you like, but not Milena. Good night." The stout man didn't give any further explanation, and she heard his heavy tread as he walked away.

The tiny room contained only a narrow bed, a table, a chair, a washbasin, and two shelves. A cord stretched across one corner did duty as a wardrobe. But Helen was holding the key to her room for the first time in her life, her own room, and she felt wonderfully happy. A cast-iron radiator gave gentle warmth. She stood on the chair to see out of the skylight and had a view of the river, wide and silent, and the sleeping city with its street lights on.

A beginning, she thought, *a new beginning. Everything will be all right.*

She went to bed, worn out by exhaustion and emotion, and as she slowly fell asleep, she called to mind everyone who had ever been dear to her:

her parents, coming back out of the night to smile lovingly at her; Paula, who must know what had happened by this time and might be thinking of her; Milos, now in the middle of his hardest fight somewhere; and Milena asleep on the other side of the wall, with her hair cut short.

The last thing she heard was the noise of a motorbike rattling down the road and fading away. *Oh no! That's Mitten riding off, and I forgot to wave from the window to let him know I was staying. Sorry, Mitten.*

PART TWO

AS THE RIVER FLOWS

I count my blessings.

—Kathleen Ferrier, British contralto,
in one of her last letters

JAHN'S RESTAURANT

Helen was so tired that she had been afraid she wouldn't wake up until midday, but at dawn the sound of a door being carefully closed and a key turning in the lock of the room next to hers woke her. At first she had difficulty remembering where she was. Then it all came back to her: Mitten, the capital city, Mr. Jahn, the room that was now her own, and Milena sleeping next door. Milena! Those must be her footsteps moving away down the corridor! Afraid of missing her, Helen jumped out of bed, flung on a shirt, and left her room. Right at the far end of the corridor a tall girl with cropped blond hair, wearing a cook's white apron tied at the back, was just starting down the stairs.

"Just a minute!" called Helen.

The girl turned. They looked at each other for a few seconds, astonished, and then ran toward each other, each of them needing to touch and hug her friend. The joy of their reunion made them laugh and cry at the same time. It was a while before they were able to talk.

"Milena! What on earth have you done to your hair?"

"Bart cut it for me."

"Bart slaughtered it! He's out of his mind!"

"No, not at all. I'll explain everything. But what are you doing here? I can't believe it."

"I ran away from school with Milos. We followed you to the mountains."

"The mountains? How far did you go?"

"To the mountain refuge."

"The refuge—but why?"

Their words were tumbling over each other. There was just too much to say all at once.

"Milos wanted to rescue you both from the dog-men. It's amazing how that haircut changes you! Only your eyes are the same!"

"Milos? Is he here too?"

"No. No, he has an injured leg. I don't even know if he's still alive. I went to get help and meanwhile they caught him. The Phalangists . . . the police . . ."

Milena put a finger to her lips. "Hush, keep your voice down. You can tell me all about it somewhere else. What about Catharina?"

"Don't worry—she's not in the Sky anymore. Milos and I took her to her consoler, Emily—remember her? What about Bart? Where is he?"

"He's here too, sleeping on the second floor. The men have the rooms down there."

She had said men, not boys, as they would have said at school.

A door opened and a plump little woman appeared in the corridor, wearing a white apron like Milena's.

"Hi, Kathleen!" she said in passing.

"Hi!" Milena replied. "This is my friend Helen. She's just arrived."

"Welcome to youth and beauty!" said the woman cheerfully, and she disappeared down the stairs.

"What did she call you?" asked the astonished Helen.

"She called me Kathleen, and you must do the same from now on."

"I'll never manage it! Where on earth did you fish that up for a first name?"

"It was a singer's name, that's why I chose it. I have to hide, you see — my face and hair, my name, everything. Are you working in the kitchens?"

"No, in the restaurant. Cleaning and waiting on tables."

"Oh, what a pity. I'm in the kitchens. Mr. Jahn put me there specially so that people would see me as little as possible. Do you have an apron yet?"

"No."

"Then get dressed quickly, and I'll take you to the linen room to get one. It's the first thing anyone does here, like getting our overcoats when we arrived at the school. Then we have breakfast down in the canteen."

Less than ten minutes later, Helen, wearing a

maid's blue apron, was going downstairs with her friend. Milena, who already knew her way around, led her along the second-floor corridor and knocked softly three times at a door on the left.

"Surprise, Bart! Open up!"

The young man put his tousled head around the door and stared. "Helen! We're all together again!"

"No, not quite," said Milena, after a moment's hesitation. "Milos ran away with her, but he was caught."

Bart's cheerfulness vanished at once. His face fell. "Caught . . . by the dogs?"

"No, by the Phalangist police."

Bartolomeo closed his eyes for a second, and lowered his voice. "We mustn't talk about it here. Let's all three of us meet outside the cemetery tonight when the restaurant closes. Do you know where it is, Helen?"

"The cemetery? Yes, in fact it's the only place I do know here."

"See you this evening, then," said Bart, ending the conversation as he closed the door of his room again.

Jahn's Restaurant was really a vast canteen for the local factory workers. It was much larger than Helen had thought the evening before. The double doors didn't open into the kitchens after all but into a second room full of tables, even larger than the first. Three boys were already busy putting back

196

the chairs that had been perched upside down on wooden tables in this second room too.

"Do you know how many people can eat here at the same time?" Milena asked. "More than six hundred! You'll see when mealtimes come—it's like a huge party."

"A lot of people must work in the restaurant, then?" guessed Helen.

"Three times too many!" said Milena, smiling. "Mr. Jahn hires everyone who's 'mashed potatoes for Napoleon,' and there are a lot of us, I can tell you! But now we won't talk anymore until this evening. Keeping quiet is the rule here."

They went down to the basement in a service elevator that shook its passengers about like some kind of angry monster. Its heavy iron mechanism was visible through the glazed doors.

"The kitchens," Milena said, when the lift reached the bottom of the shaft. They passed enormous cast-iron stoves and rows of copper saucepans hanging from the walls. "This is where I work, cleaning and preparing vegetables. Bart's in the delivery area. He loads, unloads, and carries things, and he's responsible for quite a lot of breakages. He's really clumsy! And this is the staff canteen. We eat before the customers arrive every day. Come on in."

She took Helen into an echoing room with a pleasant aroma of coffee and toast in the air. Over twenty people were eating breakfast already. Most of them were young, but some were older. There was much laughter and joking; baskets of bread were passed around, along with bowls of jam and steaming coffeepots.

"Sit here; you'll be in good company."

Helen let her friend move away and sat down beside a woman of about forty with dark, curly hair, wearing the maid's blue apron. She had round cheeks and a slight squint in her left eye; Helen noticed it at once. The woman smiled at her kindly.

"Hello, my name's Dora. Are you new?"

"Yes, I'm Helen. Do you work in the restaurants too, Miss . . .?"

"I do, so I can show you the ropes. It's not difficult. And please call me Dora."

Later, Helen always remembered those first words they exchanged and the instant liking she felt for this woman: the sense of a secret affinity and the confidence she felt in her for no reason at all. And perhaps, she told herself, it wasn't just chance that they met in a kitchen underground, a place where things were warm and went deep.

As they talked, she noticed that Dora had some difficulty in using her right hand. The fingers were oddly distorted and reddened at the joints, while her right thumb was permanently half bent.

Mr. Jahn put in a brief appearance. He said good morning to everyone with a sort of shy restraint, then drank some coffee standing up as his eyes wandered over his employees. When his glance met Helen's, he made her a discreet sign that evidently meant, *Everything all right?* She replied in the same way: *Yes, everything's fine,* and she did in fact feel hopeful.

The day passed at surprising speed. From eleven in the morning onward Helen felt as if she were caught up in a whirlwind. The two restaurant rooms filled up within minutes, and the noise went on until two in the afternoon. Luckily there was one set menu for everyone, so the customers didn't have to choose what they ate. The waiters and waitresses, all wearing blue aprons, took what the kitchens sent up in dumbwaiters and shouted orders back down the megaphones fitted to the walls: "Ten starters! That's right, ten!" or "Four main courses, please."

Helen's job was simple: she was responsible for a row of six tables. As soon as one of them was free again, she had to hurry to clear the dishes away and clean it. She often had to mop up a spilled jugfull of water, wash the floor, or sweep up the remains of a broken plate. Dora kept an eye on her all the time, helpfully showing her what to do.

As soon as her midday break came, Helen went to her room, fell on her bed, and slept like a log. She woke up just in time to go and eat in the canteen and begin the evening shift. When that was over, she had to help cleaning both restaurant rooms, and it was after eleven at night before she was finally able to hang her blue apron up behind the door of her room and leave Jahn's Restaurant.

Outside the front door, as agreed, she met Milena, who was waiting for her, muffled up in her black coat. Dora was with her and was amused by Helen's surprise. Both Dora and Milena wore the same kind of fur cap, which made them look like sisters.

"Don't worry," Milena assured Helen at once. "You can talk as freely to Dora as to me."

They walked together along the roads leading uphill from the square. It was a chilly but clear night. A few dimly lit windows cast patches of light on the somber granite facades, and Milena slipped her hand under Helen's arm. "Remember the last time we walked like this?"

"Yes, crossing our bridge. I feel as if I've lived ten years since then."

"So do I!"

Dora went ahead. She seemed to be very much on her guard, stopping and looking around intently whenever they came to the corner of a road. Twice she decided that they should retrace their steps and take a different route.

"The idiots—they hide in porches, but they can't keep from smoking. You can see their cigarettes glowing two miles away."

"What idiots?" asked Helen.

"The security police on night duty. I'd advise you to avoid them as much as you can."

"So how do I spot them?"

"Easy. They're all over the place. They're muscular and stupid, and they go around in pairs."

Higher up, Helen recognized the roads she had

gone along the night before on Mitten's motorbike. They stopped for a moment.

"Jahn's Restaurant is over there," said Dora, pointing. "Just beyond the factory. See it?"

Three tall brick chimneys reached toward the sky. In the absence of any wind, gray smoke was rising slowly from one of them. Helen could also see the Wooden Bridge to the north, with several fires flickering below it, and farther away, the Castle. Its dark mass dominated the city on the other side of the river.

When they reached the cemetery, the three women thought at first that Bart hadn't come to the meeting place. They waited a little while on the grassy promontory, watching the roads below for his arrival. The moon had gone behind a cloud, and they could hardly make out its pale disk. Helen blew on her numb fingers to warm them.

"Would it really be so dangerous to talk down there where it's nice and warm?"

"Yes," said Dora. "The Phalange has spies everywhere. There are ears listening where you think you're safest: in the corridors, in the canteen, even in your room. Mr. Jahn is closely watched. If anyone was caught criticizing the regime in his restaurant, they could arrest him and close the place down within the hour. It's the same in the city, as you'll find out. At least up here we're sure of not being overheard, we can see people coming a long way off, and the people behind that wall couldn't care less what we talk about!"

As if to contradict her, the rusty gate of the cemetery opened with a long, low, moaning sound, and the tall shape of Bartolomeo emerged from the night.

"Were you waiting in the cemetery?" Milena was surprised.

"Yes," he said, coming toward them. "Know anywhere safer and quieter?"

"Don't you find it scary being around all the dead people?" asked Helen, impressed.

"No, the dead don't make trouble. It's the living I don't trust. Now, tell me about Milos."

Helen cleared her throat and began at the beginning: their climb to the school roof, the extraordinary spectacle of the staff at their annual assembly, Van Vlyck, how they went to free Catharina, who turned out to be free already. Then she did her best not to leave out any of what followed: their flight, the night in the bus, their freezing wait in the snow, Milos's terrible fight. As her story went on, Bart shook his head, sighing. He had known that his friend was fearless and generous; he'd never thought he would take on two men and six dogs with his bare hands to protect him.

"He really did that?" he murmured incredulously.

"Yes, he did," Helen confirmed. "But he's paid such a price for it!"

She found it hard to keep back her tears as she described the way the men had thrown Milos's racked body on the sleigh like the carcass of an animal.

"Dr. Josef thinks he's alive," she finished, then blew her nose. "He said that if he wasn't, they wouldn't have taken him away so quickly."

"I'm sure he's right," Dora comforted her. "Try not to worry."

And she opened her arms. Helen fell into them, and all four stood there in silence for several seconds. In the quiet night it was like a mute prayer for their friend, a prayer that he was still alive and well. Bart and Milena too were in each other's arms, standing very close.

"What about Basil?" Bart asked at last, in a voice full of concern. "Did they keep him in the cell? Did Milos say anything about that?"

"No," Helen lied, promising herself to tell him the truth some other time. She just didn't feel brave enough to do it at the moment. "And what about you two?" she asked. "Tell me what happened to you."

They told her about their crazy expedition into the mountains, their journey down the river in the boat, their meetings with so many people who were sure that they recognized Milena as her own mother.

"Are you really that much like her?" Helen smiled. "Now I understand about your hair. But why did you turn back?"

"To fight," said Bart. "You know I've just been walking among the graves here. It may be silly, but I like it. Even at night. At school I'd sometimes go to the cemetery instead of seeing my consoler or walking around the town. Milos thought I was crazy. He said it was no way to use our few hours of freedom. But I like such places; I don't find them sad, not at all. They make you think of your own life and what you're going to do with it. And that's what Milena and I decided: we made up our minds to do something with our lives. We want to fight back against the Phalange."

"Oh, is that all?" said Helen ironically. She had spoken without malice, more with the melancholy feeling that they were powerless.

"Yes, that's all," said Bart, unperturbed. "And we may have more weapons than you think."

"Meaning?"

Bartolomeo turned to Milena. "Will you explain?"

Milena took a deep breath. "It's a love story, Helen. Do you want to hear it? Even at midnight outside a cemetery, in the freezing cold?"

"Go on."

"Right. It's the story of a girl of twenty who has a lover. One day she notices that her stomach is swelling a little too much. And then her lover leaves her; he goes off into the wide blue yonder and never comes back. The girl cries her eyes out, and a few months later she has a baby, a little girl, and calls her . . . Let's say she calls her Milena. Are you with me so far?"

"I think so. Go on."

"OK. The young mother is quite pretty, and she sings rather well."

"No," Dora interrupted gently. "She isn't 'quite pretty'; she's staggeringly beautiful. And she doesn't just sing 'rather well'; she's a contralto and her voice is miraculous. Put it that way and it makes a difference, doesn't it? She joined a choral society when she was fourteen, and all the other girls who sang with her, like me, for instance, suddenly decided to give up singing and go in for drawing or painting or something else instead! She was a soloist at sixteen. At nineteen she was engaged by the Opera House, and all the concert halls in the country were fighting over her. You have to put it like that if Helen's going to understand. Now you can go on!"

"All right," Milena continued. "So yes, she sings very well. One day a big red-headed guy happens to hear her singing in a Requiem Mass in a church. This guy is a policeman. He's married, and he has a family of kids, all redheads like him. He's not a music lover; in fact he's something of a brute. Don't ask me why, but this woman's voice knocks him sideways. He falls madly in love. He makes advances to her. She doesn't want to know him. He persists. He pesters her. He leaves his wife and children for her. She still doesn't want to know him. He's beside himself with pain and rage. He swears that she'll pay for it. His name is Van Vlyck. Are you still with me?"

"Van Vlyck!" Helen was trembling. "The man I saw at the staff assembly?"

"That's him. With less of a paunch, not so much beard, and more hair, I expect, but the same man."

"I saw him break an oak table with his bare fist." Helen remembered. "It still makes me shudder to think of it."

"Then you know what kind of man he is. I'd rather leave you to tell the rest of the story, Dora. I don't think I can manage it."

Dora spoke softly in her beautiful, deep voice, even when she had terrible things to say. In the cold, her breath made little clouds of white vapor that dispersed at once.

"The real love story, Helen, is about a whole nation falling in love with a voice. The voice of Eva-Maria Bach, Milena's mother, as you know now. You can't imagine how everyone loved that voice. It was natural, rich, dramatic, deep. It touched the heart. I was Eva's friend; I had the privilege of accompanying her on the piano when she sang *lieder* in recitals. She put so much sensitivity into them, such perfection. I never got used to it. I was always transfixed with admiration for her as I sat at the keyboard. But in ordinary life she was cheerful, lively, incredibly funny. We had some really good laughs together, even onstage! And she sang traditional tunes too, the songs of the ordinary people. She never would give those up. That's why they adored her, even if they didn't know much about music. She brought everyone together. She hated violence. And then the coup came and the Phalange seized power. Eva joined the Resistance. Shall I go on, Milena?"

Milena bowed her head and scraped the ground with the toe of her shoe. "Go on. I want to hear it again."

"Eva joined the Resistance. So did I. When it got too dangerous, we left the capital. They were checking every car leaving by the roads, so we traveled in horse-drawn carts, hidden under covers. We went on giving recitals in secret for months, in provincial towns, then in little village halls, sometimes for an audience of only fifteen. I wore my fingers out on dreadful pianos that were badly out of tune! But none of that mattered. Eva said that whatever happened, we mustn't give up. The barbarians weren't going to silence her. And word went out all over the country: 'Eva-Maria Bach sang here. Eva-Maria Bach sang there, and there, and there . . .' While she still sang, the Resistance wasn't giving up. You'd have thought that hope depended on her voice. Such persistence infuriated the Phalange. They had to silence her.

"They finally caught up with us in a little northern town early in winter. Van Vlyck was in command. They broke the door down and burst in, howling like animals. Half of them were drunk on beer. We were just finishing Schubert's song *An die Musik*, "To Music." I shall never forget it. Eva said, 'This was bound to happen sometime. Thank you for accompanying me . . .' and I thought she was going to say 'on the piano,' but she said, 'Thank you for accompanying me all this way.' Those were the last words I ever heard her say. The platform was very high. Two men tipped the piano over into the orchestra pit. It shattered with a terrible sound of jangling notes and broken wood. They took everyone in the hall away. As for me, I was given special treatment: they threw me down on the floor. One of them held my right hand flat at the edge of the platform under his boot, and another man hit it with the butt of his gun, crushing it. He brought his weapon down on my fingers and wrist at least twenty times. I fainted. When I came around, someone was shouting at Eva, 'You get out of here! And don't let us ever see your face in this country again!'

"I didn't understand. I was naïve. They let her escape into the mountains with a few companions. One of them, I learned later, was Bart's father. They let them all go, but only to have more fun killing them. On Van Vlyck's orders, they set the dog-men on them. I'm sorry, Bart. I'm sorry, Milena."

Milena was weeping silently.

"Oh, my God!" groaned Helen, and she took her friend in her arms.

"I spent four months in their prisons," Dora went on, "and then they let me out. The city had changed a lot in a very short time. People looked suspiciously at each other. No one dared speak to anyone else in the streets or on the trams. I wasn't a musician anymore. I became a cleaner. All the theaters had been closed. And they'd opened the arena."

"What arena?"

"The arena where they stage their fights. You'll find out all about that. You'll find out quite soon enough. I looked for Milena everywhere. She was only three years old, and I was her godmother, you see. I managed to get inside over ten orphanages, but I couldn't find her. I ended up thinking they'd . . . thinking they'd got rid of her. I mourned her for fifteen years until last week, when she walked right into the canteen with her short hair and her big blue eyes. It was like seeing Eva resurrected from the dead, coming toward me. I nearly fainted. But it's better now. I'm beginning to get used to it." Dora wiped her eyes, sighed, and smiled again. "Well, I think that's the whole story, isn't it? We'd better go down again. You're all frozen, and so am I. And tomorrow morning we'll have to——"

"Just a moment," Helen interrupted her. "Bart said we may have weapons to fight them. What weapons?"

"Our weapon," he said, "is Milena's voice. Dora says she has her mother's voice. Younger, of course, but Dora says it will be exactly the same in a few years' time. And she says it's a voice that can inspire people and rouse them to action."

All three of them looked at Milena, who stood there with her head bent, and they were all secretly thinking the same thing: she looked so frail, so fragile, a young girl freezing in her black coat, eyes red with weeping, one tear still hanging from the end of her nose. How could anyone imagine that what she had in her throat could "rouse people to action"? She herself didn't seem to think so at this moment.

"That's what you said, Dora, isn't it?" Bart said, as if reassuring himself. "You said her voice could rouse the people?"

"That's what I said," Dora agreed sadly. "But they'd have to hear it first."

All four of them set off, arm in arm. The moon came out again, shimmering on the slate roofs of church belfries and the steely river.

"Did you go back to playing the piano?" Helen ventured to ask after they had gone about a hundred yards.

"No, I've never played again," sighed Dora.

"Because of your hand?"

"It wasn't my hand that refused to do it. A hand can be retrained. But my heart wasn't in it anymore."

VAN VLYCK'S "MISTAKE"

Gus Van Vlyck was still in a furious temper. He was angrily pacing the corridors on the fourth floor of the high-rise building occupied by the Phalange headquarters, chin jutting out, eyes blazing. He marched into his subordinates' offices without knocking and found a good reason to get angry at every one of them. Then he went out again, slamming doors behind him, returned to his own office, and for the tenth time made phone calls to people who kept telling him the same thing: there was no more news. As he hung up, he crashed the handset down hard enough to split it, swearing furiously.

It was not the loss of Mills that had upset him so much, still less the death of Pastor, whom he hardly knew. He had felt some slight compassion for the regional police chief on hearing of his terrible end. After all, this was the man who had obeyed his orders fifteen years ago when he'd set the dogs on Eva-Maria Bach. Many men wouldn't have had the guts to do it, and Mills deserved respect if only for his absence of qualms. But as for mourning his death . . .

No, what infuriated Gus Van Vlyck so much was to know that Milena Bach, Eva-Maria's daughter, was at large and that they hadn't been able to lay hands on her. The police hadn't been so soft a few years ago, and he was going to say so at the next Council meeting. If they gave him time to speak, that is, because some of them never missed a chance to bring up the bitter memory of his mistake, now long past but coming back to confront him full on today.

When asked, just after the execution of Eva-Maria Bach, "What do we do with the child?" he had hesitated. The mother had given them trouble enough. Why encumber themselves with the daughter and risk the possibility of her reviving the singer's memory someday? Common sense called for the child's death. There was a special unit for that kind of thing, efficient men who acted fast and well. You didn't have to face the details yourself. "What do we do with the child?" All you had to do was keep your mouth shut, and the killing machines would know what that silence meant. You wouldn't even have to feel responsible.

But his opinion had been asked, and he'd been as weak as a woman. "The girl? An orphanage, as far away from here as possible. At the other end of the country!" Even as he barked out this order, he had a presentiment that it was the wrong decision. Today he knew it, and the certainty had him seething with rage.

He left the headquarters at five in the afternoon without telling anyone. Disdaining the elevator, he ran four floors down the service staircase. Seeing him emerge at the front of the building, a driver stood up very straight, cap in hand, and opened the back door of a black limousine. Van Vlyck ignored him and marched straight on ahead, his wide shoulders taking up half the sidewalk. A tram screeched to a halt a few yards away from him, but he preferred to continue on foot.

In Opera House Square, he cast a look of dislike at the abandoned theater, its door obstructed by piles of refuse, windows boarded up with planks roughly nailed across them. He spat on the ground. Why couldn't he rid his mind of such poisonous memories the way a rotten tooth can be taken out, or a gangrenous limb amputated? When would they get around to demolishing these walls, razing the building to the ground, and renaming the square itself? It was getting too much to bear! Voices came through the stones, still vibrating here after all this time. Sometimes at night he heard them echoing, joining in unison, responding to one another. Didn't other people hear them? Were they deaf?

One voice among them all never ceased to haunt him. He could stupefy himself with beer until he couldn't stand upright, he could bury his head in his pillows at night, but it still rang out, pure and deep, unchanged. There was nothing to be done about it: he would remember, he'd find himself back sitting in the front row in that church one late afternoon fifteen years before.

The young woman, the soloist, is sitting ten feet away. She is very young. Hardly more than twenty. To start with, he admires her blond hair and the delicacy of her forearms under the lacy sleeves of her blouse. What made him come into this church? He never sets foot inside a church! Perhaps he came in just because it would be cooler in here on an unbearably hot day. He got his ticket at a plain table outside in the porch and felt almost ashamed of buying it. Going to a concert! He, Van Vlyck!

The church was empty when he went in. He sat down in the front row and immediately felt so comfortable that he dozed off. Now that he's woken up, the chorus and musicians have come in. The violinists are tuning their instruments. He hasn't noticed all the seats behind him filling. He feels he is alone. He feels it's just for him that the soloist now rises to her feet and sings.

She sings effortlessly. There's only a tiny fold at the bridge of her nose, two little lines going up to her forehead. So close to him, at point-blank range, she crucifies him with her blue eyes and graceful bearing. For a full hour he observes her at his leisure: her fine hands, her fingers, her hair and the way it moves, caressing her shoulders. He sees the texture of her skin, the tender curve of her cheeks, the outline of her lips. And the woman's voice pierces his dull soul. He isn't used to such emotions, and he sheds tears. He, Van Vlyck, shedding tears! Listening to a singer and weeping!

When it's over, he stands up and claps until his hands are red. As the singers take their bows, he could swear that she is looking at him, singling him out, smiling more for him than for the rest of the audience.

Back in the street, he knows that nothing will ever be the same again; another life is beginning. My name is Van Vlyck, he reminds himself. I'm not just anybody. No one has ever resisted me yet. So why would this woman resist me?

Some weeks later he finds out that she sings at the Opera House, and he goes to a whole week's worth of performances before venturing to approach her at the end of the evening with a bunch of red roses. That's what you take singers, isn't it? He casts anxious glances around him. Suppose someone happens to see him here! At last she comes out with two other women. He goes up to her, clumsy and awkward, feeling embarrassed about his flowers. He doesn't know how to just give them to her. "Good evening. Do you remember . . . in that church the other day . . . I . . . you . . . well, we saw each other." She doesn't remember it at all.

All the same, he gets her to agree to meet him in a café next day. As she drinks a cup of chocolate, she tries to explain. "No, really, I was looking at you in just the same way as I looked at everyone else. I'm happy when the audience applauds and I smile at them, that's all. You were right in front of me; I couldn't ignore you. This is a misunderstanding, you know." He doesn't believe it. The poison has entered his veins and is streaming along them. He pesters her. He follows her to the building where she lives. He rings her doorbell. She refuses to see him. "You frighten me! I wish you wouldn't come to see me at the Opera House anymore.

Please. I don't want you to go on giving my little girl so many presents. You frighten me. You really do. Can you understand that? You frighten me!" No, he can't understand it. All he wants is to marry her and live with her. Besides, he's already left his wife and abandoned his children to be free for her. She can't let him down now! She has to be brought to understand! If only she had a little common sense!

One evening he makes his way to her dressing room in spite of her orders not to let him in. He tries to kiss her. She resists. He threatens her. He seizes her arm, pressing it too hard. She slaps his face. She slaps him, Van Vlyck! He strides away along the theater corridors with his reddened cheek, under the mocking gaze of the musicians and singers. His cheek bears the mark of his shame and dishonor.

From then on he isn't the same man anymore. After two weeks he decides to take the plunge. He's been thinking about it for a long time. Now the time has come: he joins the Phalange and takes the oath of loyalty to the movement.

That evening he and two other new recruits visit prostitutes in the slums and spend the night drinking. He goes home dead drunk and exhausted in the small hours. Passing the windows of the Opera House, he howls like a wild beast. From now on that's what he'll be, a wild beast. And he has found his pack. No one will ever laugh at him again.

When the Phalange seizes power in a bloody coup a year later, he has made headway: he gets a responsible position with the state police. He is among those who set off in pursuit of Eva-Maria Bach. "I have an account to settle," is all he explains.

His colleagues understand. "Don't worry, Gus. When we catch up with her, you can be in charge of the operation. Do whatever you like with her." They spend months tracking her down. She really gives them the runaround.

But one evening they catch her at last, in a little provincial concert hall in the north of the country. On that day he's been drinking too much again. He's not well. He doesn't enter the hall with the others; he leans against the wall outside. He hears it all: the yells, the sound of the piano breaking up.

As she comes out of the hall, astonished to be going free, Eva-Maria Bach sees him lurking in the shadows. Their eyes meet. She thinks he has just saved her. She thinks he gave the order to let her go. How remorseful she feels for her cruelty to him! How generous he is to forgive her! She takes a step toward him, but he stops her from coming any closer with a gesture. She understands: he doesn't want to compromise himself in front of his colleagues. So she simply says, from a distance, "Thank you." She finds the strength to smile at him in spite of her terror, in spite of Dora, who is still in the hall, a prisoner, her hand nothing but a mass of crushed flesh. She repeats it, "Thank you." She is thanking him for herself, but above all for her little daughter. She can be reunited with the child tomorrow and hold her in her arms. "Thank you," she says.

They push her out into the road, telling her to get out for good. Van Vlyck can't control the spasms of his stomach anymore. Resting his hands on the dingy wall of the little town hall, he throws up copiously. His vomit soils his boots and pants.

A few hours later, in the car driving through the night toward the capital, he is informed that they have picked up the little girl at her nursemaid's, and they ask, "What do we do with the child?" He feels his stomach heaving again.

217

By now, no doubt, the dogs will have done their work. He wishes everyone would leave him alone. Would let him sleep. "What do we do with the child?" his colleague persists.

"An orphanage. At the other end of the country. As far away from here as possible," he replies.

And he knows he has just made a mistake.

The sports hall at the Phalange headquarters was empty at this hour. Van Vlyck unlocked the door and strode along the echoing corridors. The entire locker room was full of the sharp odor of sweating bodies: the air, the leather, and wood all smelled of it. A jacket and pants hung from a hook. With satisfaction, he recognized them as the property of Two-and-a-Half. You always knew where to find him, and it wasn't in the library.

He changed quickly and crossed the body-building room in an old T-shirt and a well-worn pair of shorts. A regular creaking sound guided him to the opposite window, where a man with an undershot jaw and eyes deeply embedded in their sockets was doing weight-training exercises on a mat. The floorboards beneath the mat were groaning under him. Van Vlyck glanced at the number of disks on each side of the bar and couldn't hide his astonishment. "You can lift that amount ten times running?"

"Fifteen times," said the man impassively when he had put the barbell down.

Two-and-a-Half wasn't as thickset as Van Vlyck and was probably forty-five pounds lighter, but no one could equal him for sheer strength. He said no more than ten words a day, and he didn't understand jokes. His body was tough and his mind even tougher. His nickname derived from the way he never reached "three" when he threatened someone. "I'll count up to three," he would warn, but he had hardly uttered the word "two" before the subject of his threat was dead, killed by a bullet, a knife, or his bare hands. If asked why he did it, why he didn't at least give the person he was interrogating a chance, he would say, "Dunno. Guess I got no patience."

Van Vlyck got on the machine next to him and began his own exercises. They carried on together for an hour or more without talking. The two men were different in every way. Van Vlyck grunted and groaned with effort. He seemed to hate the bars or dumbbells he was lifting. He swore at them. Sweat ran down his white skin, seeping into the red hair on his broad chest and massive forearms. He often stopped to drink water and rub himself down with a towel. Two-and-a-Half, on the other hand, worked coldly on. His body stayed dry. He didn't drink anything. You could hardly hear him breathing, but the enormous weights were raised as regularly as if an indefatigable piston were lifting them.

Afterward they met in the deserted bar of the sports hall.

"A beer?" suggested Van Vlyck.

Two-and-a-Half blinked by way of assent. Van Vlyck went around behind the counter and took the tops off the two bottles himself. They began drinking in silence. Two-and-a-Half examined the contents of his glass with the same vague expression that he directed at other people. Van Vlyck wondered what he was thinking about. He felt uneasy. Was Two-and-a-Half even thinking about anything at all?

"I might have a job for you."

Two-and-a-Half didn't move a muscle.

"Information to be pried out of someone who doesn't like talking. The pay will be good."

Two-and-a-Half nodded slightly to show that he would take the job.

The wind was sweeping over the dark riverbanks. A few pedestrians, out late, were hurrying home, avoiding the puddles of water. Down on the river itself, gusts of wind turned the rain to hail as it fell, as if throwing handfuls of gravel at it. Night was falling. Two-and-a-Half followed the paved path beside the river like someone out for a stroll. He knew he might be about to kill a man, but that didn't bother him. Raindrops beat down hard on his umbrella. He crumpled the banknotes in his right-hand jacket pocket. Van Vlyck had given them to him as an advance: half the sum, the rest to be paid when he had extracted the information. It was as good as his already. He passed four bridges without crossing any of them, and stopped at the fifth.

A quick glance was enough to show him that the man he was after wasn't there. No motorbike chained to the guardrail meant no Mitten. That bike was really the common property of everyone who lived under the Wooden Bridge, but only Mitten was able to ride it. Never mind; he'd wait.

As he waited, he started over the bridge and walked along the wet sidewalk, keeping a tight hold on the umbrella, which threatened to blow away. He hadn't gone fifty yards before the noisy motorbike, still without lights, appeared at the far end. From a distance its rider, wearing a woolen balaclava, with his shoulders hunched, looked like a large, lumbering insect. He was revving the engine, but the result was pitiful: it didn't respond. Two-and-a-Half watched him coming closer, delighted. He couldn't have hoped for better working conditions: darkness, no witnesses, the bridge . . .

He waited for Mitten to draw level with him and then gave him a vicious shove. Sent flying, the tramp cried out. The motorbike fell to the ground, went into a skid on the wet pavement, crossed the road, and crashed into the opposite curb. The hot exhaust pipe broke off, skidded on the pavement, and spat out vapor.

"What's the big idea?" yelled Mitten. "I've smashed my kneecap!"

Two-and-a-Half didn't even close his umbrella. He took the tramp by the front of his jacket with one hand, stood him on his feet, and held him close in a violent grip.

"I've smashed my kneecap!" wailed Mitten. "I'm in agony!"

221

Under the soaked balaclava, his emaciated, bearded face was twisting in pain.

"Let me go! What do you want?"

"Information. About a blond girl. Milena Bach."

"Never heard of her. Buzz off!"

Two-and-a-Half was not the man to waste time in pointless chat. Most new arrivals in the city came down the river, and they stopped at the Wooden Bridge. Everyone knew that. He picked Mitten up and sat him on the metal parapet of the bridge.

"Know who I am?"

Their faces were almost touching. For the first time Mitten looked his assailant in the eye, and the pain in his knee instantly went away. He realized whose hard fingers were holding him there. If he refused to talk, he would have only a few seconds to live—just as long as it took him to fall. He would hit the icy water of the river flat on his back. His fellow down-and-outs under the bridge might hear the muted sound of his thin body as it went in. He was terrified.

"I . . . I can't swim," he stammered stupidly.

"Know who I am?" the other man repeated.

"Yeah." Mitten wept, clutching his adversary's cuffs.

"Then I'm going to count to three. One . . ."

"What was her name again?"

"Milena Bach. Two . . ."

It would be no use lying. He might gain a little time that way, but the result would be the same in the end, or even worse.

"At Jahn's . . . She's at Jahn's Restaurant. . . ."

His heart was beating hard enough to break his ribs. He guessed that Two-and-a-Half was longing to throw him into the void even after getting the information he wanted. Several seconds passed, seeming like an eternity, and then he felt the killer putting him down on the sidewalk again. The next moment, he saw the man walking calmly away. All this time he hadn't even folded his umbrella.

Mitten tried to stand the motorbike up in vain. All he did was make the pain in his knee worse. The rain was falling harder than ever. He picked up the steaming exhaust pipe and stuck it under his arm. Then he limped over to the steps and clambered down them with difficulty, holding tight to the rail.

Two-and-a-Half made three mistakes that evening. The first was not to throw Mitten into the river. It was extraordinarily tempting to do it, to watch the tramp gesticulating as he fell through the air, to hear his terrified cries and the sound of his body hitting the dark water. A little push in the chest would have done it. All that stopped him was the thought that the man might come in useful again.

Two-and-a-Half's second mistake was not to go straight home. He told himself there was no hurry, since he wasn't to meet Van Vlyck until tomorrow afternoon in the sports hall. And he liked hearing the gentle patter of the raindrops on his umbrella. He thought he would prolong that pleasure. Instead of going straight to the Upper Town, where he lived, he followed the river, and even went down the first flight of steps he came to and walked along the bank. He didn't see the three shadows going the same way, crouching low and keeping their distance. A wooden bench screwed to the paving stones offered him its half-rotten seat. He sat down, not bothering about getting his pants wet, and stayed there without moving, listening to the sound of the rain.

At that minute he didn't have long left to live, but he was not aware of that.

He waited for the rain to die down, and it soon did. The machine-gun patter of the drops above his head gradually faded, leaving only an increasingly faint rustling. Finally there was only the muted rushing of the river and the murmur of the wind. Then Two-and-a-Half made his third mistake. He lowered his umbrella to close it.

The sky exploded. Flashes of dazzling lightning blinded him, and he collapsed on the bench.

"Hit him again!" a voice breathed. "He's a tough nut to crack, he is!"

The sky exploded for the second time. He felt himself falling into a black abyss and lost consciousness.

Standing behind the bench, Mitten was brandishing his exhaust pipe.

"Do I go on, lads?"

"Not worth it," one of his companions said. "He's had it. We better get a move on now. If we get spotted from up there, we're done for. Give me a hand."

They went around to the front of the bench and dragged Two-and-a-Half to the edge of the water by his feet.

"You do the honors, Mitten!"

Mitten didn't have the strength to lift the killer. He knelt down beside him and pushed with both hands. As the man's body was about to go into the water, he hesitated. Then he thought of Milena, of Helen, of all the others taking refuge at Jahn's Restaurant who must be protected.

"One, two . . . and three," he muttered. "Bound to happen to you too someday, right?"

And he rolled Two-and-a-Half over into the indifferent and icy waters of the great river.

HOSPITAL

A jay was perching on the windowsill. It had slipped past the bars and was looking into the bedroom with round eyes. Enraptured, Milos Ferenzy looked at the big bird's bright colors, its bluish wings, the comical black mustache on both sides of its beak. He wanted to call to it by making little chirping sounds, as you do when you're trying to entice an animal, but he couldn't manage it. His mouth was too dry. Not that it bothered him. He felt completely well, as if he were in an immaterial body free of all pain, living in a state of suspended animation.

A pale ray of sunlight traced a slanting line on the whitewashed wall opposite. The room seemed to contain no furniture. A lightbulb with a metal shade hung from the ceiling. Milos noticed that he was wearing a coarse nightshirt with short sleeves. He turned his head to the left and saw the dressing on his arm. A flexible tube emerged from it, linked to a drip gradually dispensing its contents.

There was another bed parallel to his. Its occupant, a lean, muscular man of about thirty, was moaning faintly with his mouth half open. Thick bandaging surrounded his chest, but the most shocking thing about him was his devastated face, covered in terrible scars like furrows rimmed with pink flesh. His long, dirty feet stuck out from under the covers. Did they never wash people in this hospital? The pleasant sensation of wellbeing faded slightly

Hospital? What was he doing in a hospital? Oh yes, the mountain refuge. His leg. The knife in it. He gently pushed back the sheet, hitched up the nightshirt, and saw that his right thigh was painted with iodine. In the middle of the stain, his injury, stitched with black thread, looked quite small. *I'm no doctor,* he thought, *but I seem to have been quite well looked after.* At the same moment, the sheet slipped off entirely and fell to the floor. Then he saw that there was an iron ring around his left ankle, and the ring was chained to the bar at the foot of the bed. He let out a groan. The jay, no doubt hearing him, flew away with its wings rushing.

During the next hour, Milos lay completely still, worrying that he might set off some terrible pain if he made the slightest movement. Where was he? And why had he been given medical attention if he was to be kept prisoner? To take revenge on him for the dog-handler's death? The ray of sunlight had disappeared now, and twilight was slowly filling the room. The man in the next bed had stopped moaning, but he was sleeping restlessly, his breathing irregular.

Milos wondered how Helen had felt when she came back to find the refuge empty. Had she thought that he'd set off into the mountains on his own? That he didn't trust her? This worried him. He would have stayed; he'd promised to stay! But they had arrived first and taken him away on their sleigh, half unconscious. He remembered being in a sort of waking dream at the time, feeling the jolts, the cold, the sensation of being roughly manipulated, like a dead beast thrown into the slaughterman's barrow. Then he had fainted right away, and now he was lying in this room, a quiet yet disturbing place, beside another injured man.

Firm footsteps could be heard out in the corridor. The door suddenly opened, and a thickset man pressed the switch beside it, flooding the room with glaring light.

"Hi there. Slept well?"

With the jawbone of a carnivore, short hair, and a powerful chest under his close-fitting T-shirt, he looked more like a wrestling trainer than a nurse. Milos didn't like his steely blue eyes or his small, thin-lipped mouth.

"Thirsty? Here, drink this."

Milos raised his head and thirstily drank the half glass of water that the man was offering him. "Are you a doctor?"

"Me, a doctor? Not me! Mind you, I was once in

the cobbling trade, and medicine, well, it's a bit like do-it-yourself. You get better with practice. Sewed you up, didn't I? See any difference between my work and a surgeon's? Come on, be honest. See any difference? Skin's only leather, right? You just have to disinfect the material and wash your hands. That's the trick of it."

"What about that? Did you do it?" asked Milos, pointing to his chained ankle.

The man roared with laughter. "Put that on you, did they? I never noticed! What a bunch of brutes! I'll set you free."

He took a small key out of his pocket and turned it in the padlock.

You're no brighter than "they" are, thought Milos. *If you have the key, you're no stranger to this ring and chain. I bet you put them on me just to give yourself credit for taking them off again.* He knew instinctively that he would never trust this man and made up his mind to keep his distance.

"Know where you are?"

Milos looked blank.

"In the infirmary of a training camp!"

Milos still looked blank.

"A camp that trains men for the fights. Are you surprised? You must know about the fights, right?"

The man had sat down on the edge of the bed. It seemed to Milos that there was a touch of admiration in his smile.

"Come on, don't act so stupid. We know all about that business with Pastor. Hey, you fixed him good. But don't go thinking it's held against you. Nope, we really appreciate it around here. He was a fat oaf, Pastor was. Past his prime. And the winner's always in the right, eh? This time you were the winner. Good work!"

"He'd have set his dogs on us. I had to do it."

"That's it. It was you or him, bound to be. You thought you'd rather it was him! Which means you know all about these things and they weren't wrong to bring you here."

He patted Milos's arm with the satisfaction of a racehorse trainer who has just acquired a Thoroughbred. Milos made a face. The effect of the local anesthetic must be wearing off, and the pain of his injury was beginning to tug at him. The effort he was making to talk was a severe strain too.

"I'll explain about the fights tomorrow," the man said, getting to his feet. "You know enough for today. You better rest. Oh, and I'm called Fulgur. If you need anything just ask for me: Fulgur."

Before leaving the room, he disconnected Milos's drip and went to check the other injured man's pulse.

"And this guy here, he's a champion. Name of Caius. You could do worse than take him as your example. See you tomorrow, Milos Ferenzy!"

Milos dozed for a few hours, and then woke up in the middle of the night, fully alert and sweating. Fulgur meant *lightning* in Latin. And Caius was a Latin name too, wasn't it? They'd chosen such

230

strange names! And the names must be false. He had an idea that he could easily understand the mystery behind all this if he wanted to, but something in him refused to do it, or rather was trying to postpone the moment. He'd have liked to talk to the man in the other bed to reassure himself, but his companion merely groaned or muttered incomprehensible remarks in his dreams now and then.

In the early morning, pale light made its way through the window. Milos waited until it allowed him to see a little and then tried getting out of bed. Taking the strain on his arms, he managed to sit on the edge of the bed. He stayed there for some time until his dizziness wore off, then very carefully got to his feet. He made his way along the wall to the window. It opened easily, letting in a sweetish smell of damp moss. Through the bars, which were sealed in place, he could make out a tall fence some yards away and beyond it a forest of bare-branched trees. He took deep breaths. The cold air made his head go around, and he almost fainted. He was about to close the window again when the muted sound of regular footsteps approached. About fifteen young men, wearing shorts in spite of the cold weather, passed under the window at a run. They were carrying swords. Their noisy, rhythmical breathing moved away in a cloud of mist.

"Shut it!" snapped a curt voice. Turning, Milos saw Caius watching him from his bed. His fevered gaze pierced the dim light. Thick stubble was beginning to cover his scarred cheeks. "Shut that window!"

Milos shut it and went slowly back along the wall. Once he was lying down, he expected his neighbor to speak to him again, but he had to wait a good ten minutes before the man spoke in his harsh voice once more.

"Already injured when you got here, were you? Where've you come from?"

Milos hardly knew what to reply. Where had he come from? It wasn't so easy to explain. And he didn't quite know whom he was talking to. The man called Fulgur had told him to take Caius as his example, but Fulgur's idea of an example wasn't necessarily to be recommended.

"I was captured," he ventured carefully.

There was a long silence. Milos intended to stick to his decision: he would say as little as he could, commit himself to nothing, and observe as much as possible.

"'I was captured.'" Caius laughed as he imitated him. "So do you at least know where you are?"

"In a training camp, I think."

"You think right."

Milos didn't like the man's sarcastic, condescending manner. He still asked no questions, guessing that this might be the best way of actually learning something. He was right about that.

"Fact is, you're in the country's top training camp. Landing here is your best chance of survival. Give me a drink."

It was a struggle for Milos to sit up, reach the glass of water, and hand it to Caius, but he did so without complaining. He even waited for the other man to finish drinking so that he could take the glass from him again, put it back in its place, and then lie down.

"Want to know why it's your best chance?"

"I'm not asking you anything."

Caius paused for some time, probably slightly puzzled by Milos's attitude.

"How old are you?"

"Seventeen."

"Seventeen! I thought they didn't take anyone that young in the camps. What the hell did you do to be put in here with us? Bumped off one of the Phalange's big shots or something?"

For the first time Milos gave no answer.

"God, was that really it, then? You took one of them out?"

Milos did not reply.

"Not very talkative, are you? Quite right, keep it to yourself."

Conversation lapsed again. The light in the room was growing brighter. Someone went down the corridor outside but did not come in. For the second time, Milos heard men running and breathing rhythmically outside the window. He thought for a moment that Caius had gone back to sleep, but then the other man spoke again, in a very low voice and without opening his eyes: "This is the best camp because it's where you'll learn best how to hate your opponents. How to concentrate your anger. It's all in the head, you know, nowhere else, not in the legs, not in the arms. Never forget that. The man who gave me this chest injury last week had a torso and biceps twice as strong as mine, but he just wasn't eager enough to . . ."

The rest of the sentence was inaudible. Caius's voice was dropping yet lower.

"Not eager enough to do what?" This time Milos couldn't help asking.

"Not eager enough to kill me. And he was too afraid of dying. Dead before he even walked into the arena . . . already dead when our eyes met. He saw the hatred in mine; I saw the terror in his. The fight was decided before it began. My second. My third will be this winter. My wound will be better then, and I'll win for the third time. And then I'll be free . . . free . . ."

Caius stopped talking. His head fell to one side, and a few seconds later, he was fast asleep.

Attempting to make some kind of sense out of what he had just heard, Milos tried not to give in to panic, but whatever he did, the words came together inexorably into a single meaning. His pulse and breathing were racing. The Latin names, the arena, the fights: it was all crystal clear.

So he hadn't been spared either out of compassion or so he could be handed over to justice. The Phalange didn't care about any of that. They'd left him alive for an entirely different reason: to make him risk his life in front of them in the arena. To make him die or kill before their eyes, for their pleasure. A gladiator. They wanted to make a gladiator of him! Hadn't such barbarity been abandoned centuries ago? This was a nightmare.

The day brought him little fresh information. Fulgur came back as he had said he would, but only to bring in meals and check up on their injuries. The food was not very appetizing, but Milos's instinct for survival made him eat everything put in front of him. As for Caius, he was sleeping like a log, and in his few waking moments he seemed to have forgotten everything he had said in the morning.

As evening drew on, the jay came to perch on the windowsill again and stayed there for several minutes, stepping from one foot to the other.

"Hello, you!" said Milos, touched by the bird's fidelity. "Do you feel sorry for me? Did you come to tell me not to despair? Don't worry. I'm pretty tough."

When he woke up next day, he saw that Caius had gone. So had his bed. Fulgur walked into the room as abruptly as usual.

"Wondering what happened to your mate there, eh?"

"No," said Milos, more determined than ever to ask no questions.

"I'll tell you all the same: he asked to be taken back to the dormitory last night. Said he didn't fancy your company."

Dumbfounded, Milos tried not to show the slightest surprise but waited impassively to hear more. Fulgur leaned against the wall by the window, hands in his pockets. The bones of his forehead, cheeks, and jaw occupied most of the room on his face; by comparison his eyes and mouth looked tiny.

"Did you know it can be a very bad thing for a guy like Caius not to fancy your company?"

Milos said nothing.

"Now with me it's the other way around. I like you. You don't natter away like a girl, you never complain; you seem to know your own mind. I ask myself, What is it Caius doesn't like about you? Any idea?"

No reply.

"Right. Well, it's my job to explain the rules of the place to you and how it works. Are you listening?"

Silence.

"OK. This is one of the six training camps in the country. One for each province. Six provinces, six camps. Are you with me so far? Ours is in the middle of the forest. If you run away, you're fair game: you'll be pursued by a hundred men, caught, and killed immediately. So forget that idea. It's for your own good. You were chained up the other day because you didn't know about it yet. Now you do know, so there's no need for the chain. Got it?"

Silence.

"Right. You'll train here with about thirty other fighters—all of them criminals who'd have ended up on the gallows but were pardoned and sent here. Scum, the entire lot of 'em. Expect a bunch of little angels and you're in for a big disappointment. There's an arena in each camp. All of them identical: same size, same shape, same sand. And there's a seventh in the capital, just like the other six except there's tiers of seats around it for the spectators. No seats here because there's no spectators. Still with me?"

Milos nodded in assent. In fact he had never listened so intently to anyone. Every word Fulgur said was etched on his memory as soon as he heard it.

"This is where you'll train. You'll fight for real in the arena in the capital. The fights are held over three days. They'll be single combat against men from the other camps, guys you don't know. You're training with your mates here, and if you injure one badly, you'll be punished. Everything clear?"

Milos did not reply.

"Your first fight will be in three months' time, in midwinter. You have plenty of time to get better, grow some scar tissue, learn the techniques. If you win and if you survive, your second fight is in spring. Like I said, if you survive. Because the winner of a fight often dies of his wounds. Look at Caius! He came pretty close to it. Right. Then, if you win your second fight, the third's in early summer. If you're still alive after that one, then you're free. Got that?"

Milos nodded.

"In fact you're better than free. You've earned respect. You're a celebrity. The Phalange will get you a cushy, well-paid job for life, give you total protection. You're young; you've been shut up in a boarding school. You may not realize what that means, but I can tell you it means a lot. You'll only have to say your name to get the best table in all the best restaurants and free meals. You'll be able to travel in any taxi for free too. And even if you were ugly as sin, the most gorgeous women will be fighting over you. Whereas you're a good-looking lad to start with, say no more! It gives the girls a thrill to think a man's risked his life three times—even more of a thrill to know he's killed another man three times. That's women for you—can't be helped."

Milos felt himself blushing and thought of Helen. Would the idea that he was a murderer four times over make her love him more? He doubted it.

"In this camp," Fulgur went on, "you'll meet men training for their first fight, like you. They're called novices; others who have already won their fights are called premiers; and then there's the champions who've won two, like Caius. You'll soon tell them apart. A word in your ear: make sure they all respect you. This isn't a summer camp. The trainer's name is Myricus. Listen to him. He knows what he's talking about. He's a former winner—he won three times. Any questions?"

"No," said Milos, on the brink of nausea.

There was silence. Fulgur didn't move. "You don't ask whether I'm a former winner too?"

"No."

Fulgur, obviously dying to talk about himself, was annoyed by this response. "Just as you like. One last thing: you have to take the name of a fighting man. I picked Fulgur because I'm as fast as lightning. You want to find a name that suits you. I'll get them to show you the list and you can choose one."

"I don't want to. I'll keep my own."

"Just as you like," Fulgur repeated with pretended indifference. "Show me your leg."

Milos put back the sheet and uncovered his thigh. The wound had closed up well and looked clean and almost dry already.

"Excellent," Fulgur said approvingly. "I'll take the stitches out in a few days' time." And then, before Milos had time to protect himself in any way, he raised his right arm and hit the thigh as hard as he could directly on the injury. Milos screamed and almost fainted.

"So now," said the man in unctuous tones, "kindly ask me if I'm a former winner. You'd really like to know, wouldn't you?"

"Are you a former winner?" Milos groaned.

Fulgur's small blue eyes, staring into his own, were cold as a reptile's.

"Yes, that's right. I'm a former winner. I killed my three opponents. So I could be living it up in the capital, but I'd rather stay here. Ask me why I'd rather stay here, why don't you?"

"Why would you rather stay here?"

"Well, seeing as you ask, I'll tell you. I'd rather stay here because I like it. Training hard every day, seeing the fear men feel getting into the vans to go to their first fight, watching the winners, hearing about what they did, watching the losers die and hearing about their deaths, the yellow sand in the arena, the red blood flowing into it, all that—I can't do without it. It's like a drug. You wouldn't understand. I was like the rest of them at first, just wanted to save my skin. Kill my three men and get the hell out of this awful camp. But after my second victory, I started thinking what a great place it was—and liking what went on here too. It's a matter of life or death. You don't find that anywhere else except in war, but seeing as there's no war on right now. . . . Well, any more questions?"

"No," said Milos faintly, praying that Fulgur wouldn't hit him again. The pain was spreading all the way to his stomach in waves of agony.

"Right. I'll leave you, then. Thanks for this nice little chat." He turned at the door. "Yup, I really like you, Milos Ferenzy. I just love talking to you."

THE TRAINING CAMP

Five days after he had arrived, around midday, Milos felt well enough to leave his room, leaning on a pair of crutches. As he went down the corridor, he discovered that the room next to his was fitted out as a rudimentary operating room, with a table covered by a white sheet and globe-shaped medical lamp at the end of an articulated mechanical arm. Jars and bottles stood around in no particular order on dilapidated shelves. This was clearly "Dr." Fulgur's domain, the sinister scene of his experiments!

Milos shivered when he thought that he had been lying there, unconscious, at the mercy of a sadist like Fulgur. However, since his leg wasn't hurting too badly now, he ventured outside. Fulgur had shaved his head the evening before, and the cold air froze his skull and temples.

The camp did indeed stand in a clearing in the forest. You could see the bare branches of tall oaks on the other side of the wire fence. There was a watchtower at the entrance. The man in military uniform guarding it, gun in hand, gave Milos a nod. It was hard to tell whether he meant it as a threat or a welcome. Milos returned it, and laboriously made his way farther on.

After skirting the wooden huts that he thought must contain the dormitories, he came to the canteen hut. An unappetizing smell of cabbage wafted out of it. From here he could see that two more watchtowers guarded the back of the enclosure. Fulgur was right: this was no summer camp.

A square building with no windows occupied the center of the clearing on its own. It was made of tree trunks, like a trapper's log cabin. Milos had to go all around it to find the way in: a low door, unlocked. He pushed it open with his left crutch, went in, took a few steps along a trodden-earth pathway, and came to a gate made of planks. Beyond it lay the arena, like a circus ring. It measured roughly sixty feet across and was entirely enclosed by a palisade the height of a man.

Four men in canvas pants, their chests and feet bare in spite of the cold, were fighting on the sand. A handful of spectators was watching from the gallery. They glanced at Milos, registered his presence, and then ignored him. The men in the arena were not equally matched. Three of them, armed with swords, were harassing the fourth, whose head was shaved and who was fighting them with his bare hands. The unfortunate man had to keep watch on all sides at once, throw himself on the ground, roll over to avoid blows, get up again, and run. His adversaries pursued him relentlessly, surrounded him again, and threatened him with their swords. He didn't stand a chance, but he faced them with an expression of fierce defiance as if he could still hope to win.

Even from a distance Milos noticed the blunt features of his young face, his flattened nose and bushy eyebrows, his sturdy limbs. He felt as if he had met the young man before, but where? The fight went on in startling silence. No cries, no calling out, no encouragement. There was nothing to be heard but the crunch of feet on the sand and the gasping breath of the man under attack. He managed to escape his pursuers several more times, losing none of his fury and showing no sign of fear. Then a moment came when he stumbled as he fled and fell to the ground. The next moment, the man closest to him leaped up and struck him on the shoulder. Then he immobilized him, one knee on his chest, the point of his sword to the man's throat.

"That'll do," called a cavernous voice. "Let him go now."

The fighters obeyed and retreated without a glance for the breathless young man, who was dripping with sweat and swearing under his breath as he held his bloodstained shoulder.

The man who had given the order rose to his feet. He was half a head taller than everyone around him. Thick black stubble covered his angular face.

"See that, all of you?" He was addressing the spectators. "He lost because he fell. If you fall, you're dead. Never forget that. Ferox, Messor, take him to the infirmary; tell 'em to patch him up. The rest of you go and eat."

They climbed down a small flight of steps at the side of the arena—it came down to the pathway just behind Milos—and left in silence. The colossus bringing up the rear stopped. His massive size was impressive.

"You the one who strangled Pastor?"

Milos saw in his eyes the same spark of admiration as Fulgur's had shown a few days earlier.

"Yes," he said soberly.

"How old are you?"

"Seventeen."

"Good. My name's Myricus and I'm your trainer. Welcome to the camp, laddie."

With these words, he turned his back and walked away. His shoulders only just fit through the door.

Tired after his outing in the morning, Milos dozed through part of the afternoon, but around five o'clock he was woken by the creak of a bedstead being wheeled into the room. The man injured in the arena was lying there, on his back and covered by a sheet that was none too clean. The cut on his shoulder, although not very deep, had been stitched up. Fulgur hadn't been able to resist his little weakness for playing with needles.

"Doing all right?" asked Milos.

244

"Yeah, I'm OK," grunted the injured man.

There was nothing of him to be seen but his pale skull, with the hair roughly shaved. A scar traced a pink comma above his forehead. But when he turned a little to one side to spare his wounded shoulder, his face showed clearly, and Milos looked at him, his jaw dropping.

"Basil!" he cried. "I must be dreaming. It's you!"

Astonishment and delight choked him. The other young man opened his eyes and broke into happy laughter. "Ferenzy! Ha, ha, ha! I don't believe it!"

"Basil! I thought you were dead!"

"Dead? Why would I be dead? You're crazy!"

"But I saw them take you out of the detention cell! And carry you away on a stretcher! Basil, you were covered with blood!"

"You bet! So I fooled you too! Ha, ha, ha! It's easy to make yourself bleed, you know. Look at this: I got a thumbnail as hard as a bit of old iron. I nicked my scalp with it; blood flowed like someone had bashed my skull in. I wiped it all over me, my face, my neck, everything. Then I bashed my fists on the door, and when they came, I flung myself down and played dead. They thought I'd bashed my head in. Only way of getting out of that rat hole. I was getting bored, see? Only trouble is, instead of chucking me out of the school and sending me to another, same as usual, they locked me up in here. Which is worse."

"But you haven't done anything serious," Milos

interrupted. "I thought they only put criminals in this camp."

"Yeah, but they kind of explained it was . . . Oh, I dunno what now. . . . It was, like, for all I'd done, see?"

"For all you'd done?"

"That's kind of what they said. Hey, you hit the jackpot first go, right? Did you really kill a dog-handler?"

"So it seems," Milos admitted.

"Go on, tell me about it. I always like to hear how one of those Phalange guys got done in."

"I'll tell you about it, but first you tell me why they were fighting you three to one this morning. You didn't have a chance."

"It's kind of a test thought up by that trainer, Myricus. We all take it in turn. He wants everyone wounded at least once. After that, he says, you're—well, sort of baptized. Mainly it's to show what'll happen if you refuse to fight in the arena. If you just run to save yourself, after ten minutes they'll send in another opponent, and five minutes later a third if you go on trying not to fight. So the more you chicken out, the less your chance of surviving. Get it?"

"I get it. And apart from that, what's this Myricus like?"

"Myricus? Three times stronger than you and me put together. But he's no fool either. Guesses everything you're thinking. For instance, the other day he says to me, 'Listen here, Rusticus—'"

246

"Is that what you're called here, Rusticus?"

"Yeah, they gave me the name—I dunno why. Don't even know what it means. Do you know, then?"

"No," lied Milos, suppressing a wish to laugh.

"Well, he takes me to one side, says, 'Listen here, Rusticus. You know why you're not scared?' I say no. And it's true: I'm not scared. 'You're not scared because you believe you won't really fight,' he says. 'You think something will happen, you don't know what, but that's what you think, and you think no one can make you fight, isn't that so, Rusticus?' I don't know what to say because he was dead right, and I don't want to admit it. So he explains how it's the same when everyone comes here; they all reckon they'll escape fighting. 'But they're wrong,' he says, 'and that's the best way to lose a fight. No, you want to know for sure you'll be fighting.' Follow me?"

Milos followed him only too well. During the hours alone in this room, he had worked out his own secret conviction that he wasn't going to fight. Discovering that he was thinking exactly like the others was extremely annoying.

"There's some of 'em feel sure right up to the last moment they won't go into the arena," Rusticus went on, "and them, they're dead already. Listen, Ferenzy, this is what I've learned since I've been here: first, it's no use thinking you won't fight; second, it's no use chickening out when you do."

"I see," murmured Milos, although he couldn't

247

bring himself to admit that this line of reasoning had also been his own. He wondered whether it was simply a question of time—after all, he'd only just arrived—or whether his own intrinsic nature would rebel to the very end against the terrible idea of entering the arena with intent to kill.

Basil had closed his eyes and seemed to be dropping off to sleep.

"Can I ask you one last question?" said Milos softly.

"Go ahead."

"You talked to Myricus about the best way to survive, is that right?"

"Yes."

"But did the two of you talk about how to live with yourself afterward? I mean, once you've killed a man. Or two men, or three?"

"Yes, he talked about that. He said . . . Oh, I can't remember just what. . . . You mustn't worry about that."

"Meaning?"

"Well, meaning if your opponent dies, it's because his time had come."

"His destiny?"

"That's it, his destiny. And if you think you're here for some good reason, you're fooling yourself. You're just a tool, see? And then you have to . . . Oh, and he said if you ask too many questions like that, you're finished."

They remained silent for a while. Milos thought Basil had fallen asleep when his friend muttered, in a thick voice, "Hey, I'm glad I found you here, Ferenzy. Really glad."

Milos and Basil left the infirmary together the next day. They had made a kind of pact without needing to put it into words, and no doubt to compensate for their youth compared to the others: they would stay together and help each other through whatever trials they faced. They'd support each other to the last.

The other fighters were all between twenty-five and forty, and none of them seemed inclined to make friends with anyone. During training in the arena, Milos found none of the lively, cheerful atmosphere he had known in the wrestling ring. The cruel fate they all shared might have been expected to create a bond between these men, but no. Everyone here seemed solely preoccupied with becoming strong and implacable enough to survive.

Caius, only just recovered from his injuries, proved to be the most formidable of all. The rules forbade the inflicting of any serious injury on a training partner, but the definition of "serious" was very vague, and Caius was constantly trying to see how far he could go. He always had to cut or bruise his opponents, make blood flow. Myricus never told him not to. Knowing that Caius didn't like him, Milos took care to avoid him and did his utmost not to face him in the arena. He still had no idea why Caius didn't fancy his company until the night when Basil told him. The two of them often spent hours whispering from bed to bed in the dormitory that they shared with about ten others.

"Seems that the more you win, the more you get to be super — suterspi —" he began.

"Superstitious," Milos helped him out.

"That's it. For instance, if a man's won twice with the same driver taking him to the arena in the van, he'll never agree to set off for his third fight with a different driver. Or if someone sees a mouse in the arena cell while he's waiting for his fight, you can bet he'll look for that mouse second time around, and if there's no mouse, he'll be trembling like a leaf when he goes into the arena, get it?"

"Yes," said Milos. "And you think Caius dislikes me because of something like that? I mean, I never did anything to hurt him."

"Could be that. All I know is he hates cats. And I know why. When he was little, he shut himself up in a cage with a cat, just in play. Then he couldn't get out, and they stayed there together quite a while. That cat went crazy and made for him. There was no one to stop it, understand? It clawed half the face off Caius. Seen those scars he has? The cat done it. Since then he can't stand cats. But hey, you're not a cat."

"No," smiled Milos, beginning to understand. "I'm not a cat, but it seems I must have been in a previous incarnation."

"In a what?"

"A life. Someone said I must have lived before this one, and I was a cat in it."

"You a cat? Where'd you pick up that daft idea? Who said so?"

Milos felt a pang. Where was Helen now? Did she even know he was still alive? He would so much have liked to reassure her and hold her in his arms. Did she often think of him? The idea that he might have to kill three men before he could be reunited with her made his stomach contract painfully.

"She . . . she's a friend. My girlfriend. She told me one day I was just like a cat. She'd seen me climb a roof. So I expect Caius senses that, he's scared of me, he panics, and he hates me because of it."

"A girlfriend? You got a girlfriend?" asked Basil dreamily.

"Yes."

"You're in luck. Me, I got no one."

"Can we get some sleep, right?" snapped an irritated voice from the back of the dormitory.

They fell silent for several minutes, but there was still something Basil wanted to know. "Hey, Ferenzy, what kind of animal d'you think I was in my—my earlier life?"

"I don't know, Basil."

"I do. I was a draft horse, a big strong horse pulling a cart and doing what its master says. A cart-horse, that's what."

On the next night they had an impassioned discussion with two of the other novices on their chances of survival.

"One in six," said Flavius, a taciturn, short-tempered man who, so rumor said, had murdered his two wives in turn. "Three fights at odds of one in two, that makes it one chance in six."

"Wrong," said Delicatus. No one knew what he had done, but he spoke to everyone with arrogance and contempt. "We have a one-in-two chance three times running—that's nothing like one chance in six. In math they call it calculating the probabilities. But that'd be above your heads."

Milos didn't know what to think, except that each new fight would be like the first, so that the chance of survival was always one-in-two.

Basil put forward another theory, an original and surprising idea. "You ask me, we get a chance of . . . of one in four." And in spite of Delicatus's unkind laughter, he wouldn't budge from his opinion. "If I kill my three men, see, and then there's me in the fights, that makes four of us in all. And if I'm the only one surviving I have a one-in-four chance, right?"

As Delicatus could think of nothing to say, he added, triumphantly, "That shut you up, eh, Delicatus?"

The nights were never quiet. Some of the men had nightmares and woke everyone up yelling with terror; others snored or talked in their sleep; others couldn't sleep and kept getting up to go to the lavatories or walk outside. In the few calm moments you heard the wind blowing through the oak trees in the forest, and the mournful creaking of the timber used to build the arena.

One evening as he went to bed, Milos pushed his own bed a few inches closer to Basil's. Next day he found that Basil had done the same thing. They never mentioned it, but each felt better, hearing the other breathing closer to him than before, and knowing that at any time he could whisper or hear the simple words of comfort that made fear relax its grip slightly: "You all right? Are you asleep? Are you cold? Want my jacket?"

Another frequent subject of discussion at night was what kind of gladiator it was best to face in a fight — a novice, a premier, or a champion. Myricus had told them the results for the last few years, and they went over them again and again. There were six possible scenarios:

Two novices fighting each other. In this case the chances were equal.

Two premiers fighting each other. Here again the chances were equal, and it was the same when two champions fought.

A novice fighting a premier. In sixty-five percent of such fights, the premier won.

A champion would beat a premier in seventy-five percent of fights.

Finally, a novice fighting a champion. Here, surprisingly, the novice won in over half the fights.

So you could work it out that the ideal scenario was to fight a champion first, alarming as the prospect might seem, then a novice in your second fight, and finally, as a champion, a premier in order to gain your liberty.

But there was no real point in this reasoning, since the fight organizers picked pairs to suit themselves, even though it could happen that one of the Phalange leaders expressed a particular wish to see a fighter already known to him face a certain other man. They liked to put two seasoned champions against each other in a fierce, final fight. Or at the other end of the scale, they liked to see two terrified novices fighting, or to relish the pleasure of watching fights of two men or three men against one, which amounted to executions.

A week after Milos left the infirmary, Myricus gave him his sword. The trainer presented it to him with ceremony, like a priest administering the sacraments.

"Here. This weapon is your only friend now. Don't count on anything or anyone else, even me, to help you get out of this alive. Never part with it; always respect it."

Milos was impressed by the weight of the sword and its beauty. The pommel fit into the palm of his hand as if made for it. The double-edged blade bore no sign of earlier fighting. It seemed to be new, and cast golden reflections at the least movement. A coiled snake adorned the hilt.

"Thank you," was all he said, and he slipped the weapon into its sheath.

During training sessions, Myricus referred frequently to the harmony that must exist between a fighting man and his sword. "It must be a part of yourself. You must feel it in your nervous system, in your blood. It must obey your mind as swiftly as your arm and your hand, even react ahead of them. It's the extension of your desire, understand?"

Whatever the exercise—fighting, running, dodging—you kept your sword in your hand. Milos, who was left-handed, found that he liked the warm, reassuring presence of his weapon in the palm of his hand. However, that still left one question. "It's the extension of your desire," said Myricus. Presumably he meant the desire to kill. Milos felt no such thing. The dreadful memory of Pastor's bones cracking as he slowly went limp in his killer's arms haunted him all the time. Did he want to kill anyone? He did not. On the other hand, he felt a great desire to live. It had him shedding hot tears every night; it almost choked him.

His wrestling experience came in extremely useful. Day after day in the mock fights he realized that his reflexes were much better than those of his companions. His eye was far quicker. He could see their mistakes in the way they positioned their bodies and braced themselves. He knew he could leap at the best moment to knock them to the ground. Gradually, as his injury healed, he felt sure he would be able to beat almost all his opponents. All he lacked was the really crucial thing: acceptance of the barbaric idea of attacking an unknown man with the intention of killing him.

But one incident taught him a valuable lesson.

Winter was coming, and Milos had been in the camp for two months when Myricus picked him for the part of victim in the "three against one" exercise. He had to leave his sword on the benches and go down into the arena ahead of the others. He went along the path from which he had watched Basil's fight a few weeks earlier. The wooden gate was closed behind him, and he found himself alone on the sand. His first opponent appeared in the gateway opposite, armed with a sword. It was Flavius, the man with a murderer's dark eyes.

Inflicting serious injury is forbidden, Milos told himself to calm his thudding heart. Flavius took small steps as he approached and then speeded up, brandishing his weapon. Milos began jogging to keep his distance. They skirted the arena three or four times like this. Several times Flavius rushed at Milos, forcing him to throw himself to the ground, but it was more like a dance than a real attack. Flavius had obviously been told to make his adversary run and tire him out without touching him.

By the time the gate in the barricade opened again, Milos was out of breath, but he still had enough strength to avoid his second adversary for some time. However, it was a shock to see that the new man was Caius. His chest was still bandaged after his recent wound. He had hardly reached the sand before he made for Milos with a perfect diagonal approach. The nature of the contest changed abruptly. Myricus had always recommended them not to waste their energy in shouts and useless grunts. "Leave that to your opponents," he used to say. "Keep quiet; concentrate; be pitiless." But Caius couldn't refrain from making muted growling noises. His mouth twisted in fury, he struck low at his adversary twice in quick succession, and Milos realized what Caius's perverse wish was: he wanted to hit the leg that had already been wounded. Milos flung himself backward to avoid the blade, rolled over on the ground, and then, getting up in the same movement, he raised his fingers, spread like claws. Challengingly, he fixed his eyes on Caius and hissed through his teeth like a cat. The other man let out a howl of rage and flung himself into the pursuit of Milos, who was running as fast as he could go.

Up in the gallery they had all risen to their feet except for Myricus, who sat there impassively, determined to let the contest run its course. Milos was going so fast that he hit the barricade and saw Caius about to attack him. He didn't have time to avoid the sword quickly enough. Blood flowed from his forearm. He waited for Myricus to call out, "That's enough!" However, the trainer kept his mouth shut. He felt like calling for help, but that would have been no use. Leaping aside, he avoided a second cut, and fled at frantic speed. *If only I had my sword,* he thought at that moment. *If only I had my sword, I'd kill him. After all, he wants to kill me.*

He reached the other end of the arena, not too bothered by Flavius, who was now reduced to the role of spectator. Then the gate opened for the third time, and Basil came in. He looked savage. He was faster than Caius, and quickly reached Milos, who was backed up against the barricade. He struck fast and precisely, and Milos's hip was covered with blood.

"That's enough!" boomed Myricus's deep voice at last.

"Sorry—I'm sorry," stammered Basil, who was kneeling beside his friend. "I didn't have any choice. That bastard, he'd have finished you off. Took you for a cat, didn't he?"

"Thank you," breathed Milos. "I think you've saved my life."

"Don't mention it. That's OK. Me, I always liked cats."

Fulgur didn't trouble to hide his delight when he saw the injury to Milos's leg. "There's a pretty sight! Who gave you that, Ferenzy?"

"Rusticus."

"The cart-horse, eh? Think yourself lucky. He usually strikes harder. Anyone can see you two are good mates. Come on, then, I'll give you a little encore."

Without more ado, he gave Milos an injection and didn't even wait for it to take effect before setting to work. Milos turned his head aside and gritted his teeth under the piercing pain of the needle. Then, gradually, he felt it die down, until at last he felt only the unpleasant sensation of the thread as it was pulled through the edges of his wound, drawing them together.

"That cart-horse, he ever talk to you about his brothers?"

"What?"

"Rusticus. He ever tell you about 'em?"

"Tell me about what?"

Milos remembered the conversations he'd had with Basil at the school. The other boy had indeed introduced himself as a cart-horse, but without explaining exactly what he meant.

"No, he didn't," he said, careful not to insist on keeping quiet to Fulgur anymore. "He hasn't told me anything."

"Pity. You'd have enjoyed it, especially the last bit. Because it all turned out badly for them. Very badly. I could have been a cart-horse myself, you know. I had all the qualifications: I'm hefty and I didn't exactly invent hot and cold running water. Problem is, I like to be on the winning side. Yup, that's my problem."

Fulgur finished his stitching. Hearing the little sound as the thread broke, Milos knew that the brute had just bitten off the remains of it with his teeth, as you might bite the thread after sewing on a button. He preferred not to look. Fulgur completed his care of his patient by painting the place with iodine.

"There, you can go back to your room. Getting into the habit of this, aren't you? Soon there won't be space on you for any more stitching! And don't forget: next chance you get, ask your friend Rusticus to tell you all about his mates—if you want a good laugh. Ask him how Faber is, for instance. Oh yes, that's a very funny story."

Milos didn't have to wait long for his next chance to talk to Basil. Late in the afternoon, Milos was dozing in the infirmary sickroom when the door opened. His friend's large head appeared around it.

"You asleep?"

"No, come in."

Basil sat down on the edge of the bed and raised the sheet. "Dammit, I didn't miss you."

"That's OK. It's not deep," Milos reassured him.

"Sorry, but I didn't know where to strike. Finding the right place isn't easy. I mean, finding somewhere to bleed a lot that's not too dangerous. I thought of a buttock, but you didn't turn your back, and then sitting down's tricky later."

"Really, don't worry. You aimed very well."

"Caius is furious with me. Told me if I ever found myself facing him, he'd make a hole in my hide. But he doesn't scare me, just because he's won twice . . . Hey, look! A jay!"

The big, colorful bird had settled on the window-sill without a sound. It just fit between the bars and looked almost as if it wanted to come in.

"We know each other already," said Milos, smiling. "He comes visiting the sick."

The two of them fell silent and watched the jay. They were both thinking the same thing: you're free, bird. You can come and go; you can fly away over the wire fence and perch on the forest trees when you like. Do you know how lucky you are?

As if guessing, the jay turned weightily on the sill, took off, and flew away.

"Who's Faber?" asked Milos into the silence that followed.

Basil's mouth dropped open. "You know Faber?"

"No, but Fulgur mentioned his name just now. Who is he?"

Basil bent his head. He was frowning. "Faber is the leader of the horse-men," he muttered at last. "Our leader, see?"

"And . . . and something bad happened to him?"

"Yes."

"Did they kill him?"

"Worse than that."

Milos dared not say any more. Basil sniffed noisily and then wiped his nose and eyes angrily on the back of his cuff.

"They did worse than kill him, Ferenzy. They made fun of him. I'll tell you, but some other time. I kind of don't feel like it here."

IN THE CITY

If she hadn't been missing Milos and feeling constantly anxious, Helen's time in the capital city might have felt like the best days of her life. She had never known such a delicious sense of freedom before. Having a place of her own, her name on a door that she could lock and unlock with her own key, going out when she liked, getting on the first tram to come along and losing herself in unknown streets: she relished these small pleasures day after day. They never faded. Mr. Jahn had given her half her first month's pay in advance so that she could get herself what she needed. She bought an alarm clock, a brightly colored hat, a pair of woolen gloves, a scarf, and a pair of boots. The coat that Dr. Josef's wife had given her, although a little old-fashioned, was warm and comfortable and she decided to keep it. She also unearthed a dozen novels going cheap in an old bookshop near the restaurant, and lined them up on the shelf in her room. "My library," she told Milena proudly.

She came back quite dazed from her solitary walks in the city. She loved mingling with the anonymous crowd swarming over the sidewalks at rush hour. *If you could see all these people, Milos! Racing about, bumping into you without even noticing you're there. You feel like an ant among millions of other ants. If you were with me, we'd have to hold hands to not get separated. I go into shops, boutiques, hardware stores, choosing what I'll buy when I have more money. If only you were here too, my love. . . .*

But what she liked even more was walking at random, going farther and farther afield, delighted to discover a new bridge, a pretty square, a little church. She walked fast, wrapped in her warm coat, until her legs began to tire. Then she would catch a tram or a bus going back toward the city center.

Dora was right: people here weren't very good-tempered. Or rather, it was as if they didn't trust one another. You heard little laughter and few cheerful conversations. The fact was that the people of the capital seemed depressed. Sometimes Helen met a glance from a pair of friendly eyes, but they turned away at once. She soon learned to spot the Phalangist security police and the agents on night duty: men with wary faces, often hidden behind newspapers like something in a bad thriller, but you could easily guess that their ears were working harder than their eyes.

When she got off the tram one afternoon, she

found that someone had slipped an invitation to a meeting into her coat pocket, and she thought the wording suggested that it was for people opposed to the Phalange. She thought of the young man who had been sitting beside her; it must have been him who'd given it to her. He had looked attractive and rather nice. "A trap!" cried Dora. "Whatever you do, don't go!" And she advised Helen never to talk freely to strangers, however friendly they seemed. "New friends, whoever they are, must be introduced to you by someone safe, or it's better not to trust them."

A few days later, as she was going back to the restaurant on foot, she heard shouts: "Out of the way! Militia!" She had no time to move aside and was knocked down by three men armed with clubs who were chasing a tall, lanky man. They caught up with him and beat him. He fell to the ground, curling up his long, thin limbs to protect himself, but they kept hitting him on the head and the back.

"Stop!" cried Helen, paralyzed by horror as the unfortunate man huddled there while the brutes went on attacking him. "Stop it! You'll kill him!"

She realized that everyone around her was running away except for a young man, who had turned his collar well up to hide his face.

"Bastards! You'll pay for this!" he shouted in his own turn, and then he too ran for it. He was obviously counting on his burst of speed to escape the militiamen, and he was right. One of them chased him a hundred yards and then gave up.

"I've seen your face!" the young man taunted the militiaman, turning around one last time. "I've seen all your faces, and believe me, I'll know you again!"

The militiaman hurled insults at him and went back to his companions. Helen hadn't moved from the spot.

"Got a problem, miss?" he spat as he passed her. "No? Then you better get out of here."

No doubt it was because of this incident that she didn't feel like walking alone next day and asked Milena to go with her. "You could live without Bart just for an afternoon!"

"It's not Bart I spend the afternoons with."

"Oh? Who is it, then?"

Milena hesitated. "Well, if you promise you won't breathe a word to anyone . . ."

"I promise."

"Come on, then. After all, it would be a good thing for you to know."

They set off along the uphill roads leading to the Old Town. Black ice made the sidewalks shine, and they held on to each other to avoid slipping. Milena was laughing to herself, impatient now to share her secret. Helen had never seen her looking so happy and radiant before. It made her a little more aware of her own loneliness and distress. A lump came into her throat. Milena noticed her friend stiffening slightly and understood at once. She stopped and put her arms around Helen. "Forgive me."

"There's nothing to forgive. You have a right to be happy! I'm not jealous."

A sad look came into Milena's eyes. "Don't think I'm happy, Helen. I can never be really happy again now I know what they did to my mother. I could easily be inconsolable, but that doesn't stop me from feeling content sometimes. So there it is; I'm content today. Content to have Bart, content to be with you, content to go where I'm going at this moment."

When Helen only nodded, Milena stood back from her and took her hands. "Helen?"

"Yes."

"Milos is definitely alive. I can't keep it from you any longer."

Helen trembled. "How do you know?"

"From Bart and Mr. Jahn. They're sure of it."

"How do they know?"

"They'll explain. And what's more, Bart says that if Milos is alive and has one chance in fifty of getting out of trouble, he will. He knows Milos very well. So don't despair."

"I only had to get there with Dr. Josef an hour earlier!" said Helen angrily, shaking her head. "Just an hour earlier and I'd have saved him! I suspect I'm going to be inconsolable too."

"You did the impossible. Come on, we'll be late."

They set off again. A little farther up the road, when they met two women coming the other way, Milena took care to draw the hood of her coat well over her face. "Or they may go thinking I'm a ghost again!"

"So they may. Are you really so like your mother? Do you have any photos of her?"

"Yes."

"And are you?"

"Well, yes, the photos show me with clothes and a hairstyle twenty-five years out of date! Dora even gave me one with myself as a baby in her arms. I'll show it to you. And as you'll see, she was very beautiful."

The apartment building with its peeling facade stood on the corner of two streets in the most out-of-the-way part of the Old Town. It had an old-fashioned entrance hall. The girls went in and climbed a narrow staircase smelling of beeswax.

"Where are you taking me?" asked Helen as they reached the fifth and last story.

Without replying, Milena knocked on a door that had no name on it, and a smiling Dora let them in. "My goodness, have you brought us an audience?"

"Isn't that all right?"

"Of course it is. Good idea! Come in, Helen, you're very welcome. Put your coats over there on the bed."

It was like being in a doll's house without the doll. The space was tiny, the furniture plain, and the walls were bare except for a musical score pinned over the wallpaper in the living room.

"It's a Schubert manuscript," said Dora, following Helen's eyes.

"A reproduction?"

"No, an original, in his own hand. You can look at it."

Helen went closer and stared at the modest sheet of paper, slightly yellowed now, with notes written on the music as if in haste in the composer's beautiful hand.

"The ink . . . it looks as if it's only just dried. I can't believe it! It must be a rare document, surely."

"Very rare," Dora said, laughing.

"But you . . . I mean, it's valuable. . . ."

"If I sold that score, I could buy the whole building. And the one next door."

"And . . . and you don't sell it?"

"No. I'm stupid, aren't I? What do you think?"

"I don't know," said Helen, impressed.

"It's always been there. And the piano too. A Steinway! You wonder how it ever got up here. The stairs are too narrow, and so are the windows. It's a mystery. I like that; I like to imagine that they took the roof off to bring it in."

"Have you always lived here, Dora?"

"Oh, no. This is where my piano teacher used to live. She was a brilliant, crazy, impossible old woman who made herself infusions of cloves to inhale and used to throw her shoes at my back when I played wrong notes. When she died, I bought her apartment. That was when I was making money from playing the piano. I thought that was only natural. I didn't realize it was paradise. You discover what paradise means when you lose it, and what your nest means when you fall out of it. Come on, I'll make tea and then we'll get down to work."

Helen took her shoes off, sat down in an armchair, folded her knees up against her chest, and waited, motionless. Dora sat down on the piano stool, pushed up her sleeves, and shook her dark curls. Milena remained standing, one hand on the side of the keyboard, concentrating as if about to give a recital. Her ruffled blond hair contrasted with the angelic beauty of her face and enhanced it.

"Let's start, Milena. We'll go back to D. 547."

"Right, I'm ready."

Dora delicately played the first chords, and when Milena opened her mouth, the nature of the air and everything else around her seemed to change, as always when she sang. Helen was shivering.

"Du holde Kunst, in wieviel grauen Stunden,
Wo mich des Lebens wilder Kreis umstrickt,
Hast du mein Herz . . ."

"You're getting ahead of yourself," Dora interrupted her. "You're too far ahead on *'Hast du.'* Go back to the beginning, please."

As far as Helen could tell, Milena was neither ahead of the piano nor behind it, but perfect. All the same, Milena obediently went back to the beginning. Once she was past that passage, Dora nodded her approval. "Good, that's it." She smiled.

She knew she wouldn't have to repeat herself ten times with Milena. Helen felt that special pride you get when a brother or sister whose gifts you have known for a long time finally reveals them to the world. She remembered the school yard where Milena used to sing for her. It seemed so far away now. And she remembered Paula, her large consoler, asking with amusement, "How's your friend Milena? Do you admire her as much as ever?" At that moment she admired Milena more than ever.

Helen was equally fascinated to see Dora's mutilated right hand running lightly over the ivory keys. Sometimes she had to rest it for a moment and massage her aching wrist.

"I have difficulty spreading my fingers beyond a fifth these days and it's no use even trying thumb passages!"

She might as well be talking Hebrew, thought Helen. "I'd never have noticed anything," she said, intending to comfort Dora. "I think you play incredibly well."

"That just shows you don't know anything about it!" cried Dora, bursting into laughter and holding up her damaged hand. "Myself, I feel as if I'm playing with my foot!"

Helen thought her laughter was just a little too cheerful. "Are there any records of Eva-Maria Bach?" she asked suddenly.

"Yes. I have one here, but Milena doesn't want to listen to it."

"Dora's right," Milena agreed. "The idea scares

270

me. But with Helen here today I think I could summon up the courage."

"Really?"

"Yes, really."

Dora disappeared into the bedroom and came back with a black vinyl record in its sleeve. She held it out to Milena.

"There, this is all I have, and the few photos I've shown you. My treasures. I'd hidden them in a suitcase and given it to a friend for safekeeping before I left the capital. I was right to take precautions, too. They ransacked the apartment and took everything away. Everything. Except the piano, because it was too big. And guess what else those idiots left, Helen?"

"The Schubert manuscript?"

"Exactly! It was just where you see it today, pinned to the wall in full view. It's the one thing they'd have been bound to take if they hadn't been such ignoramuses! I think I'll be laughing over that for the rest of my life!"

Milena turned the record sleeve over in her fingers. It had a simple design of a bunch of pale mauve flowers on it. She read out loud, in a low voice, "High-quality recording . . . symphony orchestra . . . contralto: Miss Eva-Maria Bach . . . They called her 'miss'?"

"Yes, she wasn't twenty-five yet, remember. And unmarried."

"But she already had me, didn't she?"

"Yes. I think you were two at the time. You had chubby cheeks, and you—"

"I don't know if I will have the courage, after all. I'm all right with the photos, not so sure about the voice."

It was Helen who took the record and put it on the gramophone. Dora had lifted the heavy varnished wood lid. The "high-quality recording" crackled badly. Dora turned the volume down very low. "My neighbors are safe," she said, "but you never know; they might have visitors."

The extract began with several bars played on the violin, and waiting was almost unbearable for the two girls. It was as if Eva-Maria Bach might suddenly open the door and walk in. At last the voice rose, distant and peaceful:

"What is life to me without thee?
What is left if you are dead?"

Overwhelmed, Milena hid her face in her hands and kept them there until the end of the aria. Helen listened, entranced by the fullness and balance of the low contralto voice. She realized how young her friend still was by comparison. Dora was smiling, her eyes bright with emotion.

"What is life, life without thee?
What is life without my love?"

"That's enough for today," murmured Milena, as the aria reached its last note. "I'll listen to the rest of the record another time."

All three wiped away tears, laughing as they brought out their tissues at exactly the same time.

"Well, what do you think?" asked Dora when she had put the record back in its sleeve.

"I think I still have a lot of work to do."

"You're right. So let's get on with it!"

"Let's do that."

When Helen and Milena left the Old Town, the streetlights had already come on. They took the shortest way they could along little, sloping streets and down flights of stone steps. When they reached the square where Jahn's Restaurant stood, they met Bartolomeo, returning at just the same moment with a huge black scarf wound around his neck.

"Bart," called Milena, "Helen would like you to tell her what you know about Milos."

"Come on, then, Helen," he said. "Let's walk on a little way, just the two of us, and I'll explain."

They left Milena behind, went toward the river, and walked along the bank. Without knowing it, they stopped at the same bench where Two-and-a-Half had been sitting before Mitten hit him on the head with his exhaust pipe. The quiet murmur of the ripples accompanied their voices.

"I'm sorry I didn't tell you sooner," Bart began. "I just couldn't make up my mind."

"Is it that tricky?"

"Yes. Yes, it is. Well, first you have to know that Mr. Jahn has always been sure that Milos is alive."

"How could he be sure?"

"He knows the Phalangists and the way their minds work. If they took Milos away on their sleigh in such a hurry, that means he wasn't dead or they'd have dug a hole quite close and thrown him into it. They're not the sort to bother about an enemy's corpse."

Helen had always thought the same, deep in her heart. And above all, over and beyond all reason, she had an utter conviction that her lover was alive. It had taken firm hold of her mind. She felt it in every fiber of her being. If not, how could she talk to him silently as often as she did, by night, by day, telling him her secrets, telling him about her difficulties and her moments of happiness?

"Since then," Bart went on, "Mr. Jahn's had confirmation through the network. Milos is alive. Only what comes next is rather more worrying. That's why I couldn't bring myself to tell you."

"I'm listening," said Helen, but a shudder ran through her.

"Well, if they spared his life," Bart went on, "it was with one idea in mind."

"What idea?"

"Look, I'll repeat what Mr. Jahn said, shall I? That'll be easier. The Phalange despises weaklings and losers. They eliminate them without any scruples, just like putting down the sick animals in a litter. But they respect the strong. As they see it, Milos is strong, and he proved it by killing Pastor. What's more, they found out that he was a wrestler. So they had him looked after, and now they're going to use him in their fights."

"Fights?" asked Helen, feeling as if the blood were draining out of her.

How could Bart explain gently about the barbarity of the arena and the savage shows it mounted? He did his best, but in spite of all his efforts he could only tell her unbearable things. No, no one can avoid fighting. Yes, one of the two must die. No, no mercy is ever shown.

"The winter fights begin next month," he finished, determined to tell the truth to the end. "And Milos will be . . ."

For a moment he hoped Helen would slap his face to punish him for the horrors he was revealing. He'd have welcomed it; he hated himself so much for having to tell her.

"What can we do?" she asked at last, in a faint voice.

"I don't know," Bart replied. "Of course we've thought of getting him out of there, but even approaching the place is impossible. The army guards the camps."

"Then there's nothing to be done?" Helen was crying now.

"Yes, there is. Mr. Jahn says we mustn't give up hope. He says things are moving."

"Things are moving?"

"Yes. The network's been in turmoil for some

months now. I'm supposed to keep it a secret. I shouldn't tell you, but the hell with that."

"What do you mean? Is there going to be an uprising? When? Before the winter fights? Tell me, Bart! Tell me!"

"I know almost nothing, Helen. They give me a few scraps of information because my name is Casal and I'm my father's son, but I'm only seventeen, not sixty, like Jahn! If I learn anything at all, I'll tell you. Promise!"

"Promise!" He had fired the word at her, like Milos had, without meaning to. Helen leaned her forehead into the hollow of his shoulder. He was so tall. He gently stroked her head.

"We mustn't give up hope, Helen. I'm told that when things were going very badly, my father used to comfort everyone by saying, 'Never fear: the river's on our side.'"

They turned and looked at the dark, quiet waters, the sparkling eddies glinting here and there. Far away, on Royal Bridge, cars glided through the silence as night fell.

THE HORSE-MEN

When he heard three quiet knocks at his door, Bartolomeo thought at first that it was Milena. They often met at night; that was no secret. He put out his arm for his watch and was surprised to see that it was five in the morning. What brought her to his room at this early hour? Usually it was more like the time when she went back to her own! He got up, yawning, and opened the door. Mr. Jahn, hands in the pockets of his heavy overcoat and a fur cap on his head, saw his surprise and smiled.

"Get some warm clothes on and come with me. Don't switch the corridor light on. I'll be waiting for you downstairs."

Bart didn't even think of asking questions. He nodded and closed the door again. Then he put on his coat and boots and flung his long scarf around his shoulders.

Jahn was waiting in the dim light at the back of the restaurant. "Come on, we'll go out through the kitchens."

They took the service stairs down to avoid waking everyone in the place by using the elevator, and once in the basement went along a corridor that Bart had never found before. They left through an emergency exit that opened into an alleyway behind the building and walked a hundred or so yards through the night. Then Jahn stopped outside the double door of a garage. He unlocked it with a large key.

"Where are we going?" asked Bart, seeing the car inside.

"For a little drive. I'll bet you don't even know the place. Give me a hand, will you?"

The two of them pushed the heavy four-door car out of the garage and then all along the road. At the corner they jumped in and coasted down the slope to the avenue that ran beside the river. Only then did Jahn turn the ignition key to start the engine. They drove for about a mile before turning off to cross Royal Bridge. The yellow light of the street lamps cast living shadows on the ten bronze horsemen, and the last, a gigantic statue, seemed threatening, about to bring his raised sword down on them. As they passed through the sleeping suburbs, Bartolomeo's fingers caressed the supple leather of the seats and the chrome dashboard.

"First time you've been in a Panhard?" asked Jahn.

"First time I've been in a car at all," replied Bart.

Jahn glanced at him in astonishment.

"I arrived at the boarding school in a bus when I was fourteen, and I got on another bus when I was seventeen, running away with Milena in the middle of the night," he explained. "But that's all. Well, maybe I was driven around in a car when I was really small, but if so, I don't remember."

"You're right. Forgive me," Jahn apologized.

Day was just beginning to dawn when they reached the country. Mist hung low over the fields. Soon the horizon ahead of them grew wider. Jahn looked in his rearview mirror several times and steadily slowed down. Bart turned to look behind them. In the distance, a black car was slowing down too. He thought there were two men in it.

"They're following us," said Jahn. He sighed.

"Phalangists?"

"Yes."

"Do they often follow you?"

"They try to. But I can spot them. So I lead them sixty miles over the muddiest roads I can find, I buy a chicken from a farmer, and then I drive back. It infuriates them. I love that."

Bart didn't expect such practical jokes from the large man he thought of as placid and reserved. "So we're on our way to buy a chicken from a farmer?"

"No, I didn't wake you at five in the morning for that. I'm going to try shaking them off."

They went on driving slowly for half an hour or more. The black car adjusted its speed to theirs and stayed behind them. Just after a bend in the road, they found themselves at a junction. Here Jahn suddenly accelerated, went straight ahead, and was out of sight before his pursuers had time to come around the bend themselves.

"With a bit of luck, they'll think I turned off there."

The maneuver succeeded perfectly. They had lost the black car.

"We're going to see the horse-men," Jahn said, a little more relaxed now. "Also known as the cart-horses. Have you heard the term before?"

In his mind's eye Bartolomeo saw the large form of Basil with his unmanageable tufts of hair and his long, rough-hewn face. What had happened to him? Surely he hadn't been left to die in that cell. . . .

"I know one. He brought me my father's letter. But he never explained exactly what the . . . the cart-horses are . . . I mean the horse-men."

"I'll tell you," said Jahn, sighing. "We have plenty of time. There's a good hour's drive still ahead of us."

He lit a cigar and lowered his window to let the smoke out. Bart decided that the smell wasn't really so unpleasant. He felt well, wrapped in his warm coat, watching the winter landscape pass outside the car windows.

"No one knows exactly where they come from," Jahn began. "They're rather like a large family who have always been around. I suppose there are about a hundred thousand in the country in all. All of them are brave, tough, and strong as oxen. But they are unable to learn to read and write. They marry among themselves so regularly that these characteristics go on from one generation to the next. They used to be employed in work needing strength and stamina, particularly carrying loads along narrow streets where horse-drawn carts couldn't go. Hence their nickname of cart-horses. But you mustn't think they were despised. Far from it: they were admired for their strength and steadfastness. A good many people even saw a certain nobility in their rustic manners, if you can understand that."

"I certainly can. It's what I felt about Basil. He might seem stubborn, but he had such a generous spirit. I got the impression that he'd have died to deliver that letter to me."

"Not just an impression. I can assure you he'd have done exactly that. When you entrust a mission to a cart-horse, he's ready to die to carry it out. That's why the Phalangists wanted the horse-men on their side when they seized power. What a godsend that would have been: a hundred thousand of them, immensely strong and ready to demolish anything once they were given orders to do it. But there was one thing the Phalangists had forgotten."

"What?"

"They'd forgotten that while the horse-men need a master, they like to choose that master for themselves. And simple and uncomplicated as they may be, they don't pick just anyone."

"They refused to serve the Phalange?"

"Every last one of them! People think they are uncouth, but they know the difference between good and bad. Your father was sent to make contact with them. I thought he was the wrong choice, too reserved and short-tempered, while they think in simple terms and are very emotional. But surprisingly, they adored him and he instantly and entirely trusted them. In short, they allied themselves with the Resistance. It cost them severely. It's all very well to be physically strong, but that's not much use when you're facing armed men. Many of them were killed. Others were arrested and treated like animals in prison. When it was all over, the Phalangist police did a deal with their leader, who was called Faber.

"They'd never been able to capture him. They would release all the horse-men who had been taken prisoner, they said, in return for his own public surrender. Faber had been chosen by the horse-men as their leader not because he was the most intelligent or the wisest of them, simply because he was the strongest. The Phalangists never imagined that the unfortunate Faber would fall into their trap so easily, and next day the guards were surprised to see a giant of a man with almost no neck and large, gentle eyes — eyes like a horse's — turn up at the gate saying, 'Good morning, I'm Faber. I've come to surrender.'

"The poor fellow thought he'd done the right thing. He never suspected they were going to humiliate him. They harnessed him to a cart with ten or so Phalangist leaders in it, and he was made to pull them through the city streets by himself, bare to the waist, amid laughter and mockery."

"But I thought you said people respected the horse-men."

"Most do, yes. But they realized that there were a great many others around who backed the Phalange. These Phalangist supporters had kept well hidden up to this point, but now the fight was won, they emerged from the shadows. They let fly at Faber with all the cruelty of cowards who have nothing to fear anymore. Someone even put a cap with horse's ears on his head as the cart went up the street to Phalange headquarters. They spat at him and shouted abuse. He was treated as a cart-horse, and the name stuck."

"He took it all without protest?"

"Everything. He'd decided to sacrifice himself, and he went all the way. Any horse-man would have done the same. He braced himself to climb the hill. He took the handfuls of oats and buckets of water they flung at him without flinching. He was a proud man, and it was hard for him."

"But you . . . were you there? Did you watch this show?" asked Bart, aware of the condemnation in his question.

Jahn registered it too. "I saw the parade pass from my window, like thousands of others, and I was ashamed of doing nothing. But you have to remember that we had fought back fiercely until then, losing almost all who were dear to us: Eva-Maria Bach, your father, hundreds of other comrades. It was over. They could do anything they liked now, and they indulged themselves to the full."

"But did they keep their word? Did they release the horse-men?"

"Months later. Once they were sure there was no one left for their prisoners to follow."

"They must have borne my father a grudge, surely? After all, he'd dragged them into disaster."

"That's not the way they reason. They still think they did the right thing. And your father had given his own life for the cause. You don't bear a martyr a grudge."

"What about Faber? Did they let him go?"

"Yes, but the humiliation left its mark on him. He hardly speaks anymore, I'm told. He's withdrawn to a remote village with his family, or those of it who are left."

"And that's where we're going?" asked Bart in a low voice.

"That's where we're going," Jahn confirmed.

They didn't talk as they drove the next few miles. The landscape had changed; the car was now winding its way through wooded hills with their tops veiled in mist. Farther on, they drove past gray rocks thickly covered with lichen, looking like the backs of some strange species of animals. Bart opened his window and breathed in the moist moorland air.

He felt as if they were leaving the human world behind and entering a land of legend. He would hardly have been surprised to see an elf or a goblin appear around a bend somewhere ahead.

"The horse-men thought very highly of your father," Jahn said, breaking the silence. "They'll feel the same about you. That's why I'm taking you to see them."

The question that had been troubling Bart for some time was on the tip of his tongue. "What exactly do you expect me to do?" But he refrained from asking it. When they finally drove into the horse-men's village, he was almost dropping off to sleep, lulled by the regular purr of the engine.

A boy of about fifteen came to meet them.

"Basil!" Bart cried in spite of himself.

The boy bore a striking resemblance to his friend at the school: the same long face, the same flattened nose, the same powerful shoulders, the same unruly hair.

Jahn stopped level with the lad. "Do you know where Faber lives, please?"

"No," said the boy, frowning. "What d'you want with Faber?"

"Only to talk to him. Don't be alarmed—we're friends."

"I'm not allowed to . . ." the young horse-man let slip, without realizing that he was giving himself away.

"Is it farther on?" asked Jahn.

"That's right."

They drove slowly on and met two children coming downhill at a run, one carrying the other on his back.

"This is amazing!" exclaimed Bart. "They're all like miniature versions of Basil!"

Higher up in the village, a girl with the same long, rough-hewn face was climbing the hill slowly, carrying a bucket of water.

"Is Faber's house over there?" asked Jahn, his elbow on the open window of the car.

"Yes . . . er, no," said the girl, confused. "Who are you?"

"Friends. That's his house, is it?"

"That's right."

It certainly wasn't difficult to worm information out of these people.

Jahn stopped the car a little farther up the hill, and they came down again on foot to knock at the door. It was opened by a very tall, strong woman of about fifty with a look of sadness about her. She let them in. The curtains were drawn, and it was some time before their eyes adjusted to the dim light in the room. A large ginger cat was asleep on a chair near the fireplace. The woman wore an apron and a head scarf with locks of white hair escaping from it. Faber was in bed, she told them. "But if you're friends . . ."

She climbed the stairs with a heavy tread. No more was heard for some time. She must have been talking to her husband in low tones. Then she reappeared at the top of the stairs, leaned forward, and called down, "What was your name, please?"

"I'm called Jahn. He knows me."

She disappeared again, and the silent waiting resumed. The two men downstairs looked at each other, baffled. What could the couple be talking about up there? At last the woman slowly came down again and planted herself in front of Jahn, arms spread helplessly to show there was nothing she could do. "He doesn't want to see you. Hasn't wanted to see anyone for months. He's not well."

"Tell him this is important," Jahn persisted. "Tell him I've come with . . . with Casal."

She went off for the third time.

"But," murmured Bart, "he'll think it's—"

"Your father back again? I don't know. I just need him to get up."

As she came downstairs this time, the woman was nodding. Apparently there was news.

"He's coming," she announced, and something that was almost a smile spread over her kindly face. "Sit down while you wait."

They sat down on the benches set on each side of the table. She remained standing, automatically wiping her hands on her apron. She was a heavy woman, but the floor on the story above hadn't creaked while she was up there. Now, however, it was groaning under the weight of the man walking about as he dressed. It sounded as if it might collapse.

"He's coming down," the woman repeated.

There was the dull thud of a shoe that had gotten away, then footsteps, then two gigantic feet were placed on the top steps. Two endlessly long legs followed, and when Faber appeared on the staircase in his entirety, the sight took Bartolomeo's breath away. He had never seen such a huge human being. The man's torso in particular was twice as broad as the chest of a normal man. His shoulders, arms, and hands all appeared double the usual size. Above this enormous mass his long face suggested the head of a sad, old horse, with drooping cheeks and a soft mouth.

He didn't spare a moment's glance for Jahn but walked slowly over to Bartolomeo and stopped in front of him.

"You're Casal?"

"His son," said Bart, feeling uneasy. He had to put his head back slightly to look Faber in the eyes, not something he usually needed to do.

"You're his son?" asked Faber, and emotion made his chin wobble.

"Yes," Bart confirmed.

The giant took one more step, opened his great arms, and flung them around the young man. He clasped Bartolomeo to his chest and didn't let him go for several minutes. Bartolomeo felt as if he had been swallowed up. Held so close to this peaceful colossus, he felt that nothing bad could happen. When Faber loosened his embrace, his eyes were moist with tears. Only then did he turn to Jahn and offer his hand.

"Good morning, Mr. Jahn. Pleased to see you again."

A few moments later, they were sitting at the table with a jug of wine. Faber's wife brought him a bowl of milk, and throughout the conversation he dunked pieces of bread in it and fished them out again with a soupspoon. In his hand it looked as if it belonged to a doll's tea set.

Jahn began, cautiously, "Listen, Faber. You must be aware that a long time has passed since they did you such harm."

No reply.

"And you must also be aware that things changed some while ago."

"They did? I don't know. I don't go out. What's changed?"

"People are sick and tired of the Phalange, understand? If there's a revolt, they'll be with us."

"Why would they be with us? They did nothing when I was pulling that cart and folks threw filth at me."

"They were afraid," Bartolomeo put in. "Afraid of being arrested, beaten up, killed."

"You're right there," Faber agreed.

"And then," Bart went on, "then they thought perhaps the Phalange wasn't such a bad thing after all. It would put the country in order. They'd wait and see. So now they do see—"

"And they see it wasn't a good thing," Faber finished the sentence. He needed to have everything put into plain words.

"Exactly. They see it wasn't a good thing, and they'll support us. Are the horse-men ready to fight on our side?"

Faber put his spoon down on the table and wiped his mouth on his sleeve, looking awkward. "Us horse-men, we don't like killing."

"No one likes killing," said Bart. "But we have to defend ourselves. You saw what they did to you—to you personally and your people. You can't have forgotten!"

Faber looked at him with his large, moist eyes. "I know that, but we're used to putting up with things, we are. We're strong but we don't like fighting."

"Those of your age, perhaps, but that's changed too. I made a friend at the boarding school, a horse-man like you, and I can tell you it wasn't a good idea to cross him. The horse-men have learned not to let themselves be humiliated, I assure you. We're going to need your strength, Mr. Faber, the strength of all the horse-men. Without you we'll be defeated for the second time."

"I don't know what to say," Faber mumbled unhappily. "Who'll command us?"

Jahn, who had said nothing for some while now, looked at Bartolomeo and gave him an encouraging nod.

"I will command you," said the young man firmly. "You can count on me."

As he spoke those words, he felt that his father was there beside him, almost as if he were physically present at the table with them. He felt convinced that his father heard him and approved of what he said. His throat tightened.

"I will command you, with Mr. Jahn. I'll be back here with you when the moment comes. Until it does, build up your health again and talk to your people. You know how pleased they'll be to see you up and about. They must all be ready on the day, and it's up to you as their leader to convince them and gather them together. Prepare them to fight, Mr. Faber!"

At seventeen Bartolomeo didn't have the necessary experience to lead the horse-men himself, and he knew it. But that was not what Jahn expected of him. He had brought him here because his name was Casal, because he knew how to handle words and find arguments to persuade the huge horseman to emerge from his state of depression. And Bart had indeed found them.

"You'll have something to eat, won't you?" the large woman asked them.

"A good idea, Roberta," Faber agreed. "You must be hungry, coming all that way. You came from the capital?"

They had no time to reply, for a child of about eight rushed in, clung to the woman's apron, and whispered something to her. His nose was running.

"There's another black car driving into the village," Roberta told the three men.

"Who's in the car, my boy?" Jahn asked.

"Two thin gentlemen, sir," said the child, proud to be asked in person.

Jahn was on the alert. "Did they ask you any questions?"

"Yes, they asked if I'd seen you."

"And what did you tell them?"

"I told them I wasn't allowed to say. Then they said they'd give me money to tell them."

"And did you tell them?"

"No. I said your black car had gone on!"

Jahn swore. "The Phalange. I thought I'd shaken them off. Those idiots drove on at random and now they're here. We'll have to hide."

"Go up to the bedroom," the woman suggested. "I'll tell them there's no one here."

Jahn, Bart, and Faber quickly climbed the stairs, while the horse-child, beaming, opened his hand. "Look, Roberta, see how nice they were! I didn't tell them anything and they gave me the money all the same!"

The room upstairs was half filled by the large unmade bed where Faber had been lying only an hour ago. The other furnishings consisted of a wardrobe with one door missing and a rush-seated chair where, no doubt, Roberta sat to watch over her husband during the day.

Jahn went to the window and cautiously moved the curtain aside. The car drove slowly past without stopping. A minute later it came back downhill at the same slow pace.

"They've found my car. Now they're searching," said Jahn, "asking the way to Faber's house, and they'll find it too. We should have hidden somewhere else."

But it was too late now. They heard the sound of car doors slamming and knocking at the door. The three men sat on the bed so as not to make the floor creak by standing on it. Jahn shook his head, furious with himself for putting Faber in this situation and dragging Bart into it too. Automatically, Faber had put his pillow on his knees and was kneading it. He looked uneasy. Bart made himself calm his breathing. From below, they heard Roberta's anxious voice as she opened the door.

"Good day, gentlemen."

"Where's Faber?" barked one of the two men, without bothering to give a civil greeting.

"Not here," moaned the poor woman, terrified. "Gone out."

Then she uttered a cry. Faber clenched his fists at the sound. He hated the idea of anyone hurting his Roberta.

"He's upstairs! Go and get him!" bawled the man.

"Upstairs? Oh, not there, not at all!" cried Roberta, in a voice so obviously intended to mislead that in other circumstances it would have been funny. The horse-women were no better at lying than their children.

"Go and get him, I said!"

"He's not well," said the poor woman, contradicting herself. She didn't know what to do now to protect her husband, and her helplessness made her cry. She was sobbing as she climbed the stairs.

"They want you to go down," she murmured, kneeling in front of Faber and clasping his hands between hers.

"Are they armed?"

The large woman nodded. Yes, they were armed. Jahn was distraught. To be found with Faber and Casal's son was a terrible mistake. The Phalange would inevitably draw their own conclusions about the revival of the network. All three would be arrested anyway, and the Phalange would definitely have ways of making them talk.

It was now that Faber's huge form leaned toward his wife. "Where are they?" he whispered.

At first Roberta didn't understand what her husband meant. She looked at him with a question in her eyes.

"Are they there?" Faber asked. "There? There?" He pointed to what would be different places on the ground floor below.

"There," said Roberta. "Near the table. Both of them. If they haven't moved."

Faber rose slowly and did something unexpected: he climbed on the bed and stood there upright. His head touched the ceiling, and he had to bend slightly.

"There?" he asked once more, pointing his forefinger.

"Yes," said Roberta, and she suddenly understood what he was planning.

"You coming down?" shouted the man who had done all the talking downstairs, and he hit the living room ceiling twice, hard, probably with a broom handle. He had no idea that he was pinpointing his exact position and inviting his own ruin.

"I'm coming down!" replied Faber, and he jumped off the bed, raising his feet as high as possible so as to fall back on it with his full weight, landing on his posterior. The beam of the ceiling below him was too thin to stand up to the impact. It broke, and the bedroom floor exploded with a crash, opening up a gaping hole through which Faber disappeared. Jahn, Roberta, and Bart felt the floor beneath their feet give way, and they clung to the walls to keep from being carried down in the giant's wake. The bed itself hesitated for a moment, leaning at a crazy angle toward the hole, and then it fell through the gap to land on the floor below. The faint groaning still to be heard down there soon stopped entirely, and there was only silence.

"Faber!" cried Roberta, and she ran downstairs with Jahn and Bart after her. When they reached the ground floor, Faber was already standing up and rubbing his forehead, which had a red bump on it.

"I flattened them, but the bed hit my head. Are you all right, Roberta? They didn't hurt you?"

The couple embraced clumsily, and it was touching to see the colossus planting little kisses on his wife's forehead. The two militiamen looked as if the sky had fallen on their heads. The first was lying on his stomach, his left leg folded under him at an unnatural angle. The other man, caught between the table and the frame of the bed, had broken his neck.

"We must get rid of the bodies," said Jahn, and he started searching the dead men's pockets for the keys to their car.

They went to get the car and parked it just outside the door. Then they extracted the two bodies from the debris of broken planks in which they were entangled and put them on the backseat. As he handled them, Bartolomeo tried not to look at their faces, but he couldn't prevent himself from shaking. Faber helped too, muttering all the time, "My God, oh, my God, what have I done?" Jahn had to speak sharply to make him stop. Meanwhile Roberta was trying to shoo away the horse-children who were coming to gape, open-mouthed, at the strange spectacle.

A few miles from the village, there was a deep pond on one side of the road, half overgrown by rushes. They drove the Phalangists' car to the side of the pond and pushed it into the water, with its two occupants in the front seats once more.

"An accident." Jahn drummed the word home. "You hear, Faber? They had an accident. No one in the village saw them. If anyone makes inquiries, everyone must say the same thing. An accident."

"That'd be a lie," muttered the giant.

Jahn punched him in the chest. "Yes, but a lie to protect yourselves! Can you understand that?"

"I think so."

In the pond, the roof of the car sank right under-
water with a mournful gurgle. Reeds were already
rising erect around it again.

They drove back through pouring rain. The windshield wipers worked hard; raindrops pattered down
on the car. They said nothing for a long time, both
still shocked by what had just happened. It was
Bartolomeo who finally broke the silence.

"What was my father like, Mr. Jahn? You've
never talked to me about him."

Jahn hesitated. "Do you want the truth?"

"Yes."

"Your father was a somber, secretive man. I
often saw him at our clandestine meetings. I always
remember his deep black eyes. When he looked
at you, you felt he was reading your mind. It was
extremely intimidating, and it made him very suc-
cessful with women."

"He didn't talk much?"

"Very little. He was a taciturn man, but the
moment he did open his mouth, everyone else fell
silent. He still had quite a strong foreign accent.
What else can I tell you? He seldom made a joke.
There was a great melancholy in him. Very sad. I
don't know where it came from."

Bart said nothing.

"Not that it kept him from being a hard man
too."

"Hard?"

"Yes, perhaps too hard . . . He never hesitated

if there was any doubt of someone's reliability. He would be in favor of eliminating that person, even at the risk of making a mistake, and he wanted the same to apply to him if necessary. He insisted on taking part himself in all dangerous operations: the execution of Phalangists, sabotage, commando raids to free comrades of ours. He took a great many risks. He was destined to die and he knew it. I often wonder if he wasn't actually looking for a chance to die in his prime. Your father was no angel, Bart."

"Was he tall, like me?"

"No. Lean, but not very tall. I suppose you must get your height from your mother, but I never met her, or I'd have talked to you about her, you may be sure. I don't know much about your family."

The car drove on through the ceaseless rain, throwing up fountains of water on both sides of the narrow road. Jahn said no more. Bart pulled his coat around him. He couldn't have said if he felt sad or happy, confident or despairing. The picture of the two dead men in their car kept coming back into his mind, with their limbs dislocated like the joints of puppets as they sank into the muddy water of the pond.

A RECITAL

It was the very end of the winter, and a sudden spell of bitterly cold weather struck the city. It froze under a dirty gray sky. People stayed at home whenever possible, and after midday the squares, avenues, boulevards, and parks were populated only by large crows. They too looked frozen as they came down in hundreds to perch on the bare branches of the trees. Only the powerful river resisted the cold, and its dark waters flowed on, never freezing over.

Helen gave up her walks and spent the afternoons reading in her room. She turned up the radiator, got under the covers of her bed, and immersed herself in a favorite novel. During these days it seemed to her as if nothing important could happen, as if the world were stuck in a groove. But she also felt that something profound and unknown to her was moving in the space inside this numb, drowsy sensation. As if the sleeping earth were incubating a secret, throbbing life in the warmth of its belly. She would have to wait. . . .

Sometimes the book fell from her lap and she sat motionless for a long time, her eyes fixed on a mark on the wall or the ceiling, lost in painful reverie. *Where are you, Milos? I wish I could see your wild curls again, hold your big hands in mine, talk to you, kiss you. Are they treating you well? You haven't forgotten me, have you?*

These thoughts saddened her, but she needed to spend such moments with her absent love. She began keeping a diary in which she wrote to him every day.

Dear Milos, I was late for my shift today. Let me tell you about it. . . . Dear Milos, Dora is really impossible! You wouldn't believe what she did this morning. . . .

She confined herself to describing the small events in her life. And she imagined what the two of them would do when they were together again later, but she could never manage to write that down.

She waited for Bart to come and tell her when he had more news, as he had promised he would. He didn't come. She reassured herself by remembering what he had said on the riverbank: he knew something was going on but he wasn't allowed to talk about it. One day Milena told her that Bart had been to what she called "meetings," but she couldn't talk about them either.

An afternoon came when Helen had suddenly had

enough of her sad, somnolent state; she was tired of staying shut up indoors. She put on her thickest sweater and her brightly colored cap, wrapped herself in her coat, and went out. No trams were running; she supposed the cold had damaged their engines. She was alone on the deserted sidewalks, and it felt like walking through a ghost town. When she came to the former Opera House, she stopped and cautiously climbed the steps, which were gleaming with black ice. It was hard to imagine Dora, years earlier, climbing the same steps arm in arm with Eva-Maria Bach, both of them cheerful and happy. Then she saw the poster on the locked door covered with obscene graffiti. She didn't have time to look away. The words leaped to her eyes: *The Winter Fights . . . Arenas . . . Reservations at . . .*

The very realistic picture on the poster showed two black swords under the red beam of a floodlight, one raised in triumph and dripping with blood, the other broken, lying in the sand, the sword of the defeated man.

She lived through the next few days in a state of anxiety and nausea. She felt she was falling ill and confided in Dora one evening. In spite of the cold that stung their cheeks, the two of them were walking along the banks of the river, making sure that no one overheard them.

"But who goes to see these horrible spectacles, Dora? Do you know?"

"Practically all the Phalangist leaders, Helen.

Anyone who seems to disapprove is considered squeamish, and people suspect he might turn traitor sometime."

"That wouldn't be enough to fill all the tiers of seats, though! And apparently the arena always has a full house."

"You're right. A lot of people go."

"But why?"

"I suppose we have to believe they just enjoy it. And I imagine they also go to the arena to be seen there, so that the authorities will think well of them, as part of the family. Boys get dragged along by their fathers. They have to prove themselves capable of watching such things without being physically sick. Basically it's a kind of initiation, like rites of passage in primitive tribes. When they've watched a fight, they think they're men."

"Men? More like barbarians," murmured Helen. "It's so depressing."

"Yes. Yet they're our human brothers—in theory. I sometimes wonder whether I don't prefer animals."

"Do you think something could still happen to prevent the fights? They're in two weeks' time. That seems like no time at all to me. I'm so frightened for Milos. I can't sleep at night."

"I don't know, Helen. We have to go on hoping in spite of all the darkness around us. I remember how the worst happened within only a few days fifteen years ago. So I tell myself that something good could happen quickly too. Even though that could never bring back our dead."

"Do you believe in God, Dora?"

"I began to have doubts before it happened, but I've lost all faith since they crushed my hand and set the dogs on Eva. Still I wouldn't want to put other people off believing. You asked me a question; I told you the answer, that's all."

"But then what gives you the strength to be . . . well, the way you are?"

"The way I am?"

"Yes. You're always smiling, you comfort people, you're amusing . . ."

"No one needs strength for that. Or anyway, no more strength than it takes to be sad or cruel, right? I don't know. It must be my own way of resisting. But it's yours too. We're like each other, you know. Not brilliant but dependable!" She broke into laughter and pressed Helen's arm. "Well, there it is—not everyone can be a Milena!"

"Do you think Milena's as gifted as her mother?"

"It's a different kind of gift. Her voice isn't as strong as Eva's. Not so full, you might say. But she's more at ease in the higher registers. And she can find nuances that make you think you're hearing a melody for the first time when you've known it for years and years. Do you know what I mean?"

"Yes, I do. It always is the first time with her."

"Exactly. And then she has . . . well, grace, and I don't know how to explain that. It's something beyond technique. Perhaps the quality of her soul—it's very mysterious. But anyway, I can tell you that Milena is going to be an exceptional singer. If nothing gets in her way."

Two sturdy militiamen, fur collars turned up behind their shaven heads, passed slowly in the opposite direction, gave them a baleful glance, and disappeared into the night.

"If no fat pigs get in her way," said Helen in a low voice.

Ten days later, when Helen came into the restaurant for her evening shift, she was surprised not to see Dora there. She asked more than ten people where she was, but none of them knew. A platform had been put up against the back wall, and a piece of furniture of some kind stood on it, concealed by a blue cloth.

"What's that?"

"No idea."

No one seemed to know anything this evening.

Helen set to work, made vaguely uneasy by her friend's absence. The customers arrived as usual from seven onward, muffled up in winter coats and scarves. Within a few minutes the two rooms of the restaurant were full of noise. Helen had come to enjoy the daily ballet performed by the girls in blue aprons, the understanding between them, the challenge — also a daily event — of standing up to a tidal wave of hungry customers, serving tables, clearing away, cleaning up, and restoring the restaurant to its original state of peace and calm.

She told herself that no doubt she could do

something else with her life, but while she was waiting, she owed it to Mr. Jahn to do the job he had given her as well as she could. What would have become of her without him? Without Dr. Josef, without Mitten? All of them, she guessed, were links in a secret chain. She wondered how many of the workers sitting at these tables shared the same burning desire for freedom to return, so that everyone could talk freely again, and sing, and the Opera House could be reopened. In three months at the restaurant Helen had never heard a single word of discontent. A deafening silence reigned. But perhaps if someone dared to speak that first word, then everyone would rise up and they would all open their hearts.

She had just brought the dessert course to one of the tables, a tray of small bowls of fruit in syrup, when she heard the tinkling sound behind her. She turned to look. Mr. Jahn was standing on a chair, looking uncomfortable. His paunch swelled inelegantly under his buttoned waistcoat. He was trying to get silence by tapping the rim of a glass with a spoon.

"Please, my friends! Silence, please!"

It was rare for Mr. Jahn to assert himself. There must be some serious reason, and curiosity showed on all faces.

"Listen to me, please, friends."

Before he started speaking, Helen had time to notice a dozen men standing close to the entrance, arms crossed over their chests. Their long heads, short necks, and massive torsos left her in no doubt: they must be horse-men. She had never seen any before and was impressed by their tremendous physical presence.

"My friends," Jahn began.

At that moment the staff in the kitchens were relaxing a little after the usual frantic activity. The last dishes of dessert had been sent out; there were no more orders. They were already beginning to tidy up and clean the stoves. This was the moment for Lando, the head chef, to give his daily performance. Without pausing in his work, he cheerfully struck up an operatic aria. He wasn't always entirely in tune, but he certainly had a powerful voice. His face as red as a peony, he ended the aria on a last reverberant note, and acknowledged the applause and laughter like a diva.

Milena was washing dishes with two of her comrades, bending over one of the huge zinc tubs in the sinks. All three girls were talking cheerfully, but Milena was in a hurry to get the job done and go to the canteen to eat. She was ravenously hungry, and Bart would be there by now.

"Hi, Kathleen. They want you in the restaurant."

At first they'd had to call her two or three times before she reacted to her new name. She was used to it now, and she turned at once.

"In the restaurant? What on earth for?"

The waiter who had spoken to her spread his arms to show his ignorance. "They just want you there."

"Who does?"

"Mr. Jahn."

She took off her rubber gloves and followed the waiter. She couldn't make it out. The big man had always expressly warned her not to show her face in the public rooms, and now he himself was summoning her. And at a time when there must still be a lot of people around. She climbed the stairs, surprised by the unusual silence on the ground floor, and opened one side of the double door. Jahn was waiting for her there. He took her by the arm as if afraid she might run away.

"Come on."

Astonished, she let him lead her into the restaurant. Turning her head from side to side, she found all eyes intently gazing at her. The customers from the second room had crowded in to join those in the first, so that it was quite difficult for her to make her way past the rows of seats. Milena felt no fear, only immense amazement. And so she arrived at the far end of the room. A smiling Dora met her at the foot of the platform.

"Come with me," she said.

They went up three steps and were onstage. A waiter jumped up behind them and pulled the blue cloth away to reveal an upright piano, an unexpected sight here. So far Milena had not had the time or inclination to object.

"What's going on?" she asked, but she was afraid she knew already.

"It's a recital, my dear," said Dora. "I'm going to

play the piano and you're going to sing. We can do that, can't we?"

The accompanist was wearing a pretty cream dress, with a bright red flower in her curly black hair. With no more ado, she sat down on the piano stool and struck a cheerful chord.

"You could have warned me!" Milena protested.

"Sorry, we forgot."

Milena had no choice: she would have to sing. She took up her usual position standing beside her friend, her right hand on the side of the piano, and then froze, feeling sure that she wouldn't be able to utter a single articulate sound. All the same, she ventured to look at the room, where the lights had been dimmed, and realized that for the first time in her life she was facing a real audience.

A great many of them gave her encouraging smiles, and she was touched by their goodwill. She saw Bart perched on the back of a chair by the window, surrounded by his friends. He waved a couple of fingers at her. *If only I could entertain them,* she thought. *I'll never be able to sing.* There was absolute silence now. Expectation was at its height.

"Schubert, D. 764," announced Dora in a low voice, but just as she was about to play the first chord, she stopped and signaled discreetly to Milena, who failed to understand.

"What is it?" she murmured.

"Your apron," whispered Dora. "Take off your kitchen apron."

Realizing that it did look slightly strange, Milena

opened her mouth with an expression of such dismay that the audience burst out laughing. In her haste to untie the white apron, she only tightened the knot behind her and had to ask Dora for help, but Dora couldn't do it either. The more she struggled in vain to undo the apron strings, the louder everyone laughed. It seemed to go on forever, and in the end Milena couldn't help laughing herself, showing the audience her luminous face at last. It was a moment that overwhelmed everyone present who had known Eva-Maria Bach. They recognized the clear, laughing eyes of the singer they had loved so much in the past, her generous smile, her love of life. Nothing was missing but her long blond hair.

"Schubert, D. 764," Dora repeated, and this time they were off.

Milena had never sung so badly in her life. She felt she was making every possible mistake, mistakes she had patiently put right one by one during dozens of hours of work. She got ahead of the accompaniment, she fell behind it, she mixed the words up, her voice faltered. On the last note she turned to Dora with tears in her eyes, furious with herself. But she had no time to indulge in her distress. Applause broke out and had hardly died down when her accompanist began another song. This one went better. She gradually came to feel new confidence. Inner peace spread through her, and at last her voice rang out full and serene.

Helen, precariously seated on the very end of a bench at the back of the room, held her breath. A man of about fifty beside her was gently nodding his head, and could hardly hide his emotion.

"The child sings almost as well as her mother. Oh, if you could only have heard our Eva, young lady," he murmured to Helen. "When I think what they did to her—it was disgusting."

The sound of a scuffle and several stifled oaths made them turn. The horse-men at the entrance were overpowering a man who was obviously trying to leave the restaurant.

"No one goes out," the largest of them said calmly, lifting the man right off the ground. "Mr. Jahn's orders."

Then he put the man down in his seat again and pressed on his shoulders to keep him there, as if quelling a refractory child.

Once peace was restored, Dora and Milena performed another four *lieder*. Helen recognized the last one from hearing her friend rehearsing it: *An die Musik* ("To Music").

"Du holde Kunst, in wieviel grauen Stunden,
Wo mich des Lebens wilder Kreis umstrickt,
Hast du mein Herz . . ."

She sang melodiously, and the audience paid her the tribute of complete silence. The slightest inflections of her voice could be heard, even the tiny sound of her fingernail on the wood of the piano during a rest. And when the last note had rung out, the silence continued and no one dared to break it.

"'In My Basket'" Dora whispered, and she played two bars of the tune.

Faces lit up. "In My Basket"! Milena was going to sing "In My Basket"!

The name of whoever had written that artless and very simple little song was long forgotten now. It was to be sung slowly, in a low voice, with nothing abrupt about it. It had come down through the centuries, a light and melancholy tune, and no one tried to work out what the words meant. The Phalange had taken it into their heads, heaven only knew why, that it contained some hidden message and must therefore be banned. The ban was, of course, the best possible way of making the little tune a good-luck charm to the Resistance, in the same way as the giant hog Napoleon had become the movement's mascot. You never found out what the girl in the song had in her basket, only what wasn't in it, and no doubt that was what enraged the Phalange.

"In my basket,
In my basket, I have no cherries,
My dear prince.
I have no crimson cherries,
I have no almonds, no.
I have no pretty kerchiefs,
No embroidered kerchiefs,
I have no beads, no.
No more grief and pain, my love,
No more grief and pain. . . ."

* * *

The first to take up the melody were several women timidly raising their voices. Then the bass voice of a man at the back of the room joined in. Who stood up first? It was impossible to tell, but within a few seconds, the entire audience was on its feet. The only person still sitting down was the man who had tried to leave a few minutes earlier. The horse-man who had barred his way then took him by the collar of his jacket and forced him to stand like his neighbors. Everyone sang mezza voce, all of them simply adding their voices to the rest without raising them. The childlike words of the song rose in the air like a muted murmur from underground.

"In my basket, I have no chicken,
Father dear,
No chicken to be plucked,
I have no duck, no.
I have no velvet gloves,
Gloves neatly sewn, no.
No more grief and pain, my love,
No more grief and pain."

Helen couldn't get over it. All around her, dozens of grown men and women were taking out their handkerchiefs as tears ran down their cheeks. For a little song like that! As she clapped with all her might, she felt a lump in her throat. *Don't worry,*

Milos! We're coming! I don't know just how we'll do it, but we'll get you out of there!

The recital was over. Mr. Jahn went up on the stage, gave bouquets of flowers to both the singer and the pianist, and kissed them. They came down into the restaurant while some men took the piano away and began dismantling the platform. Helen would have liked to congratulate her friends, but there was such a crowd that she couldn't get through to them. When everyone had left the restaurant a little later, she helped her colleagues to finish the cleaning and tidying up. It was after midnight before she could finally go to her room.

In passing she knocked on Milena's door, but there was no reply. She went back two floors down and knocked at Bart's. No one there either. She went to bed, listening in vain until halfway through the night for the sound of a key in the lock of the room next door. Around four in the morning she thought she heard a shot fired outside. She got up, stood on her chair, and opened the skylight. Icy cold stung her face. Cars were driving fast over Royal Bridge. There was more firing; she heard the sound of voices in the distance, then silence. Helen went back to bed, her heart full of mingled hope and anxiety.

Not much later she was abruptly woken by the sound of a door being kicked in. She sat up in bed, terrified, thinking someone was trying to break into her own room, but the men outside were forcing their way into Milena's little room next door. It was

313

ransacked violently but swiftly. There wasn't much to be taken away or broken. As soon as the men had gone again, she got up and joined five other girls in their nightdresses in the corridor. Mute with horror, they were gazing at Milena's books lying jumbled on the floor, her broken shelves, her little ornaments trodden underfoot, her scores torn up.

"I'm scared." The youngest of the girls gulped, hugging a cushion as if it would protect her.

"Apparently the revolt began in the night," said another girl.

"How do you know?"

"Didn't you hear the gunfire? And Mr. Jahn has disappeared."

"When?"

"Last night. He left with Kathleen and her tall boyfriend."

"Bart? They've left?" murmured Helen. "They never said a word to me!"

"Or me," replied the other girl. "But my room looks out on the street behind the building. I was looking out of the window after the recital and I saw them get into two cars."

"Two cars? Wouldn't one have been enough?"

"No, there were other people with them. I saw Lando, the head chef, and those horse-men who were guarding the entrance to the restaurant. They all left together."

"Where were they going?"

"How do you expect me to know?"

"No, of course you don't. Sorry."

Helen stayed in Milena's room by herself to tidy it up a little. Among the torn-up scores, she came upon the music of "In My Basket," which had survived. She took it away to her own room and slipped it into the inside pocket of her coat.

Then she went back to bed, to keep warm while she waited for day to dawn.

FUEL ON THE FLAMES

The two cars crossed Royal Bridge together and drove away into the freezing night, going east. Jahn led at the wheel of his heavy Panhard. A young horse-man beside him, unsure where to put his long legs, was kneading the cap he held on his knees.

"I'm your bodyguard, Mr. Jahn. Is that right?"

"Yes, that's right. What's your name?"

"Jocelin."

"Well, Jocelin, your job is to protect me in case of any violence. Me and the passengers in the back seat."

"Right, Mr. Jahn. I'll protect you."

He didn't have to say any more. The fists he raised slightly spoke for him; they were as heavy as anvils.

In the back of the car Milena, Bartolomeo, and Dora were huddling close together to keep warm. Before they left, Milena had just had time to run to her room and fetch her things.

"Hurry," Jahn had told her. "We won't be back here for some time."

Flinging her clothes and a few favorite things into her bag, she had thought that perhaps they were going to take her from place to place to sing for more audiences. She wouldn't have minded. The pleasure she'd felt in her first recital promised great future happiness. But that wasn't it. On the contrary, as soon as he had left the city behind and felt certain that no one was following him, Jahn told the two women that they were going to have to hide — again. Whatever happened, they must avoid falling into the hands of the barbarians. He knew a safe place where they would both stay as long as necessary, he said.

"What was the point of giving the recital, then?" asked Milena, unable to hide her disappointment.

"What was the point?" repeated Jahn, laughing. "Do you know what will happen after tonight?"

"No."

"What will happen is that hundreds of people who heard you and Dora will tell hundreds of others about it, and they in their turn will pass on the story to thousands more. All these people will be saying that Milena Bach, Eva-Maria Bach's daughter, sang for an hour accompanied by Dora. They'll describe the way everyone rose to their feet to sing an encore of "In My Basket." Tomorrow the news will spread through the whole country, through towns and villages, all the way to the most remote houses. When you sang, you stirred the embers into

317

flames, understand? People will come out of hiding and throw more fuel on the flames — twigs, branches. They'll fan it into a blaze that becomes a vast conflagration. That's what will happen, Milena."

She didn't reply. She found it hard to imagine that she had been able to unleash such forces by herself.

"Why didn't you warn me I was going to sing?" she asked.

"It was a Resistance secret, and although you were very closely concerned, there was no need for you to know. Are you annoyed?"

"I don't know. A little. It means you thought I couldn't keep my mouth shut and Dora could. I'm not a little girl, you know. Still, what does it matter? Anyway, I'd have died of fright if I'd known in advance."

"Well, there you are."

They drove on through the countryside for about an hour, then followed a straight road through a forest of spruce trees. Dora gloomily watched the dark trees pass by in the headlights. At a junction, the second car, driven by the head chef, Lando, tooted its horn briefly and stopped. Jahn stopped too, sixty feet farther on. Turning around, Milena saw two horse-men get out of the car, propelling a man with a hood over his head in front of them.

"The Phalangist who tried to leave during the recital," Jahn explained.

"Are they going to hurt him?" asked Milena.

"No. But I'm sure that's what he expects. He's

probably half dead of fright, thinking he's going to be executed, but that's their way, not ours. We're just going to leave him here. A little walk will do him good, and he's not about to raise the alarm with his friends, because the nearest phone is almost twenty miles away."

The two cars set off again. The Phalangist watched them go, holding his hood and astonished to find himself still alive.

Milena put her head on Bart's shoulder. They drove on through the forest and then past fields with mist hanging over them. She was just falling asleep when they reached a village with rows of brick cottages. They looked drab in the faint light. At the very end of the road, Jahn stopped his car outside a small house just like the others.

"Here we are, ladies."

They all got out except Jocelin, the young horseman, who preferred to stay in the car to keep watch on the road. The air was sharp and cold. There was a loose brick in the wall to the right just above the door frame. Jahn stood on tiptoe, dislodged the brick, put his hand into the hole, and brought out a large key. The door opened, squealing, to reveal a small room with rickety, old-fashioned furniture. A single lightbulb dangled from a wire. Dora ran a finger over the dust on a chair and made a face.

"What luxury! Oh, you really shouldn't have! See what a lovely life we musicians lead, Milena! Such a grand hotel! Such comfort! How many stars does this place have?"

"You won't be staying here long," said Jahn, sounding rather put out. "And you'll be safe; that's what matters most. Everyone in this village supports us."

"Wonderful. And if we get bored, we can always do the housework. Guns for you, brooms for us, right?"

Milena, who knew Dora very well by now, realized how furious she was.

"Dora, please don't think that—" Jahn began, but she gave him no time to go on.

"I don't think anything!" she snapped, looking him straight in the eyes. "I just know one thing: fifteen years ago, Eva and I hid as if we were ashamed to be ourselves. We traveled covered by stinking blankets, we could wash only every third night, and we scurried into hiding like insects. And what for, at the end of the day? To be captured. To be tortured in my case and killed in hers. I'm sorry, Jahn, but I have no intention of playing the same part again. That role doesn't suit me."

Jahn was not used to opposition and was left speechless by the angry woman now already on her way to the door and about to march out of it.

"I am not staying in this hole!" she went on. "Nor is Milena. We're not dolls to be taken out to make the place look good and then put back in the cupboard once the visitors have gone."

"I just wanted to make sure you avoided any risks," Jahn pointed out calmly. "You two are very valuable to the cause, as you well know, Dora."

"Save your breath, Jahn," Dora interrupted him. "I'm very fond of you, but it's no use arguing. This discussion is now closed. Come on, Milena."

Bartolomeo was torn between astonishment and admiration. He had never before heard anyone speak to Mr. Jahn so fiercely.

After this outburst, oddly enough, the atmosphere in the car was more cheerful and relaxed. It was as if Dora's anger had done everyone good, first and foremost herself; it had been on her mind for a long time. Jahn too, for he was tired of secrets and the necessity for silence. And finally Bart and Milena, who would now be able to stay in the fight together.

The two men replied freely to questions now, describing the hundreds of meetings that had been held over the last few months in cellars and garages, the underground work of thousands of invisible but determined partisans. Their supporters were waiting only for the signal, they revealed, and then the revolt would begin. It was a matter of days now, no more.

The two cars had turned back and then branched off on a road going north. Bartolomeo soon recognized the moorland landscape and the moss-grown rocks. This time it seemed only a short way to the horse-men's village.

Faber and his wife had waited up late to welcome their visitors. They were upset to think they had received them so grudgingly last time and were determined to make up for it. They succeeded.

Roberta was wearing a pretty flowered dress and pink lipstick. Her husband was barely recognizable in a suit that could have accommodated two men of normal size. A comb had left shining furrows in his black hair.

Seeing the gigantic horse-man appear before her, Milena felt that she was suddenly in one of the stories she had read as a little girl, tales in which peaceful giants held children in the palms of their hands. Bart hadn't been able to keep from telling her how Faber had crushed the Phalangists in his kitchen. She had doubted the story, but now that she saw the colossus in front of her and the new ceiling above their heads, she had to believe it was true. Jahn made the introductions. As soon as he said that Milena was the daughter of Eva-Maria Bach, Roberta clasped her hands, saying breathlessly, "Oh, how like her mother she is! Oh, my God, she's so like her! And can you sing too, Miss Bach?"

"I'm learning," Milena modestly replied, to the great amusement of those who had heard her a few hours earlier.

They sat down at the table—a new one, like the ceiling—and Roberta brought in beer. Faber dispensed smiles all around, delighted to have all these people in his house. The gradual revival of the leader of the horse-men was complete now, and it was a pleasure to see the change in him.

"Well, Faber?" said Jahn. "Have you managed to assemble your men?"

"I think so, Mr. Jahn. There are groups all over the country, ready to fight. A good number here in this village. I don't know quite how many, but a lot. You'll see them tomorrow morning."

Then Lando, the head chef, raised a particular problem: how to bring this fighting force of horsemen to the capital when the moment came? None of them could drive.

"Walking's best," replied Faber. "A pair of legs never breaks down. It'll take three days; that's nothing."

"Three days is far too long," growled Lando.

"No, Faber's right," Bart put in. "If they go on foot and separately, it'll be harder to pick them up than if they're traveling by bus or car. They'll be on all the roads coming from the north, the south, everywhere. And the rest of the population will join them. It'll be a human tide converging on the capital. The Phalangists can't intervene everywhere. They'll be overwhelmed."

He went on in this vein, picturing the irresistible advance of the horse-men while all the other supporters of a free society rallied to them. His black eyes were blazing. Milena looked at him with love and admiration. He might be only seventeen, but he wasn't afraid of arguing with older men, and they treated him as an equal.

"I'll speak to them tomorrow," he added, without waiting for anyone to agree with him. "I'll explain what's at stake, and they'll listen to me."

"Yes," Faber confirmed. "They're expecting you to speak to them anyway, Casal."

Now Jahn spoke, but gradually Milena realized that she was no longer following what he said. His words echoed around in her head without making sense. She felt dizzy, lost consciousness, and came around in the powerful arms of Roberta, who was laying her down on the bench, pushing the men aside.

"White as a sheet, poor little thing! Has she had anything to eat recently?"

The others realized that in fact Milena had eaten nothing the evening before, nor indeed had Dora. A long day's work, all the emotion of the recital, the drive, the cold, and a glass of beer on an empty stomach had been too much for her.

"You great brutes!" the tall horse-woman scolded them all, cutting a slice of cake. "There you go, starting revolts, and you don't notice a girl fainting under your very noses! And Miss Bach at that! I won't let you forget this in a hurry!"

The incident brought the evening to an end. The visitors were to sleep in the nearby houses. Milena and Dora, after having something to eat and drink at last, were given the Fabers' huge double bed; its owners were staying the night with relatives at the other end of the village. Bartolomeo and Lando went to the house of one of the horse-men who had been on the drive with them. The enormous Jocelin flatly refused to leave Jahn and insisted on putting him up at his own house. "I'll protect you day and night, Mr. Jahn, that I will!"

* * *

When they woke up, Dora and Milena heard the staircase creaking. Still drowsy, they emerged from under the eiderdown to see the large figure of Roberta coming upstairs with a tray in her hands.

"They tell me musicians and suchlike artists have breakfast in bed, so here we are! Coffee, bread and butter, jam. Anything else you ladies would like?"

"This is more than enough for us ladies!" said Dora, laughing. "It's paradise!"

"Now, you mustn't make fun of us. I'm sure you've stayed in the best hotels."

"I'm not making fun, Roberta. This is much better than the best hotels. You're very kind."

"Mitzi didn't bother you too much?"

"Not at all," said Milena. "She slept in her own chair like a good kitty. Look at her."

The large cat twitched one lazy ear to greet her mistress. Curled up in the chair, she looked like an enormous ginger cushion.

Roberta put the tray down on the bed and opened the shutters. Cold air and white light invaded the room. "There's fog and frost this morning," said the horse-woman. "You'll need to wrap up well to go out. There now, I'll leave you to eat your breakfast."

Sure enough, the two women couldn't see more than five yards ahead of them in the village square, where they joined a group of some twenty men, including Faber, who towered half a head above everyone else; Bartolomeo, muffled in his black

325

scarf; the head chef, Lando, who was freezing; and Jahn, with the faithful Jocelin still beside him.

"What's going on, Bart?" Milena asked.

"Faber wants to introduce me to his people so that I can greet them and speak to them. They've gathered at the way out of the village."

The little group set off through the fog and had soon left the last houses behind. Bart wondered what to expect. Faber had said that a great many horse-men had gathered here, but what did that mean? A hundred? Perhaps two hundred? He walked on beside Jahn, never guessing that he was about to experience one of the greatest moments of his young life.

At first he saw only a dozen rows of horse-men standing motionless in the mist. The vapor of their breath half hid their massive faces. They wore warm clothing and boots. Most of them had bags on their backs or slung over their shoulders. Clubs could be seen sticking out of some of the bags, while other men held clubs in their hands. Bart was impressed by the sense of power radiating from these dark, silent, colossal figures.

"How many are there?" he whispered to Faber. "I can't see them all."

"A great many, as I said. They're waiting for you to speak to them. Right, get up there and off you go."

"But they won't all hear me. My voice isn't loud enough."

"You don't have to shout. Just speak to the ones

in front. They'll pass it on. They'll repeat exactly what you say till it gets to the back row. We always do it that way here — no need for anyone to yell."

Bart gave Jahn an uneasy glance. Jahn shrugged. He couldn't help, nor could Lando or Milena, who gave him a little signal of encouragement. He took a step forward, slightly at a loss, and got up on the wine crate that had been put there for him to stand on. What was he to say? Why hadn't he had the sense to prepare a speech in advance? Well, too late now.

"Good morning, friends," he began. "My name is Bartolomeo Casal."

He was about to go straight on, but Faber stopped him with a gesture. He had to leave time for the sentence to be repeated. The horse-men in the front row turned around and passed it on in low voices to those in the second row:

"Good morning, friends, my name is Bartolomeo Casal . . ."

who passed it on to the third row:

"Good morning, friends, my name is Bartolomeo Casal . . ."

and so on.

Soon the message was lost in the mist, but he knew it was still passing from one man to the next. It took a long time. Now and then Bart looked inquiringly at Faber — *Can I go on?* — but Faber shook his head: no, not yet. After long moments of silence, the low note of a horn was heard in the distance. Faber nodded: the message had reached the end of its journey.

Bartolomeo realized how precious words were in such circumstances. He mustn't waste them. He had to find the shortest way to say what had to be said.

He went on: "In the past, my father led you . . ."

"In the past, my father led you . . ." repeated the horse-men in the front row.

"In the past, my father led you . . ." the men in the second row passed it on.

"And he lost his life, like many others."

"And he lost his life, like many others."

"And he lost his life, like many others."

"Now I will take up the fight again, with you!"

"Now I will take up the fight again, with you!"

"Now I will take up the fight again, with you!"

"Trust me!"

"Trust me!"

"This time the people will be with us . . ."

"This time the people will be with us . . ."

"And we will defeat the barbarians!"

"And we will defeat the barbarians!"

Punctuated by the horn calls in the mist, the simple sentences they repeated took on unexpected weight in the silence as they made their slow progress on. There was time to weigh every word, and every word weighed heavy: rebel . . . *rebel* . . . fight . . . *fight* . . . freedom . . . *freedom* . . .

He asked them to set off for the capital that morning. When he had finished, the last horn call set off a roar that sent a shiver down his spine.

"Go and greet them," Faber told him. "Walk among them; they'll like that."

"No," protested Bart, getting off his crate. "I can't do it. I don't like the idea of some kind of personality cult. I'd feel ridiculous."

Jahn took his arm. "Go on, Bart. You mustn't disappoint them. And those of them who knew your father will be happy to see him again in you."

Bartolomeo hesitated for a few more seconds and then made up his mind. "All right, but you come too, Milena."

He took Milena's hand and led her forward. The first rows opened before them, and they let themselves be swallowed up by the peaceful crowd of horse-men, the vapor of their breath hovering almost motionless above their heads. It was an unreal moment. There were not hundreds but thousands of people ready to fight. In their heavy winter clothes, with caps or balaclavas on their heads, they seemed to have come out of another time. There were many women among them, and boys too, some of them no more than twelve. These lads were proudly brandishing their pikes or clubs. In the ghostly light of early morning they all made way for the two young people, offering them smiles and words of friendship.

"Are we in a fairy tale?" whispered Milena.

"That's how I feel," said Bart. "Either that or we're dreaming the same dream at the same time."

Soon they had lost their sense of direction and didn't know which way to go. Wherever they turned, they saw the same multitude of backs, shoulders, kindly faces, and there were the same large hands to shake. Immersed in the warmth of this human throng, they no longer felt concern either for what the next day would bring or for the biting cold of winter.

"Which way is the village?" asked Milena at last, feeling dazed.

A young horse-woman heard her and took her arm. "Would you like me to take you back? Follow me!"

She set off ahead of them, very proud to be their guide. She was bare-headed, and her straight hair, growing untidily, stood up on her strong skull in tufts. There were deep folds around her neck. Her man's coat flapped around her legs, and now and then she turned to see if they were still following her. When she saw that they were there, she smiled with delight. Once she took her opportunity to whisper to Milena, "Oh, you're as beautiful as a princess!" Then she turned away very quickly, moved with emotion at her own daring.

"You're the beautiful one," Milena murmured to herself. "Much more beautiful than me."

Back in the village they all met at Faber's house again. Jahn left briefly, accompanied by the inevitable Jocelin, to go to the post office, the only place in the village with a telephone. He came back looking very pale to announce his news: the uprising had begun in the capital during the night, and the army had opened fire, terrorizing the population. There were dozens of dead, and this morning the

Phalange had restored order. However, in several northern towns, young people had put up barricades, which they were defending doggedly, and those barricades were still holding.

"Good God!" swore Lando. "Things are moving much too fast! It's far too soon!"

"Yes, it's too soon," Jahn agreed, "but there we are. The fire has been lit. No one can put it out now."

RETURN TO THE VILLAGE

As soon as she woke up, Helen realized that this wasn't going to be a morning like any other. After her fright when the militia broke into Milena's room, she had fallen asleep. It was a heavy, dreamless sleep, and now she was sitting on the edge of her bed, feeling numb. Her alarm clock told her that it was nearly ten in the morning. She had never gotten up so late since coming to the restaurant. She washed, dressed hurriedly, and went out into the silent corridor. The sight of Milena's shattered door brought last night's violence straight back to her. She passed it without stopping and went downstairs, feeling vaguely that the whole world was out of joint.

On the second floor, she went to Bartolomeo's door, and saw that it too had been forced open. She glanced inside the room, where the same chaos reigned as in Milena's after the barbarians had ransacked it. Objects were lying around on the floor, broken and crushed underfoot. Her stomach muscles cramped with fear: what would happen if her two friends ever fell into the hands of these men?

The two restaurant rooms were empty. Helen took the elevator down to the basement. In the silence its iron machinery seemed louder than ever. Passing through the kitchens, she finally heard a faint sound coming from the staff canteen, and then voices. She opened the door and saw about thirty of her fellow workers sitting there, crammed into a space too small for them. They were in the middle of such a lively discussion that they hardly noticed her arrival.

"We can manage the meals no problem without Lando," a boy sitting at the corner of the table was saying. "I mean, we're not total idiots!"

"It's not a matter of being idiots or not," said another boy, wearing a warehouse man's gray apron. "It depends on whether we can serve the customers anything. The suppliers know that Mr. Jahn has gone away, and we haven't had half this morning's deliveries: no vegetables, no bread. So what do you think we're going to give people?"

A young woman leaning on a cupboard said placidly, "I'm perfectly happy to serve anything we have, but I don't think anyone's likely to turn up. They say the factory's on strike."

"Exactly," agreed a man beside her, smoking a cigarette. "There was a scuffle at the entrance."

"So what are we going to do?" one girl asked.

The discussion went around in circles like this for

several minutes, until a young man of about twenty suddenly got up on his chair. He was clearly angry. "Look, I'm sorry, but you're really getting me down with all this talk about vegetable deliveries!" he cried. "Going on about carrots and potatoes when people were putting up the barricades last night. You heard them too, I suppose. What are we waiting for? Let's get moving!"

"Hear, hear!" another young man agreed. "I've no intention of sitting here twiddling my thumbs. I'm off into town to see what's going on. Coming?"

The two of them put on their jackets and marched out.

"Be careful!" the boy smoking the cigarette called after them. "They're saying people died last night!"

There was a long and weighty silence.

"I wonder what Mr. Jahn would say," one of the cooks, a girl in a white apron, said with a sigh.

"What would he say?" replied another girl, getting to her feet. "He'd say he's not our father, and maybe we should learn to manage without him. And not be scared anymore! Those two boys are right. I'm going after them. Who's coming with me?"

It was Rachel, a friend of Dora's. Helen knew her well.

"I'll come," she said, surprised to find herself so bold.

Going along the corridor to her room, she felt a sense of elation. There were three days left before the winter fights. Only three days. But suppose the revolution was already beginning? Suppose the city was suddenly in chaos? Wouldn't the Phalangists have more urgent things on their minds than going to watch gladiators die? Surely they would! They wouldn't go to the arena. They'd stay away and the fights would be canceled! For the first time in months, she saw hope ahead. A faint hope, but a real one.

Looking around her little room at her few ornaments, the two bookshelves, her clothes hanging from the cord, she asked herself an unusual question: what do you take with you when you're a girl of seventeen going off to build barricades in the street to save your lover? Unable to come up with any satisfactory answer, she put on her brightly colored cap, her scarf, and her winter coat, and set off.

The other three were waiting for her outside the restaurant. They conferred briefly and decided to go to the factory. From a distance they saw that the tall gates were guarded by a dozen armed militiamen. They turned away and went along small streets, taking care not to slip on the black ice. The boy who had spurred them into action in the canteen was still talking passionately. "They want to prevent crowds from gathering, but they won't do it! We only need people to stop being frightened and come out into the street, that's all!"

"Don't talk so loud," the other boy warned him.

"I'll talk any way I like," his friend retorted. "I've kept my mouth shut for years and I'm sick and tired of it, do you hear? Sick and tired!" He shouted it out at the top of his voice, and then roared with laughter. "Oh, how good that feels! Why don't you all try it?"

Luckily, the tram was running normally. They boarded it, and immediately noticed three militiamen sitting at the back, clubs in their hands and pistols at their belts. The enthusiastic boy calmed down a little but still stared defiantly at them.

"Got a problem?" inquired one of the men.

"No, just admiring your uniform," replied the boy. He not only had the gift of gab; he had guts too. The few passengers on the tram smiled, and the militiaman clenched his jaw.

As they approached the city center down the long avenue leading to Opera House Square, the tram filled up more at every stop. Helen thought there was a special kind of excitement on the passengers' faces, as if they were waiting for something. Or was she just imagining it? She leaned her forehead against the cold window. The tram stopped.

"Shall we get out here?" asked Rachel.

"At the next stop," one of the two boys said.

The automatic doors were just closing again when Helen froze, transfixed. There on the sidewalk—on the other side of the road! No, she couldn't be dreaming. . . .

"Wait!" she cried, leaping to her feet. "Open the doors! Let me out! Please!"

Frantically, she pulled the stop cord. Rachel took her arm, "Helen, what is it?"

"Over there. I saw . . ." Helen murmured.

As the tram set off again, she jostled passengers aside and went to stare out of the back window, ignoring the militiamen and moving so impetuously that they made way for her. The two figures were disappearing down a little side street. She didn't know one of them, an old woman walking unsteadily, dressed in black and holding a shopping bag, but the other . . . She could have sworn . . . ! How could she mistake that face? She'd have known it among a hundred thousand! She was just in time to see them go through the front door of an apartment building—the second in the street, she thought—and then disappear from sight.

"What did you see?" Rachel asked again.

"Someone I know! But I can hardly believe it."

The tram was packed now. The journey between the two stops seemed to last hours. Helen made her way to the doors and jumped out as soon as they opened.

"I'm off!" she called to the other three, and then she ran back along the sidewalk, her heart thudding.

Suppose she was wrong? No, there couldn't possibly be such a likeness! Back at the last tram stop, she set off breathlessly along the side street, which rose up a slight slope. The apartment building had a gray facade. She was certain, as she opened the second door inside the entrance, that this was where the two figures had disappeared. A dark corridor lay ahead of her. She tried the light switch, but it wasn't working, and she groped her way on until she reached a small yard with broken paving. Dingy grass grew in the cracks, and there were dustbins standing around. Close as it was to the big avenue, the place seemed to be in a bad state. Two staircases led to the upper floors. At random, she chose the one on the left, a blackened spiral staircase. There was a smell of mold.

On the first landing she stopped and listened. She did the same on the next floor, with no more success. Then on the fourth floor. It was as if no one at all lived in the building. Perhaps it had been condemned as a health hazard. She went down to the yard again and tried the other staircase. This was lighter and better maintained, and the electricity on it was working. On the first floor she found two closed and silent doors, the same on the second and third floors, but right at the top, under the roof—the clear, child's voice inside made her heart turn over.

"It stings!" the voice was complaining. "The soap hurts my eyes!"

Now she was in no doubt at all. She knocked vigorously on the door. It was opened by the old woman she had seen in the street, her sleeves rolled well up over her pale, wrinkled arms, a washcloth in her right hand. Helen ignored her and marched straight to the big tub of steaming water in the middle of the room. Octavo stood up, stark naked and dripping, and flung himself into her arms.

"Helen!"

"Octavo! Oh, I'm so pleased to see you again! I am so pleased!"

She hugged him close for a long time, then kissed his cheeks and his hands hard. "What are you doing here, Octavo?"

"I'm staying with Auntie Marguerite, of course. Are you crying?"

"No. Well, yes. Auntie Marguerite?"

She let go of the child, suddenly aware of her own incivility. "I'm so sorry," she said, turning to the woman. "Just bursting in like that!"

"Oh, never mind! I think you must be the famous Helen?"

"I don't know about famous, but I'm Helen. And you're — ?"

"I'm Paula's elder sister, Marguerite."

That was obvious. She had the same gentle chestnut-brown eyes and the same nose as Helen's large consoler. Only her girth and her age were different. Marguerite must be ten years older and weigh four times less than her "little sister." Helen often remembered the story of her childhood that Paula had told her. *"I remember, my sister, Marguerite and I had caught a hedgehog. . . ."* It was funny to see the second character in that anecdote suddenly appear, at least half a century older. This frail lady who wasn't very steady on her feet would never be able to run after hedgehogs now.

"Paula sent Octavo to me on the bus this

339

winter," she said, explaining the little boy's presence.

"That's right," the child agreed. "But she'll soon be coming to find me. I wrote her a letter. Without any spelling mistakes, and I did her a drawing."

"Very good, Octavo. And how's your Mama Paula?"

"She's fine."

Marguerite nodded, but her sad smile obviously concealed another story. As soon as she could, she drew Helen into the kitchen and closed the door.

"How is Paula?" Helen asked for the second time, steeling herself for the reply.

"I haven't heard anything from my sister for over a month," said Marguerite, and she burst into sobs. If she would let go like that in front of a stranger, the poor woman must have been wanting to pour her heart out for a long time.

"Are you afraid something's happened to her?"

"Oh, yes, I am! Octavo had a letter for me in his pants pocket. You can read it—look, it's over there on the dresser."

Paula's careful, cramped writing filled half a page. Lovingly, Helen imagined her consoler's large hand moving over the paper. She read to the end without raising her head.

Dear, dear Marguerite,

I'm sending you Octavo by the bus tomorrow. I shall put him in the care of someone who will take him to you. It's getting too dangerous here. Several young people escaped from the boarding schools this winter. Poor children, they set off for the mountains or down the river, and God knows what's become of them. The Phalange people accuse us of being their accomplices (and for once they're not wrong) and they're threatening to teach us a lesson if that kind of thing goes on. But it does go on. They say they'll know how to punish us. They say we all have our weak points. So I'm putting my own weak point on the bus. Please look after him as if he were your own. He's a good child. I hate parting from him, but I'll come for him as soon as possible. I know you're not in very good health, but he won't give you any trouble. Of course I'll reimburse you for all your expenses. Send him to school if you can; he likes learning things.

With all my love,
Your sister, Paula

"There, you see!" cried Marguerite as soon as Helen had finished reading. "I've heard nothing since that letter. There was no reply when I wrote back. I'd have gone to see her, but the journey's too much for me. I have a weak heart, my hip gives me trouble, and then of course I can't leave Octavo."

Helen thought for some time. Several young people had escaped? Did Paula mean just Milena and herself and the two boys, or had there been others? Had their escape brought a wind of change and freedom blowing down the dismal school corridors, a wind that couldn't be contained? What had become of Catharina Pancek, Vera Plasil, and the others? And above all, what had become of Paula? Her silence was worrying. The idea that her

341

consoler might be suffering was unbearable to Helen.

"Do you know what time there'd be a bus going up there?" she asked.

"There's one that leaves from the bus station at twelve thirty, but you're surely not going to . . . Why, you haven't even eaten!"

Helen was already on her feet. "If I run, I can catch it."

She put her coat on, checked that she had enough money in her purse for a ticket, and ran back to Octavo, who was still splashing about in the tub.

"I'm off again, Octavo darling. Sorry."

"I know. You have to leave because if you're not back, they'll put someone else in the black hole."

It took Helen several seconds to realize what he was talking about.

"Oh no, that was at the school! I'm not there anymore now. I'm free. I can come and go at random!"

"Where's Random? Will you take me there with you?"

She burst out laughing. "I mean I can go where I like. And yes, I'll take you around with me sometime."

"Promise?" asked the child, drawing a design in bath foam on Helen's cheek.

"Promise. As soon as things are better again."

She hugged Marguerite as if she'd known her forever, and ran down the stairs. "Any message for your sister?" she called up from the yard.

"Yes, tell her I've put Octavo down for school!"

She ran along the riverbank, the front of her coat still wet from Octavo's bathwater, retracing the way she had gone several months earlier in the middle of the night when she was looking for the Wooden Bridge. She hadn't known at the time that she was soon to be reunited with Milena. And now she'd lost touch with her again.

The bus station was quiet, but Helen noticed several soldiers pacing up and down in their khaki uniforms, with guns in their hands. They were clearly on a war footing. She swiftly boarded the almost empty bus bound north. Once she was seated, she had time to think about what she had done. Yes, she was leaving the capital just at the moment when it looked as if the fighting were about to begin; yes, she would have to be back in a few days' time for the winter fights, supposing they were held. But a force ten times stronger had made her catch this dingy bus to go find Paula. She couldn't abandon the woman who had been so good to her, not after Paula had comforted her when sadness and despair threatened to overwhelm her. She wouldn't let Paula down. She could never forgive herself if she did.

With nothing to read, it was a long journey. At every village people got out of or onto the bus, taking no notice of one another. The red-faced driver manhandled his vehicle around the bends and up slopes, tooting angrily at everyone else on the road as if they had no right to be there. Late in the afternoon he stopped outside a café, went in, and didn't come out. Gradually the passengers followed him, and soon they were all inside. The room was dark and smoky. Helen sat down at the end of one table. Steaming bowls of soup were passed over her head, and plates of ham or omelettes. Her stomach was crying out with hunger. She looked in her purse, but it contained just enough for her to buy her return ticket.

"Aren't you eating anything, young lady?" the man on her left asked. She recognized him as one of her neighbors in the bus.

"No, I'm not hungry."

"Not hungry or short of cash? Come on, I saw you counting your pennies; there's nothing to be ashamed of. Everyone has a right to eat, you know!"

He was about fifty. She had no time to protest; he was already summoning the waitress. "An omelette for the young lady, please."

As she emptied her plate, he turned away from her to talk to other people, perhaps to keep her from feeling awkward.

"Where are you going?" he asked when she had finished her omelette.

She told him her destination, and he looked surprised. "Do you think you'll get that far?"

"Why not?"

"They say there's trouble there. Barricades. No one's being let into the town. Now, how about a coffee?"

344

Night had fallen by the time they set off again. The shared meal had loosened the passengers' tongues, and for several miles the cheerful sound of conversation mingled with the purring of the engine. Then the conversation gradually died down and most of the passengers dozed off. Helen, who had no one sitting beside her now, took off her shoes, put her feet up on the seat, and used her coat as a blanket to keep her knees and elbows warm.

As she dropped off to sleep, she thought of Octavo wanting to go to "Random" with her. Then she wondered again how Paula came to have her little boy and who his father was. Her consoler had told her many of her secrets, but never that one! She just used to laugh and call Helen nosy if she persisted in asking.

She was woken by the cold. The bus had stopped, and the folding doors had opened, letting in a blast of icy air. The driver was standing in the aisle, looking at her impatiently.

"Here you are, miss. This is where you get out."

She got to her feet, looked around her, and saw that she was the last remaining passenger. The bus was empty. Night surrounded them.

"But we haven't reached the bus station!"

"I'm not going there. There's fighting. I can do without any trouble."

Helen stood on the step, frightened. "Surely you're not just going to leave me here!"

He didn't even bother to reply.

"At least tell me where the town is."

"That way. Follow the road and you'll get there. Or you can take the shortcut over the hill there. Got a flashlight with you?"

Helen was surprised. "The hill? You mean where the consolers live?"

"That's the one. Good night, then." He touched her shoulder with his fingertips, not even trying to hide his impatience. "Make up your mind, won't you? Want me to push you out?"

She wasn't going to spend any longer arguing with the driver. She got out. Did the man have a daughter of her age, she wondered, and if so would he have liked the idea of her being left alone in this deserted spot in the middle of the night?

She didn't have a flashlight. She decided that the best thing would be to go on along the road, reach the town, and then take the route she knew so well over the bridge and on into the village. She stood there motionless until the sound of the engine had died away entirely and then started walking. After going only a little way she stopped short: she caught the sound of dogs barking over in the direction of the town. Their excited yapping could be distinctly heard in the silence and seemed to be coming closer. She shivered, turned on her heel, and made for the hill.

The moon shed faint light on the rising path. She stumbled on rocks several times but reached the top of the hill without hurting herself. The wind was blowing in gusts, and her teeth were chattering.

The rooftops of the first of the consolers' houses came into sight below her. She tried to see the town or the river in the distance, but they were hidden in the night.

Following the road through the village, she felt nervous. There was something wrong here. The place was sleeping, certainly, but it was an uneasy sleep. She saw one front door standing wide open. A shutter swung in the wind. She quickened her pace. When she came to the fountain, she took the familiar little road to her right. Marguerite's words came back to her: *"I haven't heard anything from my sister for over a month."* What would she do if Paula wasn't at home? Where would she sleep?

The farther she went, the more certain she was that the houses to the right and left of the road had been abandoned. She could sense their empti-ness, as if the large forms of the consolers no longer warmed them with their sheer size. She stopped at Number 47, her heart thudding. The light of a candle trembled on the other side of the window. She looked through the window and saw Paula.

She was sitting in her armchair, head tilting slightly toward one shoulder, fast asleep. Helen opened the door, closed it quietly, knelt down at her consoler's feet, took her hands in her own, and looked at her for a long time. She had never seen Paula asleep before, and it was strange to feel that her mind was so far away. In the end she began to feel almost embarrassed. She shook her, gently.

"Paula . . . Paula!"

The large woman opened her eyes and showed no surprise. It was as if she had fallen asleep like this with Helen already kneeling there, and now that she woke up, they were still in the same position.

"Oh, my beauty," she murmured. "Look . . . just see what they've done."

Only then did Helen notice the state the room was in. The chairs were broken, the table turned upside down, shelves pulled away from the wall. The dresser lay on the floor, gutted. It was easy to imagine the furious hatchet blows falling, bent on destruction.

"I didn't get back until this afternoon. After a month. I've tidied the kitchen up a bit, but I haven't touched anything in here. I'm so tired. I ought to have gone up to the bedroom."

Her voice was shaking, near tears.

"Where were you for that whole month, Paula?"

"Why, in their prison, my beauty."

"In prison? You?"

"Yes, four of them came and took me away. They were very rough. They hurt my arm and my head. It was because of the young people running away."

Helen felt her own mounting fury.

"More than twenty of them escaped," Paula went on. "You were one of the first, my beauty, and the others followed your example. We gave them clothes and food, poor children, and we hid them when necessary. So they arrested us—Martha,

Emily, and me. The others were turned out of the village. And then the men came back and smashed everything. Did you see it? Not a house was spared. And Octavo isn't here. . . ."

She uttered a long, sorrowful sigh, and closed her eyes.

"Oh Paula," Helen whispered.

"What will become of me now?" moaned the consoler. "The revolt has started, you know. There are barricades up in the town, and the Phalangists will be swept away within a few days, that's for sure. Everyone hates them so much. I ought to be glad of that, but I can't really manage it. I liked comforting young people, you see. I liked it better than anything! I don't think I'll ever be able to do anything else except cooking. The doors of the boarding schools will be opened now, and all the children I loved will go away. Oh, my beauty, what will become of me? I'll be nothing but a fat, useless old woman. And Octavo isn't here. . . ."

This time her tears flowed down her plump cheeks in torrents.

"Dear Paula," Helen repeated, overwhelmed. She got up, went around the chair, and took Paula's hot, heavy head in her hands. She kissed her and stroked her hair and her wet face. "Don't be upset, Paula. Octavo is fine. I saw him at Marguerite's, and she's sending him to school. He's working hard. Did you get his letter?"

Paula nodded.

"You know what we'll do now, Paula? We'll go upstairs to the bedroom. You'll sleep in your own bed and I'll sleep in Octavo's. And tomorrow we'll both catch the bus and go to join them in the capital. I'll take care of you. Don't worry about anything. I love you as if you were my mother, you know I do. You're the only mother I ever knew."

The consoler nodded again, and buried her face against the breast of the girl who had knocked on her door for the first time four years earlier—the girl she had described as a little, lost kitten at the time.

THE WINTER FIGHTS

Milos kept looking for the jay through the week before he left the training camp. It was all very well trying not to be superstitious, but he couldn't help hoping that the big, brightly colored bird would reappear and bring him luck. Every morning and late every afternoon he went around behind the infirmary to where he had seen the jay in autumn, but it never turned up on the windowsill, on the other side of the bars, or anywhere else. Milos felt it was a bad omen.

He wasn't the only one watching out for signs. One of the premiers fell into a furious rage because someone else went to sit in his usual place in the refectory. He picked up the bench, tipping the other man off it, and laid into him with his fists shouting, "Want to get me killed, do you? That's it—you want to get me killed, you bastard!" It took two other men to separate them.

Their training had taken a more violent turn for some time past. As the fights came closer, the gladiators seemed to be trying to toughen themselves up even more, to shake off any weakness. On their last night in the camp, Myricus summoned them all to the arena after their evening meal. There were no floodlights on, but torches fixed to logs of wood cast red light on their somber faces. The men moved away from each other and stood motionless, swords in their hands. Myricus walked slowly among them, then went up to the gallery and addressed them in his deep voice.

"Gentlemen, look around you. Look at one another, all of you: Caius, Ferox, Delicatus, Messor . . ."

He listed all thirty names without omitting a single one, taking his time about it. That grave recitation instantly conveyed a disturbing solemnity.

"Take a good look at each other, because in a few days' time, when I call you together again in this place, many of you will be dead. So look at one another now."

There was an oppressive silence. All the gladiators kept their eyes focused on the sand. None of them lifted their heads when Myricus told them to look up.

"At this moment, as I speak to you," the trainer went on, "the gladiators in the other five camps are listening to a similar address. Like you, they are surrounded by torches, and every one of them is wondering: *Will I be among the dead or will I survive?*

I tell the novices among you, and I repeat it for the benefit of the others: hatred is your only weapon. Hate your opponent as soon as you see him appear on the other side of the arena. Hate him in advance for wanting to take your life. And make sure you're convinced that his life is not worth yours."

He paused. The gladiators remained silent, deep in the turmoil of their own thoughts. A little way ahead of him, Milos saw the shaved nape of Basil's neck and his massive shoulders rising and falling to the regular rhythm of his breathing. He took comfort from the sight, and then he wondered which of the two of them would fight first. He prayed that it would be him, not Basil.

Myricus went on speaking for some time. He conjured up the names of the great gladiators of classical antiquity: Flamma, who had won thirty fights; Urbicus, a winner thirteen times, and then defeated because he held back from striking the mortal blow and gave his unfortunate opponent a chance.

"We set out tomorrow," he concluded. "Leave your swords here on the ground. You won't be needing them during the journey. We'll collect them and give them back to you when the time comes for you to fight."

That night was not disturbed by any nightmares. An unreal calm reigned in the dormitories. Probably none of them really slept. Every time Milos thought he was dropping off, he gave a start and was wide awake again, as if he were determined not to sleep away any of the hours that might be his last. Basil couldn't sleep either.

"What's your girlfriend's name?" he asked in the middle of the night.

"Helen," Milos whispered.

"What?"

"Helen." He had to repeat it in a louder voice, and it felt like speaking to her in the silence.

"What's she like?"

"Well . . . normal."

"Come on," Basil insisted. "You can tell me. I won't repeat it."

"Right," said Milos, slightly embarrassed. "She isn't very tall, she has short hair, her face is rather round . . ."

These general remarks weren't enough for Basil. "Tell me something special—oh, I don't know, something she does well."

"She . . . well, she's good at climbing a rope."

"There we are, then!" said the young horse-man, satisfied, and he turned over.

Next morning, the camp gates opened, and three military vans drove in and stopped outside the canteen, followed by two tarpaulin-covered trucks full of armed soldiers. The gladiators were assembled in the wind and drizzling rain. It was Fulgur's job to divide them into groups and handcuff them to chains linking them together. He did it with perverse pleasure, scanning their faces for signs of fear. Milos did his best to hide his emotions, but his sickly, pale face gave him away, and when Fulgur gave him a meaningful wink, as if to say, *Got the jitters, have you?* it was all he could do not to rush the man and headbutt him.

He looked desperately for the jay until the last moment. Please come back! Let me see you! Just for a second. Let me see you one last time, and I'll take your bright image away with me, the image of life!

He had to be pushed to make him climb into the van.

Fulgur had taken care to separate him from Basil. He was put in the second van with a number of others, and sat on one of the wooden benches running around the sides. The convoy set off and drove out of the camp, with one of the trucks full of soldiers going ahead and the other bringing up the rear. Any attempt to escape would have been sheer suicide. A small barred window had been cut in the side of the van, and for a long time they saw the complex pattern of the bare branches of oak trees moving up and down past them. Around midday they finally left the forest, joined the main road, and drove south toward the capital.

A little later a bus with a noisy engine coming from the north overtook the convoy, which was driving slowly. When it drew level with the second van, the two vehicles went along the road side by side for about fifty yards. Paula was sleeping at the back of the bus, her hands on her knees. Her large posterior occupied two whole seats. Beside her, in a seat by the window, Helen was trying to read.

She raised her eyes and looked absently at the van carrying Milos, handcuffs on his wrists, his heart heavy.

For a few seconds there were no more than ten feet between the two. Then the bus accelerated and parted them again.

The convoy reached its destination in the middle of the night. Those of the gladiators who had never been in the capital before pressed their faces in turn to the little barred window, but all they saw of the great city was the facades of dismal gray buildings. When they got out of the vans, they all shivered in the damp cold of the night. The headlights of the vehicles, now maneuvering to leave again, swept across the base of an enormous, dark structure: the arena. So this was the end of their journey. Their last journey?

Milos, handcuffed and under guard, was pushed toward the building with his thirty or so companions in misfortune. They passed through a heavy, wooden double door that was closed behind them and barred with a beam as thick as a tree trunk. The floor of the arena building was trodden earth. They passed beneath the tiers of seats, followed a corridor, and entered their prison cell, a vast room with clay walls giving off a strong smell of mold. Straw mattresses on the floor were the only furnishing. As soon as their handcuffs had been removed, the gladiators fell on their beds. Most of them, exhausted by the journey on the hard seats in the vans, buried themselves under the blankets at once, hoping to sleep; the others remained seated, eyes burning, trying to read some secret sign telling their fortune in the marks on the walls. Four armed soldiers guarded the door.

"Aren't they going to give us anything to eat?" asked Basil. "I'm ravenous."

They had to wait an hour before they were brought a bowl of thick soup and a large roll each.

"Better than we had in the camp!" said Basil, pleased. "Don't you think? I guess they want us to be in good form tomorrow!"

Milos smiled at him bitterly. For once he had difficulty swallowing, and he was not the only one. Basil, however, found himself the recipient of three bowls of soup and three rolls, all of which he ate with relish.

Guards came to take away the bowls and spoons. Then the soldiers left, and they heard the sound of keys turning. The lights all went out at the same time, except for a night-light behind wire that gave a pale glimmer above the door. Hour after hour they heard the noise of new arrivals in the rooms nearby, the sound of their unknown voices. Their opponents. The men who were going to kill them or be killed.

In the morning, Milos woke feeling somehow outside himself. He wondered if he had slept at all, if he was still in a dream, or if this was reality. The place stank of urine. One of the gladiators must have relieved himself in a corner of the cell.

He turned to Basil and saw that his eyes were wide open and that he was pale as a sheet.

"All right, Basil?"

"No. I feel ill."

"What's the matter?"

"Must have been that soup. It didn't agree with me."

The door opened, and Myricus came in with a piece of paper in his hand, flanked by two soldiers. "Gentlemen, I've come to give you today's timetable. It's eight o'clock now. The first fight will be at ten. It's you, Flavius, so get ready."

All eyes turned to the short-tempered gladiator, who hadn't spoken a word to anyone for days. Sitting on his mattress with his knees drawn up to his chest, he acted as if none of this concerned him.

"You'll fight another novice. Good luck. Your victory will encourage all the others. Is there anything you want to say to us?"

Flavius didn't move a muscle.

"Right," Myricus went on. "I've given the youngest of you the privilege of fighting this morning. I know the waiting is hard to bear. Rusticus, you'll fight second, and Milos third. You're fighting a champion, Rusticus. As you know, that's the best-case scenario."

"The best . . . what?" muttered the young horseman, his jaw trembling. Milos thought his friend was about to throw up.

"It gives you the best chance of winning," Myricus

explained, remembering who he was talking to. "When a novice fights a champion, he very often wins, remember?"

"I remember. So I'll win, will I?"

"I'm sure you will, Rusticus. Just avoid looking him in the eye. His stare is stronger than yours."

"So I don't look at him, right?"

The trainer didn't bother to reply, but went on. "Milos, you're to fight a premier. I saw him this morning. He's a tall man. Watch out for his long reach. And remember, let him think you're right-handed until the last moment and then change your sword hand as you attack. Don't forget! One last piece of advice: don't turn all soft when you see him. Anything you want to say?"

Milos shook his head and heard no more of what Myricus was saying. Turn soft? Why would he do that? He lost track of the names of the others who were going to fight. Rubbing the palms of his hands together, he found they were damp. Next moment the shattering knowledge struck him that he was about to fight to the death. He thought he had known it for months, but he realized he had only just understood. He remembered what Myricus had said. "Right to the end, you think something will happen to prevent the fight—you won't really have to go into the arena." It was true. In spite of himself he had been living in that impossible dream, and now the facts struck him in the face. He felt overwhelmingly tired, unable to fight a kitten. Would he even have the strength to raise his sword?

Around nine o'clock they were brought pots of coffee and some bread. Basil didn't touch either. From being pale, his face had turned green. Milos made himself chew slowly and finish his breakfast. *I have to eat,* he told himself without believing it. *I have to eat to keep my strength up.*

Myricus had gone away again. The painful wait began. Flavius, deep in gloomy thoughts, was as still as a statue. Near him, Delicatus was working hard to keep a sardonic, mocking smile on his face. At the far end of the room, Caius, emaciated as ever, was darting glances at the others from his black eyes. For a moment his mad gaze met Milos's, and the two of them defied each other in silence.

They all felt relieved when the swords were brought in. Picking up his, Milos felt better. He stroked the handle, then the hilt, and ran his fingers over the shining blade. Several men rose to their feet, took off their shirts and sandals, and began their routine exercises: jogging with their swords in their hands, jumping, rolling over on the ground, taking evasive action, leaping forward. Some got together in pairs to practice.

"Come on, Basil," said Milos. "You have to warm up."

"I can't," moaned the boy, curled up under his blanket. "I have a stomachache. Any moment now . . ."

"No, Basil! Don't let yourself go! This isn't the right moment. Come on out."

The young horse-man's long head slowly emerged, and Milos saw that the soup wasn't the only reason for his friend's sorry state. His eyes were full of terror, and he was trembling all over.

"Right, Basil, I'll leave you there for a bit, but you must get up as soon as Flavius has gone—will you?"

"If I can."

Milos mingled with the others and put his mind to the movements he had automatically carried out thousands of times during training. They all suddenly froze when the door opened and two soldiers came in. The sound of the arena came to their ears, both distant and menacing: the muted growl of a monster lying in wait somewhere out there. They were going to be delivered up to it. Myricus came in too, and his voice rang out. "Flavius!"

The gladiator, bare-chested and gleaming with sweat, walked slowly toward the door, eyes fixed. He was clenching his jaw; his hard features expressed nothing but pure hatred. His companions felt it and flinched as he passed them.

As soon as the door was closed again, Milos flung himself on Basil and shook him by the shoulders. "Basil! Come on!"

When his friend didn't move, he raised him from the floor, put him down on his feet, and put his sword in his right hand. "Come on, Basil, fight!"

The unhappy boy stood there before him, a pitiful sight, arms dangling, clearly sick at heart.

"Fight!" Milos encouraged him, slapping him on the arms and thighs with the flat blade of his sword to provoke him.

The young horse-man didn't react. However, he raised his sword, making Milos think he was about to join in the action. Next moment he dropped it on the ground and ran full tilt for a corner of the room, where he brought up the contents of his stomach, bent double by the spasms.

A scornful and unpleasant laugh from Delicatus wasn't echoed by anyone else. Basil ignored it too. He went back toward Milos, wiping his mouth on his forearm, and smiled faintly at his friend. "That's better!"

There was a little color in his cheeks again. He took off his shirt, and they exchanged a dozen blows. His friend's fencing struck Milos as very inconsistent.

"Wake up, for God's sake!" he shouted. "Don't you realize you'll be fighting for real in a few seconds?"

He felt like flinging himself on Basil to hurt him, even wound him if he had to, just to get him to react and defend himself. He was making up his mind to do it when the door opened again. Myricus came in followed by the two soldiers.

"Rusticus!"

The young horse-man stared at him, panting. "Is it my turn?"

"Yes. Come on!"

"What about Flavius?" someone asked.

"Flavius is dead," the trainer replied briefly.

Since Basil still made no move, the two soldiers took a step forward and impelled him toward the doorway with the butts of their guns. He started slowly walking. His chin was trembling like a child about to burst into tears.

"I don't look at him, right?" he asked Myricus.

"No, don't meet his eyes."

Milos went over to give him a hug, but Basil pushed him gently away. "Don't worry. I don't care about this champion. They don't need to know I'm scared. I'll be back. I'm not like Flavius."

The wait was unbearable. The worst of it was being unable to hear anything or imagine what was going on. Milos couldn't go on warming up. He crouched down by a wall and hid his face in his hands. *Basil, my companion through all this, don't leave me alone! Don't die! Please come back!*

It went on for a long time. Other gladiators were exchanging fast and furious blows around him. The air vibrated with the clash of their blades. There was a brief respite in which he thought he heard a muted roar from the arena in the distance. What was going on there? His heart was racing. This fight was going on for an eternity, much longer than Flavius's fight, anyway. What did that mean?

When the door opened again, hinges squealing, he didn't dare to raise his head. All he heard was the sound of feet on the concrete, then Basil's faint voice: "I got him."

The young horse-man walked in, flanked by Myricus and Fulgur. He was in shock.

"I got him," he repeated, as if to convince himself. But his triumph was a joyless one. Thick blood was seeping from a wound in his side. He dropped the reddened sword from his hand and murmured, "He was going to kill me . . . had to defend myself . . ."

"He fought bravely and he won!" Myricus announced. "The rest of you follow his example!"

Fulgur, delighted to have a winner who was also wounded on his hands, was already leading Basil away. "Follow me to the infirmary. I'll fix that for you."

Basil started moving, right hand holding the edges of his wound together. At the door, he turned and looked at Milos. There was no triumph in his eyes, only an expression of profound sadness and disgust at what he had just done.

"Good luck, friend!" he said. "See you soon. . . . Don't let them get you, right?"

"See you soon," Milos managed to say. The words stuck in his throat.

Myricus went off too, recommending that he should not stand about motionless now. There were two fights between gladiators from the other camps before his, he said. Milos immediately began his exercises, but he noticed, with a sense of panic, that fear was changing all his perceptions: the weight of his sword, the length of his arm, the speed of his legs. It was as if he had suddenly lost control of his body. When he ran, he seemed slow; when he started a movement, it seemed uncertain.

"I can't feel anything," he groaned, close to panic.

"It's normal," said a voice close to him. "It's always like that before you go in. Try a bout with me."

He recognized Messor standing in front of him, offering to act as his partner. The two of them had never exchanged a word before this day.

"Thanks," said Milos gratefully.

Their few sallies brought him out of his lethargy, and when Myricus appeared at the door again with the two soldiers, he had regained a little confidence.

"Milos!" called the trainer, without any apparent emotion.

As he went out, Milos felt a need to salute one of his companions. Since Basil wasn't there anymore, he chose Messor, who had shared these last few moments with him. He went up to the man and shook hands.

"See you later, my boy, and good luck," growled the gladiator.

In the corridor, Myricus repeated the same advice as before. "He's a tall man. Watch out for his long reach. And remember, let him think you're right-handed until the last moment. Don't forget!"

Milos got it, but his trainer's words were distant and unreal. Twice he almost fainted, but his legs went on carrying him and did not give way.

The four men followed the corridor and came out under the rising tiers of seats. Voices and the sound of the spectators' feet mingled above their heads.

The planks were groaning under the weight of the audience. A horn blew three long, low notes. Milos realized that they were announcing his arrival. The two soldiers stopped at a gate, and a guard opened it to leave the way clear. Myricus gently pushed Milos in the back, and the young man walked into the arena.

The violence of the shock left him reeling. All at once thousands of eyes were on him, and the bright beam of the floodlights on the yellow sand was dazzling. It's like being born, he thought. Babies must feel this violence when they're pushed out of their mothers to begin life.

Everything he had been told was true. The arena here was similar to the arena in the training camp, and so was the consistency of the sand underfoot. However, nothing else was the same. Here the space rose on and on upward: beyond the palisades, rows of seats wound their way toward the roof, coiling like a gigantic shell, and they were crammed with people. Myricus led him to the grandstand, which was occupied by a dozen Phalangists in overcoats. Among these men sitting in the best seats he immediately recognized the bearded, red-headed giant he had seen at the boarding school several months ago: Van Vlyck!

He saw himself again lying flat in the school loft, Helen beside him — two accomplices. He remembered her laugh, the touch of his shoulder against hers, the sound of her breathing so close to him, and the emotion he had felt at that moment. Could such sweetness really have existed? Was that really him? He had felt invincible at the time—so long ago! Now the barbarians had him in their clutches, and he would have to fight to the death for them—for their pleasure and for his survival. And to see Helen again. She was waiting somewhere; he was sure of it. For her sake he must forget everything he had believed in all his life: the rules of fair play in sport, respect for your opponent. He must be nothing now but fury and the desire to kill.

Burning sweat ran into his eyes, blinding him. He passed his hand over his face.

"Milos!" announced Myricus, to the governmental representatives. "Novice." And he named the camp they had come from.

A small, thin man sitting next to Van Vlyck narrowed his eyes. "Milos Ferenzy?"

Milos nodded.

"Then let's see how you go about killing people," said the man, laughing.

Milos didn't move a muscle. Myricus took his arm and led him to the other side of the arena.

"Mind his reach. Use your right hand at first," he repeated one last time before walking away.

The gate opposite opened, and Milos saw his opponent appear. He was a tall, thin man with his skull shaved, followed by his trainer, who was a head shorter. The two of them made for the grandstand in their own turn. At the distance now between them, Milos couldn't hear the name of the man he was to fight or the camp he came from.

Silence suddenly fell when there was no one in the arena but the two gladiators facing each other. About sixty feet separated them. Milos took a few steps toward the other man, who imitated him. He had the bent shoulders of men who are too tall; his chest was flabby and wrinkled, covered with white hairs. His sword was held at the end of an arm that seemed to go on forever; there was gray stubble on his hollow cheeks. Milos put his age at over sixty. There had been no one of that age in the camp where he himself had trained. *He's a grandfather,* he thought, *I can't fight him!* The full sense of what Myricus had said hit him now. *Don't turn all soft.*

When there was no more than fifteen feet between them, they made the same movement: both bent their knees and reached out the arms holding their swords. Milos resisted the pressing temptation to shift his weapon to his good hand. They stayed watching each other like that, hardly moving.

A few whistles came from the seats, then shouts of "Go on! Attack!," followed by grotesque encouraging noises as if they were inciting animals to fight.

They can't wait to see our blood flow, thought Milos with disgust. *They sit there safe in their seats, sure that nothing can hurt them. Is there a single man among them who'd have the courage to jump the palisade and come down to fight on this sand? No, they're all cowards! They don't deserve me to give my life up for them.*

He was less than ten feet from his opponent now.

The other man's forehead was deeply lined, and he read in his eyes the same fear that he himself felt. He made himself ignore it. He had to hate this man, not feel sorry for him. He breathed out noisily through his nose, made his glance steely, clutched his sword so firmly that it hurt, and took one more step. The other man chose that moment to lunge forward suddenly like a fencer. His blade stung Milos's bare ankle, and then he broke away at once. Milos cried out with pain and saw blood cover his foot, while applause and laughter greeted this unusual move. The vague pity that Milos had felt a moment before instantly vanished. This thin, elderly man was here to kill him, and he'd do it at the first chance without any scruples. He realized he couldn't let his guard down.

As the other man came toward him again, he suddenly shifted his sword to his left hand and began moving rapidly with small, sideways steps, making his adversary turn his weaker side to him. The man seemed disconcerted for a few moments and then lunged forward again, once, twice, again and again, always thrusting at Milos's legs or feet. *You think you'll get me like that?* thought Milos, amused, recovering a competitive wrestler's reflexes. *You're planning to attack me low down there ten times, make me lean forward ten times to protect my legs, and the eleventh time you'll attack from above and open up my chest, right? Come on, then. I'm ready for you . . .*

They went on with their deadly dance like this, each sticking to his strategy. The old man kept attacking low down by Milos's feet. Milos hopped and skipped around him. The fight hadn't been going on long, but there was such tension between them that they were both already breathless and dripping with sweat.

Attack from above! Milos begged, for his own sake. His foot was burning, leaving a red trail in the sand at every step he took. *Please, attack me from above. Just once. Look, I'm leaning over, offering you my chest. Come on, don't hesitate.*

It worked. The old gladiator suddenly rushed forward, his sword horizontal at the end of his long arm. He uttered a piercing cry, more of despair than rage. Milos was ready for him. He dodged but stumbled and fell on his side. The other man was thrown off balance himself by the failure of his attacking move. Now he too was lying on the ground, face in the sand. Milos was quicker to get to his feet: he was standing up in a fraction of a second, and then he leaped. He smashed his knee into the small of his slower adversary's pale, sweating back, and with his elbow raised in the air he set the point of his sword to the wrinkled neck.

With his free hand, he immobilized the man's head, and his lower body held his opponent's leg trapped. But there was no need for that now. The old man was a pitiful sight, gasping for breath, saliva running from his twisted mouth and mingling with the sand. A faint wail rose from his lips. The crowd had been roaring; now it was waiting for the human sacrifice it had come to see. For a few brief seconds, Milos felt a violent sensation of delight: *I've won!* But it was instantly dispelled by a terrible feeling: he was reliving a nightmare. Here he was once more, against his own will, master of the fate of another human being who was at his mercy.

A few months earlier, in the cold and solitude of the mountains, he had brought himself to do that terrible thing to save Helen, trembling with fear and cold there behind the rock, and to protect their other two friends who had escaped. Now he had to kill to save himself, and it was happening under the dazzling beam of floodlights, before the eyes of spectators whose excitement made them rise from their seats to see better, row after row of them. What did they want to watch? His humiliation? Did they want to see him kill an old man who could be his grandfather?

He knew he couldn't give them the death they wanted. How could he push his blade farther into a defeated man's body? How could he go on living after that? He'd thought he could do it in self-defense, to save himself. But this was nothing short of murder. He wasn't going to give them that pleasure. He would relax his hold, stand up, and then what was bound to happen would happen. The old man would be declared the winner. As for him, he would be handed over unarmed to a gladiator, then to two at once, then three if necessary, and he would die at their hands. *We'll see*, he thought. *We'll see.*

The crowd was shouting now, yelling words he

didn't understand. He leaned over his opponent again, almost lying on him.

"What are you doing?" the old man groaned. "Kill me. And save yourself. You're young."

"I can't do it," said Milos.

He raised his sword—the point had traced a bleeding scratch shaped like a comma on the man's old neck—threw it six feet away from him, knelt down, and waited. Go on, do whatever you want.

At that moment, instead of the protests he expected, a strange silence fell, as if preceding some terrible event like an earthquake. The dull sound of a heavy impact shook the arena. Mouths opened, ears were strained, and then came the second impact, just as heavy and with just as deep a sound. The Phalange leaders got to their feet and fled headlong from the grandstand. Other spectators did the same. Uneasiness was spreading to all the tiers of seats.

The old man, pale-faced, had gotten to his knees beside Milos. "What's going on?"

But no one was taking any notice of them.

"They're breaking down the gate!" a voice shouted.

It was the signal for panic. People began running in all directions among the rows, jostling each other as they looked for a concealed exit.

Who were "they"? Who was breaking down the gate? Milos, kept in ignorance of the outside world for months, could hardly believe it. And yet he had to admit the evidence of his eyes: the Phalangists had gone, a few baffled soldiers were waiting for

orders that didn't come, and the audience was trying to leave the arena in a mad stampede. Who but
the Resistance could have set off such a headlong
flight?

At the moment when Milos and the old man
got to their feet again, hearts beating wildly, the
gates on both sides of the arena opened and the
gladiators, liberated from their cells, surged in with
a terrifying noise, brandishing their swords in the
air. They invaded the arena and attacked the palisades. Their fierce faces and wild cries spread terror
among the frightened audience.

"Basil!" Milos called, looking for his friend among
the crowd of gladiators. Basil wouldn't know he'd
survived his fight, and he had to reassure him. Then
he remembered that Basil had been wounded and
was bleeding from his side. It might be a serious
injury. Where could he find the "infirmary" that
Fulgur had mentioned? It must be somewhere close
to the cells. He made his way against the human
tide. He passed through the gateway and underneath the stands—which were shaking with the
turmoil of the audience trying to get out—went
back along the corridor, and soon reached the large
cell where he and his companions had spent the
night. It was empty. Nothing was left lying on the
floor among the straw mattresses but the shirt and
sandals that had belonged to Flavius, so recently
dead in the arena, and his own. He had survived.
He put them on and went out.

"Basil!" he called.

This time he turned right, opening all the doors he came to as he passed. Right at the end of the corridor a steep, worm-eaten wooden staircase led up through an open trapdoor to the story above. He dropped his sword and climbed the stairs.

"Are you there, Basil?"

He put his head up through the trapdoor to inspect the room. It was empty, lit very faintly by a tiny opening in the adobe wall. He went down the stairs again and as he turned, he saw Caius barring his way, sword in hand. His own sword had landed farther away, out of his reach.

"Well, cat, not spitting anymore now?"

Milos froze.

"Caius, don't! Stop that. We're free now."

The other man wasn't listening. He advanced, madness in his eyes, crouching with knees bent and arms apart, ready to spring. He was gripping his sword so hard that his knuckles were white.

"I'll teach you to scratch, you bastard!" he hissed through his teeth. The scars on his hate-filled face seemed uglier than ever, forming a pattern of purplish lines.

"At least give me my sword!" asked Milos, careful not to make any sudden move. "I'm a gladiator like you! I have a right to defend myself. Give me my sword—do you hear, Caius?"

There was no reply.

"Caius," Milos breathed. "Please! This is so stupid! We're free now. Do you realize? We're free. And I'm not a cat, you know—I'm not a cat."

Caius didn't hear him. No words could touch him in his delirium. And Milos saw that he was in deadly danger. He shouted at the top of his voice. "Help! Someone help me!"

There was no reply. The corridor was too narrow for him to escape that way without coming close to Caius, who as he saw was about to attack him any moment. Without thinking anymore, he leaped back to the stairs behind him and climbed them, using both his hands and his legs. Two steps collapsed under his weight. Once at the top, he found himself up against the wall. Caius had already joined him there.

And the dreadful confrontation began again, but in the half-light this time. Milos tried in vain to find words that would halt the madman in his tracks. He could see nothing of him now but a dark shape six feet away. They stood like that for a few seconds, breathing heavily.

And suddenly, from a furtive movement, from a change in the speed of his opponent's breathing, Milos guessed that Caius was about to fling himself on him and strike him down. He got in first, lunging forward at the other man.

It all happened very fast.

The blade went into his stomach with a long, cold, burning pain. It was the only blow that either of them struck.

Dazed, Milos fell to his knees.

When he recovered consciousness, he was alone. In the distance, the thudding on the entrance doors to the arena was still echoing through the building. He was lying on his side, curled up. His head lay on the damp, cool ground. A little way off, a gray mouse was looking at him gently. He felt like stroking its soft fur. The pretty agate of its black eyes shone behind its twitching whiskers. It wasn't afraid of him. *The mouse can see I'm not a cat.* He tried to move; his body wouldn't obey him. He wanted to call out, but he was afraid that his own cries might tear him apart and kill him. He felt as frail as a flame in the wind. The least breath of air would blow him out.

His stomach was sticky with blood. *My life is flowing out of it,* he said to himself, pressing both hands to the wound. "Help," he moaned. "I don't want to die." His tears fell to the ground and left a muddy little trail there. The mouse came closer with tiny steps, hesitated for a moment, and snuggled close to his cheek. *You're not entirely alone,* it seemed to be saying. *I'm not much, but I'm here.*

Then the pictures began to come.

First he saw Bartolomeo on the bridge, hugging him in his long arms and then striding away. "We'll see each other soon, Milos! We'll meet again somewhere else. We'll all meet again, the living and the dead."

"Why did you let me down, Bart?" he asked.

The tall young man didn't reply. He simply knelt

beside Milos and smiled at him, friendship in his eyes.

Basil came too. His faithful, rough-hewn face was a good sight. He stammered several clumsy, reassuring words. "Don't you worry, friend . . . I'm all right. Look!" And he showed Milos his own wound, healed.

Then other faces came. A wrestling coach from the past. "No strangling, boys, I repeat, no strangling." Milos saw himself, very young, rolling over and over on a mat in the gym. Other faces, forgotten, came back from the past: small companions of his in the orphanage offering to swap marbles; friends from the boarding school slapping him on the back. "All right, Milos?" they cheerfully asked. "Good to see you again!" His consoler let them in, she told them to sit down, scolded those who made too much noise. She wanted to know if anyone was hungry, and went to make something to eat. Milos wondered how she would be able to do any cooking, how all these people could fit into this tiny room, and it made him laugh.

And then at last there was Helen. She seemed to be freezing under the hood of her school coat. Snow was falling, white and soft, on her shoulders. She knelt beside him too, and took his face between her icy hands. "Don't go, Milos," she said. "Don't go away, my love." He looked into the deep eyes of the young woman leaning over him, he saw her round cheeks, and he thought there was no one

377

more beautiful in the world. "I won't go away," he wanted to say, but his lips were made of stone. So he told her, with his heart alone: *I won't go away, my love. I'll stay with you. I promise.*

And then all of them who had been leaning over him — Bartolomeo, Basil, the friends he had known through his life, Helen, who had brightened that brief life with such a dazzling light — they all gently moved aside and turned to the doorway, where a man and a woman stood, young and elegantly clothed. The pretty woman wore a spring dress and a flowered hat. The man was tall and strong, with the same laughing eyes as Milos. Although his own eyes were already closing, Milos smiled at them both, and they came to kneel beside him at once. The woman passed her hands over his shaven head, caressing him. "What happened to your hair, my darling?" she asked. The man, a little way behind her, nodded and looked at him with intense pride. There was no uneasiness on their faces. Far from it: they seemed as confident as if seeing someone they loved after a long absence, knowing they would be able to live happily together for always.

"Father," murmured Milos. "Mother. Have you found me?"

"Hush," said the woman, putting her forefinger to her mouth.

And so did the man. "Hush," he said.

So Milos became a good little boy again. He curled up in a ball to keep all this warmth and love inside his body and to take it with him wherever he was bound.

And then he closed his eyes and let himself go.

The gray mouse scurried up and down his leg a little longer, over his back, up to his shoulder. It went back to rub against his face. Not moving now, it stayed there for a few minutes, its soft nose quivering. It was waiting for a sign of life, but there was none. Suddenly, in the distance, came an impact stronger than the others, followed by an ominous crack. The beam barring the gate had just given way. Frightened, the mouse scuttled over to the wall and disappeared down a hole.

THE ROYAL BRIDGE

Milena sat down on a rock and took off her boots to massage her sore feet. She did that every time they stopped to rest. Gerlinda, the young horse-girl who had called her as beautiful as a princess and never left her side, was already busy lighting a small fire to boil some water.

"Will you sing me something if I make you a mug of tea?" she asked.

Milena smiled. Any excuse would do to get her to sing. She had only to begin, without even raising her voice much, for people to gather around her. And if they knew the tune, they would sing along.

They had started out on the long march to the capital two days ago, and it reminded her of her travels with Bart when they had run away in the autumn. She remembered their elation as they talked the situation over in the immensity of the bare mountains. But she also remembered their terrible uncertainty, their fear of what the next day might bring. Now, on the contrary, she felt that nothing could prevent them from reaching their journey's end, surrounded as they were by the friendly horsemen with the persistent odor of their wool and corduroy clothing. The natural strength of these people, their kindness, and their peaceable innocence were infectious. They were reassuring; they made you feel confident for no real reason. Milena had felt the same with her consoler, Martha, during her years at the boarding school, but there was only one Martha. Here she had the impression of a huge, multiple, ever-changing body of people, an irresistible force.

As they went on toward the capital, the numbers marching with them grew. Hundreds and then thousands of men, women, and children had rallied to them in small groups making their way through the countryside. Coming down from the hills and out of the woods and fields, they joined in human streams that swelled into rivers. The doors of houses were opened to them as they passed by. They were offered food, their bags were refilled, they slept overnight in barns.

Gerlinda came over with a mug of steaming tea for Milena.

"Now, what about my song?"

"All right, but only for you. I don't feel like singing for an audience of fifty. Come closer."

A smile lit up the young horse-girl's blunt face,

and she leaned her ear close to Milena's mouth. Milena began quietly:

"Blow the wind southerly, southerly, southerly . . ."

But as others came over to hear the song, she rose abruptly, mug in hand. "No, I've finished now! Another time . . . this evening!"

She put her boots on and went to join Bartolomeo and Dora, who were sitting a little way off wrapped in their winter coats. Their breath was escaping from their mouths in little blue clouds. *The two people I love most in the world,* she thought as she went over to them. *I only need Helen and Martha here as well and the magic circle would be complete.*

"I'm sure Jahn and Faber will have reached the bridge by now," Bart was saying, sounding impatient. "I should have stayed with them."

"They'll send for you if they need you — they promised they would," Dora replied.

"Yes, I just hope we don't arrive too late. The winter fights in the arena begin tomorrow morning. Milos may not be due to fight on the first day, but we don't know. We have to get into the city fast."

Milena nestled against him. "We must trust the others. We'll be there tomorrow, after all."

"Yes. The Phalange will never dare fire on us. We're unarmed, and there are women and children with us — they won't be able to do it."

"No, they won't," Milena comforted him. "And

you'll soon see Milos again. You've always told me he had a real talent for survival."

"Yes, so I did. And a talent for happiness too. More so than me."

"Happiness?" said Dora, joking. "Is there such a thing? It must be so boring!"

They kept close together as they went on along narrow paths and over bad roads during the hours that followed. Gerlinda never left Milena "in case she got lost." Who was leading their advance? It was impossible to say. They were carried along on the tide. As evening fell, they reached the hills above the city and were amazed to see that the hillsides were teeming with people as far as the eye could see.

They knew that the population had rallied to the Resistance, but the sight of that great crowd surpassed their wildest hopes. How could anyone for a second imagine that the Phalange might be able to resist such a force? A rumor was soon circulating that they would enter the capital at dawn, and until then they must wait and keep warm. Cries of joy were heard, as if the battle were already won. Gerlinda jumped up and down and hugged Milena.

"Are you so pleased with the prospect of a cold night in the open?" Milena asked in surprise. "We'll all be frozen before sunrise!"

Gerlinda looked at her blankly and then said simply, "Oh no! People will help us."

She was right, and the night that had promised to be so uncomfortable was a miraculous experience. Within a very short time firewood was found, fires were crackling, and red flames were shooting up into the dark sky. Had Milena feared the cold? She often had to insist on leaving her place close to the fire; people took turns there in an orderly fashion. Had she been afraid they would go hungry? If anything, there was too much to eat! Every bag heaved with loaves of bread, ham, pâté, apples, wine, chocolate! As soon as she sat down, someone would come to kneel behind her and hug her to warm her up. The first time it happened, she thought it was Bartolomeo or Dora or Gerlinda. Who else would venture to take such a liberty? But it was a horse-woman she had never seen before. In her own turn, Milena warmed up people she didn't know and soon realized that it was as sweet to give as to receive.

At dawn they were all numb, stupefied by drowsiness, tramping up and down on the ground in an attempt to warm their feet up, but they had a sense of having survived together, having reached their journey's end, and they felt that something great lay ahead. Thin plumes of smoke were still rising from fires that hadn't been entirely extinguished. Yesterday's clouds had lifted, and in the biting cold they saw the other hills also covered by thousands of shapes, with figures already on the march on the plain below, and in the distance the sparkling ribbon of the river.

The crowd began to move slowly, and it was good to be advancing in company again. Someone began humming:

In my basket,
In my basket, I have no cherries,
My dear prince.
I have no crimson cherries,
I have no almonds, no. . . .

And everyone took up the song, the tall horsemen and all the others, whether they could sing in tune or not.

"I have no pretty kerchiefs,
No embroidered kerchiefs,
I have no beads, no.
No more grief and pain, my love,
No more grief and pain. . . ."

They all repeated it except for Milena. Their voices rose around her—ordinary, clumsy, hesitant, but all vibrating with fervor and certainty.

"Aren't you singing?" asked Gerlinda.

"No," she replied, with a lump in her throat. "I'm listening for once. I have a right to listen too."

A horse-child of about twelve, short and sturdy, red-faced and breathless with running, suddenly plucked Bartolomeo's sleeve. "Mr. Jahn wants you. With your lady."

"With my lady?"

"Yes, your lady Milena."

"Where's Mr. Jahn?"

"At the bridge. I'll take you."

"I'm coming too!" said Dora, and without waiting for any reply, she fell into step with them.

"And me!" cried Gerlinda, starting to follow.

First they had to make way through the crowd, using their elbows and shoulders. Then the child suddenly went off to the left at a tangent, and after a little way they found themselves miraculously alone, going down a sloping path.

"I see you know some shortcuts!" called Bart.

"Yes," said the child. He was going ahead of them, kicking pebbles out of his way. "I live here!"

"Where?" asked Milena. She couldn't see a house anywhere near.

The child ignored this question and quickened his pace. They were at the bottom of the hill now, skirting coppices that sparkled with frost. The frozen grass crunched under their feet.

"Wait for me!" called Dora, already lagging behind with Gerlinda. "That lad must be wearing seven-league boots!"

But the small messenger didn't turn. He forged straight ahead at high speed. From behind, he now looked light and graceful, as if he had grown taller. Soon Milena was out of breath herself.

"I can't go on at this pace!" she told Bart. "I'll catch up with you down there. You go ahead!"

The young man made off in pursuit of the child, who ran nimbly on as if airborne. He was almost level with the boy in a few strides. "Not so fast! We can't keep up with you."

As the sky turned pink and blue in the east, the sharp sound of their footsteps echoed over a long distance like a crackling fire. The two figures, one tall and one shorter, hurried on their way, leaping down slopes and over ditches. Bartolomeo had never in his life covered so much space in such a short time. The cold morning air whistled around his ears. He was stunned by the noise of his own breathing.

"Is it much farther?" he asked after a while, intoxicated with emotion.

"No," said the child, suddenly stopping. "We're here!"

He stood motionless, hands on his hips, and there was something angelic about his ingenuous face. Bart was astonished to see that the boy was hardly out of breath and, above all, that he looked so changed from when they had first seen him. He might have been a different child.

"Incredible!" said Bart, disconcerted. "You must be some kind of magician!"

"Yes," replied the child, and he pointed to a tumulus on their left. "Climb up there! I'm not allowed to go any farther."

Rather perturbed, Bart began clambering up the mound on all fours. He turned when he was halfway up, and saw that there was no one else near him. He looked in vain for his strange little guide and then, sure that the child had disappeared, he went on climbing. When he reached the top of the tall mound, he found himself less than a hundred yards from the entrance to the Royal Bridge. And what he saw there made him freeze with horror.

On his side of the river a staunch troop of horsemen, armed with pikes and clubs, was trying to cross the river. A dense cloud of vapor hovered in the air above the crowd. On the opposite bank, invisible in a hundred covered trucks parked at an angle to the bridge, soldiers armed with guns were firing to prevent them from crossing. The bridge was littered with about a hundred large bodies, lying dead. But the worst of it was that the horsemen in the front line were doing all they could to mount an assault, ignoring the bullets decimating them. Bart saw two young men running forward together, brandishing clubs. They hadn't reached the middle of the bridge before shots rang out. One of them was hit in the chest, performed a grotesque little dance, flung his arms in the air, and fell headfirst. The other, wounded in the leg, went limping on for ten more yards before he too was shot down. As he fell, he furiously threw his club toward the soldier who had just fired the shot that killed him.

"Stop!" shouted Bart, horrified.

But a compact formation of ten more horse-men was already going into the attack. They held all kinds of objects in front of them as makeshift shields: wooden planks, pieces of rusty sheet metal. In spite of their strength and energy they didn't get much farther than their comrades. A murderous burst of firing mowed them down. Only two of them, gigantic figures, were left on their feet. They staggered as far as the first truck and seized its undercarriage to tip it over. The soldiers must have let them get as far as that to amuse themselves, because it took only the two shots that now rang out to finish the unfortunate men off.

"Stop!" shouted Bart, and he raced toward the bridge.

He was immediately drowned in a sea of arms, backs, and powerful torsos, but it was far from the soothing sensation he had felt a few days earlier when he and Milena walked through the crowd of horse-men, with Gerlinda as their guide. This time anger distorted the heavy faces that were usually so tranquil. Tears of rage were running down their cheeks.

"Jahn!" Bart shouted. "Anyone know where Mr. Jahn is?"

"Here!" roared a voice, and the huge figure of Jocelin suddenly appeared in front of him, an expression of dismay on his face. "Quick! He wants to see you!"

In spite of the cold, Jahn was bathed in sweat. He took Bartolomeo by the collar of his coat and shook him. "Stop them, Casal, for God's sake! They won't listen to me anymore! They won't listen to anyone!"

"What about Faber?"

"Faber wanted to go and speak with the soldiers. He was shot down. That maddened them! They're all going to get themselves killed!"

Bart left the stout man and shouldered his way through the crowd toward the bridge. The closer he came, the denser the crowd of bodies. He just managed to get through, and when he was finally on the other side of them, he realized that the horse-men were preparing for a mass attack. A bearded young man in shirtsleeves, with Herculean shoulders that reminded him of Faber, had appointed himself their leader, and he was haranguing his men.

"All together this time!" he urged them. "We'll show 'em what we're made of!"

Bartolomeo planted himself in front of the man and spoke sharply. "Shut your mouth! You don't know what you're saying!"

Although he was much less broad than the other man, he was almost as tall, and his voice echoed forcefully. "Don't do it!" he went on, turning back to the horse-men as they prepared to charge. "Don't cross the bridge! They'll shoot you down one by one! They're just waiting to pick you off!"

Anyone else in Bart's place would have been swept aside by the furious giants, but his name was Casal—and they listened to him.

"They killed Faber!" cried a high voice.

"And they'll kill you too if you charge them," replied Bart. "You're not cattle going to the slaughter!"

"I don't care if they kill me!" said the last speaker, a boy of hardly sixteen.

"I forbid you to go any farther!" thundered Bartolomeo. His black eyes were darting flames as he raised his fist in front of the lad's face.

"If your father was here—" someone else began.

"My father would tell you exactly the same!" Bartolomeo cut him short. "I speak as he would!"

As the fighting horse-men saw his determination, doubt crept into their ranks.

"I know you're brave. I know you are ready to die," Bart went on. "But what's the use of that, just to give them the satisfaction of killing you? What's the use of it? I ask you."

"So what do we do, then?" asked one of the men. "We're not retreating!"

"And we're not leaving our comrades dead on the bridge!" added another.

They had a good point. Looking beyond their furious faces, Bartolomeo saw the vast crowd waiting farther off, unaware of the drama being played out here on the bridge. The light of dawn, low in the sky, now showed massed throngs all the way to the hills on the horizon. And he looked at the other side of the river. Behind the lines of gray-green trucks where the enemy was concealed, implacable and silent, the city seemed to be holding its breath. He had to admit that he had been wrong, just as Jahn, Lando, Faber, and all the others had been wrong: the soldiers had indeed opened fire. They had obeyed orders, ruthlessly shooting down those poor souls armed only with clubs.

What could he say now to men who had just seen a friend, a father, a brother fall dead before their eyes? And Faber, their much-loved leader! Bart had succeeded in keeping them from rushing to their doom for the moment, and he had managed to save the lives of a few of them, but he wouldn't be able to contain their despair and fury much longer.

"Come on!" shouted the young man who was so keen to lead an attack. "Let's charge them!"

"No one move!" shouted Bart. "I order you not to move! Leave this to me!"

And without knowing just what he hoped for, he started over the bridge himself, walking straight down the middle of it. He moved a dozen paces.

"What are you doing, Bart?" someone called behind him. "Come back!"

He recognized Jahn's voice but did not turn.

There was no sign of life on the other side of the river. They'd wait until he was halfway over the bridge before they fired. He'd be a better target there, closer, easily visible. He went another few feet. What did he want to do? He didn't know.

Then he remembered what Jahn had said about his father, and the words began dancing around in his head: "*I often wonder if he wasn't actually looking for a chance to die in his prime. . . . There was a great melancholy in him. . . . I don't know where it came from. . . .*"

He shuddered, afraid of detecting the same

sinister temptation in himself. Did he, Bartolomeo, have the same melancholy in his heart? The same profound sadness, so that putting an end to his life was almost a seductive idea? He went on walking straight ahead, stumbled on a uneven paving stone, walked around the distorted body of the young horse-man who had thrown himself into the attack beside his friend, and went another five yards. His black scarf was streaming out in the cold morning wind. From where he was now, he could no longer hear the cries of the horse-men or the sound of the great crowd behind them. All that came to his ears was the peaceful murmuring of the river. *I'll walk to the end of it,* he told himself. *There's nothing else I can do. I'll walk it to the end.*

And suddenly Milena was by his side.

"Milena!" he exclaimed, stupefied, seizing her by the shoulders. "Get away from here!"

She shook her bare head. Her short blond hair stood out like a halo around it.

"No, I won't! We'll cross the bridge together. Come on."

She took his arm and led him slowly on, looking serene, her back very straight.

"They'll fire on us, Milena. You know they will."

"On you perhaps, but not on me."

"They're capable of it! Look, they fired on boys of thirteen! We're walking over their bodies."

"They won't fire on me, Bart. They won't fire on Milena Bach. I'm not hiding anymore. Let them see who I am! Let them take a good look!"

For a moment Bartolomeo wondered whether she had gone out of her mind. He stopped her by force. "Milena, listen to me! What are you hoping for? Do you want to be a martyr? Martyrs don't sing, you know."

He stroked her cheek. It was soft and icy.

"No one will dare order them to fire on me, Bart. No one!"

"Milena, they set the dog-men on your mother fifteen years ago! Have you forgotten that?"

She gazed deep into his eyes, her own blue and burning. "They did it because they were up in the mountains with no one to see! My mother died all alone in the darkness of night, understand? She can't even have seen the teeth that tore her to pieces. We're in broad daylight here, Bart. Look around you! See all these thousands of people! They're watching. Their eyes will protect us!"

Bartolomeo turned and saw the troop of horsemen starting over the bridge after them. But their anger had died down, for now at least, and they were advancing slowly and in silence, shoulder to shoulder. Their grave faces and the dark folds of their clothing made them look like stone statues with life breathed into them, marching on like an invincible army. Bart raised the palm of his right hand to them, and they stopped. Their obedience to him expressed a greater and more formidable force than the disorderly attacks just now. Beyond their figures, armed with pikes and clubs, Bart looked at the countless crowd coming down from the hills: men, women, children. Far in the distance you could imagine yet more of them, like tiny mites floating in the air.

On the other side of the bridge, the guns were silent. *Milena is right,* he thought. *If they fire on us at this moment, they'll set off such fury that it will carry them away, they'll be lost forever, and they know it.*

In spite of this conviction, he still knew he was playing a deadly game. A single bullet would be enough. And another for Milena . . . Yet he felt no fear, only an awareness that he was living through the crucial moments of his life and that he was at peace with himself.

He held Milena's hand, and they took several more steps together. In the middle of the bridge, they stopped and saw that twenty yards behind them the horse-men had stopped too. They glanced at the dark waters of the great river flowing below. It had brought them here at the beginning of winter. Why would it let them down now? The wind had dropped. The whole world seemed to be waiting.

"We mustn't stop," said Milena. "Come on."

They walked on as if suspended in midair, avoiding the broken bodies still lying where they had fallen. Among them they recognized Faber's. He was facedown, and his immense arms, open like spread wings, seemed to be trying to seize and lift the entire bridge. A red trickle of blood ran from his head, making its way into the cracks between the gray paving stones.

The trucks on the opposite bank still didn't move.

It was disturbing. They took twenty more paces, still at the same speed. Milena's hand in Bart's was soft and sure. He turned his head to look at his companion. Everything about her was youthful and luminous. *No*, he told himself again, *they can't fire at her without condemning themselves.*

And suddenly he knew they had arrived at the precise point where they would not be allowed to go any farther. Something had to happen now. He felt Milena's hand trembling in his. Had the same idea come to her too? They did not stop. Every step farther they took represented a victory, yet every step going was a terrible threat.

It was then that they heard the engine of the first truck on the bank starting. It maneuvered out of its parking slot and drove slowly away down the avenue. A second followed it, then another, and yet another. Soon the entire convoy was on its way south toward the army barracks. At first there was an incredulous silence. Then shouting broke out among the horse-men.

"They're leaving! They're clearing off!"

It was the signal for a great roar of voices that rose to the hills and echoed back from them. Bart and Milena, feeling they were waking from a dream, realized that they had crossed the entire bridge. The last trucks, the ones barring the exit from it, were starting up in their turn and driving away. They saw the frightened faces of the truck drivers quite close. Some of them couldn't be much older than themselves. They hardly had time to step aside: a human wave was already sweeping toward them, and nothing could contain it. A similar torrent of men and women shouting for joy poured over the two neighboring bridges. The city lay ahead.

In a few minutes, the banks had been invaded, and the great peaceful army led by the horse-men flowed into the icy avenues of the capital. Windows were opened as they passed; people shouted acclamations. Shouts of hatred for the Phalange could be heard too, as if no one had ever wanted anything but to see it fall. Then the liberated citizens came out into the road to join the crowd, and the immense procession made for Phalange headquarters in the New Town.

"The arena!" cried Bart. "We must go to the arena!"

"Yes," Milena agreed. Gerlinda, in tears, had miraculously found her again in the excited crowd.

There were no trams running, and no cars on the streets. The three of them raced down small side roads, Bartolomeo in the lead, the two young women following him. Making their way through the Old Town, they reached the square outside the arena fifteen minutes later, out of breath. To their surprise, there was turmoil there already. The crowd was a mixture of a number of horse-men, people from the city, and gladiators looking as if they had come from another age, bare to the waist or in their shirtsleeves despite the bitter cold. The two halves of the great gate were closed, but a dozen horse-men were advancing on it in single file, an enormous beam found on a nearby building site under their arms.

"Out of the way!" they shouted. "We're going to break the gate down!"

A space opened out ahead of them, and they charged the gate at a run. It was made of solid oak and groaned at the impact. They moved thirty feet back and ran at it again.

"They'll never do it," said Bart.

A gladiator with a stolid face, head shaved, was standing close to him. He was still holding his sword and looking around him, dazed, as if unable to understand where he was.

"Has there already been fighting in there?" Bart asked him.

"Yeah."

"A boy called Milos—did you see him?"

"Dunno."

"How did you get out here?"

"Small gate around the back. Don't have any tobacco, do you?"

"N-no," stammered Bart, taken aback by this unexpected question, and then he set off to go around the building, with Milena and Gerlinda behind him.

There was indeed an exit at the back, a narrow gate already under the control of a group of horsemen and insurgents holding weapons. They were letting out the gladiators and ordinary spectators but seizing any members of the Phalange who tried to escape by mingling with the crowd.

As she reached the place, Milena was not expecting another experience as strange as the one she had just shared with Bart on the Royal Bridge. Yet an extraordinary thing happened: a powerful man with a red beard, wearing a heavy overcoat, came up to the gate, his head lowered, in the vain hope of passing unrecognized. Fingers pointed his way at once.

"Van Vlyck! That's Van Vlyck!"

Two horse-men seized him firmly, and a third handcuffed him. He seemed to be demoralized and put up no resistance. As they were about to lead him off, a woman's voice rose in the crowd.

"Wait!"

Milena stood before him. They did not say a word, but simply stood there face-to-face.

Van Vlyck, mouth open, wild-eyed, stared at the girl, and one could guess that for him time had been wiped out. He saw before his eyes the one person he had ever loved, the woman for whom he had unhesitatingly sacrificed all that was best in his life, and whom in the end he had delivered up to the murderous Devils. She stood there younger and fairer than ever, fascinating, immortal. In this girl's blue eyes he saw his devastated past and his dark future.

And Milena found that she could not hate him. In his eyes, as if in a magic mirror, she saw the image of her living mother. *I'm looking at the man who killed her,* she told herself, but the words did not get through to her mind. *I'm looking at the man who . . . who loved her,* she thought instead, *the man who wept one evening fifteen years ago when he heard her singing in a little church in this city and who never got over it. I'm looking at a man who loved her to distraction, who looked at her as he's looking at me now. . . .*

And when Van Vlyck moved away, led off without ceremony by his horse-men guards and taking no notice of what was happening, it was as if he took away a living memory of the dead woman, a memory in the flesh that no photograph or recording could ever equal.

Milena felt shattered. It took her some time to return to reality, but a tremendous crash accompanied by shouts of triumph brought her out of her daze. Bartolomeo took her arm.

"The bar across the main gate has just given way, Milena—we can get in through it now!"

They ran back, still followed by the faithful and dogged Gerlinda. The battering ram had indeed broken the gate down, but those wanting to go in clashed with those in a hurry to get out, either gladiators or spectators who were ashamed of being there, and there was turmoil. The three young people managed to get through the crowd by dint of sheer determination. Bart shouted more than twenty times, "A boy of seventeen named Milos! Anyone seen him?"

No one replied. Milena even asked a gladiator with a face horribly mutilated by scars, standing proud as if a wild beast had once mauled him.

"Milos Ferenzy! A gladiator, seventeen years old! Was he in your camp? Do you know him?"

The man shook his head, looking dazed, and went on his way. Soon they gave up asking and climbed to the top of the tiers of seats, shouting as loud as they could, "Milos! Milos!"

Gradually, as the arena emptied, they came to the conclusion that their friend wasn't there.

"He could be somewhere else in the building," Milena suggested.

But it seemed unlikely. Why would he have hidden? He must have left, and they had missed seeing him; their paths had crossed.

They went along corridors at random, opening the doors of deserted cells to left and right. In the end they had gone all around the building and were back where they had started.

"Milos!" called Bart one last time.

His voice echoed under the vaulted ceiling and died away, leaving the place in total silence. As they were about to leave, Gerlinda pointed to the far end of a corridor.

"There's stairs over there."

They made for the staircase. Two worm-eaten steps were missing. Bart went up carefully in case any more collapsed under his weight. Halfway up, he stopped.

"Have you seen something?" asked Milena.

The young man disappeared from view without replying. She waited a few seconds and then, hearing nothing, asked again, "Bart, have you seen something?"

There was still no answer. Fear was churning inside her. She went up in her own turn. A faint light came through a small opening in the mud-brick wall. Bart was kneeling beside a body curled up in a perfect curve like a sleeping cat. She made her way over on all fours and leaned against her lover's shoulder.

Milos was wearing a dirty white shirt, its front soaked with blood. One of his feet, black with dirt, had been bleeding too. Unable to say a word, they looked at his tranquil face. It was like the face of a child of twelve.

"Milos . . ." murmured Bartolomeo.

"Oh, Helen!" cried Milena.

And with their heads close together, they mingled their silent tears.

Gerlinda's frightened voice came up to them from below. She had stayed behind alone in the dark corridor. "Is there anything up there? Hey! Is there anything there?"

SPRING

It seemed as if winter would never end that year. In the middle of March there were a few faintly spring-like days, but then the cold returned. Deep snow fell again, as if Nature couldn't shake off her covering of ice and frost. She might stretch and shift, but she always fell back under it, exhausted, frozen, defeated.

Helen spent a long time shut in her little room at Jahn's Restaurant, coming out only for her shifts, doing her work like a robot. Milena and Dora, the only people she would see, did all they could to make her eat a little, forced her to talk, to wash and brush her hair. Twice they managed to take her for a walk beside the river.

At last, one afternoon, she said she wanted to go with Bartolomeo to see Basil in the hospital. The young horse-man's wound had turned out to be much worse than it seemed at first, and he had a perforated stomach, which caused him great pain. The hospital was on the hills, in a park planted with larch trees. Basil, looking sad and thin, was lying in a white room that didn't seem the place for him at all. On this first visit Helen just listened to the two young men talking.

"Do you need anything?" Bart asked.

"Yes," said Basil, fretfully. "I'd like to be able to eat real food—by mouth."

As they left, Helen hugged him and told him she'd be back. She was good to her word and visited every day, first with Bartolomeo and then alone until Basil was discharged.

She had to go through the city to get to the hospital, and she took the tram to its terminus. The cheerfulness of the other passengers passed her by, but the final fall of the Phalange and the return of freedom had brought new light to their faces. Helen couldn't understand it. *What do all these people have to smile about?* she asked herself. *Don't they know my love is dead?* Then she walked through the park with her head bent to reach the hospital, where everyone came to know and greet her.

First she asked Basil about the boarding school. She got him to tell her about his first meeting with Milos the day when he gave Bart the letter and it all began. "Was it a fine evening?" she asked. "Or was it raining? What was Milos wearing?" Then she wanted to know about the training camp. What exactly did they eat there? Who shaved their heads? Who was the man he called Fulgur? Did they train barefoot or in sandals? Basil had to tell her every detail and was impressed by the attention she paid. No one else had ever listened to him so intently before. He frowned with concentration as he tried to remember everything.

"Did Milos . . . did he ever talk to you about me?" she ventured to ask one day.

Basil might not be very clever, but his heart told him what to say. "You bet he did! Couldn't stop!"

"Oh—what did he say?"

"Well . . . all sorts of things. Said you were very pretty."

"What else?"

"All sorts of things, like I said. For instance . . . oh, I dunno . . . said you were very good at climbing ropes."

And in this way, as the days and their conversations went on, they came to that last morning, the morning of the fights in the arena. First Basil told her about his own. He did so without much emotion until he had to describe the moment when he gave his opponent the death blow, at which point he unexpectedly burst into huge sobs.

"He—he wanted to kill me, see?" he stammered. "I didn't want to die. Wanted to live."

Helen bent over and stroked his forehead. "Don't cry, Basil. You were only defending yourself—you know you were. It wasn't your fault."

"I know, but we horse-men, we don't like killing folks."

She left it there for that afternoon, but as soon

as she was at his bedside the next day, she began again. "Basil, tell me about Milos, please. I mean his last day in the arena. Tell me all you can about it. I need to know."

For once the young horse-man began at the end. "It was Caius who killed him," he said gravely. "I'm sure it was. He thought Milos was a cat."

"A cat?"

Basil told her about Caius and his murderous insanity, and he went on to describe Milos's fight with the old gladiator. Fascinated, Helen listened. Every word she heard was transformed into pictures of Milos alive. She clung to them with all her heart.

"Did you see it yourself?" she asked when Basil had finished. "He really spared his opponent?"

"Yes, I saw from behind the gate. I was just back from the infirmary. Fulgur had been sewing me up. Milos almost lay down on top of the guy; they talked, then Milos took his sword away. You have to be brave to do a thing like that! Then there was the battering ram at the gate, and after that it was all chaotic. I didn't see him again, and my stomachache was terrible. I wonder what he was doing there at the end of the corridor — Milos, I mean. Everyone was running for it, and he went back. . . . Maybe he was looking for me."

Helen nodded.

"I'm sure that was it, Basil. He was looking for you. You deserved it."

* * *

As May approached, winter finally retreated. The sky was full of migrant birds returning, and the sun came out, warming everyone. Helen felt the claws of grief that clutched her heart relax their hold slightly. She went out more, caught herself laughing at Dora's amusing remarks and the jokes the others made at work. Slowly her love of life was coming back with a light and hesitant touch. It felt like she was breaking out of the prison of her mourning, just as the city broke out of the ice of winter. But sometimes in a light-hearted moment she felt as if it were treachery, and the idea plunged her into grief deeper than ever.

One Sunday the city celebrated the return of freedom. In holiday mood, the capital hailed its heroes: the horse-men and the Resistance. There was dancing in the squares and on the streets all day. Every part of the city was full of music and singing. That evening a horse-drawn trailer arrived in Opera House Square, and when the tarpaulin over it was removed, Napoleon the giant pig appeared in all his glory, a monumental and astonishingly clean vision. Although applauded as a hero, he ignored his triumph, merely waggling his large ears, grunting, and snuffling around for food. He was hoisted up to a platform in the middle of the square by means of a system of lifts and straps.

People were mingling cheerfully everywhere, waving tankards in the air. Stupefied by beer and the noise, Helen was clinging to Dora's dress. In the middle of the festive crowd she caught sight of

Mitten, limping, toothless but happy, dancing for joy. He recognized her, rubbed his stomach with both hands and shouted, pointing to the pig, "Told you so! Now we'll have a hog roast!"

A little later she was greeted by Dr. Josef, who had brought Napoleon. He must have known about Milos, for he hugged her close with his eyes bright, and said nothing.

As evening fell, microphones were put up in the courtyard of the Opera House, and a series of musicians performed there. Toward midnight, Milena stepped forward alone, wearing a blue dress that Helen had never seen before, and began to sing.

"In my basket,
In my basket, I have no cherries,
My dear prince. . . ."

Everyone fell silent. Those who were wearing hats took them off, and when the chorus came, thousands of voices joined in, raising the little tune to the sky. At first Helen's throat felt so tight that she couldn't utter a sound, but then she managed to sing after all:

"I have no pretty kerchiefs,
No embroidered kerchiefs,
I have no beads, no.
No more grief and pain, my love,
No more grief and pain. . . ."

She sang, her voice mingling with the voice of Dora, whose hand was on her shoulder:

"In my basket, I have no chicken,
Father dear,
No chicken to be plucked,
I have no duck, no.
I have no velvet gloves,
Gloves neatly sewn, no.
No more grief and pain, my love,
No more grief and pain."

She sang with all the others, and it was her own way of returning once and for all to the land of the living.

Helen worked in Mr. Jahn's restaurant for a few more months and then found a job that suited her better in a bookshop in the New Town. During the next few years, she had the pleasure of seeing several old friends come into the shop, former students at the boarding school who had found out where she was. She saw Vera Plasil, now a young woman in full bloom accompanied by her husband, and a few weeks later, just as she was about to shut the shop, in came Catharina Pancek, who had hardly changed.

Milena Bach and Bartolomeo Casal stayed together. Right into the evening of their lives they were a luminous, inseparable couple. Bart was a brilliant university student and became a famous lawyer. As for Milena, she didn't waste her talent. Dora found her a singing teacher and made her work hard. Over the years her natural voice gained in depth and balance, and she became the incomparable singer that she had always promised to be. She sang in the most famous theaters in the world, but she never forgot her origins, and every season she gave a recital in the Opera House of the capital city, the theater where her mother had once sung. Helen reserved her seat for this occasion months in advance, and was always there sitting in the front row.

Even with a symphony orchestra behind her, Milena never failed to give Helen a private, loving little wave from the platform. It said: *Do you remember the school yard? Do you remember the icy dormitory and the long winters?* And then her voice rose, vibrating with humanity. Helen let that familiar yet mysterious voice carry her away, as you might let yourself be carried away on a ship. And during her voyage she let the secret images of her heart come before her eyes: the great, tranquil river flowing under the bridges, the infinite love of the consolers, the faint memory of her dead parents, and then, always and forever, the smiling face of a boy with brown curls.

EPILOGUE

Evening was falling in the garden. Helen breathed in the honeyed scent of the clematis with pleasure. She slowly finished taking the washing off the line. It was going to be a mild night, and the young woman was in no hurry to go in.

"Mama, it's for you!" a little girl suddenly called to her from the open sitting room window.

Leaving her laundry basket under the line, Helen went in. The child held out the receiver, forming the silent syllables with her lips: "A gentleman."

"Thanks. Go and put your nightie on. I'll come in a minute."

She didn't know the deep male voice. "Is that Helen Dormann?"

"Yes," said Helen, although she had changed her surname some years ago.

"Hello, Helen! This is Octavo. I'm so pleased to have found you—I had difficulty finding your number."

"Octavo?"

"That's right, Paula's Octavo. You remember?"

Slowly, she sat down. She hadn't seen Paula for ages. A hundred times she'd told herself she would go and visit her, and a hundred times she had put it off until later. The bookshop, her children, the distance . . . As for Octavo, she had lost track of him entirely.

"Good heavens, Octavo!" she cried. "How are you? It feels so odd to hear you with a grown-up voice."

"I'm calling from the village," he said. "Paula has just died. I thought you'd want to know."

She caught the bus next morning. All the way, memories were overwhelming her, and she couldn't manage to read the novel she had brought. Octavo welcomed her to the little brick house in the consolers' village, Number 47. She would never have recognized him. He was tall and strong; his chin and cheeks prickled her when they kissed.

"Come upstairs. She's on her bed there. As you'll see, she's at peace."

Paula lay there with her hands crossed over her breast. The perfect calm of her face was as reassuring as ever and seemed to be telling those who came to pay her a last visit, *You see, it's not too bad, nothing to make a song and dance about!* Helen, who had shed all her tears during the journey, was beyond grieving now. She kissed the forehead of the woman who had been like a mother to her and sat at her bedside for a long time.

She helped Octavo with the funeral arrangements. He had a car, and she was to go back to the capital with him when it was all over.

On the morning of their departure, she asked him to wait for another hour. She went down the hill and easily found the exact place where she and Milena had met Milos and Bart fifteen years ago. It seemed like yesterday. She followed Donkey Road and crossed the bridge, marveling at the infinite patience of the four stone equestrian statues. The sun was hot. She slung her sweater around her shoulders and walked on with her arms bare. The water of the river shone.

She found the barred gates of the boarding school open and walked in. The Skeleton's old-fashioned lodge was still there. As she passed it, Helen felt goosebumps, almost expecting to hear the woman's acid voice all of a sudden: "And where do you think you're going, young lady?" But there was no sound apart from the twittering of sparrows in the trees in the yard.

Following the wall of the building, she found the refectory door unlocked and went in.

"It's closed. Are you looking for something?"

The place was unrecognizable without its tables and chairs. Reels of electric cable lay around on the floor.

"Can I help you?" the electrician asked, screwing a switch into place.

"Yes . . . no. That is, I was a student here long ago . . . at the boarding school. I just wanted to look."

"Ah, yes, but it's closed. The holidays, see?"

"Of course. I'm so sorry. I don't want to bother you. Do you happen to know if it's possible to get through that little door at the back there?"

"The door to the cellar? I don't know. But there's a bunch of keys hanging from the nail there. If you want to try it. . . . Here, you can borrow my flashlight. It's in the toolbox there."

The third key she tried opened the lock. Helen turned the beam of the flashlight on the darkness and went down the stairs. Once at the bottom, she went along the tunnel. Its ceiling was covered with dusty cobwebs. The door of the detention cell, torn down and smashed to pieces, barred her way. She stepped over it. A smell of mold met her nostrils. The bunk was broken too, lying flat on the floor. A rusty bucket with holes in it lay in a corner.

There was no picture left, no Sky, nothing.

The birds had flown away. All of them.

The hardest moment, and Helen hadn't expected it, was when Octavo had to turn the key and lock up Paula's little house behind him. Neither of them could hold back their tears on the steps outside.

But they talked cheerfully on the drive back, telling each other about their lives and recalling the past. "Do you remember about going to Random?" asked Helen. "And a fox—a foxess?" Octavo, who had forgotten, roared with laughter. He was an amusing man, very vivacious.

He dropped Helen at her home in the middle of the night. They parted, promising to see each other again from time to time and talk about Paula. Helen slipped quietly into her sleeping house, but as she opened her bedroom door, another opened at the end of the corridor, and her daughter came out.

"Can't you sleep, darling?"

The little girl shook her head. She was twisting the front of her nightdress and wasn't far from tears. "I had a bad dream, Mama, and then you weren't there."

Helen took her in her arms, put her back to bed, and sat beside her to reassure her. She stroked her daughter's hair and talked to her quietly.

And it seemed to her that the love she had received from Paula flowed into her caressing hands and her voice, and she in turn was passing it on, a love as powerful as the river.

"I'm back now," she said. "Go to sleep, my beauty, go to sleep. Everything's all right."

ACKNOWLEDGMENTS

I would like to thank several people who have accompanied me through the writing of this novel: Thierry Laroche of Gallimard Jeunesse, for his helpful and always friendly comments; Jean-Philippe Arrou-Vignod of Gallimard Jeunesse, who reassured me about the darker side of the story; Dr. Patrick Carrère for his advice on medical subjects; Christopher Murray, musician, for his equally valuable help with musical matters; Rachel and my children, Emma and Colin, who all three give me the inestimable gift, constantly renewed, of being there for me.

And finally I would like to express my great gratitude to the memory of Kathleen Ferrier, the British contralto, whose voice and whose story both moved me deeply and have gone into this story. But for her, this novel would not have been written.

Estacada Public Library
825 NW Wade St.
Estacada, OR 97023

WITHDRAWN